BY PETER MAAS

NONFICTION
In a Child's Name: The Legacy of a Mother's Murder
Manhunt
Marie: A True Story
King of the Gypsies
Serpico
The Valachi Papers
The Rescuer

FICTION
China White
Father and Son
Made in America

Peter Maas

CHINA WHITE

SIMON & SCHUSTER

New York London Toronto Sydney Tokyo Singapore

SIMON & SCHUSTER
Rockefeller Center
1230 Avenue of the Americas
New York, New York 10020

SIMON & SCHUSTER and colophon are registered trademarks of Simon & Schuster Inc.

Designed by Irving Perkins Associates, Inc.

Manufactured in the United States of America

1   3   5   7   9   10   8   6   4   2

Library of Congress Cataloging-in-Publication Data
Maas, Peter.
China white/Peter Maas.
p.   cm.
I. Title.
PS3563.A2C48   1994
813'.54—dc20   94-20327
CIP
ISBN: 0-671-69417-0

For my sons, John-Michael and Terrence

CHINA WHITE

1

THE CLIENT STATUS of Mr. Y. K. Deng of Hong Kong became a prime topic of discussion near the end of the quarterly management review of the New York law firm of Needham & Lewis, a meeting that till then had been all gloom and acrimony.

Billing goals for the year clearly were not going to be achieved. It was not as though the firm would shut its doors tomorrow, but the stagnant revenues of the late 1980s had taken an alarming turn for the worse. As a traditional "white shoe" firm, Needham & Lewis had been ill prepared to compete in the frenzied new business world of junk bonds, mergers and acquisitions, and hostile takeovers.

James B. Needham, the firm's patriarch and surviving founding partner, yearned for the days of bedrock relationships, when you didn't have to pitch your wares like an account executive hustling a new advertising campaign, when clients sought you out, when you could lunch or golf confidently over the years with a corporate CEO without worrying about waking up one morning to learn that the company had been purchased by German or Japanese interests who promptly brought in their own management, their own bankers—and their own law firms.

The shortfall in projected revenues this year, according to the comptroller's estimates, looked to be close to five million dollars, severely denting the expected profit for the firm's thirty-two partners.

"We've got to cut costs," snapped Gregory Howser, the new head of the litigation department. "Carrington and Addison—and I can name plenty of others—haven't brought in a dime's worth of business since I've been here. Get rid of them." Howser was one of the young turks Needham had enlisted in hopes of revitalizing the firm. It was, however, a decision he was beginning to regret. Still the arrogant pup had brought with him two major brokerage houses that were fending off dozens of court actions following the collapse of the junk-bond market, so for now at least he had to suffer Howser in some silence.

"My God, man, maybe they're not rainmakers, but they've done valuable work within the office," said old Albright, the head of trusts and estates. "You can't simply throw them out like that. They have wives, children, mortgages."

"Fuck 'em!" Howser said.

"Please," James B. Needham said. "Could we move on to more productive areas?" He turned toward Sam Gladdis, whom he had placed in charge of new business. "Sam, what's the situation with our Chinese friend, Mr. Y. K. Deng?"

"At this point, from what I've been able to piece together, it's down to us and Baker, Hammerfeld in San Francisco. They have the advantage of a Hong Kong office. On the other hand, from what Mr. Pei from Chinatown, Mr. Peter Pei, tells me, Mr. Deng would prefer to locate in New York. As you'll recall, it was Pei who originally approached us on Deng's behalf, unsolicited by anyone here. He said simply that Deng had heard good *joss*—that was the word he used, *joss*—about us. I didn't press him any further, but a friend of mine at the Asia Society tells me that the word means very favorable things, good luck, fine reputation, all rolled up together."

"What's Pei's relationship to Deng?" a member of the review team asked.

Gladdis shrugged. "All I can tell you is that Pei's an established figure in Chinatown. And an American citizen from way back, which is out of the ordinary, considering our past exclusionary policies against the Chinese. I believe he was actually in the U.S. military during World War Two. He and Deng are what they call Chiuchow. Very tight, I'm told. They both come from around Swatow, which was a small fishing village until the British turned it into a major port right after colonizing Hong Kong in the nineteenth century. They transformed it into one of their first entry points for the opium they forced on China. You've all heard of the Opium Wars, how British trading companies got half of China hooked on opium?"

"For Christ's sake, spare us the history lesson," Howser interrupted.

Gladdis glared at him. "I was just trying to fill everyone in. Anyway, as for Deng himself, it appears he arrived in Hong Kong some time in the early nineteen-fifties. Just how he got started in business isn't clear, but today he's chairman of Hong Kong/Kowloon Enterprises, Limited, which according to Pei has holdings in shipping, banking, restaurants and hotels, as well as casino gambling in Macao, the Portuguese colony next door. What Deng wants is guidance and representation for his U.S. investments. He wants to be low-key, Pei says. He's very conscious that, ah, certain attitudes prevail in some quarters about the Chinese."

"Nineteen ninety-seven is what this is all about," Needham said. "Come ninety-seven, China gets Hong Kong back. When the Brits announced they were honoring their commitment to pull out, about which they didn't have much choice, everything went south in Hong Kong. Then when it looked like the Beijing regime was loosening up, there was another boom. Next came Tiananmen Square and, bingo! another nosedive. It's like a goddamn roller coaster. Now Beijing is saying they'll give Hong Kong special status and guarantee capitalism there for fifty years. Well, who the hell knows? Fellow like Deng has to hedge his bets."

"I looked him up in *Who's Who in Hong Kong,*" Gladdis continued. "It's brief, but it pretty much matches what Pei said. He also has a daughter, who Pei tells me is a student here in the States. Oh, and I almost forgot: Deng's a steward at the Royal Hong Kong Jockey Club."

"OK, OK, Sam," Needham said. "We've got the message. Deng's obviously a catch for us. We do for him the kind of job we're capable of, the word'll get around. He isn't the only important Chink—strike that! I mean Chinese—who'll be arriving. We get him, we'll get plenty of the others. And on that score, Sam, how are we doing with the recruitment of young Tom MacLean?"

Before Gladdis could reply, Howser said, "MacLean? The Tom MacLean in the U.S. attorney's office?"

"The one and same."

Everyone stared at Needham, as if struck dumb. They all knew who MacLean was. Every lawyer in the city, if not the entire nation, knew about him. He had just successfully prosecuted one of the most famous trial lawyers in the country, Arthur Green, for systematically defrauding clients.

"Jesus, do we want some Savonarola nut like that running wild in the office?"

Needham rather enjoyed Howser's discomfiture. The only recent complaints on billings concerned the hours Howser and his litigating team had recorded. It all had been settled amicably, but still, it was upsetting. "Listen, Greg," he needled, "weren't you bitching about all our alleged dead weight? An aggressive new fellow like young MacLean sounds just about right to me. You know, aggressive *and* ambitious." Needham paused for a beat. "Like you."

Then Needham's tone turned somber. "The fact is that MacLean's joining the firm could be the crucial difference in netting Deng. MacLean spent part of his boyhood in Hong Kong. And I understand he speaks Chinese, at least some Chinese."

"Ah, so," Howser mocked, "Confucius say talkee Chinese is now a partner prerequisite."

"Don't be such a smartass, Deng speaks perfectly good English," Gladdis chimed in, delighted to take the offensive. "He isn't some Chinatown fishmonger, for God's sake."

"It's simply a gesture, a *beau geste,* if you will," Needham said. "I'm told the Chinese especially appreciate that sort of thing. Recognition of face. Far more important, though, is that the Chinese believe in relationships, beginning with family and then spreading outward to others close to them, surrogate family. I'm led to understand that MacLean's father had such a relationship with Deng way back when in the Agency."

"And what's that supposed to mean?" Howser demanded. Instantly, he regretted his swift mouth. When Needham said "Agency," it meant, of course, agency with a capital *A*—the Central Intelligence Agency. Looking at the seventy-three-year-old Needham, with his permanently pink countenance, his friar's fringe of hair, his substantial paunch, it was hard to imagine that he once had been a derring-do member of the OSS—the Office of Strategic Services, precursor to the CIA. He had parachuted into Yugoslavia during World War II to work with the partisans and dropped behind German lines in France to blow up a key railroad bridge. The old-boy network may have broken down in the legal profession but, as Howser knew, it was still alive and well in the intelligence community.

Gazing contemptuously at Howser over half-frame reading glasses, Needham did not bother to respond.

"Oh," said Howser, his voice suddenly diminished.

2

AMONG THE GLEAMING GREEN-GLASS COMMERCIAL TOWERS along lower Park Avenue, the ancient brick-and-mortar Racquet and Tennis Club sat like an island of smug probity that was, indeed, unto itself.

Inside, Tom MacLean stood at the reception desk. He was a lanky six feet two, with an unruly cowlick in his light brown hair that conspired to make him appear even younger than his thirty-four years. He asked for James Needham.

A smartly uniformed attendant peered at a clipboard for a moment and said, "Mr. MacLean?"

"That's me."

"Mr. Needham is waiting for you in the bar. Second floor, to your left off either the elevator or stairs."

MacLean chose the stairs, passing on the way up a walk-in humidor, redolent with the scent of fine cigars. On the second-floor landing, directly ahead of him, was a large sitting room facing the avenue. Occupants of wing chairs were engrossed in newspapers. Several backgammon games were in progress. To his right, down a wide corridor, he heard the click of billiard balls.

By the bar's entrance, clams and oysters on the half shell lay on glistening beds of ice. A mahogany bar ran along one side of the room, its brass rail testifying to a daily polish. Racing and hunting prints adorned the walls. Grouped around the floor were oak tavern tables with sturdy captains' chairs. At this hour, six p.m., about half of them were filled with men in conservatively tailored suits of dark hues, risking nothing more adventurous than a chalk stripe. There was an occasional blue blazer. No women were to be seen.

MacLean was led to a corner leather banquette where Needham was seated. "My boy," Needham said, extending his hand, "good of you to come."

"My pleasure, sir."

An elderly waiter, Irish in appearance and accent, immediately hovered over them. "Another Macallan's, Mr. Needham?"

"Thank you, Vincent." Needham turned to MacLean. "A taste of the ancestral land for you? Single malt, you know. Smooth as you could want."

"Actually, I'm only half Scot. My mother's folks came from Germany."

"By God, nothing wrong with that," Needham said. "Good stock, all around. Proud heritage. So what'll you have?"

"A Budweiser would be fine."

The waiter appeared rocked by the request. "I'm afraid we don't serve, uh, that."

"Heineken!" Needham exclaimed. "How about a Heineken?"

"Good enough," MacLean said.

"I like your style," Needham said. "Man of the people. Stands you in good stead with juries, I'll wager. Funny thing. Had extensive work done on my country place in Westchester. Threw a cookout afterward for the contractor and his crew. Ordered cases of imported stuff, Heineken, Beck's. The contractor came up to me and said his men were asking was there any Bud? Sent right into the village for it, of course. Never can tell, can you?"

After the drinks were served, Needham said, "First off, I want personally to congratulate you on that Arthur Green conviction."

"That's nice to hear. It's not exactly a unanimous opinion, at least among a lot of lawyers."

"Is that right?"

"Yes, they seem to think I went overboard on it. Hey, what's the big deal? A lawyer overbills. Not quite a man-bites-dog story. Frankly, there was even some concern in my own office that it should have been a disciplinary procedure for the bar association, not a federal prosecution."

"What made you go after him?"

"Well, I don't want to sound holier-than-thou, but the law means something to me. While my dad gave me all the help he could, I basically worked my way through law school. I genuinely believe the law is really what keeps society from falling apart. So the bond between a lawyer and client ought to border on the sacred—maybe not up there with priest and penitent, but close. And Green wasn't just overbilling, he was stealing thousands in phony expenses. What got me was that two of the firms he'd been with pretty much knew something wasn't kosher and didn't say a word about it because he was bringing in a ton of business. So that eliminated the possibility of any disciplinary action before the bar association. Green had to be the most surprised guy in the world when he was indicted."

"Makes my blood boil," Needham said. "Ruins everything for everyone else. One of the reasons I'm anxious for you to join us. Sends a message out there we're foursquare in these trying times. Honest in the practice of law. Honest in billings." Needham paused. "This Green was a Jewish fellow, was he?"

"Yes, but so was one of the three young associates at the last firm Green was with who couldn't stomach what he was doing. David Goldberg was one of my key witnesses. Smart, terrific kid."

"Good to know, good to know," Needham said hastily. "Good for his kind, too. Bad business, stereotyping people."

At least, he made the effort, Tom MacLean thought, amused more than anything by Needham's clumsy attempt to regain high moral ground, to beat down prejudice undoubtedly bred in his bones. Keeping a straight face, he said, "I couldn't agree with you more."

"Well, now," said Needham, plunging on, "let's see, now. Northwestern law degree, was it? After that, a year at Cromwell, Becker in Chicago. What made you leave?"

"The truth is that I married the boss's daughter, and it just got to be an uncomfortable situation for me. Maybe I overreacted. I don't know. Anyway, I wanted big-city action. Chicago obviously was out of the question, so I applied to the U.S. attorneys in New York and Los Angeles. New York came through first."

"Still married?"

"No. Kay made the move with me, but she didn't have that many friends here. I was working long hours, so she was alone a lot. Plus she could never understand why I didn't stay with her father's firm, live the good life in Chicago. I don't mean to imply it was her fault things didn't work out for us."

"Understand, understand perfectly. Been married better than forty years myself," Needham said, intent on making his next point, seemingly oblivious to the non sequitur. "Two daughters is what I've got, but one of them has given me a grandson. In law school, he is. I'm on the last lap of my life, but I want this firm to be around for him. Continuity! I need someone to take up the reins, lead the firm into the twenty-first century, and I'm of a mind that you fit the bill, if you're interested."

"That's very generous of you."

"Not generous at all. *My* self-interest at stake here." After ordering another round of drinks, Needham studied MacLean for a moment. "Been a prosecutor about eight years now, correct?"

"Yes, mostly business and securities fraud."

"So you've seen the bad side of corporate conduct?"

"That's fair to say."

"I seem to recall you were involved in the Hammond Aerospace investigation. Major contract chicanery on a new Navy fighter plane. But you didn't indict. Why?"

"That was a close call. What Hammond did was to charge cost overruns to other projects. But when I looked into it, it was clear to me that the Navy was just as culpable. How much was criminal intent or plain bureaucratic indifference was hard to say. There also was another factor to consider. It's a depressed area out where Hammond is. Literally thousands of innocent people could have lost their jobs. And I satisfied myself that there wouldn't be a repeat performance."

"You're not a zealot then, everything black and white."

"Zealot? I like to think I know right from wrong. But a zealot, no. The world's a hell of a lot more gray than black and white, at least from what I've been able to see."

"You plan on prosecuting all your life?"

"I wouldn't be sitting here talking to you if I did."

"Like that. Don't mince words, do you?" Then, abruptly, Needham asked, "How's your father?"

Caught off guard at this sudden turn in the conversation, MacLean couldn't conceal his astonishment. "You know my father?"

"No, it's not been my good fortune to meet him. But I know of him, certainly. A great patriot. Unsung hero. One of those who quietly answered his country's call."

"Well, to answer your question," said MacLean, still trying to recover, "he's retired now. He does some consulting work, and some teaching, too. His specialty is the Far East. Southeast Asia. He spent a lot of time there."

"That I'm aware of." Needham drained his glass and fixed his eyes on

MacLean. "I, ah, once labored in the same general vineyard as your father: A little before his time, naturally."

MacLean began to reevaluate Needham. All his rambling, his apparent guilelessness, simply had been a smoke screen to get to this point.

"Tell me," Needham said, "your father ever mention a Hong Kong fellow named Deng, Y. K. Deng?"

"Not that I remember. Dad was pretty circumspect about what he was doing."

"Understandable. Secret world he was in. All important to maintain secrecy, security. America's enemies lurking everywhere." Summoning Vincent, Needham ordered another round.

"Even in Hong Kong," MacLean said, "when he finally told me who he was working for, he didn't get into any specifics about what he was doing." It was eerie, he would think later, how Needham had managed to unleash a haunting past. Maybe it was Needham saying that his father was a great patriot. It was nice to hear that. Nice to know that there were people who held his father in such high esteem.

MacLean looked away for a moment. *Hong Kong!* The war in Vietnam was raging then. His father would be absent for weeks at a time. He remembered the afternoon when he was just a kid and he and Freddie Carradine were exploring deep into one of those forbidden tunnels the Japanese had dug into the hillsides during World War II, how dark and spooky it was, and how they came at last to a chamber at the end of the tunnel and in the wavering beams of their flashlights, they saw a desk and a bed—and a skeleton!

The next day, his father had returned from one of his mysterious trips, and he related his adventure with Freddie. "Dad, do you think it was a Japanese soldier?"

"Probably. You know, though, you're not supposed to go into those tunnels."

"I know, but Freddie Carradine is always saying the English are braver than anybody, that's how they conquered the whole world, like Hong Kong and everything, and he dared me. You won't tell Mom, will you?"

"No, son, I won't. A promise is a promise. It'll be our secret."

And then young Tom MacLean, age eleven, said, "Dad, what do you do exactly? I mean, you're away all the time, and the other day at school everyone in class had to say what their father did, and I didn't know what to say. Afterward Mom said to say you worked for the State Department, but even the boys whose fathers are at the consulate ask me what you do. It's sort of embarrassing."

He remembered how his father held him by the shoulders and stared at him for the longest time before he replied, "You're right, son, it's not fair, so I'm going to put my trust in you. I haven't told you before because I thought you weren't old enough not to tell your friends. But now I think you are. You have to promise to keep this a secret, though, between us, just like you and the tunnel. Can you do that?"

"Yes, sir."

"Well, what I do is work for the Central Intelligence Agency. Do you know what it is?"

"Gosh, yes. Are you a real spy?"

"No, nothing like that. What I do, the best I can, is to try to protect our country from anybody who might want to do it harm. The thing is you can't tell anyone. I'm not even supposed to tell you."

"So what'll I say?"

"What Mom said. That I do special things for the State Department."

"But that's not true, and you always told me that I was never to lie."

"This is a little bit more complicated, son. I'll explain it all to you one of these days."

But, of course, that day never came.

In the bar of the Racquet and Tennis Club, Tom MacLean turned back to Needham and repeated, "Even in Hong Kong, he never got into any specifics. To tell you the truth I still don't know what he did. It's kind of understood that it's a subject that's out of bounds."

"As it should be, as it should remain," said Needham, nodding vigorously, dewlaps quivering. "By the by, speaking of Hong Kong, you speak Chinese?"

"I picked up some Cantonese from our amah, the woman who took care of our house. But if you're interested in me because of my fluency in Chinese, you're making a big mistake."

"Doesn't matter, just wondered," Needham said. He rubbed his chin, peering at MacLean. "Well, now, how much you making downtown, you don't mind me inquiring?"

"Not at all. That's not much of a secret, for sure. Ninety-two five."

"Well, how does two-fifty sound to you? To start."

"Mr. Needham, I hope you're not counting on me to bring in a whole bunch of business. That'd be another mistake."

"I'll be frank with you, my boy. No sense beating around the bush. You may be the connection we need. This fellow Deng I mentioned before. Could be a mighty important client. Had some relationship with your father. Bumped into him somewhere or what during the Hong Kong days, I don't know. Don't know the details. Probably, like you, never will. But this is what a source of mine told me, and my sources are pretty good. So what do you think?"

"I think I'd like to think it over."

"Not for too long, I hope."

"I'll get back to you in a couple of days."

"Good, good. One thing I can promise you. The bar in the partners' room will be well stocked with Bud. For imbibing at day's end only, of course."

3

S HORTLY PAST NOON the following day, Tom MacLean was crossing St. Andrew's Plaza, headed for one of the hot dog stands clustered next to the federal courthouse, when he heard her shout, "Hey, Tom!"

He turned to see Shannon O'Shea, slim and five foot three, with a mop of reddish blond hair, freckled nose and an impish grin. She was wearing gray slacks, a white blouse with a floppy bow and a black jacket a size too large, the better to cover the SIG-Sauer nine-millimeter semiautomatic that MacLean knew was at her waist. Eight rounds in the clip and one in the chamber as opposed to the sixteen-shot model favored by most male FBI agents.

"Ah, the Mick herself, bless us all," MacLean said. "What welcome fate causes our paths to cross?"

"Chinatown. Checking out a new restaurant. You free? Care to join up?"

"Your timing couldn't be better. I've just been stood up by a ravishing witness named Wanda who was going to help me bring all the crooks on Wall Street to their knees. Also, possibly myself."

"Oh, Tom. As incorrigible as ever."

Tom had first met Shannon O'Shea when she was fresh out of the FBI Academy. The case that brought them together involved major criminal fraud, A Cosa Nostra crime family had secretly backed the construction and management of a music theater just north of New York City. Outwardly it appeared to be a typical cash cow for the Mafia, to be milked into inevitable ruin.

What mystified MacLean about the operation was that the biggest entertainment conglomerate in the country, with assets of two billion dollars in movies, cable television and music, had invested a modest three hundred thousand in the theater. Even more puzzling, close to a million and a half more also had been paid to a mob-connected "theater consultant." These checks were promptly cashed, less a ten-percent fee, and the money returned to the conglomerate. Shannon had been sent in undercover as a secretary in the corporate treasurer's office. She quickly found that the laundered cash was being used by the conglomerate to buy cocaine for the music groups it had under contract, hardly expenditures that could be reflected in its audited financials.

Now, walking past the federal Metropolitan Correctional Center, MacLean and O'Shea started across Columbus Park on the edge of Chinatown. A bunch of Chinese kids, undaunted by their lack of height, were racing up and down a basketball court. "Not too many dunk shots there," she observed.

"Don't worry. Give them time, and one of them will make MVP in the NBA."

Suddenly she stopped and turned to him. "Tom, forgive me. I meant to write you a note about Arthur Green. That was a wonderful job. One for the Force against the Dark Side."

"Thanks, but I may be moving over to the Dark Side myself."

"You're kidding."

"I'm not. I've been thinking about it for a while, and I've just gotten a hell of an offer. The office hasn't been the same since Funderbunk was appointed."

Henry Funderbunk was the new U.S. attorney. MacLean hesitated before he said, "There was a very unpleasant sidebar to the Green case. The first thing Artie did was hire one of Funderbunk's former law partners as his counsel. And before I knew it, there was Funderbunk sidling up to me to ask if this case warranted a federal prosecution. Wasn't it really a bar association problem? After all, sooner or later, I'd be going into private practice, and did I want a decision to go after another lawyer, an important lawyer, on my résumé?"

"Honestly, Tom, that's not enough reason to quit. The point is you did it."

"OK, but there's more. I've been a prosecutor for eight years. I can feel myself getting a little jaded. Fresh people with newly minted outrage have to take over. And the law will need the likes of me on the other side to keep them from running amok. Anyway, what are you up to these days?"

"Narcotics."

"More cocaine?"

"No, heroin. China white. I'm primary relief on the Asian Drug Task Force."

In FBIspeak, primary relief meant the second in command, and MacLean said, "You're moving up fast. Am I actually going to lunch with the Bureau's first female director-to-be?"

"Don't bet the farm on it. Just here in New York, there're six layers of bosses above me. And on this one, I think I lucked out. Some genius in personnel suddenly discovered my unique qualifications. Otherwise, I'd still be chasing car-theft rings. I mean, how many agents do you think there are who speak Mandarin, Cantonese and Hakka? I'll save you the trouble. You're looking at her."

MacLean would never forget the moment he had learned of Shannon O'Shea's linguistic skills. During the music-theater case, they'd gone to a Chinese restaurant on a dinner break and she had suddenly started spouting Cantonese to the waiter. He'd said, "Wait a minute. How does a Mick from Woodside, Queens, get to speak Cantonese?"

"Simple. I was a Maryknoll missionary in Taiwan for five years. You wanted to reach out, you had to learn the lingo."

"You were a . . . a *nun?*" he had managed to sputter.

"You got it."

"And now you're an FBI agent?"

"My God, MacLean," she had said, "you sure do know how to put two and two together. Stop being so sexist. Where I grew up, the good guys became priests or cops, it's not such a big leap. But being a girl, it was a little difficult for me, priestwise."

On the far side of Columbus Park, they started up a narrow street, not much wider than an alley, lined with trading-company storehouses that had Chinese characters painted on grimy windows.

"I thought Colombian coke was the drug of choice," he said.

"Still is, and that's where all the emphasis is. But I'm here to tell you that the feature attraction for the nineties will be good old smack—number four heroin, a/k/a China white. It used to be heroin from Turkish poppies, refined in Marseilles. The old French Connection. We paid off Turkey to stop poppy cultivation, and we thought that was the end of it. Next cocaine and crack overshadowed everything. But we forgot about the

Golden Triangle. And then Chinese traffickers made the great discovery that there was a huge, untapped market in America. Fifty thousand American kids died in Vietnam, Tom. And another fifty thousand came back hooked on heroin. It isn't the French Connection anymore. The Chinese are coming and so is China white, more than you can possibly imagine. It's the Chinese Connection now. It makes everything that came before look like play school."

"Come on, Shannon. What is this, shades of the Yellow Peril? Fu Manchu time? The Chinese are wonderful, smart people. They are going to enrich us. Every time I turn around there's some Chinese violinist prodigy, some math genius, or a computer whiz kid."

The quiet, narrow street they were on, Park Street, ran into the Chinatown end of Mulberry Street. Once there, they entered a clamorous, chaotic world, apart from the rest of the city. Oriental faces surrounded them. Palpable energy filled the air. They were assaulted by the smell of fish that lay in boxed open displays on dripping crushed ice, and by the savory scent of sizzling fried dumplings. Curbside peddlers hawked made-in-Taiwan dolls and watches. A gaunt herbalist measured out ancient medicinal remedies into paper cones, ground antler and ginseng.

Shannon O'Shea hopped over some blue crabs scuttling away from a corner seafood market. "Listen," she said, "I know they're wonderful, smart people. But that doesn't mean that they don't have plenty of smart bad guys, too."

"What are you pitching me," MacLean said, "a Chinese Mafia?"

"Sort of. You've heard of the Hong Kong triads, haven't you?"

"Sure, the famous secret societies. Although since everybody seems to know about them, they're not very secret."

"Yes, well, everybody doesn't quite know everything. There're now five dominant triads in Hong Kong. We know that much. They claim to be fraternal, patriotic organizations, of course. What's secret are their criminal cores and who runs them, who the dragon heads are."

They turned north on Mott. On the other side of the street a group of Chinese youths, in their late teens and early twenties, lounged against the window of a tea shop. Hair carefully spiked, they were all wearing black leather jackets, designer jeans and black boots. Three of them had cigarettes dangling from surly lips. The stream of passersby gave them a wide berth.

MacLean saw their eyes fixed in his direction. Then he realized that they were staring not at him, but at Shannon O'Shea. "Those kids look like they know you," he said.

"Yes, my undercover days are over. They're part of the Gray Shadows gang. Their big rival is the White Eagles, which is more established. There're at least four major street gangs," she told him. "The local tongs—benevolent business associations, quote unquote—use them to protect territory."

"The street gangs into dope, too?" he asked.

"We assume so. Till now, it's been mostly shakedowns, protection rackets, collecting weekly payments from illegals that were smuggled in. There's been a lot of shoot-outs recently. We figure it's because of the white powder. Too much of it coming in. Too much money."

"And they know who you are?"

"Sure, word gets around fast. They even have a name for me."

"What?"

"The Dragon Lady."

"Are you serious?"

"Yes." She mimicked clawing at him. "Pretty ferocious, huh?"

MacLean surveyed the youths again. Even though he knew Shannon carried the semiautomatic and was a dead shot, he worried suddenly at her vulnerability in the face of such undisguised hostility. "I hope you're watching out for yourself," he said.

"Come on, Tom, I'm a federal agent. Even Mafia wiseguys know better than that."

"Yeah, but didn't you say the Chinese are different?"

The restaurant Shannon took him to was on Bayard Street, a block south of Canal. At first, all MacLean saw were Chinese characters on the curtained window. Then he saw the discreet lettering in the corner that said in English: "Inner Peace Rest." Obviously, no attempt was being made to attract the tourist trade.

"It features the Chiuchow cuisine," she said. "Just opened. The first one in Chinatown, so there must be a clientele. I thought I'd take a look. The Chiuchow are big-time traffickers in Hong Kong and Thailand. They come from Swatow, which to them is what Sicily is to the Mafia."

"Where's Drug Enforcement in all this?"

"Way ahead of us, which isn't saying much. But DEA was the first to spot the new high-level purity of the heroin coming in. It used to arrive already cut and then was cut several times more at the street level. What was left was maybe five percent pure, ten at most. Trouble was there was a ceiling on consumption. A lot of people didn't like tying rubber tubing around an arm to pump up a vein and sticking in a needle. So now they don't have to. With China white, eighty to ninety percent pure, they can snort it like cocaine to get their high."

"So the FBI decided to play catch-up, just in case?"

"You've got it." Shannon O'Shea grimaced. "I'm trying to learn Chiuchow every chance I get. That's what makes Chinese organized crime so tough. Besides the Chiuchow, you've got major Cantonese, Fujianese and Hakka triads, each with its own dialect. Just trying to romanize a name for a positive ID can land you in a padded cell."

The restaurant was about eighty feet by twenty. Along one wall was a long mural depicting misty mountains, a river winding its way down to the sea, a village at its mouth. Old Swatow, Tom thought.

The teak tables were about two-thirds filled. All the other customers were Chinese. They were led to a table in the far corner. The menu had no English translations.

Tom listened as Shannon discussed dishes with the waiter in what he presumed was Chiuchow. The waiter seemed to evidence no surprise at her command of the dialect.

After he left, MacLean said, "Was he just being inscrutable, or is he aware of who you are, too?"

"Who knows?" she said with a sigh. Suddenly she leaned forward, a mischievous grin brightening her face. "Hey, all I know is it's really great to see you again."

He clasped her hand momentarily in response. If it had been anybody other than Shannon, he might have thought she was coming on to him. But he knew that wasn't her way. She was naturally buoyant and enthusiastic, treating him as if they were old comrades in arms. Which, in fact, they were. He remembered that once, during the music-theater case, he had thought about asking her out. It never happened, though. It was right after he and Kay had separated. He seemed to recall that Shannon was seeing someone. Besides, the possibility of an involvement with a former nun was, well, inhibiting. Maybe he wasn't as sophisticated as he liked to believe. For any other guy, it probably would have been a big turn-on.

The waiter reappeared with a pot of tea and tiny cups.

"It's Chiuchow tea," she said. "Strong and bitter. Fabled for curing whatever ails you, including your love life. You must have had it when you were a kid in Hong Kong."

"Actually, no. Because my dad worked at the consulate, we had access to the commissary. Once in a while, we'd have a Cantonese dinner, but mostly it was meat loaf and milk." He couldn't help smiling at the memory. "And lots of creamed chicken and rice."

"How awful. The Ugly Americans. What was your dad doing?"

"He was, you know, in commercial stuff, international trade." It was amazing, he thought, how easily the lie came after all these years. The compact with his father.

When the first course arrived in an earthenware pot, MacLean realized that the meal wasn't going to include the usual standbys like moo shu pork or shrimp with lobster sauce. Shannon served him expertly with her chopsticks. No knives or forks were visible.

"God, this is delicious," he said. "What is it?"

"The waiter said it was a house speciality. Sliced goose tripe in goose blood."

"I'm glad I didn't ask first." He caught the amusement in her eyes. "Is goose tripe also a fabled aphrodisiac?"

"If you're in love, anything you eat is."

"That last time we ate Chinese, I almost asked you for a date."

"No way. You were married. Separated, but married. A rebound girl never gets the fellow. Even in a nunnery, they know that."

"Wait a minute. You were going with someone then. You still seeing him?"

"No." Abruptly, her face grew thoughtful and a little wistful. "When you're female and you're an FBI agent," she said quietly, "you really can't maintain a relationship with someone unless he's on the job, too, and I would never consider that. Too close to home."

The main course was placed before them, a bubbling, unfamiliar casserole dish.

"This time I'm not asking anything," MacLean said.

"Don't worry. It's a mix of pomfret and pork. Lots of garlic." Then, chopsticks poised in midair, she said, "Well, well, look who else is sampling Chiuchow specialities today."

"Who?"

"See the wizened-faced man sitting with the bald one, at that table for six against the wall. Kind of frail, with a shock of white hair. That's Benny Wong. Must be pushing eighty. Chairman of the Bountiful Bowl Tong. Also president of the Greater Chinese Association, which is the umbrella organization for all the tongs. He's the unofficial mayor of Chinatown. What he doesn't know isn't worth knowing. Got here when he was, like, nine years old."

"How could that happen with all the exclusionary laws we used to have against the Chinese?"

"If you're clever enough, there are ways around everything. Back then, if you were a legal resident here, even though you were denied citizenship, and you claimed a son alive and well in China, the chances were you could get him in. Who knew about a family tree in some rural village?"

Between mouthfuls, she went on, "About fifteen years ago, a Harvey Ng fresh from Hong Kong mounted a challenge against him. Harvey wound up in a pool of blood outside his office on Canal Street. Benny was heard to remark that when you ascend stairs, you should do it one step at a time. If you try to race up, you could trip and fall. Benny, of course, denied any involvement, and the murder is still unsolved. When questioned, he said, 'Sixty years someone builds up respect and someone else thinks he can knock it down in one day?' He explained that it was just a general observation on life."

"Who's the man with him?" MacLean asked.

"I don't know."

"She recognized us," Benny Wong said.

"No, not us, *you*," said Peter Pei. "You are the notable personage. I am a nobody. Why should she know of me?"

It was, of course, the most obvious flattery, but Pei was surprised to see how Wong accepted it with such a self-satisfied air, as if it were his due. He wondered if senility had finally wormed its way into Wong's brain. Wong reminded him of those old men in Beijing, intent on hanging onto power until they were carted off in boxes. Still, like them, he was devious and dangerous, a force to be reckoned with. Pei had known Wong when the population of Chinatown was almost entirely male, deprived of women, save prostitutes. And he had privately despised him because of the way he had sought the limelight (which Pei himself had studiously avoided), purportedly speaking for all of Chinatown, currying political favor with the *kwai lo,* the barbarians. He was with Wong now only because he was under instructions that he could not disobey.

He was certain, moreover, that the white woman at the far end of the restaurant, the Dragon Lady, had no idea who he was. Still, it was unsettling—an ominous omen?—that she'd seen him alone with Chinatown's so-called godfather, that she was even in this restaurant, which had opened its doors not a week before. Would she remember his face? Was his picture on file somewhere?

"It is true," Benny Wong was saying. "I am well known because of my dedication to the community. And you have also prospered."

"I try, in humility, to make ends meet."

"It amazes me," Wong said, "how excellently you do in your alcohol business."

"The gods looked kindly upon me. There was no competition. I seized the moment."

"And you have your various holdings in land and buildings. This worthy establishment, for example."

"Ai!" Peter Pei said, a hand raised in mild rebuke. "It is not my establishment alone. I have many clansmen, who participate."

"Ah, yes, from our troubled, ancestral home."

"It is natural. They seek investments now, here in the Mountain of Gold, as they say."

"Do you continue to broker imports?"

"I have provided commercial services for many goods. Delicacies from the sea that our people favor. The finest teas. Even vases of the Ming dynasty."

"And sets of mahjong tiles?"

The question sent a jolt through Peter Pei's entrails. With difficulty, he held his chopsticks steady as he reached for thin noodles nestled in a vinegar and sugar sauce. *How does he know that?* "I *did* import mahjong sets," he said, emphasizing the past tense, choosing his words carefully. "The game is quite popular with barbarian women of the Jewish faith. And while it returned a decent profit, I recently am preoccupied with other enterprises." He paused, pretending to savor the noodles, before venturing, "Why do you inquire?"

"It's of no importance," Benny Wong said. "A representative from one of the big department stores, I believe Bloomingdale's, visited me for ideas. The store is considering opening a Far East specialty section. I suggested sets of mahjong. He said that they were well stocked from Swatow Trading. That's your company, if I'm not mistaken."

He didn't know whether to believe Wong or not. Was a hidden message being sent? Abruptly, Pei decided to change the subject, to get to the point of this meeting. "What *amazes* me," he said, "is how you have maintained your exalted position, the respect you command, despite all the great transformations that are taking place in this community and all our other communities across America."

Nodding his head in agreement at the assessment, Wong said, "I am the necessary link between our world and the outside."

"And you were brilliant in organizing the community so that each tong was supreme in its own territory," Pei said, scarcely able to disguise his disgust at Wong's pomposity.

"Stability and order is the natural way."

"Yes," said Peter Pei, at last able to relish, however briefly, his role as a bad-news messenger. "But now much has gone awry."

"What?" Wong asked, peevishly.

"The youth gangs. They have upset everything. First, they began swaggering through the community, extorting our restaurants, demanding protection money from our shopkeepers, robbing, plundering, seizing the innocent for ransom. Then the tongs made the error of employing them to guard their interests, which only increased their impudence. And then the shootings began. Once-peaceful streets run with blood."

"Ai!" Wong said, raising his hands in protest. "Crazy youths. So many of them! They came so fast!"

Ignoring him, Pei pressed on. "Worst of all, they start to trade in the white powder, selling it themselves to the blacks and the Hispanics, selling it openly on the street, inviting the attention of the police, creating an animosity among the *kwai lo*. Listen to me," Pei said. "Circumstances that you well understand are causing powerful cousins in Hong Kong to contemplate residing here. They do not wish to arrive in an atmosphere of police scrutiny, of public hostility and concern."

Pei saw that he had Wong's undivided attention. "What can be done then?" Chinatown's unofficial mayor demanded.

"Are the tong chieftains clawless and toothless? You are their exalted leader. To begin with, the street trading in the white powder must cease. It is, in the phrase of the *kwai lo,* detrimental to our image. I speak to you as a friend. If you cannot do it, I assure you, the arriving cousins will."

Pei's pleasure in Wong's loss of face was short-lived. Unease gnawed at him again as he watched Shannon O'Shea and Tom MacLean exit the restaurant. What had prompted the Dragon Lady's presence here?

The month had begun so auspiciously. A new batch of Citibank personal and corporate deposit slips had been forwarded by his Chiuchow clansman Ho Shu-shui for the accounts that had been opened in Hong Kong to receive wire transfers from New York.

Like an exquisitely crafted watch, Peter Pei's private little network had operated with unfailing perfection for a long time now, meeting every requirement of the Internal Revenue Service.

Soon, though, the dragon head of Pei's triad, the Righteous and Peaceful Society, would be in New York and Pei could not afford a single misstep. After his lunch with Wong, Pei hurried down Mott Street to his liquor store and went directly to his office in the rear. He had planned on spending the afternoon working on the books. It was tedious labor and his biggest headache, doctoring them to show a profit, to avoid explaining to the authorities why year after year he ran a business that was actually losing money.

But first he had a far more urgent matter to attend to. He did not trust Benny Wong. For nearly a decade the mahjong sets—with the same sender, the same consignee—had routinely passed through U.S. Customs. There were twenty-four sets in each crate. And in the middle of a designated crate, one hundred forty-four tiles in one set were hollowed out to contain the white powder.

So now Pei wrote a message in Chinese characters in quick, practiced brush strokes and inserted it in his fax machine. Not knowing whether Ho Shu-shui was presently in Bangkok or Hong Kong, he dispatched his message to both places: "Desist from all mahjong shipments until further notice."

4

SEVERAL BLOCKS NORTH and a world away from Pei's liquor store, in Manhattan's Little Italy, Frank (Big Frank) Lucano stepped out of his Mulberry Street social club. Lucano, age sixty-two, was the boss of one of New York City's last surviving Cosa Nostra crime families. Where once there had been five families, there were now but two of any stature. And if Alphonse Carparti, the other family boss, some twenty years Lucano's junior, had his way, there would soon be only one.

The moment Lucano appeared, two young tough up-and-comers personally picked by Funzie DiBello for added security sprang to full alert. Until recently, Funzie, who accompanied Lucano wherever he went, was all the security Big Frank required. Until Carparti, that is. Funzie was good people. He'd been in Special Forces in Vietnam. He *liked* being in Vietnam. Not like them fucking college kids that needed a haircut running around burning the flag and everything. Being in Vietnam was good practice, Funzie said.

As Lucano was about to enter his Lincoln Town Car, an elderly woman in black, lines crosshatching her face, made her way haltingly along the sidewalk, bowed slightly and whispered, "*Buon giorno, Don Francesco.*"

Lucano nodded and returned the greeting. Across the narrow street, by the park where the old guys played cards, he saw a knot of men staring at him. One of them waved tentatively. Lucano raised a hand of acknowledgment, which triggered more waves. Big Frank smiled. Hey, he had an ego like anybody else. Maybe Big Frank Lucano wasn't a household word to the public at large, not like Carparti, but here on Mulberry Street they knew who he was, all right.

"Let's walk a little," he said to Funzie.

At a corner vegetable and fruit store, he paused to examine a bin of apples. He could have taken one, of course; nobody would have uttered a word of protest. But he did not. Lucano waited until the proprietor spotted him and came rushing out. "*Padrone*," he said. "What a pleasure!" The proprietor reached for an apple and burnished it carefully with a cloth before offering it to Lucano. "Cortlands, *padrone,* the best. Fresh from my brother-in-law's farm upstate."

Lucano bit into the apple. "Yeah, you're right. So juicy. Not like that cardboard crap you find in them supermarkets."

"May I prepare a basket for you?"

"*Grazie,* no."

"Another time, then. You must come more often. We don't see enough of you these days."

As Lucano proceeded south on Mulberry, people on the crowded sidewalk stepped aside to let him pass. They murmured salutations, their heads inclined toward him. To each Lucano nodded back. No one, though, had the temerity to try to shake his hand, or to otherwise touch him.

At the corner of Mulberry and Grand, Lucano paused. He pointed to his left and said to Funzie, "There's that good cheese place, Di Palo's, down on Grand. Get me some mozzarella."

Funzie turned to one of the two young toughs standing not more than two feet away and said, "There's that good cheese place, Di Palo's, on Grand. Go get some mozzarella. Tell them who it's for."

A circle of gawkers had gathered around Lucano, but they maintained a respectful distance. A man with close-cropped graying hair called out in Italian, "You are looking well, *Don Francesco.* Good health to you, always."

"Thank you. I feel good, thank God."

A boy, perhaps ten, clutched his mother's dress. Big Frank bent toward him. "What's your name?"

"Anthony."

"That's a fine name. You live here, Anthony?"

"No, I live in New Jersey. Me and my mom, we're visiting my grandmother."

"See," Lucano said to Funzie, "the old neighborhood's breaking up. The young people, they're all in the suburbs. It's a shame."

As if on cue, a stirring *canzone* from an espresso café filled the street. Even though there were Italian enclaves throughout the city—Bensonhurst in Brooklyn, Ozone Park in Queens, Arthur Avenue in the Bronx, as well as large parts of Staten Island, where, indeed, Lucano himself resided—it was Little Italy, with Mulberry Street at its heart, that epitomized the Italian-American experience. It was here, on Mulberry Street, that the great celebration, the feast of St. Gennaro, was held annually, attracting throngs not just from the city but from around the nation.

Suddenly, in these last few minutes, the gloom enveloping Big Frank Lucano throughout the past week vanished.

And make no mistake, it had been a miserable week for Big Frank. Sitting right in his own kitchen, the FBI agent Sullivan, a fucking Feebie, told him that Alphonse Carparti had marked him for a hit and that it was going to happen at Miriam Feinstein's place.

Miriam was Lucano's girlfriend. Probably whack her, too, Big Frank thought. Showed you the kind of prick Carparti was, fucking looneytunes with his two-thousand-dollar, double-breasted silk suits and fifteen-hundred-dollar crocodile shoes. Lucano shook his head in disgust. It wasn't like this in the old days. The last time a thing like that happened—when was that, thirty, forty years ago?—was when Little Augie and that broad he was with got clipped in the car outside that motel by La Guardia Airport. There'd been a big sitdown about that afterward. Women were supposed to be left out of it. That was the rule. It was right there when a member was being made, when he said the oath with the holy picture burning in his hands. The oath said it all: Fool around with another member's wife, you're dead meat. Period, no exceptions. The oath didn't say nothing about the wife, even if, you know, maybe she started it.

It just showed how Cosa Nostra was going to the dogs, the sour prospect of it welling up in Big Frank's gorge like one of his periodic gastric attacks. Look what happened to Angelo down in Philly, a boss blown away on his own doorstep in front of his old lady. Was that the right way? But whenever the idea crossed his mind that he might be presiding over the last days of Cosa Nostra, he comforted himself with a reassuring thought. What could possibly take its place?

In his kitchen, Lucano said to Sullivan, "So how come *you're* telling me this?"

"Frank, it's our sworn duty to warn any citizen of any information that comes our way about impending physical harm that might befall him."

Lucano stared into the agent's mocking blue eyes. Clearly, he was enjoying his sworn duty. But the information had to be solid, Lucano reasoned. It was the Miriam part that cinched it. He wondered if the Feebies had bugged her place. He felt his cheeks flame. He'd been having trouble getting it up lately. *Jesus, Joseph and Mary!* Had they been listening to that?

"When's this supposed to go down?" Lucano asked.

"Next week. Tuesday or Friday. Those the regular nights you go there, right?"

If they knew that, the apartment had to be bugged. They could have gotten in easily when Miriam was at her manicurist job at the Waldorf. That's how they first met. "Jeez," he had said when she was massaging his fingers, "you got some wonderful touch," and she'd said, "I just love relaxing people who appreciate it."

Lucano couldn't help himself. "You telling this around to anybody else?"

"Why would you say that?" the agent said, his eyes open wide in mock innocence.

Why? Lucano struggled to maintain his composure. That's what every wiseguy in the city would ask, he thought. *Why?* Why would the Feebies tip Big Frank Lucano that Al Carparti was setting him up for a hit? Why would the Feebies give a shit? Well it didn't matter. He knew he had to take care of this thing himself, shoot down any whispers that he had been talking out of school.

So the first thing Lucano did was to get the word out himself. Better it came from him, evidence that he had nothing to hide. Then he sent Iannuzzi, his consigliere, to a sitdown with Carparti's man, Tony Blades, who denied everything. Which nobody believed, but it put everything on ice, for a while anyway.

The next thing was to arrange to meet with his brother, Father Paul Lucano, four years his senior, in one of the confessionals up at the Church of the Holy Sepulcher. Not even the Feebies would go so far as to bug a confessional. He knew that some smartasses whispered that Father Paul was the real brains behind the Lucano family interests. That was because he was a stand-up guy. "Mafia?" Father Paul had told a reporter who did a feature on the Lucano brothers and the disparate careers they had chosen. "What Mafia? Stop bothering me with this nonsense. Why don't you people write about the real issues in this city, the poor, the homeless, the disenfranchised?"

But while all this talk about Father Paul running things really riled Big Frank, he did secretly seek his brother's advice and counsel. And the truth was that it was because of Paul that Big Frank had built and consolidated his hold on New York's garment center. In former times, Cosa Nostra crime families had extorted protection money from individual manufacturers to safeguard against the extreme likelihood of hijackings. But Father Paul was a visionary who devised a better way, one which eliminated the mayhem and subsequent headlines that hijacking necessarily entailed.

What Big Frank did was take control of all the trucking in the garment industry. Trucking was the choke point, as Father Paul had perceived, and nothing moved except in a Lucano truck, or one owned by his original minority partner, the old Lucchese mob, which had been absorbed by the Carparti family. Comforted by this new stability, to say nothing of the guaranteed soundness of their kneecaps, garment manufacturers immediately acquiesced and passed on the cost to the American consumer. All over the country, for every hundred-dollar sale on a dress or suit, around three and a half went to Lucano's combine.

For his advice and counsel, Father Paul got five hundred thousand in cash every year, tax free. Frank wondered what his brother did with the money, but he never asked. And the old Lucchese mob was happy with the million it got annually. And why not? They didn't have to lift a finger for it. When Carparti appeared on the scene, however, everything changed. Right away he wanted to know why the split wasn't fifty-fifty down the middle.

When Lucano called the rectory and asked for his brother, he was informed that Father Paul was golfing at one of the country clubs he belonged to. So it wasn't until the following day that he got to see him in church. Upon entering, he saw the usual collection of old biddies scattered about in the pews doing their novenas. Big Frank hated the sight of them. One of the big drawbacks about having a sitdown with Paul in the confessional was that he had to do it on his knees. He'd asked Paul if he couldn't slip in a stool or something, but Paul said those biddies had sharp eyes and loose tongues. It wasn't worth the risk.

Big Frank told Paul what Sullivan had said about the hit Carparti had planned.

Obviously, Paul responded, Carparti's aim was to take over the garment center.

"He wouldn't know how to run it."

"Yes, but he doesn't know that."

"*Fuck!*"

"Please, Frank. Watch your language. Not so loud."

Choking with rage, Lucano said, "He'll kill the chicken that lays the golden egg."

"Goose, Frank, it's a goose."

"I know, I know. I just get so fucking mad when you mention Carparti, I forget what I'm saying."

"Well, calm down. You need the family on your side to protect yourself against Carparti. This is what you must do. You will keep the garment center for yourself, of course. But you will announce that from now on members of the Lucano family no longer will have to pay the usual tribute to you as the boss, that as boss you will not expect a piece of the action from their street rackets, the shylocking, bookmaking, the numbers, construction shakedowns, labor protection, fencing, the heists. It is a revolutionary concept that will instantly leave them astonished and grateful. And it will cause great unrest in the Carparti family and turn his attention away from you. It will give you time. The important thing is that you've been forewarned. Given enough time, Alphonse Carparti's big ego will do him in."

"Gee, Paul," Frank Lucano protested, "there's real good money in shylocking. You try getting a bank loan these days?"

"Frank, there can be no exceptions. And while I'm at it, I remind you of one more thing. You are to declare that trafficking in narcotics is forbidden. It, above all else, arouses the public. This edict, given the mentality and avarice of your members, will naturally be ignored. But you must repeat it as often as possible, as if you were reciting the rosary, especially when you suspect a room is being bugged or a phone line tapped by the FBI or the narcotics agents. That will serve you in excellent stead when, as will inevitably occur, a soldier or a *capodecina* in the Lucano family—or better yet, in the Carparti family—is arrested and turned into a Judas."

"All right," Big Frank said. "It makes sense, what you're telling me."

"Good. Now I'll hear your confession and give you your penance."

"Hey, Paulie, I got nothing to confess. And I already done my penance here on my knees. If I can stand up and walk, it'll be a fucking miracle."

As Big Frank Lucano emerged from the Church of the Holy Sepulcher, Funzie said, "Where to, boss?"

"Downtown. Mulberry Street."

On the way, Lucano continued to brood about Carparti. Maybe the Feebies would take care of the way he was shoving their faces in it, doing his nutty Hollywood high-wire act, thumbing his nose at them in the papers and on TV, even posing for the cover of *GQ,* could you believe it? Paul was right. He just had to be patient.

Still, Carparti was nobody to fuck with. All you had to remember was what happened to that deaf-mute that saw the Prizzo snatch. Prizzo was a soldier in the Carparti family who Carparti suspected of skimming some of his shylocking money. Prizzo ended up in the trunk of a green Skylark out by Sheepshead Bay. When Carparti found out the deaf-mute was good at sign language, he had all the deaf-mute's fingers chopped off. "Let's see the dummy talk now," Carparti said.

As they pulled up in front of the family's social club, Lucano wondered why he bothered to come there. For sure, it was no longer a place to do business. The Feebies and the narc agents had bugs planted everywhere. Paul was right. Dealing in junk had done the families in. It wasn't even safe to step outside to do business—it turned out there was even a bug in the parking meter in front of the club. And "walk arounds" were also out. The lawyer, Koenigsberger, had tipped him that the Feebies had laser mikes, which they aimed right at a person and picked up everything he was saying. That was when Lucano invented the "ride around." If he desired a meeting, he would send Funzie out to rent a car. Let the Feebies chew on that. "Let's see them bug every sedan at Hertz, Avis, whatever, they got nothing else to do."

In the club, even after his third espresso, Lucano couldn't suppress a yawn. One of his *capodecinas,* Giuseppe (Joe Woods) Ruggiero, had finally finished bitching about the cost of his daughter Angelina's forthcoming wedding. Joe Woods ran one of the biggest bookmaking rings in the city. He got his name because whenever he was confronted with a problem, he would always say, "You dumb fuck, you can't see the woods for the trees." According to Joe Woods, nothing would do for Angelina at the wedding except daisies, tens of thousands of daisies. "This ain't the right time of the year in New York for daisies," Joe Woods had said. "You got to bring them in from California, air freight. You know how much they charge for them daisies from California? A fucking arm and a leg is what.

I say, 'Angelina, baby, what about roses from Guatemala? I can get a deal on roses. Can't you see the woods for the trees, Angelina?' But no, it's got to be daisies, you believe it?"

Idly, Lucano wondered if the Feebie tape reels were spinning. He could see them listening and thinking hard. What was daisies a new code word for? Or roses?

The thought of Feebie bugs brought back an image of Carparti and another gastric onslaught. Lucano stuck out his hand to Funzie. "Tums," he said.

"Yeah, right here, boss."

Then Big Frank said to Funzie, "Let's go." His intention was to head back immediately to his home on Staten Island. One thing was certain: tonight Miriam Feinstein's place was out of the question.

And then, on the sidewalk, the old lady saying *"Buon giorno, Don Francesco"* changed his plans and his humor.

Now, after waiting on the corner of Mulberry and Grand for the arrival of the mozzarella, delivered on the run, Lucano resumed his stately stroll down Mulberry, passing Paolucci's restaurant, where Vito Genovese, once the undisputed *Capo di Tutti Capi,* Boss of all Bosses, had broken bread each day during his narcotics trial in the late 1950s. As a young man, Lucano had stood in the street, watching while the stolid Genovese, trailed by his entourage and his lawyers, came up from the federal courthouse and climbed the steps to the restaurant. It was an article of faith in Cosa Nostra that it was a frame; Genovese did not deal in drugs. But then it became known that although this might be so, Don Vito had accepted kickbacks from those in his family who were involved in drug trafficking.

Worse yet, in his paranoia in the federal penitentiary at Atlanta, Genovese wrongly decided that another inmate involved in the case—*Joe Valachi!*—was his betrayer and had bestowed on him his famous "kiss of death." This, of course, caused Valachi, a hitherto unknown lowly soldier, to reveal the structure and inner workings of Cosa Nostra, and now, outside Paolucci's, Lucano shivered in the remembrance of this convoluted chain of events and what it had wrought.

Big Frank was ready to turn back. Ahead, two short blocks distant, Mulberry for all practical purposes ceased to be of any interest to him.

Although Mulberry retained its name when it crossed Canal Street, it was most definitely different. On the other side of Canal lay Chinatown. For better than a century, Canal had been an inviolate barrier, however invisible, between two alien cultures.

Suddenly, Lucano heard popping noises ricocheting off the ancient Mulberry tenements. He ducked instinctively behind a parked car. He felt Funzie's hand tighten on his arm. There was another round of pops. And still another. But after a second's reflection, there seemed to be a disarming quality to them. Funzie confirmed this. "Sounds like a bunch of firecrackers," Funzie said.

Lucano stood up and peered in the direction that the popping noises had come from, down toward Canal. Bright red pennants, strung from the facade of a building, fluttered in the breeze. He could see a crowd gathered, spilling into the street. Curious, Big Frank drew closer. There was another burst of firecrackers and then he heard the beat of a drum. And the clang of cymbals.

He went past the Graziano Funeral Chapel, where he had been in grave attendance more often than he liked to recall. Then Funzie cleared a path through the crowd for him.

In the open semicircle formed by the onlookers, he saw a green and black papier-mâché lion about ten feet long, its polyester mane bobbing up and down. There were two pairs of prancing, crouching legs underneath the lion, one pair inside the head, the other at the tail. The lion's eyes glowed an eerie yellow. It took Lucano a moment to realize that they must be battery-operated. A Chinese stood to one side, banging the drum. Another one was clanging the cymbals.

A man next to Big Frank was snapping photographs. From his flat drawl, Lucano could tell he was a tourist. Lucano heard him say to a woman beside him, "It's a good luck ceremony, Martha, to drive away the evil spirits. That's what the guidebook said." Jeez, Lucano thought, he had to listen to this shit from an out-of-towner.

A big sign in the window said "Grand Opening."

Dumbfounded, Lucano stared at it. Right in front of him, right across the way from Umberto's Clam House, where the late Crazy Joe Gallo was gunned down, his head lolling in a rapidly reddening bowl of linguine, was this new restaurant, a restaurant featuring . . . *dim sum!*

One of Lucano's muscular retinue, the one who had scurried off for the mozzarella, uttered his first words that afternoon, exclaiming, "You believe this, skinny-assed little yellow slants putting their chopsticks right down on our turf?"

Lucano did not respond. For an instant, in some inner recess of his mind, he glimpsed a forbidding future. *Fucking Chinks! What do they think? They can go anywhere?*

PETER PEI'S NEPHEW, Duncan Lau, waited on the platform of the elevated No. 7 IRT subway line at the Broadway stop in Jackson Heights, the Borough of Queens, New York City.

A slender five foot seven, he was wearing jeans, sneakers and a green and white New York Jets football jacket. He was nineteen years old, although he looked a good deal younger. He had a shock of straight black hair and a smooth angular face with a slightly ocherous cast. A few days before, just after he walked past two girls, American girls, he had heard one say to the other, "Did you check out that cool Chinese guy?"

He adjusted the strap of the book bag over his right shoulder. Inside the bag were five packets of cash—in denominations of twenties, fifties and hundreds.

The amount of cash in the packets varied, ranging from nine thousand four hundred dollars to nine thousand eight hundred. In preparing and banding the packets, Duncan was careful, as Uncle Pei had instructed, to keep the total in each under ten thousand. That was to avoid the scrutiny of the Internal Revenue Service and other interested law-enforcement agencies, which required notification of any banking transaction that involved ten thousand dollars or more in cash.

From the elevated platform, Duncan could see the four-story brick apartment building two blocks away on a quiet tree-shaded street where he had spent the night. Until Uncle Pei began sending him on these missions, Duncan had never ventured out of Manhattan, and it never ceased to astonish him that even in such bucolic surroundings he was still well within the city limits, not much more than half an hour by subway from the densely packed, clamorous streets of Chinatown. In Chinatown, whenever Duncan looked out a window, all he saw was another tenement, so close that he could practically reach out and touch it.

Duncan himself no longer lived in Chinatown, although his parents were still there. At Uncle Pei's suggestion—which was really an order—he had moved away, choosing the Gramercy Park area, six subway stops uptown. The subway, he had come to realize, determined Chinese migration in the city.

In the past twenty-five years, after the immigration barriers fell, the population of Chinatown had exploded from thirty thousand people to more than one hundred and fifty thousand, bursting out of its traditional ghetto confines below Canal Street into the old Lower East Side Jewish settlements, initially flanking and then directly invading Little Italy. Still, there was never enough space.

So another one hundred and fifty thousand new arrivals began flocking along the same elevated line where Duncan Lau now waited, past La Guardia Airport and Shea Stadium in such profusion that the No. 7 subway train rattling on its elevated tracks had become known as the "Orient Express." Most of them continued all the way to the end of the line, to the decaying neighborhood of Flushing in the far reaches of Queens, and created a bustling new Chinatown.

It was the greatest single ethnic influx since the great immigration waves of Irish, Italians, Jews and Germans a century ago. And these numbers were only the official count. Uncounted tens of thousands of other men and women had been brought in illegally by smuggling syndicates as cruelly indentured laborers in businesses owned by the tongs until they worked off fees that ranged up to thirty thousand dollars.

For a time, Uncle Pei had maintained an apartment for operational purposes in Flushing similar to the one in Jackson Heights. But he had vacated it for the same reasons that caused him to move Duncan out of Chinatown—too many prying eyes, loose tongues, warring youth gangs, and, worst of all, paid informants. Jackson Heights was an ideal solution. A number of Cantonese-speaking immigrants from Hong Kong, instead of following the crowd all the way to Flushing, had decided to cluster there in a relatively compact pocket, large enough so that the sight of a kid like Duncan would not arouse curiosity, yet, at least for the time being, small and peaceful enough not to invite undue police attention.

There were twelve apartments in the building Duncan had just left. The lobby registry indicated that the occupants of eight of these were Chinese.

Uncle Pei's two-room apartment, however—3C—bore no tenant's name. Something else was also different. Its door and the door frame, although they appeared to be identical to others in the building, were solid steel, with two dead-bolt locks. This extra security had been possible because Uncle Pei's Swatow Realty Inc. was the landlord.

Inside the furnishings were spartan. The rear bedroom, looking over the backyard, contained only a cot. In the front room was a sofa, a table and three chairs. The front room walls were bare, except for a big chart. Down one side of it, Duncan Lau had listed the addresses of forty Citibank branches, all in Manhattan, none above Ninety-sixth Street and none in or around Chinatown. And across the chart's top were the numbers of thirty checking accounts. Fifteen were personal and the other fifteen business accounts. Duncan had drawn vertical and horizontal lines on the chart, so that the accounts and bank branches had cross-indexed squares. In each square, he marked the date and amount of every transaction, making sure that no account got more than a single deposit the same day.

At first, only personal accounts had been on the chart, but Duncan told Uncle Pei that he often wasted a lot of time standing in line. He had noticed, though, that most branches had special tellers on hand offering express service to handle the banking requirements of businesses.

"Ah," Uncle Pei said, "very good idea." And within a couple of weeks, he gave Duncan a list of fifteen new accounts of companies, all incorporated in Hong Kong, complete with packs of deposit slips. For his suggestion, Duncan received a thousand-dollar reward in addition to the normal two hundred dollars he got for every deposit he made.

Duncan had come to the apartment the previous evening after getting a call from Uncle Pei. "It is time," Uncle Pei had said, in the agreed-upon code. "Four seven one."

Inside, near the door, he found a canvas duffel bag. Sometimes there would be cheap vinyl suitcases. Once, in Flushing, Duncan remembered, even Hefty trash bags were used. When he unzipped the bag, he saw the bills crammed in it. He switched on the one contribution he'd made to the apartment, a portable CD player, put on a Fleetwood Mac disc and to the beat of "Love Is Dangerous" he began counting. "Always count the money," Uncle Pei had told him. "Money never grows passing from hand to hand." But the total exactly matched the number Uncle Pei had given him over the phone—four hundred and seventy-one thousand dollars. In the morning, Duncan banded the first five packets—he had been cautioned to limit the number of deposits to five a day—filled out the deposit slips and loaded them in his school bag. Then he left the apartment.

Two of the Cantonese restaurants he passed on Roosevelt Avenue were still ladling out bowls of southern China's traditional breakfast staple, *jook*—a steaming soy-milk broth on which customers could sprinkle condiments like pickled lettuce and cucumbers and then dip in tiny balls of fish and pork, or slivers of chicken and beef and sliced preserved duck egg, along with twisted lengths of fried dough.

Duncan Lau went past these places to a coffee shop where he ordered orange juice, coffee and a Danish pastry.

He wondered what Uncle Pei ate for breakfast. He had never eaten breakfast with him. Certainly, his choice of the coffee shop would have met with approval. No one prying, "Oh, you're a student! What school do you attend? What do you study?"

Probably it would never occur to Uncle Pei that Duncan actually preferred the coffee shop fare he was having. "You are Chiuchow," Uncle Pei would tell him. "Never forget it. *Chitkagnin*," he would say. "By ourselves, alone."

All ethnic Chinese refer to themselves as the Han, dating from the Han dynasty around 200 B.C., which marked the decline of feudalism and the definitive rise and expansion of "the Central Country"—*Chung kuo*. China!

Among the Han Chinese, there are several major cultural groupings, each with its own dialect. The Chiuchow were the last to submit to central authority and remained notorious for a special independence, a defiant cohesiveness, against other Han Chinese as well as the white devils, the despised barbarians, the *kwai lo*.

Each time Uncle Pei reminded him of his heritage, Duncan would nod gravely, although the truth was that his own sense of being Chiuchow was tenuous. If he ever drew a distinction, it was that he was an ABC, American Born Chinese, as against an FOB, one Fresh Off the Boat.

He had been born at the New York Infirmary in lower Manhattan, so he had, of course, no memory of the village of Ch'ao-an on the Han River, just above the Chiuchow port of Swatow, where Uncle Pei came from and where his own parents lived until the Communist takeover of China. Nor did he have any recollection of their flight to Hong Kong, where they remained until Uncle Pei arranged their entry into the United States.

Growing up in Chinatown, Duncan was a latchkey kid. His father was a waiter in a restaurant from eleven a.m. to eleven at night. Until he was in the fourth grade, his mother worked half days as a seamstress in a sweatshop loft. Then she tied an apartment key around Duncan's neck so he could let himself in after school and resumed her sewing chores full-time, ten hours a day, six days a week. One or the other of his parents would phone to check on him. As he grew older and occasionally slipped out to roam the Chinatown streets, he would simply take the phone off the hook and claim later that he had been talking to Uncle Pei.

The mere mention of Uncle Pei instantly ended any complaints. Duncan both revered and feared him, not only because he was his *ah souk,* his mother's older brother, a good deal older in fact, but also because he knew him to be a powerful and mysterious figure, a man not to be trifled with, who had been in America for many, many years. Once he had tried to find out more details from his mother, who snapped in some alarm, "Don't ask so many questions! He is our benefactor. Is all you need to know."

Duncan was almost fourteen and about to enter Seward Park High School on the edge of Chinatown when Uncle Pei took him under his wing. "Beware of the gangs," he warned. "Inform me at once if you're approached."

It occurred in the school playground near the end of his first year at Seward.

"Who?" Uncle Pei asked.

Duncan told him that it was Unicorn Frankie Chin, the *dai lo,* the big brother, of the White Eagles. "From around Pell Street."

"Yes, I know. He has the big, hairy mole sprouting between his eyes. What he say?"

"He said he needed more ABCs, who speak good American."

"And?"

"They surrounded me. One of the White Eagles, the one they call Fat Monster, hit me in the stomach and showed me his knife, which he said would be used next against me. Then Unicorn Frankie pissed in a can and held it under my nose. He said I had until tomorrow to decide. If I didn't join, he would piss in the can again and I would have to drink it. Then he smiled and put his arm around me and told me not to worry. After I joined, I could have all the girls I would want."

"You say to him you are unable to oblige because you are occupied working for me, here in the store, Pei Liquors. You say I say so."

Duncan struggled to hide his concern. Unicorn Frankie was a fearsome figure, powerfully squat with his big mole and pockmarked face. He was a Hakka born in Hong Kong. The "guest people," the Hakkas were called, wanderers like gypsies, filtering down from the north of China a thousand years ago—hard-bitten people who, alone among ethnic Chinese, never had the feet of their women bound. By comparison, Uncle Pei, with his balding pate, slight stoop and little potbelly, seemed unprepossessing.

But Uncle Pei appeared to be preoccupied with other thoughts. As Duncan turned away, he said, "Stay away from girls. They talk too much."

The next afternoon, after classes, Duncan saw Unicorn Frankie waiting for him with other White Eagles in the playground. He was holding the can.

Duncan, his stomach knotting, repeated what he had been instructed to say.

Unicorn Frankie looked astonished. "He's your uncle, not just your uncle, your family uncle?" he said.

"Yes, why would I lie?" Sensing that he had the advantage, Duncan challenged him, "Why don't you ask him yourself?"

The Hakka stared at him. Suddenly, he flung the can away and said, "Who needs you?" and stalked off, his followers trailing behind.

Uncle Pei told Duncan it would be best now if he actually came to work in the store after classes. He would be paid five dollars a week. "What about your studies?" his mother protested. Duncan knew that every dollar in the household counted, and he said that he would give four dollars of his pay to her and keep only a dollar for himself. He further mollified her by saying that he would be able to study at the store. There really wasn't that much to do besides sweeping the floor, washing the window once a week and keeping the dust off the stock.

And it was true. Duncan wondered how Uncle Pei could make any money selling liquor. When a customer did come in, it was usually to purchase a present. The Chinese do not as a rule drink at home, and when they go to a restaurant for a special occasion, or to a club, they buy their favored alcoholic drink, French cognac, by the bottle on the spot. Uncle Pei's shelves featured all the expensive brands of cognac. There also was a selection of rice wines. The main whiskey displayed was Johnnie Walker Black Label. What puzzled Duncan, though, were five gift-boxed bottles of Black Bush Irish whiskey that stood in place untouched for months.

Then, just before Christmas, a police sergeant from the Fifth Precinct named Dowd dropped by. All smiles, Uncle Pei immediately gathered up the Black Bush bottles and gave them to Dowd. "For the boys," he said.

Like a terrier with a bone, Uncle Pei appeared unable to relinquish one aspect of Duncan's report of his encounter with Unicorn Frankie. "Do you often think of girls?" he suddenly asked.

Duncan decided to tell the truth. "Yes, I can't help myself."

Uncle Pei scrutinized him for a moment. "It is the natural way," he finally said.

The following Friday evening he took Duncan with him to a refurbished tenement around the corner from his store. They mounted two flights of stairs and stopped by a door with a peephole. Uncle Pei pressed a button and Duncan heard chimes ring. Then the door was opened by a diminutive Chinese woman of a certain age wearing a high-collared, embroidered brocade dress that brushed the floor. At the sight of Uncle Pei, she bowed her head deferentially. Duncan trailed behind them into a sitting room, discreetly lit with porcelain lamps that had golden-tasseled shades. Not having been told what to do, he sat in a corner chair. Fragrance from joss sticks filled the room. The walls were lacquered dark red, and hanging on them were a number of drawings picturing various forms of human copulation. In each, the female or females were uniformly submissive. The males all had immense penises. Staring at them, Duncan felt his own pulsing erection.

Uncle Pei and the woman, in between sips of tea, continued to converse in tones so low that Duncan could not make out what they were discussing. Then, suddenly, his uncle acknowledged his presence. "This is my nephew," he told the woman. "I wish to introduce him to the delights of your house."

Duncan saw the woman press a button on the wall. Moments later, a girl appeared, dressed in a *pao,* a silk robe, cinched with a sash. Duncan could see her nipples clearly outlined against the silk. He was transfixed. She had lustrous black hair. Her eyes were delicately mascaraed. Her face was a pale ivory, her cheeks lightly rouged. Duncan saw his uncle appraising her, then the woman said something to her, and she turned toward Duncan, smiled and beckoned him. Duncan glanced at his uncle, who nodded. He followed her into a chamber with a canopied bed, the first one he had ever seen. She unbuttoned his shirt and then undid his belt. She slipped out of her robe, took his hand and led him into a bathroom. The tub was filled. He could smell the perfumed water. She motioned him to get into the tub. She crouched by it and gently began to sponge him. Duncan saw his erection poking up through the water. Her fingers ran teasingly inside his thighs. He felt them caressing his testicles. Instantly, to his horror, he watched the spurts of semen shoot straight up. He shut his eyes in embarrassment. When he opened them, he saw her regarding him with amusement. "*Ngo dik siu toe,*" she said, giggling. "My little rabbit."

She toweled him off and took him to the bed, where this time he experienced a more satisfactory ecstasy. After he had dressed, he went with her back to the sitting room. No one was there. At the front door, Duncan didn't know what to say, so he said, "Thank you."

The next day at the liquor store, Uncle Pei repeated, "It is the natural way. You are young and you have these urges." He gave Duncan a card with a telephone number on it. "When you have the urge, call this number, identify yourself and ask for Madame Chang. But you also must learn to control yourself. Do not abuse this privilege."

At that moment Duncan Lau realized that he would do anything for Uncle Pei.

On the elevated station in Jackson heights as the No. 7 subway bound for Manhattan rumbled in, Duncan mused that it had been quite a while since he had visited Madame Chang's, really not since he moved to the Gramercy Park area. It was a lively neighborhood with lots of bars, restaurants and clubs in which singles and young marrieds gathered. He had met and slept with several girls, none of them Chinese, and whenever he was asked what he did, he said that he ran a messenger service.

He had been in his junior year in high school when Uncle Pei advised that it would be well for him to establish a legitimate source of income. And that summer he obtained a vacation job as a messenger for a large advertising agency through the agency's chief executive, who frequented the restaurant where Duncan's father had become his favorite waiter. Duncan soon became the swiftest messenger, entrusted with the most urgent and important deliveries. He continued to work part-time at the agency, with Uncle Pei's blessing, during his senior year. By then, he had learned that the outside service the agency also used was charging ten dollars per delivery. So Duncan, after graduating, recruited and trained a number of his high school pals who had no immediate employment future, and contracted with the agency to provide the same service at half the price. He had since expanded his clientele to include the New York office of a major motion-picture studio and a public-relations company. He made daily rounds to the offices of his clients to make sure everything was running smoothly and carried a beeper in case of a crisis. And there were still the deposits to be made for Uncle Pei, which was why he had suggested the addition of business accounts to save valuable time in his crowded schedule.

During the past year alone, Duncan had made four hundred and forty-eight deposits adding up to four and a half million dollars, thus earning himself eighty-nine thousand six hundred dollars in cash. As a dutiful son, he gave three hundred dollars a week to his parents, and kept the rest in safe-deposit boxes, which currently contained a total of almost a hundred and twenty thousand dollars. Duncan was thinking of investing some of it in real estate in still another blossoming Chinese enclave in the Sunset Park section of Brooklyn. He also was considering the possibility of a Chinese take-out restaurant around the corner from the office building where the ad agency was located and where he had become such a familiar and popular figure.

In any event, he planned on asking Uncle Pei's advice. These days he met with Uncle Pei only to supply him with the deposit duplicates once a particular cache of cash had gone into the banking system, or if the amount stashed in the apartment did not tally with the coded figure he was given over the phone. "It is best that we are not too much seen together," Uncle Pei had said, and Duncan did not demur. He was under no illusion about the source of the great sums of money he was handling. He did not know any of the details of how it was arranged, nor did he desire to. It was simply business, he told himself, and none of his business at that.

The morning rush hour was over when Duncan boarded the train. His car was empty save for a homeless man stretched out snoring on one of the benches. At the far end were two burly men he recognized as Koreans. They must be coming in from Flushing, he thought. Following the Chinese, Asians of every variety could be found there.

Two lanky, boisterous blacks around Duncan's age got on at the next stop, roughhousing with each other. They eyed Duncan, who instinctively scrunched down trying to look like a schoolboy with not a nickel in his pocket. Then he relaxed. He saw the Koreans staring at the black kids as if *they* wanted to start something. There was plenty of bad blood between African-Americans and Koreans. Duncan had heard that in the Korean all-night markets that dotted the city an automatic pistol always lay by the cash register, ready to be pulled out if a black guy came in and so much as looked crossways at the storekeeper.

In Manhattan Duncan's initial deposit was at a Citibank branch on Third Avenue. Then he worked his way across midtown. Not much more than an hour had elapsed before he made his fifth and last stop at a large branch at Fifty-sixth Street and Broadway. Standing in the priority services line, he was lost in thought, contemplating the prospects for the take-out restaurant. As soon as he was finished at the bank, he intended to pass by an empty store that was available for leasing.

He was at the teller's window, reaching back in his bag for the final bundle of cash, when he heard a voice say, "Oh, it's you again. I don't believe it. Where do you get all this money?"

Stunned, Duncan looked up and saw disaster in the form of a round-faced young woman with brown hair whose name tag said "Pam Erikson."

He remembered her at once. It had been about three months before, at another, smaller Citibank branch at Sixty-fifth and Madison Avenue. He had been making a personal deposit and she suddenly commented on how much cash was involved. Duncan quickly replied that he was making the deposit on behalf of his father, that it was savings his father had accumulated to send to relatives struggling to make ends meet in China. "It is a tradition among our people to help those of our family who are less well off."

She must have been promoted and transferred to priority services, Duncan thought. He cursed himself. *Why* hadn't he noticed her and gone to another line? How could he have been so stupid?

And then, as he desperately tried to think of what to say, he recalled sensing that she really hadn't cared about the money. She'd been trying to engage him in conversation.

It was his only hope. So he smiled at her and said, "I was asking for you over on Madison Avenue and they said you were here. Listen, I'll explain everything if you have dinner with me."

He held his breath. Then she smiled back and said, "Sure, why not? I have to work late tonight. I'll be through at six."

"It's my lucky day," he told her.

Before picking her up, Duncan changed into a jacket and slacks. He took her to Pete's Tavern on Irving Place, right below Gramercy Park, which attracted a young crowd. He counted on this to make her feel comfortable. But most important, he was known there, and she would realize that he was somebody.

He was pleased when the night manager came by and said, "Hey, Duncan, how's it going?" and when he asked her what she wanted to drink, she said a margarita with salt and when he asked what that was, she laughed and said it's a Mexican drink that she had for the first time herself the other night.

"I'll have one, too," he said. "To celebrate my good luck."

She told him she was from Cleveland, Ohio, and that she had come to New York seeking some excitement, a goal that had thus far eluded her. "I've never been out with a Chinese fellow before," she informed him.

Then, halfway through dinner, after he had explained how he had launched his messenger service, just when he began to entertain the notion that she had forgotten what triggered all of this, she said, "So what's with those cash deposits?"

He had spent most of the afternoon rehearsing his explanation, and now he leaned forward, lowering his voice, intent on conveying his ultimate trust in her—that, indeed, he was literally placing his life in her hands. What he was doing, he confessed, was kind of illegal. Thousands of Chinese immigrants were arriving in America. Hardly any of them spoke English. They slaved night and day and had little money for a few precious moments of relaxation and entertainment, even to go to a movie. And they yearned more than anything for the escape that movies provided, movies they could understand. The cash he was depositing was from pirated videotapes made in Hong Kong and China and sold here at a discount price these people could afford. While he received a small commission for each deposit, it was really like robbing the rich to help the poor.

"If you report me," he said with all gravity he could muster, "I will have to go to jail."

"Oh, wow," she said. "I think I want another margarita."

6

Shannon's merry green eyes, with their flecks of brown, danced in Tom's memory all morning the day after their Chinatown lunch. He was about to call her, when she phoned him instead.

"I was just thinking about you," he said. "What a terrific time I had yesterday."

"And all I've been hearing is about you. It's all over the office that you're leaving. The agents are real upset. So are the postal inspectors and the IRS guys. I didn't realize you had so many admirers. Male ones, that is. No chance of you changing your mind?"

"Nah. It's time for me to find out what the world out there's like. Listen, let's talk about something important. Like when can I see you again. You free tonight?"

"I wish. But that's always the problem. I'm working." She paused. "Tell you what, though. You haven't quit yet and we've got something interesting going down. More education for you."

"When and where?"

"Be in front of the courthouse. Six o'clock. I'll pick you up."

It was nine p.m. Shannon had parked on a side street off Main Street in Flushing, Queens. The closest Tom had ever been to Flushing prior to tonight was to watch a baseball game when the Chicago Cubs played the Mets at Shea Stadium in Flushing Meadow. But where he was now could just as well have been a million miles from New York City, or at least the New York City he knew. He felt totally discombobulated, as if he were the butt of some bizarre geographic joke.

Physically, Main Street had the appearance of any small town main street, U.S.A., with low-rise wood and brick buildings. The only thing lacking to complete the picture was a Civil War monument. Except for the street names, however, there was scarcely a sign in English. Instead, the whole area was ablaze with neon Chinese characters, and teeming with people, like Mott Street in Manhattan's old Chinatown, but without any sense of being cloistered, closed-in.

He could see the glow from where they were parked. And beyond it, in the distance, the Manhattan skyline, including the lighted towers of the World Trade Center and the Empire State Building.

"I can't believe it," he said.

"Hey, *you* can't believe it?" Shannon said. "How about me, mister? Remember, I'm a Queens girl." She pointed to a four-story apartment building. "That's where it's supposed to be stashed. Apartment 2H."

The information was from a hot new CI the Bureau had developed, she had said on the drive from Manhattan. A major cache of China white.

Ah, the fabled CI, MacLean couldn't help thinking, without which law enforcement, or at least most of it, would be helpless. CI used to stand for confidential informant. Then some alert semanticist in the Department of Justice decided that anything smacking of informer carried undesirable connotations for a jury. So the new tag for a CI—cooperating individual— was ordained. It had a much better ring, implying dutiful citizenship, doing the right thing.

This operation was to be a joint effort of FBI agents and city police, with the FBI, in the person of Shannon, in charge. Tom watched as the shadowy figures under her command moved around them. An agent in a blue jacket with "FBI" in yellow letters on the back came up to Shannon. "OK, we're ready," he said. "The rear's covered." MacLean could see the bulk of the bulletproof vest underneath the agent's jacket.

"Fine. Let's do it," she said.

In the building lobby, Shannon, also in a jacket and vest, drew her semiautomatic. All at once, her jaw set, she didn't look so vulnerable to MacLean anymore. Four other agents were standing by, along with three cops who wore "NYPD" jackets. One of the agents was carrying a hydraulic pump with flexible metal prongs the size and width of credit cards. Two of the cops held the handles to a battering ram, about six feet long, with a solid steel ball at one end. Everybody else had shotguns.

As they started climbing the stairs, another agent, already positioned on the second-floor landing, waved them up. "Stay back," Shannon O'Shea whispered to Tom. "You never can tell."

He watched them move down the corridor. Where in earlier decades there might have been the smell of Jewish cuisine, perhaps stuffed cabbage or potato pancakes, tonight they were greeted by the scent of food being stir-fried in woks.

Apartment 2H was at the far end of the hallway, directly facing them.

The agent holding the pump wedged the prongs between the door locks and the doorjamb. He glanced behind him and nodded.

Shannon shouted, "FBI!"

Instantly, the agent worked the pump. The locks, under the enormous pressure, popped in less than a second. Almost simultaneously, the two cops slammed the steel ball of the battering ram against the door.

The door fell in with a crash. The agents and cops rushed inside the apartment, Shannon with them. Tom MacLean heard the shouting, the commotion, but no gunshots.

Then he saw her back in the corridor, beckoning to him as she returned her semiautomatic to her holster. He followed her into the apartment. In the front room, three young Chinese facing a wall were being handcuffed. Two handguns were on a coffee table.

Shannon screwed her face up in theatrical disgust. "No China white," she said. Then she broke out in a big smile. "But lookee, lookee! We got something else!"

She took him into a second room. Tom's eyes widened. He had never seen so much cash in his life. Reaching almost from the floor to the ceiling were bundles of bills, mostly hundred-dollar bills. They seemed oddly compressed. On a table, he saw a strange contraption made of welded steel with clamps and a lever.

"That's what they use to press heroin bricks," she told him. "You keep reading in the papers about seizures—so many kilos or pounds, right? But the Chinese have an ancient weighing system of their own. We call it a unit. They call it a *jin,* roughly seven hundred grams, or about a pound and a half. Now a kilo of cocaine, two-point-two pounds, is going for maybe ten thousand bucks. But a unit of China white, which is not much more than half that, goes for nine times as much—up to *ninety thousand,* coin of the realm. And," she said, waving at the stacks of money, "what you're looking at over there, coin of the realmwise, squished for easier transportation out of the country, are the wholesale proceeds. God knows what it brought on the street."

"How do they get the money out?"

"Probably just in suitcases, although it's a little riskier nowadays. Customs is starting to inspect more outgoing baggage to suspect destinations like, say, Hong Kong. So you go the other way, via Europe. And once you arrive in Hong Kong, you're home free. Carrying cash into Hong Kong, believe me, is not a felony."

"Well, anyway," MacLean said, "there must be millions here. You've made a real dent."

"I wish. This is maybe three months' worth of sales and it's only one operation. The stuff pours in every way you can think of. Parcel Post. Even FedEx. Mules, people who swallow condoms of it. In picture frames. In golf cart tires." She shook her head. "Inside those big fancy goldfish people decorate their ponds with. Of course, they're dead, but there are always some dead fish in every batch. A few weeks ago, it was porcelain vases in open crates. A few cross strips of wood holding the vases in place. Nothing hidden there, you'd think. Except the posts of each crate were hollowed out and filled with China white."

They went into the front room. An FBI agent was reading the youths their Miranda rights in English. "You have the right to remain silent . . ." They stared blankly at the agent.

A cop, Chinese, yelled at them in Cantonese. More blank stares.

Suddenly, Shannon began jabbering at them in a dialect MacLean was unfamiliar with. For the first time, they appeared startled, the blank stares gone. First one and then another answered, haltingly, as if they could not comprehend how this strawberry-blond young woman could be speaking to them in their own tongue.

"They're Hakka," she said. "Probably fresh recruits right off the boat, the *sai lo,* little brothers they call them, in the White Eagles. That's a gang run by a Chinatown tough guy named Unicorn Frankie Chin. Getting to be big-time, Unicorn Frankie is. Oh boy, I wish he'd been here, but the top ones never are. Two of them admitted knowing who he is. But that's all. They claim some stranger offered them a hundred bucks each to baby-sit the money. The guns were here when they arrived. And then we arrived. Period. End of story."

"What are you going to do with them?"

"Book them. See if any of them are illegals. Trace the guns. See if we can flip one of them. See if their parents have any influence. The trouble is the White Eagles are undoubtedly the only real family they have. Not every Chinese kid is another Albert Einstein. Kids like these can't hack it in a new environment. They're embarrassed, humiliated, in school, and then along comes Unicorn Frankie to fix them up with money, girls, clothes, cars. In court, as it now stands, they'll walk." She frowned at the prospect of the judicial process, then brightened. "I didn't mean to down-play the significance of all that cash in the other room," she said. "This is a big score for our side."

On the way back into Manhattan, he asked, "How much of this stuff is coming in, do you think?"

"Tom, it's all guesswork. For years, the estimate was five hundred thou-sand addicts. Now, it's been bumped to a million. The truth is nobody re-ally knows." An undercurrent of anger and frustration crept into her voice. "But I'm here to tell you it's not simply a ghetto addiction, a thought America likes to comfort itself with. It's all over the place, in the South Bronx, no argument, but it's also spreading out to every suburban mall in the country. China white isn't a party drug, like cocaine, that everybody talks about. It's a solitary splendor."

At the first red light on the Manhattan side of the Midtown Tunnel, two blacks in their twenties advanced toward her car with squeegees for an unwanted windshield cleaning, an event that united every white middle-class driver in the city in fear and loathing. Before Tom could wave them off, Shannon suddenly rolled down her window and said, "Beat it."

They stopped, frozen, then retreated. "Yo, lady, we ain't no muggers," one of them said. Marvelous, he thought. There was a true sense of jungle out there. Somehow, they knew this was the wrong car to pick on.

"I've got to go back to the office," she said.

"I'll come with you. Maybe we can grab a bite afterward."

"OK. That'd be great."

Shannon O'Shea turned off the FDR Drive at the Brooklyn Bridge exit and drove to Federal Plaza, where the FBI's New York headquarters is lo-cated. When she and Tom got off the elevator, several agents still on duty applauded. Then a stylishly coiffed gray-haired man, in a blue blazer and gray slacks, came out of an office and walked toward them.

"That's my boss, Wakefield," she whispered. "Thinks he's quite the fashion plate. Must have rushed down from the Twenty-one Club. You'd be surprised how many of our major citizens are delighted to buy him drinks. Look, he's smiling. I must have done something right."

"Oh, yes, MacLean," Wakefield said after Shannon introduced him. "Great work you're doing across the street. He scrutinized them both, obviously trying to puzzle out what they were doing together.

"Tom," she said, "my office is over there. Be back in a flash."

MacLean sat at her desk. He noticed a pile of copies of the *South China Morning Post,* Hong Kong's dominant English-language daily. And on the desk, folders of clippings from it. They all seemed to be about the colony's Chinese tycoons. One had a headline: "Men with the Midas Touch."

After a few minutes, Shannon returned. "I couldn't resist," she said. "I told him rumors of your resignation might be premature. You might be taking over organized crime and drug enforcement in the U.S. attorney's office. He's all atwitter." Then her face turned solemn. "I'm sorry. I'd like nothing better than to be with you. But the rest of the night's gone. The assistant director here wants me on the phone. And so does Washington. And I have to write up the events of the evening, pronto."

"I figured as much, but tell me something," Tom MacLean said, pointing at the folders with the clippings. "What's that all about? They all look to be about upright citizens, the Hong Kong elite."

"It's just a personal hangup I have. Practically every one of them arrived penniless in Hong Kong in forty-nine or so, fleeing the Communists. They're all connected, somehow. At least, a lot of them. I like to keep track, is all."

"You're kidding. Triads?"

She looked at him a little sheepishly. Finally, she said, "Yes. You know how they're always talking about Cosa Nostra infiltrating legitimate businesses. Well, the triads have been doing it for hundreds of years. Sometimes, I think Marco Polo brought back what became the Mafia's initiation rites from China along with the silk and spices."

She phoned Tom in the morning. "I didn't get out of the office till four a.m. They're holding a big press conference at noon to show America the FBI's on the ball. Show the DEA we're in the game. They counted the money. Eight million six hundred thousand. That translates into about a hundred and forty pounds of China white, wholesale, I remind you."

"Listen," Tom said. "Could you do me a favor?"

"Name it."

"Would you look in those fabulous files of yours and see if there's a man named Deng in them anywhere. I only have the initials. Y. K."

7

H<small>E WAS BORN</small> Deng Yue-keung. It means a strong friend. But from that time in Shanghai in 1949, normal ties of friendship meant nothing to him. All he demanded, and got, was fearful respect.

He was then sixteen years old and a university student. It was a period of great foreboding. The Communist forces under Mao Zedong, coming from the north, were driving through central China. For months, his father spoke wearily of the militancy of the workers at his cotton mill. His father had come from his native Swatow to establish the mill. As for many enterprising Chiuchow, Swatow was too much of a backwater compared to the great sprawling seaport of Shanghai, bursting with global commerce. His father nonetheless advised him constantly, "You are Chiuchow. You are special."

Then one afternoon, after the daily lesson in the English language that his father insisted that he take to prepare for the challenges of a changing world, he returned to his neighborhood, turned a corner and saw the smoke rising from his home.

He ran into the house somehow knowing what he would find.

His father's dismembered body was in a sitting room on the ground floor. His head had been hacked off. There was a sign on his bloody torso. It said "Exploiter of the Masses."

His mother's corpse was in an adjoining room. She was naked. She had been disemboweled, a gaping wound rising from between her legs up over her abdomen.

He found his older sister in her bedroom. Her thighs were smeared with blood. Her breasts were cut off. Her throat was slit. The sign placed on her read "Capitalist Whore." Her eyes were still open, gazing sightlessly at him.

He shuddered, walked to her and gently closed her lids. He kissed her on the forehead.

To his own surprise, he did not erupt in an explosion of grief. Instead, he was enveloped by an icy rage, the chill of which had never deserted him.

Almost immediately, two strangers arrived and spoke to him in the Chiuchow dialect. One of them, named Ho Shu-shui, was a short, muscular man in his early twenties. After introducing himself and extending his condolences, Ho said that he was from the village of Ch'ao-an in the mountains surrounding Swatow. "We are of the Righteous and Peaceful Society," he said. "We offered our protection to your father, but he declined. Your father was a noble and respected man who did not comprehend that he could not stand alone."

Deng, of course, was aware of the Righteous and Peaceful Society. His father had explained how these secret orders came into being centuries ago as patriotic defenders of China, but eventually had become criminalized. The turning point occurred when Chiang Kai-shek used them to break the Communist labor unions in Shanghai. As a reward, they were freed by the government to do as they wished. They dealt in opium, his father said.

"We offered our help to your father," Ho Shu-shui said. "Now we offer it to you. We will be your brothers. The police," he said, "are useless. There have been seven other incidents in the city today, such as the tragedy that has befallen the house of your father."

"I accept," Deng replied without a moment's hesitation. "I accept, with gratitude."

The Society made the funeral arrangements. He took photographs of his father, mother and sister, packed one bag of clothing and left the house. The evening after his family was buried, he was inducted into the *Hung* brotherhood in a ceremony of ancient tradition.

The incense master wore a white robe, the color of mourning, in reverent memory of the First Five Ancestors.

The incense master spoke of the one hundred and eight monks, trained in the martial arts, who gathered so long ago at the Shaolin monastery in the province of Fujian to fight the northern invaders, the Manchus. And he spoke of the betrayer among them who had caused the forces of darkness to surround and set aflame the monastery, and how all perished in the fiery holocaust, save for a precious few who lay protected under the yellow curtain that fell so miraculously over them in the great hall, enabling them to breathe. And of those few, how only five in the end—the First Five Ancestors—finally managed to escape in billowing smoke after chopping a hole through the monastery walls.

And now at the altar, in front of the incense master, Deng and other chosen initiates slipped through the bamboo hoop with serrated strips of red paper at the top and bottom symbolizing that jagged hole in the monastery wall, reliving the moment of avenging rebirth. "It is thus," each one repeated, "that the vagina of my mother has teeth."

And then, said the incense master, after many travails and much suffering, the First Five Ancestors prayed for divine guidance in the night and the *hung* light, the red light, appeared in the eastern sky, whereupon they declared themselves to be men of the *Hung*.

In unison, the initiates chanted the litany of oaths. A bowl of wine was brought forward, and after that a live cock. The cock's head was severed and held over the bowl. "This cock's head sheds fresh blood," the incense master proclaimed, "and brings with it loyalty and righteousness and the enjoyment of longevity. Only the wicked and the treacherous need fear the fate of this cock."

The incense master held up a silver needle with a long red thread. He punctured the middle finger of Deng's left hand and, as a drop of his blood appeared, it too was added to the bowl.

The yellow woven scroll hanging over the altar on which the oaths, thirty-six in all, were inscribed was burned in homage to the life-saving monastery curtain. Then its ashes were stirred in the bowl. Each initiate stepped forward and drank from the bowl.

"We are now of one blood," the incense master chanted. "We pledge that we, the brethren, shall be as if from one womb, as if begotten by one father, as if nourished by one mother."

His dead mother's handmaiden, wailing hysterically, provided the names of the two troublemakers at the mill who led the mob that slaughtered his family. Accompanied by Ho Shu-shui, he sought them out. On their knees, they pleaded for mercy. He shot them both with the revolver that his new blood brothers had given him. He aimed first at their genitals, and as they lay writhing on the ground, screaming, he paused for a moment, relishing their agony, before bending forward and emptying the rest of the bullets in the cylinder into their faces.

In the weeks that followed, under orders, Deng executed seventeen members of the local Communist Party cadre one by one. He did not know anything about his targets, other than where they could be located, nor did he care. Ho marveled at his methodical efficiency. "You never show the slightest emotion."

"Don't worry," he replied. "I take the greatest pleasure from my work." Within three months, he was officially designated an officer of the Society, a red pole, an enforcer. But Chiang Kai-shek's Kuomintang armies continued to crumble against the Communist troops, and by the end of 1949 Chiang himself had fled to Taiwan.

Deng went south with Ho to Swatow, but he found he had no links left there. His father's brother, a Kuomintang general, had died fighting the Japanese, and Deng had no idea what had happened to the family.

So he accompanied Ho to Ch'ao-an to collect Ho's sister, An-shui. Deng was immediately taken with her. She was a sturdy girl, the same age as he, and much fairer than her brother, with wonderfully expressive eyebrows and a forthright manner that he found so much more pleasing than the cloying coyness of the female students in Shanghai. She clutched his hand tightly as they boarded a junk one night in Swatow bound for Hong Kong, and it suddenly occurred to Deng that while he had personally killed nineteen men, he had yet to know a woman.

Tens of thousands of refugees were swarming into the English colony, and they had no difficulty in landing undetected on the Kowloon side, separated from Hong Kong Island itself by the narrow straits of Victoria Harbor.

Ho led the way to Kowloon's Walled City, where the Righteous and Peaceful Society was gathering to regroup.

Nothing could have prepared Deng for what he was about to enter as he descended the steps of an alley not more than two feet wide. Roughly four hundred by seven hundred feet, the Walled City was said to contain some fifty thousand human beings, the most densely populated real estate on earth.

Festering and decaying, it was a nightmarish place in which the sun never shone. Instantly, a pervasive stench assailed Deng's nose. An-shui again clutched his hand. If Ho had not chosen the right entry, where a Society member awaited them, they might have wandered endlessly, lost.

Structures as high as fifteen stories rose in a crazed, honeycomb fashion. The widest passageways were five feet. Most, twisting and turning, leading up and down, were no more than two or three feet across. Occasionally, a dim naked bulb lighted the way. Overhead were grimy, spidery networks of wires and cables. Underfoot there was one slimy puddle after the next, and every wall was damp to the touch. Yet in this truly unholy place, life went on. He passed windows through which he glimpsed bakers at work, miniature factories turning out machine parts and plastic toys, stores displaying foodstuffs, others stocked with clothing.

It also was a place where the police did not venture.

The room provided to him, Ho and An-shui was eight feet by ten. It had pallets, a solitary bulb, a gas burner, a basin and a porcelain toilet hole in the floor in one corner. Outside, in the hallway, was a water pipe with a spigot.

The look on Deng's face must have betrayed him. "I suppose," Ho said, "this doesn't suit your pampered past. I regret the lack of silken pillows."

The memory of his burning home and what he had found inside rushed through him. And then Ho saw another look on Deng's face, one that was the last image seen by nineteen men who were no longer alive.

"I'm sorry, my brother," Ho hastily said, backing off. "It was a stupid joke. I'm sorry."

Deng struggled to quell his anger. Finally, he said, "I'm sorry, too."

The close proximity with An-shui night after night increased his desire for her until he no longer could bear it. "I wish," he at last told Ho, "to make your sister my wife."

Ho's response acknowledged what tacitly had become the reality of their relationship. Despite Ho's older age and much longer membership in the Society, Deng had become the leader. "I am honored," Ho said. "My sister has spoken to me of her deep feeling for you." He bowed his head deferentially. "I welcome you again as a brother. And I will seek other space for myself."

They were married in a Buddhist ceremony. To celebrate, Ho produced a bottle of the finest cognac. "It's stolen, of course," he chortled, "which only makes it taste better."

Within a month, Deng was summoned to the Walled City quarters of the Righteous and Peaceful Society's dragon head, its *lung tao,* whom he had never met. He was a chubby man about sixty, with sly eyes. Deng instinctively disliked him, but personal feelings were of no consequence in the brotherhood. The thirty-sixth oath said, "After entering the *Hung* gates, I shall be loyal and faithful to all my sworn brethren."

The dragon head said, "Elements of two Kuomintang armies, as well as the Ninety-third Division, have gathered in Yunnan Province along the border with Burma and Laos. The Americans, I am told, hope to use them to launch a counterattack against Mao." As he said this, the dragon head raised a limp, deprecating hand, as if already dismissing the prospect of success.

"The commander of the Ninety-third Division," he continued, "is General Li Wen-huen. He is well disposed toward us. His father is Yunnanese, but his mother is Chiuchow. His mother's late brother was a *pak sze sin* in our Society and we have made the general aware of it."

Deng listened intently, unsure of what the purpose of this was. A *pak sze sin,* a white paper fan, was a dragon head's chief counselor.

Then the dragon head got to the point. The Society's finances must be replenished to enable it to gain its proper place in Hong Kong. It was imperative to make an arrangement with the general to share the benefits to be derived from the *ya pien,* the opium poppy.

"General Li," he said, "controls much of the poppy fields. I have chosen you for this mission. While you are young, you have proved yourself steadfast and, more important, resourceful. Your uncle was also a Kuomintang general, which will be of great significance to Li. Above all else, what we seek for the Righteous and Peaceful Society is a continuous, dependable supply. Trust therefore is vital, particularly as regards payment, which, you are to inform the general, will be arranged through Chiuchow banking procedures. You should not go alone. Who do you wish to be with you?"

"Ho Shu-shui."

"Yes, as I anticipated. I hear you work well together. Remember, however, you work on behalf of all of us."

They traveled by boat to Bangkok and north through Thailand to the Golden Triangle, armed with identity documents expertly forged by Society technicians inside the Walled City. In Thailand, they would be among friends. Of all the Chinese who had settled there, the Chiuchow

were the most populous and powerful—especially in *hu kwan,* the underground banking system, a system that flourished wherever the Chiuchow had established themselves, a system based on trust, impervious to
governmental currency controls. In the winding maze of streets that
make up the Western market district of Hong Kong, interspersed among
the commodity trading houses, are obscure finance and gold shops.
Someone walks into one of them, deposits cash and gives the name of a
recipient in Bangkok. The coded information is relayed to a sister shop in
Sampeng, Bangkok's original Chinese quarter. The recipient is then noti-
fied, usually within the hour, and told, "Your money's ready." There is no
physical or wire transfer of money, no paper trail exists. Billions of dollars change hands throughout Southeast Asia in this manner, not just
from overtly criminal enterprises, but in flight capital and to avoid taxes
as well.

From the frontier village of Mae Sai, in northern Thailand, a Chiuchow
resident, for a modest sum, led Deng and Ho on an arduous trek through
jungle trails to the Yunnan border. Their guide pointed to a dirt road,
which would lead them to General Li's encampment.

The general was a youthful, pear-shaped man with a round, jolly face
offset by piercing eyes as black as olives. He greeted Deng warmly. "I did
not know your uncle personally," he said. "But he came to lecture us at the
military academy. He was a man of courage and honor."

Deng was appalled by Li's bedraggled, ill-equipped troops and understood why the dragon head dismissed the likelihood of success against
Mao's armies.

The next morning, though, he was awakened in his tent by the drone of
aircraft. When he looked out, he saw scores of parachutes in the air carrying crates of what turned out to be arms and ammunition. "It is from
the Americans," the general said. "The Central Intelligence Agency."

"What's that?"

"I'm not sure myself," the general said. "But they have promised to re-
inforce us. That's why we built this airstrip."

More planes made drops the following day, and then others actually
landed, all of them unmarked, bringing equipment too heavy for parachutes. Then, the third and fourth days, even more planes arrived. This
time they also carried a thousand elite Kuomintang soldiers from Taiwan.

Among them was an American big nose from this strange agency, who
introduced himself, through his Taiwan interpreter as, "Cox, CIA." He was

a florid-faced man in a safari jacket, a holstered revolver at his side. He spoke rapidly, emphasizing his words with windmill-like gestures. Even his interpreter had trouble following him.

"What did he say?" the general asked.

In Chiuchow, Deng interrupted. This Cox, he said, wanted immediate preparations for an assault on the provincial capital, Kunming.

"You speak English?" General Li said to Deng, also in Chiuchow, which the Taiwan interpreter clearly did not know.

"Yes." Then, with impulsive boldness, Deng added, "I think what he really wants is a sacrificial second front because of the war between the Americans and the Communists in Korea."

"I agree," the general said grimly. "But I need these arms for the war that will really count. Control of the poppy fields."

"What did he say?" Cox demanded of his interpreter, who turned helplessly to Deng.

"He says he agrees completely," Deng said, and the general, nodding his assent, said, "Yes, completely."

Cox, mollified, gazed curiously at Deng.

"Remain with me for a time," General Li told Deng. "I want to know exactly what is being said."

A week later Deng and Ho returned to Thailand. And with them were mules bearing a thousand pounds of raw opium in their saddlebags, escorted by Li's soldiers. Li had not even demanded prepayment. "You will promptly receive your money," Deng told him.

"Of that, I have no doubt," the general said. "You are a man of trust." Li permitted himself an expansive grin. "Besides, if I don't, it will be the last of the poppy that the Righteous and Peaceful Society will ever get from here."

Then the opium was hidden in produce being trucked south. But even this precaution was not really necessary, since in those days, drug control was practically nonexistent. With equal ease, they voyaged back to Hong Kong aboard the same tramp steamer.

Shyly, An-shui told Deng, "I am with child. I hope you are pleased."

To Deng's surprise, flickers of emotion, of feeling, stirred within him. Yes! He had lost a family in Shanghai, but now he would start a new one. He held his wife gently. As soon as he completed his present work, he assured her, they would be able to vacate the Walled City. "I will find a home where the child can be raised in good health."

One of the problems in converting the opium to morphine base was the vile, distinctive fumes that the process produced. Often, to avoid police detection, boats were used as floating laboratories. Deng proposed to the dragon head that they send in chemists and establish laboratories, protected by General Li, right where the poppies bloomed. He was certain that Li would agree. It would simply mean more money for him.

Deng and Ho found that the general had moved south of the Yunnan border into the Laotian highlands. The CIA-sponsored attack on Kunming had ended in disaster. The elite troops from Taiwan were decimated. Little was left of the other Kuomintang forces. "I myself suffered casualties," General Li said, speaking of his own Ninety-third Division. "But fortunately," he added with a straight face, "I kept most of my men in strategic reserve to be ready for any eventuality."

Cox was also present. Deng served again as Li's interpreter. "Tell him I must have more weapons," Li said.

"He'll get them. By God, he has my word," Cox exclaimed. "They'll be parachuted in, whatever he wants. We can't give up. We've got to keep the fucking Commies busy. This isn't over by a long shot."

Later, Cox sought out Deng. "I notice you're pretty tight with the general."

"Tight?"

"Close to him, I mean. Very friendly."

"Oh, it's because of my uncle. My uncle was a general who was killed by the Japanese."

"Is that so? Uh, where'd you learn English?"

"In Shanghai. My father wished me to do so. My father also has joined his ancestors."

"The Commies?" Cox said.

"Yes."

"You live in Bangkok?"

"No, Hong Kong, where I rebuild my life."

"We need all the help we can get. Whatever happens up here, the Bamboo Curtain has fallen."

"Bamboo Curtain?"

"Yeah, like, you know, in Europe. The Iron Curtain. You have contacts inside China?"

Deng hesitated. Then he said, "At the moment, personally, I do not. But I know people who do."

"Tell you what," Cox said, fishing out a card. "We're all in this together. You ever have any information about China, what's going on, call this number in Hong Kong. Ask for Mr. Sentry."

DENG LEFT HO behind at General Li's headquarters to prepare the laboratory sites. In Hong Kong, he hurried to the Walled City. He had been absent much longer than he expected and was intent now on fulfilling his promise to his pregnant An-shui to move to proper quarters to raise their child.

But just as he was stepping into the dark alley, he was intercepted by a Society member. "I grieve to tell you, brother, that your esteemed wife is with us no more." There had been, he said, an outbreak of diphtheria that took thousands of lives among the colony's refugees, especially in the Walled City. "I will take you to those who desire to comfort you."

When Deng received an urn with her ashes, the same cold rage he had experienced in Shanghai crept through him, masked by an outward stoicism that even the most ruthless of his secret brothers marveled at—and feared. Behind his back, they nicknamed him "the Ice Man."

Privately, he lit joss sticks in An-shui's memory, but he did not pray. He did not believe in divine providence. He had a single photograph of them taken at their wedding and he placed it with those of his mother, father and sister.

Then he sent a message to Ho. "Brother," it said, "my wife, your sister, is no more."

With a regular flow of morphine base from the Laotian laboratories, various members of the Righteous and Peaceful Society began to form their own trafficking rings. Other *Hung* societies also began to participate. But

Deng and Ho, who stayed on in Thailand, were the key brokers, the ones who set the wholesale price and determined the amounts to be distributed from the moment the shipments departed the domain of General Li. Consumption was almost entirely in Southeast Asia. Deng was aware of another market in Europe and America that was supplied from the Turkish poppy fields, but, at the time, it sounded so remote and limited—so foreign.

He moved out of the Walled City, although he stayed in Kowloon. As his wealth accumulated, he began to speculate in real estate and advised Ho in Bangkok to follow suit. For relaxation, he took the ferry across the harbor and went by bus to the Happy Valley racetrack on Hong Kong Island. The intricacies of handicapping horses fascinated him. Racing was not mindless, like so many Chinese gambling games where luck, whatever that was, was the principal factor. At Happy Valley, he had at least some sense of control over his destiny.

Every so often he would look at the card that the big nose, Cox, had given him. Finally, he made the call. Relationships were all-important. Who could say where they would lead? It was, in retrospect, a decisive moment in his life, second only to that night in Shanghai when he drank from the ritual bowl of wine and blood.

The information he possessed came from a Society member, recently returned from Beijing, who had made a fortune smuggling oil into Mao's China after trade sanctions were imposed during the Korean War. Deng disapproved of such endeavors. The decision, however, had been made not only by the Righteous and Peaceful Society, but by all the brotherhoods that had fled to Hong Kong. You did what you had to do to survive and prosper.

In English, he asked for Mr. Sentry.

Instantly, over the phone, a voice said, "What can he do for you?"

"I have news for him."

There was a brief pause and then the voice gave him a time for a meeting the following afternoon at an address on Pollock's Path on Victoria Peak, the highest part of Hong Kong Island. The meeting would take place in what Deng came to know as a "safe house."

He rode the cable tramway up to the Peak. He had never been there before. It was where the English rulers of Hong Kong resided. The change from below was astonishing. No clamor, no oppressive heat, no jostling crowds, no claustrophobic crunch of buildings. Stately white houses, built in the colonial manner, with large bay windows and sweeping verandas were discreetly scattered on greenswards among lush bamboo and fern, Chinese dwarf pine and brilliantly hued giant hibiscus. Magpies chattered. Sparrow hawks swooped by.

There was disappointment as well. He had looked forward to observing what he had been told was an unparalleled vista from the Peak, a vista that swept up the Pearl River to Canton, into China itself. But the Peak that day, as was often the case, was enveloped in clouds, swirling around him like fog, without the slightest hint of the bright sunshine that he had left less than an hour before. He always remembered that first visit, and later, when he had become Y. K. Deng and could live anywhere he wanted, he chose not to reside on the Peak.

There was a gate at the address he was given. After he had pressed the bell and identified himself, the gate swung open. The man who met him on the veranda was not, as he expected, the swashbuckling Cox. Bespectacled, of medium height, in a gray suit and blue tie, he said, "Hello, I'm Mr. Sentry. We have looked forward to hearing from you." He escorted Deng inside to wicker armchairs.

Declining an offer of tea, Deng wasted no time. He said a compatriot had just returned from the north. The compatriot had met with high officials in economic development. The lack of oil was slowly strangling China. There had been a meeting in Moscow. The Soviets refused to intervene in Korea. Beijing was more than receptive to a face-saving Korean resolution, a cease-fire.

"How can we reach you?"

"I think that would be difficult at this time," Deng said.

"Can you tell me who your compatriot is?"

"Ah, that would be even more difficult. Events will have to bear me out."

And, of course, they did.

Although unknown to Deng, he was assigned the CIA cryptonym DH/ROGUE. The DH designated Hong Kong. ROGUE was a random selection. The initial notations in the file on him read: "Reticent re personal history. Taiwan confirms deceased uncle was KMT general. Father, ditto deceased, apparently well-to-do industrialist prior to ChiComs taking power. Appears to be in early twenties. Well educated. Speaks good English. Staunch anti-ChiCom. Close, repeat, extremely close to Gen. Li Wen-huen, cdr. ex-KMT 93rd Div., now 3rd Chi Irregulars, Laos, Burma.

Info so far excellent. Prime asset potential. Continued cultivation highly recommended."

The file swelled from time to time as Deng made additional trips to the Pollock's Path safe house. Twice, he refused an offer of a monthly retainer. He did, however, eventually agree to use a contact box at the Hong Kong General Post Office, which he promised to check periodically.

And it was then, fifteen years later, in 1967, while the Vietnam War was raging, that he responded to an urgent request for a meeting at a new safe house at the Peak on Plantation Road.

He was received by still another American he had not met before, a tall, lean man with blond hair and an easy athletic grace named John MacLean, who welcomed him, stumbling over the words, in Cantonese.

Deng was pleased by the effort. MacLean, at least, was the first CIA big nose who had made a stab at acknowledging his heritage. "Thank you," he said in English. "But it is not necessary to address me in the Cantonese manner. I am not Cantonese."

"Really? I apologize. What are you?"

"Chiuchow."

"Chiuchow? I hope I haven't offended you. I didn't know."

"It's unimportant. It is simply that we are a proud people." Deng stared at MacLean. "And unto ourselves, as we traditionally say."

"Gosh, again I apologize. Will you take some tea with me? It'd make me feel better. I really mean it."

This time, for the first time in all the years Deng had journeyed to the Peak, he accepted the offer.

"I've got my family here," John MacLean said. "I hope my kid, my son Tommy, gets a chance to learn Chinese, gets to know the Chinese. You have children?"

"No," Deng replied. "Unhappily, no."

"Well, I hope that changes for you. In the end, kids are what it's all about, aren't they?"

"Yes, perhaps. I have considered it. Perhaps it will come to me one day."

After tea was served, MacLean said, "I'll tell you why I wanted to see you. We have a real problem. The war in Vietnam is not going well."

"I must say," Deng said, "I have never understood why your country is there."

"It's the domino theory," MacLean said. "Vietnam falls and the ChiComs—your Communist countrymen—take over all of Southeast Asia, including Indonesia and Malaysia. That's what Langley says, anyway."

"Langley?"

"Forgive me. That's where the CIA headquarters is."

"The theory is ridiculous," Deng said. "Every schoolchild in China knows that the Chinese and the Vietnamese despise one another."

"If that's the case, we're in deep shit. But what can I tell you? I'm only a soldier in the trenches. The big thing right now is the Ho Chi Minh trail, the supply route south for the North Vietnamese. We've got to interdict it, mobilizing the Laotian hill tribesmen. The objective is to occupy the Viet-cong and their allies, the Pathet Lao, by conducting a secret war, secretly financed by insuring that the tribesmen can earn enough money to sustain themselves, make it worth their while."

"As you must know, their only reliable cash crop is the opium poppy."

"Yes, and with the war going on, they're having a lot of difficulty getting it to market. We propose to remedy that situation."

"It is always so, isn't it?" Deng said. "We do what we have to do."

The two men remained silent.

John MacLean did not tell Deng that he himself had questioned the project and had been curtly informed, in writing, by coded cable from the chief of the Far East Division: "Re your query, opium and derivative consumption unfortunately widespread throughout Southeast Asia, but nonetheless longtime fact of life. Latest data available shows Golden Triangle narcotics production currently only five percent worldwide. Priority issue here is successful prosecution of Vietnam war."

"What is it that you wish of me?" Deng said at last.

"General Li Wen-huen. Our relationship with the general has been, well, a little shaky since the adventure in Yunnan in the fifties. To put it bluntly, the general doesn't trust us. We know, though, that he trusts you, and we hope you trust us, our commitment. The general's the critical element in our game plan. It's that simple."

So it was that Deng, in the company of John MacLean, found himself back in the mist-shrouded mountains of northwest Laos where the lime-stone bedrock provided the soil with the high alkaline content ideal for nourishing the delicate poppy plant. General Li's mule caravans brought the raw opium to the field laboratories, where it was dissolved in heated water in oil drums. Ordinary lime fertilizer was added to precipitate out waste matter, allowing the morphine to float chalky white near the surface. It was then filtered through cloth, reheated and, with the addition of concentrated ammonia, filtered again and transformed into chunks of morphine base, about a tenth the weight of the original opium.

From crude landing strips, the CIA-owned airline, Air America, flew it to Vientiane, the Laotian capital. Deng had it taken to a Pepsi-Cola bottling plant owned by a Chiuchow associate of his, where, under cover, it was converted first into heroin base and then heroin in a tricky, dangerous process that required the expertise of master chemists.

And a great deal of it was the new powdery white number four heroin, injectable China white. A big new market right in Southeast Asia had suddenly opened up—the American GI, seeking solace from a deadly, futile war.

But the source remained a shameful secret. An official U.S. government report declared: "While opium growing is centered in regions of Laos and Burma adjacent to southwestern China, cultivation is closely controlled and none of the crop is believed to be channeled illicitly into the international market. Much of the crop is most likely being converted into morphine for medicinal purposes."

For John MacLean, the disillusioning truth, once discovered, meant immeasurable personal anguish, but by then it was too late. For Deng, heroin was simply a commodity that meant immeasurable profits. He brought Ho Shu-shui from Bangkok to Saigon to receive the shipments flown down by Air America pilots. And Ho brought in a clansman from his native Ch'ao-an, a clansman named Peter Pei, then residing in New York City, an American citizen, who, as a former U.S. Army soldier during World War II, was able to arrange excellent Army wholesale contacts in South Vietnam, especially with a Green Beret, an Italian-American, also from New York, whose name was Funzie DiBello.

And now, the morning after Shannon O'Shea had transmitted a query about him to the Hong Kong police, Deng rose from his silk sheets, donned a robe and began his daily round of shadowboxing exercises, his *tai ji quan.* From his window, he could see his private beach and the expanse of Deep Water Bay on the south side of Hong Kong Island. The house, a long, slightly curved white villa, paralleling the curve of the beach, with a red tiled roof, had been constructed for him with the advice of a master in *feng shui,* the harmonious physical interplay of natural and cosmic forces that supposedly resulted in *ch'i,* fortunate destiny.

The house was situated at the rounded head of the bay, thus achieving an auspicious balance for spiritual and material blessedness, or so the *feng shui* master claimed. The driveway in front was circular. "To have it coming directly to the entrance," the master further explained, "would have the headlights of vehicles rushing toward you like tigers stalking in the night."

Deng believed in none of this. He believed only in himself. But it was important to many of those who dealt with him. "Ah," they would say, "he's a prudent man. He had good *feng shui.*"

He could have had a much grander home if he wished, but he disdained the ostentation of some of his fellow stewards at the Royal Hong Kong Jockey Club. The wife of one of them actually flaunted blue and pink mink coats to match the colors of her twin Rolls-Royces. She chose one or the other, she had announced, to reflect her emotional state at any given moment. And unlike them, confident in his whispered renown, he did not have elaborate security systems, armed guards on patrol, or video cameras and electronically controlled gates to protect him. He had only his personal red pole and his driver, a *sze kau,* an ordinary Society member. Nor had he, as so many others of the Hong Kong elite, in their drive for social status, adopted an English given name. The initials "Y. K." were as far as he would go.

He preferred being close to the sea. It was in the Chiuchow tradition. His sole display of showy wealth was his sleek, Italian-built, seventy-foot Riva yacht, which he had purchased for two million dollars, and on which he would sail to Macao to visit his casino, or dally over part of a weekend with one of a stream of available young women of diverse ethnicity, all intent on gaining his favor.

That morning, as he completed his exercises, he was fifty-eight, a lean man, at five feet eleven well above average Chinese height, with black hair combed straight back from a slightly receding hairline, high cheekbones and eyes that never smiled.

On a bedroom table were the photographs of his mother, father, sister, first wife—and second wife. He had remarried immediately after his return from Laos. His wife was from a prosperous merchant family, dutifully alert to his desires. Halfway through her pregnancy, her doctor, a Chiuchow, confided to Deng the discovery that she suffered from pulmonary stenosis, a serious heart condition. The stress of birthing might prove fatal.

"I want the child," Deng said.

His wife died during delivery.

He had hoped, of course, for a son. And although he got a daughter instead, it didn't matter. He named her Li-po, which meant precious beauty. And he also kept her photograph in the room, by his bedside, quite apart from the others. Finally, he had achieved an emotional connection.

She had grown into a lovely, willowy creature with a flawless complexion and delightfully pouty, laughing lips. What pleased him even more was how, under his guidance, her mind developed. He would put her up against the son of any man he knew. But glancing now at her portrait, he frowned. He had sent her to America, to Yale University, where she was majoring in economics. Her grades were uniformly excellent and he had every expectation that she would join him in business, at least that portion of his business that was publicly joinable and—after all, who could really predict?—perhaps the other part, too. Now, though, there was a potentially ominous cloud on an otherwise serene horizon, one that he should have anticipated, but had not.

After dressing, he went into the dining room where he breakfasted on the steaming bowl of *jook* the cook had prepared. Alongside it was a copy of the *South China Morning Post.* He stared at it as never before. There, on the front page, were two photographs of himself, one standing by his colt, Avenger, the winner of the racing event of the year, the Queen's Cup, and another of Deng at the celebratory ball afterward conversing with the English queen's own sister, Princess Margaret. He squinted at the photographs, tilting the page, to decide if they were flattering to him. An instant later, he castigated himself for such weakness. They were the first published photographs of him since his arrival in Hong Kong. Other horses running under his silks had won major races, but he always had his trainer take the bows, and he had never gone to the ball previously or, for that matter, to any other public event that invited publicity.

This time, though, there was a purpose. Now he wanted those photographs included in whatever information was being collected about him. Possibly, they might even appear in the American press.

Only one file had ever concerned him, where he had *hok tei,* the dark background. And that had been in a folder of the Royal Hong Kong Police—a file that detailed suspected triad membership, suspicion of opium smuggling, complicity in extortion in the construction trade, conspiracy to murder. But a Chiuchow police sergeant, a member of the Righteous and

Peaceful Society, had removed these paper records just before computeri-
zation was to commence. He had given them personally to Deng, who
read them, burned them and then ordered the execution of the two informants who had been named in them.

Deng's Mercedes sedan, relatively unremarkable compared to the
Rolls-Royces that seemed to be the order of the day in the colony, awaited
him for the trip to the central business district on the north side of the island. He passed the vast, tightly packed armada of junks and sampans in
Aberdeen Harbor on which the boat people lived and swung around the
Western market district, amused as always that they were, despite their
names, the most un-English parts of Hong Kong.

At his offices at Hong Kong/Kowloon Enterprises, Ltd., his secretary
greeted him, giggling. Then he saw the copy of the *Post* on her desk featuring the photographs.

"Congratulations, sir."

"To work," he said.

From the windows of his private office, he could see the towering sky-
scraper of the Bank of China, seventy-two stories high, the tallest building in all of Asia, dwarfing every other edifice in central Hong Kong. Its
sharply irregular angles were said to engender bad *feng shui*. Apparently,
the dour rulers of the People's Republic in Beijing did not care. Out of curiosity, Deng had gone to the top when it was finished in 1990. From that
vantage point, mighty Hong Kong appeared to be a miniature toy town, a
plaything. He often wondered grimly if that was also Beijing's view.

His secretary brought in a report of the last twenty-four hours of casino
receipts from Macao, as well as the previous day's receipts from the two
restaurants he owned, one on the island, the other in Kowloon, which
were so favorably recommended in the tourist guides. There also was a
daily status rundown on his shipping interests in port and on the high seas.
There were updated rolls of his rental property and progress reports on
condominium sales. And still another report from his broker on the current state of his portfolio, while, in a corner of his office, a computer
screen, which he rarely looked at, flickered with the latest quotations on
the Hong Kong stock exchange.

There was also a fax from Ho in Bangkok confirming his arrival in
Hong Kong the next day.

Deng then read the third alarming letter he had received from his
daughter's amah, who had been with her since birth and whom he had

sent with Li-po to America, to Yale University, to attend to her needs—
and to look after her. Li-po, the letter said, was seeing the *kwai lo* more
frequently than ever. Twice in the last week, she had missed her curfew.
The *kwai lo* was a young professor teaching Chinese culture, the amah
wrote. He had been in China more than once. The amah was at her wit's
end. Li-po had regressed from a remarkably stable, studious twenty-year-
old into a simpering teenager. The amah said that she had told Li-po that
she would report her behavior to her father, and Li-po had replied defi-
antly "Tell him anything you want!"

Lips pursed, Deng toyed with the letter. The fact was that there was
nothing he could do from Hong Kong. To order Li-po to return was self-
defeating. Well, he would address the problem soon enough.

Then he took a call from Sir Roger Ma, O.B.E., whose wife boasted the
matching minks and Rolls-Royces. Ma congratulated him on Avenger's
victory. His wife, he said, adored the horse and he offered a staggering
purchase price. For another fifty thousand U.S., Deng said, it was a done
deal. He smiled inwardly as he heard the catch in Ma's breath. Ma had
had no expectation that Deng would consider selling the colt, he had just
been going through the motions for his own ego. Deng was famous for being possessive about his stable, but Ma, of course, was not aware of Deng's
immediate plans. And for Ma to back out now would entail unacceptable
loss of face.

"Joyful news," he replied weakly. "I will inform my wife at once."

Late in the morning, he reviewed the figures for the Bank of the Han
River, a bank he personally owned and had nostalgically named, through
which he moved large amounts of cash from time to time and from which
he also borrowed at extremely friendly interest rates. In Hong Kong, there
were no banking regulations. As it was often said, "What may be a vice
elsewhere is considered a virtue in Hong Kong."

Shortly after one p.m., Deng lunched with the head of his construction
subsidiary and the representative of a German consortium that wanted to
put up a new office tower on one of the last available island parcels.
Deng's firm had been the low bidder. "We have most excellent relations
with the building trades," he explained modestly.

Like an old woman fingering worry beads, the German kept fretting
about what would happen in the colony after it was ceded back to China
in 1997.

"Don't concern yourself," Deng assured him. "Beijing will never kill
such a goose of gold as this."

"Ach, you think not."

"Without question, my dear sir."

Then, just before four o'clock, he left for his meeting with the CIA station chief, Malcolm Colby. He had met Colby, newly posted, once before. He was the eighth station chief Deng had dealt with. But, unlike every other meeting, this one would not take place in a safe house. It would be, at Deng's suggestion, in the great lounge of the Mandarin Oriental Hotel. There wasn't a more public spot Deng could think of in central Hong Kong, and that was exactly what he wanted, just as it had been at the ball the night before. However recent Colby's arrival, and despite the rather mundane title he had at the U.S. consulate, everyone who was anyone knew within days who and what he was.

As he entered the hotel, Deng was besieged by more congratulatory well-wishers, including complete strangers, hailing his colt's triumph. He posed, smiling, for more photos.

Colby rose and also congratulated him. The setting was so incongruous. Beautiful Chinese women, the best money could buy, undulated seductively by in their silk, slitted *cheongsams,* while a string quartet played Viennese waltzes in the background. The station chief was drinking a gin and tonic. Deng contented himself with tea. He had not touched a drop of alcohol since the cognac Ho had uncorked the night of his first wedding in the Walled City. The memory of his hangover the morning after had never left him.

"It's good to see you again," Colby said effusively. "You know, the first time we met, I barely had a chance to review your file. I made sure to take another look. Boy, it's really something, I must say. And it goes so far back! The first to let us in on that uranium gas diffusion plant in Lanchow. And the plutonium facility up there at Pao-t'ou. Jesus! The whole nuclear ball of wax. To say nothing of Laos, the arms shipments to Iran . . ." The station chief's voice trailed off, as if he suddenly realized where he was. "And," he whispered, "uh, all the rest."

Deng permitted himself a barely perceptible nod. "You are too kind."

"What do you think is up ahead, ninety-seven and so forth?" Colby asked, his voice still lowered.

Deng answered cautiously. "It's difficult to know, since not even the new Standing Committee of the Politburo in Beijing knows. In the end, I believe, it is the army's view that will be decisive."

"So you're off to the States. Hedging your bets?"

What effrontery! Deng thought. "Yes, that is my present intention," he said. "I've never been there. It's time. And I have a daughter who is a student in your country."

"I know that. I saw it in your file."

Ah, you know so much, he reflected. And yet so little.

"Well, the paperwork's all finished. You should have your permanent resident visa in a couple of days, with our heartfelt appreciation. Two visas for your household staff and six work permits, what we call green cards, correct?"

"Yes, for my business associates that I desire to bring with me."

Ordering another gin and tonic, Colby hoisted his glass. "Here's to great success for you," he said. "Remember, you're going to find it a little different over there."

"Thank you for your precious advice," Deng said.

Colby had not been in Hong Kong long enough to realize, and perhaps he would never learn, that Deng's response, which he found so gracious, was actually a polite Chiuchow way of saying "Go fuck yourself."

At her desk in New York, Shannon O'Shea clipped the *South China Morning Post* edition featuring the pictures of Deng with his horse and with Princess Margaret and started her personal Y. K. Deng folder.

The Hong Kong police reported that he had a clean sheet. The sole mention of him was a notation that he had been seen recently at the Mandarin Oriental Hotel in the company of a man believed to be the new resident CIA station chief.

Guess that tells us all we have to know about clean-as-a-whistle Mr. Deng, she thought, as she made copies of the clips and sealed them in an envelope for Tom MacLean.

Then she had another thought. Why would someone like Deng let himself be seen so openly with the CIA? Maybe he was the one deciding what story was told. She kept this possibility to herself, however. She could just hear Tom remonstrating, "Come on, Shannon. *Enough,* already!"

9

T HE CONFEDERATION of the Hong Kong dragon heads, the *lung tao*, assembled one by one at the marina where Deng's yacht was berthed. Deng greeted them in the ancient manner, placing his left hand over his chest, thumb pointing up, little finger down, the three middle fingers curled back against the palm. Each returned the gesture, which like the pictograms in Chinese writing signified their rank. The upturned thumb represented the head of the dragon, the downward little finger its tail.

It was a rare convocation. The Confederation had not met formally in six years, not since it organized a cooperative response to an embarrassing onslaught of hit-and-run gangs coming in on high-speed boats from mainland China, machine-gunning their way, undoubtedly with Beijing's blessing, into scores of the colony's jewelry stores that paid protection money to the local triads. The loss of face was enormous and only regained after body parts of the intruders began bobbing up in the waters surrounding the colony.

"I salute you, venerable one," Deng said to old Fong, the seventy-seven-year-old Cantonese *lung tao* of the 14K Society. Fong's grandfatherly appearance was deceiving. The triad he presided over was as tough and hard as its namesake gold. Deng extended a hand to help him on board. "You continue to amaze us with your vibrant well-being."

"Girls, girls! The younger the better!" the old man cackled. "I recommend them highly."

Desiring a harmonious spirit above all else this evening, Deng saw the frozen disdain on the face of Shing Heung-tang, standing within earshot as Fong loudly pronounced his prescription for long life. Also Cantonese and dragon head of the Three United Association, Shing was equally renowned for youthful companionship—in his instance, boys. But his sexual preference in no way impeded a cold-blooded grip over Hong Kong's flesh trade, both male and female. Besides, it could be argued that he was simply honoring the memory of many of the revered Shaolin monks, among whom pederasty was not unknown.

Deacon Kau, the sober, bespectacled *lung tao* of the Fujianese Red Sky Society, smoothed over this awkward moment. "In matters of longevity, having drunk, all of us, the cock's blood, each must find his own path," he said diplomatically. "Is it not written? Strength through diversity."

All of them, Deng included, were attired in conservative business suits, indistinguishable from members of the colony's executive elite, of which, indeed, they considered themselves to be an integral part, innovative entrepreneurs dealing in essential goods, providing necessary services. To a man, they'd been seated prominently at the banquet welcoming the new governor-general dispatched from London to oversee the final years of English rule.

All, that is, except the last to arrive, Stanley Chow, the Hakka dragon head of the Glorious Together Association. Deng heard the screeching tires of Chow's bright red Lamborghini as he pulled in, driving himself, alongside the chauffeured Rolls-Royces of the others parked at the marina. He seemed to go out of his way to flout every convention. The license plate numbers for the Lamborghini were four sevens. In Chinese numerology, seven invited disaster. It meant death. Still, on the Hong Kong docks, not one container of cargo moved, nor did any public transport on its streets—from the lowliest tourist rickshaw "boy" to the most elegant limousine for hire—without Chow's acquiescence.

Deng watched as Chow swaggered toward him in a white silk turtleneck and houndstooth jacket. After giving him the sign of the dragon head and receiving a perfunctory response, Deng said, "I am told you had a profitable evening last night at my fan-tan tables in Macao."

"Humbly, I cannot deny it," Chow said, his angular, wolfish face breaking into a toothy smile. "You have my myriad thanks."

Fan-tan is the most popular Chinese game of chance. Porcelain buttons are swirled inside an inverted bowl. Bets are placed on how many remain in the last batch after the bowl is lifted and the buttons removed four at a time.

"It is said," Deng continued, "that your hearing is of such acuteness that you can accurately gauge the number of buttons beneath the bowl at the commencement of play."

"Ah," Chow replied, "is it not the curse of our culture always to invoke the occult? But in truth I must say that I am blessed with the most excellent ears. Just this afternoon, I have heard that you sold your champion horse to the insufferable Ma. Astonishing news."

"I beg your indulgence. Soon, all will become clear."

Deng signaled the captain to cast off, then joined the others in the main salon and savored for a moment the face it gave him as they wandered about the sleek interior. The yacht was named *Grass Sandal,* for it was related that after the First Five Ancestors had fled their burning monastery, their path was blocked by a large body of water. But a grass sandal of one monk was miraculously transformed into a boat by benevolent gods, enabling them to escape their Manchu pursuers. A large painting in the salon depicted the event, and Fong told Deng, "It brings you honor that you remind us of our true and mysterious heritage."

It was a cloudless, moonlit evening. Ahead was the jagged outline of Lantau Island, whose rural villages Deng would sometimes visit in a spasm of vague nostalgia for a life he never knew. They cruised past the glittering lights of the floating restaurants in Aberdeen Harbor. To the north Kowloon's blazing neon jungle and the Wanchai nightlife district in Hong Kong proper reached into the sky, threatening to outshine even the moon.

Deng felt a tinge of regret that such sights would shortly become a thing of the past for him as he motioned the others to chairs around the large burnished teak table in the center of the salon. Ceremonial cups of tea were served. The salon fell silent. There was now only the throb of the yacht's engine and the soft rush of the sea.

In the annals of organized crime, the power of these five men was unparalleled. The brotherhood had spread throughout Hong Kong and Southeast Asia like some monstrous underground fungus creeping unseen in the earth, dividing and subdividing and replicating again into new cells, each mirroring exactly in miniature the form of the whole, each with its own leader and circle of advisers, office bearers they were called, who conducted day-to-day operations. Only a handful of officers at the highest echelon knew the identity of those seated around the teak table on Deng's yacht, in whom final authority was vested, whose edicts affected not only each society in all of its multiple branches but its relationship to other societies. Never did any of the decisions come down as formal directives, but word of them became instantly known, as if carried on the wind.

Unlike the Cosa Nostra, to which it was often compared, the brotherhood reached into every stratum of life. Deng could not think of a single rags-to-riches Hong Kong tycoon—and the list of them was nearly endless—who did not belong to one of the secret societies, for none of them, no matter how inventive or enterprising, could have succeeded without paying his required dues.

But there was also a profound ethnic impulse that gave the secret societies such power and leverage. Among the Chinese, the concept of allegiance to "family" is paramount. And the brotherhood, of course, was the ultimate extension of family. Deng was not unaffected by this emotional tie. Still, ever the realist, he was comforted by a far more practical bond. More than the blood oath of loyalty they had taken, each of the men at the table had the capability of bringing down the other four.

This delicate balance made possible the peaceful resolution of conflicts that inevitably cropped up in the management of prostitution, the scores of "girlie" clubs, the hundreds of unlawful gambling parlors, the illegal licensing of more than twenty thousand street vendors, the "security" afforded the most elegant shops and boutiques as well as the film, television and music industries, the movement of produce in the markets, the shipment of goods by sea and air, the availability of labor in hotels and restaurants, the apportionment of rights in the construction of residential and office buildings and the "interior decoration" of same—in whatever enabled Hong Kong to function by day and by night.

And, of course, dwarfing everything else, was the constant flow of money from the magical elixir of the opium poppy, with which, it was said—rather poetically, Deng thought—all pain and anger were lulled, all sorrow forgotten.

Tonight he would propose to drown America in that elixir—the white powder.

10

NORMALLY, WITH THE DIVERSE tribal dialects—Chiuchow, Hakka, Fujianese and Cantonese—represented by the men at the table in the salon of the *Grass Sandal,* Deng would have spoken in China's official language, Mandarin, to avoid loss of face. The aged Fong, for all his years, had never bothered to master Mandarin and recruited his number-one son to translate when necessary. Tonight, however, there were no interpreters present. So Deng chose Cantonese, the prevalent dialect in Hong Kong.

"*T'ien pu pa,*" he began with a smile, staring at Fong. "Heaven I don't fear. Earth I don't fear. I only fear a Cantonese trying to speak Mandarin."

It was a joke familiar to them all, but it still earned appreciative chuckles. The correct comradely tone had been set. Fong, in particular, was beaming. "You better fear the Cantonese," he said gleefully. "And for other reasons."

"Honorable brothers," Deng continued, his features suddenly grave, "we confront a crossroads in our destiny. The Year of the Buffalo is fast upon us when the English will return to the Beijing usurpers this territory that is in fact ours. The lackeys of the Politburo promise that special economic status will be granted. Perhaps so, perhaps not. But for us, of the *Hung,* all we have built here is soon finished. They denigrate our glorious past as feudal superstition. I have no doubt they have learned who we in the Confederation are. They intend to deprive us of what we have labored so assiduously to create, if for no other reason, despite their pious words, than that they desire our riches as their own."

"Yes, yes!" cried Fong, stirring his tea clockwise in vigorous assent. "It is true. We must think of the future."

Deng couldn't help a moment of inward amusement. The old man, he thought, must believe that he had another fifty years left in him. "Ah, precisely," he said, "the future is that which I intend to address. *Our* future."

He got to his feet to assume a more commanding presence. "It is clear we cannot remain here under conditions that at the most favorable will be uncertain, and most likely quite onerous. Clearly, we must leave behind the endeavors that have so richly rewarded us. That is not to say that we can't reestablish them in another place. But that demands time and financing. What we can take with us immediately, however, is the white powder. It is our salvation."

Deng paused to let his words sink in. "America obviously offers the greatest advantages. Our countrymen have settled there in increasing numbers, not only in the traditional cities of New York and San Francisco, but in cities called Boston and Philadelphia, Washington and Atlanta, in Chicago and Dallas, in Los Angeles and Seattle. In all of them, and more," he said, raising a clenched fist, "there are populous communities where the Han people steadfastly preserve the culture of our ancestors. But, as we know, in every opportunity, there is also danger. And in these communities, there are bad omens. Gangs of our youths have been"—hesitating, Deng searched for the right word—"have been . . . *yes! Americanized!* They strut about the streets like shameless peacocks. They terrorize and extort without subtlety. They kidnap, rob and murder brazenly. As long as they preyed only on our people, the American police paid little heed. But these gangs have run amok. *Kwai lo* tourists are caught in crossfires. *Kwai lo* women are raped. Such incidents cause the American press to write articles that link the gangs to the *Hung* brotherhood, to the Hong Kong 'triads,' which then serve to energize the authorities."

He brandished a page from *The New York Times* and translated the headline: "Immigrant Waves from Asia Wash an Underworld Ashore Here."

"Ai!" Deacon Kau interrupted. "These unfortunate occurrences you cite are but normal human events. What can be done?"

"We must control our destiny," Deng replied. "The Americans in Vietnam developed a great appetite for the *tai sei,* what they call heroin number four, and thus brought great riches to us. I have studied the situation with care. Among the Italians, there is an organization that is a pale imitation of the brotherhood," Deng continued. "For years, it operated successfully until its membership became involved not only in the importation of heroin from the poppy cultivated in Turkey, but directly in its distribution in the United States. That was its downfall. Public outrage became widespread, and was increased by the arrival of the cocaine narcotic in great quantities from South America. But there was a difference. The cocaine barons have no intention of departing the small countries in which they live and remain secure. That is an option denied us. The lesson history provides is unmistakable. We must avoid the stupidity of the Italian Cosa Nostra."

"Ai," Kau repeated, still annoyed. "I speak confidently for my brothers assembled at this table that none of us has even laid eyes on a packet of the white powder in many celestial years. What does this have to do with us, the Confederation?"

"Everything!" Deng said. "If we wish to lead tranquil and profitable lives in America, we cannot be associated in any way with the *tai sei*. It is one thing for the Golden Triangle to be known as the source. It is quite another for the Han people to be selling it on the street. The total of the white powder reaching America is great, but it comes in myriad fashions, in small amounts, by courier and post, in commercial shipments of every conceivable sort. The sheer volume enables the American Drug Enforcement Administration and the one they call the FBI to make random seizures, which they trumpet to the press as evidence of a new menace to American society, what is portrayed as the 'Chinese Connection.' "

Deng crumpled the article in the *Times* and threw it on the table in disgust. "We also must share the blame," he said acidly. "Within the last moon in New York, receipts in the care of the youth gang the White Eagles were guarded so sloppily that eight million six hundred thousand dollars were seized by the agents of the FBI. Not even the Italians could be so artless."

There was an uneasy silence. The raid led by Shannon O'Shea had made all the Hong Kong papers, both English-language and Chinese. Everyone around the table was aware that the White Eagles were Hakkas with close ties to Stanley Chow's Glorious Together Association.

Stung, Chow exploded. *"Tiao mi kouet gnin!"* he shouted in the Hakka dialect. "Fuck the Americans!"

"What did he say?" Fong asked.

Before anyone could translate, Chow repeated himself, this time in Cantonese. *"Diu mi kwok yan!"*

"Oh," said Fong.

Chow was on his feet, facing Deng. "Like my learned brother," he said,

"I, too, have studied the lessons of history. And history teaches us that the foreign devils forced the opium poppy on our people, enslaving more than fifteen million of them, reaping great fortunes. Let the wheel now turn. Let fifteen million Americans fall under the spell of the white powder, *twenty million, thirty!* As for myself, I will watch with pleasure from afar. I will go to Taiwan, where I will not have to suffer the indignities of the barbarian big noses."

"The estimable *lung tao* of Glorious Together is historically correct," Deng said, careful to keep his voice calm in contrast to Chow's outburst. "But vengeance for its own sake offers no real reward. Blowing up a bear with dynamite brings no meat to the hunter. We must act as one for our common benefit. We can't all go to Taiwan. A society of the brotherhood, the United Bamboo, is already there, in close alliance with the government. Our arrival will only beget unrest, while America, the land of opportunity, as they say, beckons us."

"He speaks undeniably," said the flesh peddler, Shing, aware of the impossibility of transporting his thousands of male and female prostitutes out of Hong Kong. "My dear Chow, sit down. Hear him out."

"Brothers," Deng said, "I have a plan. We will dry up the tributaries that form the great river of white powder. We, the Confederation, will become its single source, like a mountain lake. We will accomplish what the OPEC nations tried to do with oil. Control the supply and price of a precious resource."

"But OPEC failed," Deacon Kau protested.

"Yes, because they were composed of dissimilar peoples—Arab, African, South American—with different needs. We are the Han, bound by blood and common purpose. OPEC also failed because the West reduced its consumption of oil during that period. No user of the *tai sei* will ever reduce his consumption, I assure you," said Deng.

"Each of us will contribute two million dollars," he told them. "Five million will be paid to our compatriot in Laos, General Li Wen-huen, for fifty tons of raw opium. Five million will be reserved for the refinement process and the cost of transportation. Analysis shows that the greatest risk of interception is during the hundreds of individual shipments currently being made. Our five tons of pure white powder bricks will arrive in America in one shipment, where it will then be stored for distribution."

As Deng expected, the objections began at once.

"General Li no longer holds sway over the poppy fields," said Fong. "He is being overwhelmed by the renegade warlord, Shan Wa, in Burma. Wa is mix-blooded, half Burmese. He sells to anyone."

"My plan takes that into account."

"It is impossible to transport five tons of the powder through Thailand to Bangkok in the manner you suggest."

"That also has been anticipated."

"Ai," Deacon Kau said, "it's against our nature to risk all on one throw of the dice."

"Exactly," Deng shot back. "That's what the Americans will think. And what is our risk? At the most, we each lose two million U.S. Someone," Deng said, "has just lost more than eight million dollars and I have heard no outcry." Deng waited for Chow to say something. But he remained silent.

"Who will distribute the product?"

"We will use the Italians."

"How?"

"Honorable brothers," Deng said. "In this, and other aspects of the shipment, you must place your trust in me. Listen! The wholesale price per unit, a *kwai lo* pound and a half, is now ninety thousand U.S., so the value of the first five tons is nearly six hundred million dollars. This provides a return to each of us of over one hundred and sixteen million, more than enough to enable us to settle respectably in America if we wish and to invest in whatever we choose. And that does not encompass the return in years hence from additional shipments."

Deng knew there would be a last objection. And it came from Deacon Kau. He could almost hear the abacus beads sliding back and forth in Kau's head. "According to your estimates, the rightful division of income from five tons should include at least an additional eighteen million dollars."

"Ah," Deng said, "although I have to have your approval, I am the one who must arrange and manage every step of this venture, while you remain passive participants. I would require a three-percent commission of the gross income for my services."

"Eighteen million U.S.!"

"Yes."

"It is fair," Fong broke in at last, his voice abruptly matter-of-fact, abandoning the jolly-old-fool guise he was so fond of adopting. "Let us remember it was Deng Yue-keung who first journeyed to the Golden Triangle to make the arrangements with General Li, the fruit of which all the societies have shared."

Finally Stanley Chow spoke. "That was bound to happen. It could have been any of us."

"Perhaps," Fong said. "But it *was* Deng. We must ponder his words with care." Fong nodded at him. He rose immediately from his seat and went out of the salon.

Deng joined his captain at the wheel of the *Grass Sandal*. He donned a jacket a mate brought him to ward off the chill of the sea breeze. They were still headed westward at a leisurely speed toward Lantau Island. He could see the lights of a night jetfoil crossing in front of them, racing to Macao, a seventy-minute trip ferrying gamblers. It amazed him how so many of his countrymen would work so diligently through the day and, spurred on by a belief in lucky days, lucky numbers, lucky omens, would then rush off to his casino tables to lose their hard-earned money. It was, he decided, the insatiable drive for "face." Big money meant great face. And if you couldn't get it any other way, there was always fan-tan and the other games.

It was even more amazing to him that the English would outlaw gambling in the colony except at the racetrack, forgoing huge tax revenues. Their sanctimonious reason was that it would corrupt public morality, as if that were possible in Hong Kong. Stanley Chow was right. The *kwai lo* had subjugated China by means of the opium poppy and now their cries of alarm and anger about the white powder were simple hypocrisy.

Deng had no doubt that his plan would be endorsed. After the *lung tao* had recovered from the shock of the scope and apparent daring of what he proposed, he had seen the glitter in their eyes as he outlined the profits to be reaped. And when Kau raised the question of his commission, he knew he had won them. In their minds, they were already banking their shares.

Of all the dragon heads, Stanley Chow gave him the most unease. Perhaps it was because he was Hakka, the wandering people, Chinese gypsies—of the Han race, but still apart from it, clannish like Chiuchow, yet different, unruly, infinitely more rootless and reckless. In preparing his plan, Deng had read much about the Italian underworld in America and had found an analogy in the papered-over hostility that existed between Sicilians and Neapolitans. If he were Italian, Deng concluded, he would be Sicilian.

He knew that Chow envied him, not only because of his recognized intellect, but especially because of his control of casino gambling in Macao. Deng had been the first to perceive the opportunity, and under Confederation rules, he enjoyed a monopoly. As Deng watched still another jetfoil skimming over the moonlit sea toward Macao, he wondered what Chow was saying. But what *could* he say? Deng thought he had handled the issue of the White Eagles gang with exquisite tact, stating the facts so that Chow could not take direct personal offense, was reduced in his fury to railing blindly against the Americans. Undoubtedly, Chow was furious that he himself had not thought of such a grand plan as Deng had presented.

And it was a grand plan, brilliantly conceived in every respect, he reflected with satisfaction, a plan of indisputable genius.

A crewman approached him and said, "Sir, your guests invite you to rejoin them."

"Soon, we will be turning back," Deng told the captain. "Tell them to prepare the food."

Every eye was on him as he stepped into the salon and took his place at the table.

"Brother," Fong said, "we have considered and debated. We have voted unanimously to adopt your meritorious proposal."

Deng was about to rise, as custom dictated, to accept and applaud their wisdom.

But Fong lifted a cautionary hand, and Y. K. Deng remained seated. No one at the table stirred.

"We have also decided," Fong continued, "that in an endeavor of such magnitude, two *lung tao* should oversee it. You, obviously, and one other. It is the prudent and practical way. The ancients have taught us the yin and yang of success in life. And if some ill fortune should befall one of you, the other will be prepared to step forward immediately. Thus it is the decision of the Confederation that Stanley Chow shall join you for the mutual benefit of all and divide with you the commission you ask."

Deng was dumbfounded. He glanced at Chow, whose face was impassive. He couldn't tell whether Chow was gloating, or as unhappy as he. What Fong had said sounded reasonable enough on the surface. *But why*

Chow? Suddenly, it dawned on Deng. Everyone there knew he and Chow so deeply mistrusted each other that they would never be able to come together to betray the rest of the Confederation, as Deng, on his own, might. So much, he thought, for brotherhood.

He sensed their anxiety, as they awaited his answer, that he might possibly rebuff them. What small minds they really had, he thought, his fellow dragon heads, lacking, for all their cunning, any vision. To reject their verdict, though, would kill the plan entirely, and that Deng was unwilling to do.

He rose, clapping his hands softly. "Yes, I accept your words. They are well chosen," he said. "I should have thought of this myself."

"Wonderful!" Fong exclaimed. "So it's settled. We must drink to our success."

"Of course," Deng said. "At once." He noticed that Chow, alone, was not smiling. Deng pressed a button summoning a servant who brought bottles of Hennessy Paradis cognac and snifters of shimmering crystal.

Business was concluded. Therefore dinner could begin. At every setting were solid gold chopsticks, engraved with the character for the family name of each dragon head. Fong tested his chopsticks with his teeth, bobbing his head in approval. "Good, very good," he prattled. "Fourteen karat. Very hard."

Deng had gone to great pains to select a menu ensuring representative dishes that included Chiuchow bird's nest soup and oysters fried in spiced egg batter, Hakka-style baked duck stuffed with rice and lotus seeds, a Fujianese pork casserole and fish that was steamed in the Cantonese manner in fresh ginger, tender onions and sesame oil.

As usual, there was no conversation as the dragon heads hunched over their bowls, gobbling the food rapaciously, tossing down glass after glass of cognac. Only Deng abstained.

The meal was just ending as the *Grass Sandal* nosed back into the marina. "A wonderful repast," Fong said. "Unifying. One that pays homage to us all."

As the others left for their waiting cars, Stanley Chow lingered behind. "That was very clever of you," he told Deng, "causing me to explode like a madman."

Deng didn't reply.

"But the truth is that you're the mad one with this scheme of yours."

"Why didn't you speak up in my absence? Or did you?"

"How could I after you had them hypnotized with those mountainous sums? That's all they could think about."

"We will see then, won't we?"

"Yes. And, of course, they also fear your legendary intelligence. They believe that you have insights they don't possess."

"You don't?" Deng inquired.

"As I said, you're very clever."

They gazed at one another. Then Chow added, "It wasn't my idea. It was the old man who said that the two of us would be in perfect counterbalance."

"Ah, he is a canny fellow, isn't he?"

"The others appeared quite relieved that I will be at your side."

"As you can imagine, it is also of great comfort to me," Deng said, unable to resist the barb.

They walked toward the parking area. As they approached Chow's Lamborghini with the four sevens on its license plate, Deng said, "I've always wondered why you choose to display such an unlucky number."

Again, there was that wolfish grin. "Because, like you, I don't believe in luck. The difference between us is that I don't disguise it. As you remarked earlier, it is said that I like to hear the rattle of the buttons under the fan-tan bowl before placing my bet."

"Then rest assured. You have heard them."

The next day Ho Shu-shui arrived in Deng's office from Bangkok.

"The general remains amenable to our proposition?" Deng asked.

"Yes, and for reasons beyond money. He has suffered big loss of face. Only last week, the entrance to one of the residences he maintains in Thailand, in Chiang Mai, was bombed. Everyone knows that it was the work of Shan Wa. In the tea shops, they whisper that General Li is finished. The general remains secure in Laos, but his caravans are continually attacked along the mountain trails when they cross into Thailand, making delivery on his contracts questionable. So the traffickers, naturally, turn to the half-breed, Shan Wa."

"The Confederation," Deng said, "has approved my plan."

"Excellent. It is the right moment. Peter Pei advises from New York that there appears to be aroused street activity by the DEA agents because of the seizure of the money in the care of the White Eagles gang by the FBI. It has given the FBI much face. And there is much chagrin, too, that it was a woman who led the raid, a woman they call the Dragon Lady."

"I must tell you," Deng said, "that in this endeavor, we will have a working partner, Stanley Chow." He observed Ho's evident dismay. "Why do you frown, brother?"

"The *dai lo* of the White Eagles is a youth they call Unicorn Frankie Chin. Pei has also informed me that he proclaims to be Chow's blood nephew. It is his wildness that has caused special trouble."

Now it was Deng's turn to frown. "I knew the White Eagles were Hakka. I did not know, however, of this intimate connection." Then, abruptly, he smiled and said, as if enjoying the prospect, "I believe we can use this to our advantage. Even Chow cannot resist the profits my plan will bring him. I will speak to him privately about his nephew. This nephew will be his responsibility. He must learn that sometimes it is far better to appear to be a paper tiger than a real one."

A desktop lunch of steamed and fried dim sum was served. The two men ate in silence. Afterward, over cups of Chiuchow tea, Ho observed Deng lost in thought again. "Stanley Chow is still of concern to you?" he ventured.

"Ah, no, my brother. Forgive me. It is a personal matter." Deng hesitated. After his family's murder in Shanghai, he had anesthetized himself against every wound life could inflict. It was the only way he knew to survive and remain strong. To have acted otherwise would expose unacceptable weakness. Yet there were so many other times when he had yearned to cry out in pain or anger or fear—or love. Suddenly overcome by a profound loneliness, he stared at Ho. No one had been closer to him during his days of travail and triumph, yet Deng had concealed even from Ho his innermost feelings. "It's silly of me, isn't it?" he blurted. "Our people cherish a son so much more than a daughter. But I have a daughter I cherish above all else. And now I am in danger of losing her. In America, I have been told, she has taken up with a man . . . a *barbarian*."

Ho Shu-shui shifted nervously in his chair, searching for the right response. Such emotion from Deng caught him off guard. Should he provide counsel or consolation?

But before Ho could say anything, as though none of this had occurred, Deng, busily rearranging some papers on his desk, said, "Well, I suppose I should meet personally again with General Li."

Relieved, Ho said, "That would be wise. He is currently in Bangkok to have a cataract in his eye removed, and after the assault on his residence, a visit from you would be of great comfort to him. Every man from time to time requires it." He wanted to add that he wished to be of solace now to Deng. But he dared not, since to speak thus, unsolicited, to a man like Deng, was unthinkable.

L IKE JUNGLE BEASTS drinking communally on a riverbank after a day's ferocious combat, the Force and the Dark Side would gather at The Place to cut deals that enabled the criminal justice system to escape terminal gridlock. A pub on Manhattan's Upper East Side, The Place began as a hangout for FBI agents. Prosecutors and defense lawyers soon found it expedient to follow.

It was a testament to the high regard for Tom MacLean that, in lieu of the usual courtroom witness room pressed into service, the hat had been passed around the U.S. attorney's office to hire the backroom of The Place for his going-away party, complete with a buffet of cold cuts and waiters serving pitchers of beer.

Over the raucous din of some fifty-odd assistant prosecutors and assorted investigators, Ed Carmody, the chief of the organized crime section, at last yelled, "Quiet down. We are here to honor Mr. Warmth himself."

A chorus of cheers. Laughter.

As they all knew, the sobriquet was bestowed after his first session with the crooked lawyer, Arthur Green. It'd been a wintry day in which the office heat failed. Green, his two attorneys, a postal inspector and an IRS agent huddled in overcoats around Tom's desk.

Tom started low-key, so the story went. "These three shirts on your expense sheet. One hundred seventy-five each?"

"Yeah, well, I didn't know I'd have to stay over in Philly. You want I should represent my client in a dirty shirt?"

"But that was in November. According to American Express, you purchased these shirts October sixth and it wasn't in Philadelphia."

"You, uh, got my AmEx records?"

"Among other things, yes. Now about this trip to the Kentucky Derby."

Four hours and three hundred and ninety thousand dollars later in fraudulent expenses, the matter of overbilling yet to come, everyone remained bundled up save Green, who, his Chesterfield cast aside, jacket off, shirt collar unbuttoned and tie yanked down, was frantically dabbing his brow with a handkerchief.

"Oh, Mr. Warmth casts a glow wherever he goes. Just ask our female assistants. He hasn't met one he doesn't like, depending on the number of beers he's consumed. We've cleaned out his office." Carmody dangled a bra. "It's a thirty-four D cup. Obviously the property of Annette Taylor in civil rights."

"Oh, Tom," curvaceous Annette cried unfazed, beer in hand. "How could you?"

As was customary, wit did not reign supreme at these affairs.

Carmody exhibited several panties. "Also lost and found. No wonder he labored such late hours behind locked doors. What's his fatal attraction?"

There was a high-pitched giggle. "He's single!"

"He's the only assistant who gets along with every defense lawyer in town," intoned Carmody. "They all hate him."

"And now he's gone over to the Dark Side," someone shouted. "Defender of sleaze, Wall Street scum, so long as they can afford him."

"He's sold out!" The chant reverberated in the room.

"It's my pleasure to present him with a token of our esteem," Carmody said. "A twenty-five-dollar gift certificate to the Armani emporium. At least, that'll get him through the front door."

Finally, unsteadily, Tom rose to his feet. The expectation was that he would respond in kind. Instead, he told them, "Be prepared. I will torture you all. Luke Skywalker exists no more. You see before you the Prince of Darkness."

"He isn't kidding," Rick Montebello muttered to a lissome assistant fresh out of law school that he had been vainly trying to bed down. "He was always better at cross than direct." Montebello was to replace Tom MacLean as head of the frauds section. He remembered a drug-money-laundering case Tom was prosecuting. Usually, Tom was very matter-of-fact about the adversarial nature of the law, refraining from caustic comments about creepy-crawly shysters, but after the conviction, he had remarked with surprising passion, "I could never represent a drug dealer."

Idly, Montebello now wondered what the Prince of Darkness would do if that moment of truth should ever arrive.

Elsewhere in Manhattan that night, in a fourth-story loft on a deserted stretch of Division Street, on the eastern fringe of Chinatown, the three young White Eagles arrested in the Flushing raid sat bound to chairs.

The windows of the loft were painted black. There were a half-dozen naked lightbulbs hanging from the tin-plated ceiling. Perhaps a dozen mattresses were scattered on the floor. In one corner was a hot plate and a refrigerator. Containers of leftover food littered a table.

Unicorn Frankie Chin stalked back and forth. Behind him stood his two lieutenants, Fat Monster and Flying Pig, both with pistols in their belts.

Unicorn Frankie's lower lip was still badly swollen. A bandage covered the wound on his cheek, a memento of his hasty flight to Hong Kong. In a house in Kowloon, he had stood before his uncle, Stanley Chow, who had nodded to his red pole enforcer, who, armed with brass knuckles, had smashed a fist into Frankie's jaw.

"Rise, you noxious worm," Chow had said in the Hakka dialect. "If you weren't the son of my second sister, you would never get up."

Frankie had staggered to his feet, holding his jaw, blood seeping between his fingers.

"You have brought disgrace upon me," Chow had said.

"Uncle, these things happen," he had mumbled.

Chow motioned to the red pole, who had stepped forward again, fist raised.

Frankie had fallen to his knees, kowtowing. "No, no, uncle, I beg your forgiveness. I have committed the unpardonable. I am unworthy in every respect. I deserve to die like the dog I am. I ask humbly only to be allowed to discover how this occurred."

"Big American gangster," Chow had sneered. "That information would mark an auspicious beginning of your redemption. Your future hinges on it."

And now, in the loft on Division Street, Unicorn Frankie glowered at the three trembling *sai lo* of the White Eagles. "How did the Dragon Lady know about the apartment?"

All three, whose street names were Melon Head, Whiteface and Itchy Ass, glanced nervously at one another.

"When you met Simon Hsu from Chicago and he gave you the stuff, it was at the hotel by La Guardia Airport, is it so?"

The three nodded.

"And nobody followed you to the apartment in Flushing?"

Three heads shook in unison.

"Fuck your mothers!" Unicorn Frankie screamed. "You lie, you fucks." He turned to Fat Monster. "Shoot them."

Fat Monster took out his pistol, a snub-nosed .38. Everyone heard the hammer cock. He pressed the barrel against the forehead of the one called Itchy Ass.

"*No!*" Itchy Ass cried, lips quivering. "It was Whiteface. Whiteface was busy fucking his girlfriend when Simon Hsu called from the hotel. He told Simon Hsu to bring the stuff to the apartment. We would meet him there."

"So Simon Hsu knew where the apartment was?"

"Ai! So what, big brother?" Whiteface protested. "Simon Hsu is one of us."

"You stupid fuck," Unicorn Frankie said. He told Fat Monster to untie Itchy Ass. Then he drew a Ruger .22 from his pocket, wiped the grip clean with a handkerchief and handed it to Itchy Ass. "Blow his fucking brains out," he said, pointing to Whiteface.

Afterward, examining the results, Fat Monster said, "Whiteface still breathes."

"Untie the other stupid fuck."

"Look," Fat Monster said, smirking, "Melon Head wet his pants."

"You shoot him, too," Frankie told Melon Head. "I don't want White-face breathing no more."

The body was placed in heavy-duty trash bags. "Dump him somewhere," Unicorn Frankie ordered. "See if you can do it without getting caught. You better not get caught. I'm keeping this Ruger with your fingerprints on it. You fuck up again, it goes to the cops."

At that same hour in his apartment off Gramercy Park, Duncan Lau marveled again at the strange quirk of fate that had turned what seemed to be unmitigated disaster into such good fortune. It was always this way after he and Pam Erikson made love, and he listened contentedly to her soft rhythmic breathing as she slept, snuggled next to him.

She had moved in a week after that dreadful encounter at the bank, when he had thought all was lost. Right away, she replaced Duncan's pallet with a queen-size bed and a down quilt, purchasing with her own money bright throw pillows, getting rid of the plastic window blinds and sewing and putting up curtains in their stead, making sure there were always fresh flowers in the vase next to the bed.

He couldn't resist a satisfied smile. She had given him a sense of stability and order, of belonging, that he had never before experienced. As much as the success of his business ventures—the messenger service, which had expanded to still another client, a brokerage house, and the take-out restaurant, which would have its grand opening in a few days—Pam's presence by his side trumpeted his successful arrival in the *kwai lo* world.

Only yesterday, quite unexpectedly, his feelings for her struck home. As he walked down a street with Pam, hand in hand, one of his old Chinatown chums happened by and hissed at him in Cantonese, "Banana." It was the worst possible insult. It meant yellow on the outside, white inside.

"What did he say?"

Without hesitating, Duncan had lied. "He said, 'Lucky fellow.' "

"Oh, God, I'm so happy."

"So am I," he said, and at that moment he had meant it.

Of course, there remained his responsibilities at Uncle Pei's apartment in Jackson Heights. About a hundred thousand dollars was still to be deposited. But even here, Pam, who continued to work at Citibank, was invaluable. Duncan was so busy setting up the restaurant, dealing with all the permits that were required, that she volunteered to make the deposits for him.

News of the money seizure in Flushing had left Duncan shaken, and when he approached the Jackson Heights apartment, it was with increasing trepidation. Everywhere in Chinatown it was whispered that Unicorn Frankie Chin was a *bot fun kwai,* a white powder ghost—a heroin dealer. And his messengers reported being taken aside by employees of his various accounts, from executives to secretaries, and asked, "Do you have any connections downtown for, you know, the, uh, white stuff?"

He would, Duncan decided, complete his current commitment to his benefactor, Uncle Pei, and that would be the end of it.

12

In the crowded partners' room at Needham & Lewis, James B. Needham led Tom MacLean to the refrigerator by the bar and opened the door with a flourish. Inside was a row of gleaming cans of Budweiser. "You see," Needham exclaimed. "I'm as good as my word."

"Tell you what. This time I think the occasion calls for a Macallan's. On the rocks."

"Couldn't have said it better myself," Needham said, beaming. "You've already made the transition." He turned to the black bartender, the only black in the room, who doubled during the day as the maitre d' in the partners' dining room. "Eldridge," he said, "you heard the order. Meet our newest partner, Mr. Tom MacLean. Tom, this is Eldridge Jones."

MacLean extended his hand. "Pleasure to meet you, Mr. Jones." It took Eldridge a moment before deciding that Tom wasn't patronizing him. "My pleasure, too, sir."

"May I have your attention!" Needham shouted. "For those of you who haven't made his acquaintance yet, I wish to present Tom MacLean."

Over applause, Needham continued, "Gentlemen, I have a story for you. There was a young attorney who died unexpectedly and arrived at the pearly gates pretty sore about it. 'There must be some mistake,' he insisted to St. Peter. 'I'm appealing. My time hasn't come. I'm only thirty-four.'

" 'Really?' St. Peter said. 'Let me look you up.' And then St. Peter came back and told him, 'Look, it's right here. According to the hours you've been billing, you can't be thirty-four. You have to be at least seventy-four.' "

When the chuckles died down, Needham said, "You know, these days lawyers rank right down there with journalists as objects of public disdain. The addition of Tom to our partnership reaffirms that Needham &

Lewis is what it has always been. A law firm of honor, integrity and talent. I ask you to join me in raising a glass to Tom and to welcome him here. Tom, perhaps you have a few words for us."

"Thank you, Jim," MacLean said. "I want to say that at thirty-four myself, I'm not ready for St. Peter, either. I also want to say that there's been a lot of talk, too much for my money, about my prosecuting another attorney. But I'll let you in on something. Before we went to trial, he turned on me and said, 'Why don't you grow up? I haven't done anything any other lawyer hasn't done. You think a lawyer who bills a client sixty hours a week worked those sixty hours? *Come on!*' Well, I don't buy that. Nor do I think this firm does. Which is why I'm delighted to be with you."

"Well said," someone called out.

"I just hope," Gregory Howser chimed in, puffing on one of his trademark Cuban cigars, "that we haven't let the fox in the chicken coop. Hey, only kidding," he added quickly as a chorus of boos filled the room.

Having been given a rundown on Howser by Needham—"Basically, he's a first-rate lawyer, he just likes to bulldoze people," Needham had said—Tom retorted, "Not to worry, Greg. Just so long as you don't walk past the no-smoking sign in my office with that stogie lit. That'd be very prosecutable."

"Praise the lord," someone else yelled, "law and order arrives at last in this hallowed place."

As the other partners began to drift off, Needham said, "Wonderful performance, Tom. Wonderful. Made plenty of friends, you did. Humbled Howser. Good for him. Good for you. Good for the firm. Wonderful." Then, shifting gears, Needham lowered his voice and said. "Something's come up. Have to talk to you."

Needham's inner sanctum was lined with signed photographs—presidents, generals, corporate pashas. The two most prominent featured General "Wild Bill" Donovan, the World War II spymaster who first proposed creation of what became the Central Intelligence Agency, and the late CIA director William Casey, who also had served under Donovan. "Great men, they were," Needham had said when Tom was given his first tour of the premises. "Guarded the nation day and night against all who would trespass against us. Don't make them like that anymore."

Now, behind his massive mahogany desk, Needham peered at Tom. "Well, now, it's a small thing, but it's the small things, I've learned, that count. I've just received a communication from Mr. Y. K. Deng. He advises he's arriving in the near future. Meanwhile, he's got a daughter at Yale, majoring in economics, biz admin, something like that. Her name is . . . wait a minute." Needham fumbled through a file folder. "Oh, yes, here it is. Li-po. Deng, of course. Li-po Deng."

"Deng Li-po," MacLean corrected him.

"Yes, well, whatever. Anyway, Deng would like you to look in on her. See how she's doing. This past summer she insisted on remaining in New Haven. And naturally Deng's a bit concerned. Not unusual. I'm told the Chinese dote on their children. And why not, I say."

"Yes, that's true if the child happens to be a son. In the Chinese culture, the birth of a son is cause for jubilation, but the arrival of a daughter is a major disappointment. They don't make any bones about it."

"Maybe so, maybe so. But our Mr. Deng doesn't have any sons that I'm aware of. And apparently he dotes on . . . on this Li-po."

"I didn't realize," Tom MacLean said, not bothering to conceal the sarcasm, "that my responsibilities include day care duty."

Needham flushed. "Listen, I don't know what Deng's plans are. I gather, though, he intends to involve his daughter in his investment program. That's the reason he had her educated in the States. And if she looks to us, *you,* for guidance and counsel, obviously that could mean a great deal for the firm. Just touch base, is all I'm asking."

"OK, OK, I surrender."

"Wonderful, Tom, just wonderful. I knew you'd see my point," said Needham, beaming ingenuously again.

"When do you want me to go?"

"As soon as possible. Uh, ah, there's one more thing."

Oh, boy, here it comes, Tom thought, by now used to Needham's circumlocution. "And what might that be?"

"Seems she's gotten involved with a Yale professor. Name's Robert Logan. Chinese scholar. Archaeology, anthropology, I'm not sure. According to Deng, he's been to China two or three times. No problem getting in. Apparently welcomed with open arms. Deng's worried. Cozy with the Commies, is that what it is? Deng has strong feelings about that. He would like us to look into this fellow, Logan. You have all those Justice Department contacts. Check him out. See if he's on the up-and-up."

"*You* want me to find out if the FBI's got a file on him?"

"Not me, son. Y. K. Deng, our client."

"No way. For Christ's sake, using the FBI like that because of some father's paranoia, client or not, about his daughter's boyfriend is outrageous. If this professor doesn't have a file now, he sure will the minute I start asking around."

"The thought was you could do it, you know, kind of unofficially."

"Absolutely not. Forget it."

Needham threw up his hands. "All right, all right. Just figured I'd throw it out. If you were a father, you might look at it differently. Just mull it over."

"Hell, Jim, now I'm not even sure I should see her."

"My boy," Needham said quietly. "You've already agreed to it. That part's a done deal."

Shannon O'Shea had been away, attending an international narcotics conference in Vancouver, British Columbia. "We'll just sit around telling each other what we already know we don't know," she had said. "But I have to be there. Everybody's on the edge of their seat waiting for a big explosion in heroin traffic and trying to figure out how to say they're on top of it."

Earlier that day, she called, "I'm back."

"We still on for tonight?"

"You bet."

A loyal Chicago sports fan since his days at Northwestern, Tom had gotten tickets to watch the Bulls play the Knicks. He also knew that she liked basketball, that in fact it was because of basketball that she had joined the FBI.

"Basketball? Explain, please," he had asked.

It was simple, she had replied. After she left the Maryknoll order, she applied to become a schoolteacher, and one night her brother, a New York City firefighter, took her to a Knicks game where she got into a conversation with a nice-looking fellow sitting next to her. Eventually, she told him she was an ex-nun.

"A *nun?*" he had said.

"Yes, something wrong with that?"

"No, no," the fellow had stammered. But he seemed to lose all interest in the game and kept staring at her. It turned out he was a recruiter for the FBI and he said, "Have you ever considered the FBI as a career?" and gave her his card.

Of course, she said, she didn't know then that the FBI, like practically every federal law-enforcement agency, was scrambling around trying to hire enough women to ward off sex-discrimination suits.

But when she considered it, she thought, Why not? Community service was a family tradition. Her brother was a firefighter. Her dad was a battalion chief in the Fire Department. And her mom was a nurse. Certainly, being in the FBI was community service. "Just like being a nun," she said, a little too glibly.

Tom had wanted to debate that. Vows of chastity and poverty. Total commitment to God's work. A hard-knock life under the best of circumstances. Was that just another form of community service? But he decided not to pursue it. Instinct warned he was edging into dangerous waters. Instinct said to drop it, at least right then.

They had planned to meet in front of Madison Square Garden, but late in the day, right after Tom's session with Needham about Li-po, she called again and said something had come up. She would be late and he should leave her ticket at the will-call window.

It was halftime when she finally arrived, grim-faced. "You remember those White Eagle kids from Flushing? The body of one of them was found wrapped in plastic in an alley off Mott Street. Three twenty-two-caliber holes in his head at close range."

"Was he talking?"

"Not that anybody knows. After they were booked, a bondsman was right down to post bail. Lawyer, too. The hearing was a nightmare. They claimed they couldn't understand English, which was a lie. Or Cantonese, even a bigger lie. We had to beat the bushes to find an interpreter who spoke Hakka, since I obviously wasn't acceptable. They stuck to the same story. A stranger, Chinese, offered them a hundred bucks each to guard the money. One of them explained to the judge that it was in the grand Chinese tradition to help a fellow Chinese. 'Oh, yes,' the judge said, 'I've heard that.' The guns were already there, they said. Never touched them. They never saw any heroin. The judge granted bail."

Shannon shook her head. "Remember how scared they looked when we grabbed them? Well, you haven't seen scared until you meet their parents. The minute I explained who I was, they started shaking. 'No know nothing. No can do nothing. Please, missy, go away, chop, chop.' It was like they were terrified to be spotted talking to me."

After Michael Jordan beat the Knicks with a last-second flying dunk, they went to The Place, filled as usual with the familiar faces of prosecutors and defense attorneys. "I hear you got quite a send-off while I was gone," she said. "All the female assistants tearing their hair out at your departure. Really have a way with the ladies, don't you?"

It annoyed him that the best he could manage was a sheepish grin. Shannon was different from other women he had been involved with. She had an indefinable quality that he found compelling. He had searched his mind vainly for the right word. Then an old-fashioned one occurred to him that seemed perfectly descriptive. *Moxie!* He looked it up in the dictionary: "[Slang] courage, pluck, perseverance, etc.; guts." For all her forthrightness, though, there was a wall around her. Inside of which, he sensed, demons lurked.

He was still trying to come up with a retort when the night manager, Dan McGuire, said, "Tom, I wondered if we'd ever see you again, now you've moved into such fancy Park Avenue digs. I'll have a table now any second. Going well, is it?"

Once they were seated, Tom said, "What'll you have?"

"I don't see any new cordon bleu additions to the menu. Therefore, a hamburger medium-rare. Side order of chili. And a light beer." She looked at him. "Since Danny boy brought up the subject, how *is* it going?"

He scowled and told her about the assignment to visit Deng's daughter.

"Hey, brighten up. We know she's an heiress. Maybe a beauty, too. Pearl of the Orient. And think how you could brush up on your Chinese."

"She's got a boyfriend." Then he told her about Needham's other request. "Can you believe it? An inquiry like that coming from me might really damage the guy. You know how compromising raw files can be."

"Tell you what," she said. "I'll do it for you. I won't pinpoint a name, just run through the data banks. Chinese-American cultural relations. Student exchanges. And so on. If he's in any of them, he'll pop up. Robert Logan. Yale."

"Listen, I want it clear that I'm not asking you to do this."

"Never fear. You know I have an insatiable curiosity about Hong Kong tycoons. You're probably right. Just a father worked up about his daughter." She gazed blankly out into the room. "Just like my dad," she said, her voice trailing off, as if she were talking to herself.

Which was why he didn't ask what that meant. He felt as though he had been caught eavesdropping.

She dug into her chili. "Excuse," she said. "I'm not very good company tonight. It's the murder of that White Eagle kid. Damn! Something's going on and I haven't a clue what it is."

"What about that CI you said you had?"

"No help. And I've got to believe him. He faces twenty years of hard time if he doesn't cooperate. Works out of Chicago brokering heroin shipments coming from Hong Kong. He was getting big commissions, but like a lot of Chinese, he's also a compulsive gambler who owes the wrong people. So on the last batch, the one we thought we'd find in Flushing, he helped himself to a unit and was caught selling it to an undercover agent."

She shrugged her shoulders. "Nobody knows this, so we figure the shipments will keep coming—they arrive in Chicago in golf cart tires—and the next time out, we hope to nail everybody. Maybe even the Hong Kong shippers. There are unconfirmed reports that the Hakka triad there is run by a Stanley Chow. Unlike your Mr. Deng, I have plenty of clips on him."

After finishing coffee, Tom escorted Shannon the two blocks to her apartment building, near where the New York FBI headquarters had been located until it was moved downtown to Federal Plaza.

In the vestibule, she melted against him as he kissed her and said, "Can I come up?"

She hesitated. She was really taken with him. It had been that way ever since their Chinatown lunch, that same rush of pleasure—and desire—each time she saw him. But she knew he was a lady-killer. Other agents in the office were already kidding her about it. And she didn't want to end up as another of Tom's trophies. She had to be sure. She needed a sign before she gave herself to him. She had worked too hard to become her own person. All she could do was hope she wasn't making a mistake when she said, "I need some time, Tom. Please."

He gazed at Shannon and decided not to push her. "Look," he just said, "we've got to start ending these evenings together."

"I know. Soon."

Tom MacLean arrived in New Haven just past noon. The address he had been given was for a house on a pleasant residential street adjoining the

Yale campus. He had phoned Li-po in the morning, identifying himself, and she had told him to come up; she had no Saturday classes.

When he rang the bell, and a series of locks were unlocked, an elderly Chinese woman looked out, a heavy chain still in place.

"Is Miss Deng in?"

The door started to close.

He tried to remember his Cantonese. Yes! *Pen you.* Friend! *"Li-po dit pen you,"* he said haltingly, "Li-po's friend," hoping he had the correct intonation. If you didn't get it right, it could convey a completely different meaning.

The door shut with a bang.

Christ, he thought. He was about to ring the bell again when he heard a voice say, "Mr. MacLean! Hi!"

He turned toward the sidewalk. The first thing that struck him were her bewitching eyes, their corners crinkling in amusement at his discomfiture. She was wearing an oversized Yale sweatshirt and jeans. She carried a bag of groceries.

"I'm sorry, really," she said. "I thought I'd be back before you got here. Auntie Mei—that's my amah who slammed the door on you—doesn't like to go out. I can't blame her. This street's OK, but it gets bad real fast. Crack, coke, heroin, whatever your pleasure. Your typical Ivy League community." Her laughter had an infectious quality that made Tom laugh with her.

"I think it was my Cantonese that scared the daylights out of her," he said. He held the bag of groceries, while Li-po took out a ring of keys and began opening the locks. Inside, he passed the amah, who still looked at him with undisguised suspicion.

"Anyhow," she said, "I thought I'd get something for lunch. Robert's coming by. I'm sure you want to meet him."

"Robert?"

"Robert Logan. Oh, come on, Mr. MacLean. My father didn't send you up here to see how I'm doing in Keynesian theory. *I know my father.*"

"Well, I don't, at least not yet, Miss Deng. And I'm his lawyer, not another amah for you."

She laughed her silvery laugh, as if it weren't worth arguing about. "Why don't you call me Li-po and I'll call you Tom," she said. "I have to get lunch started. Very, very Chinese. Southern fried chicken. Robert's from Kentucky, as you also undoubtedly know."

"No, I can honestly say I didn't."

Logan arrived a few minutes later. He was lean and square-jawed, dressed in khaki trousers and a tweed jacket, twenty-eight and was, as it developed, an archaeologist.

"How'd you get into it?" MacLean asked.

"Back in the Boy Scouts. I was twelve. We were on a camping expedition and I remember to this day finding an Indian arrowhead, and then another one and then sitting there trying to imagine the man who made them and what his life was like. And eventually at college, here at Yale, who could resist China? I mean, you had Beijing Man—what was called Peking Man until the Communists insisted on changes in phonetic spellings—the first man to use fire to cook meat."

Since Logan was the one who had mentioned the Communist regime, Tom said, "No problems getting in and out or gaining access to archaeological sites?"

"Not until recently," Logan said. The goals for everyone were to advance knowledge. He had been to China four times. The last trip had been to Hubei Province deep in central China, where the great Yangtze River began its flow to the sea. Two skulls had been unearthed that indicated that perhaps the progenitor of the modern human being, always thought to have been African, might have evolved independently in China. Of course, this had triggered great controversy. An exercise in Chinese hubris? But the trip was a bummer, he said. It was 1989. After trying to arrange at least to have plaster casts of the skulls made, he returned to Beijing just in time for the crackdown on the student democracy movement in Tiananmen Square. Suddenly, the skulls were unavailable. He hadn't been back since.

"How did you two meet?" Tom asked.

"I had finished a lecture on the late Neolithic period and was walking across a quad," Logan said, "when I spotted this gorgeous creature coming toward me. And in my best Mandarin, I said, '*Tsao. Ni hao ma,*' which more or less means, 'Hi, how are you today?' and what I got back was a torrent of words, not one of which I understood, but which I subsequently learned was Chiuchow. Basically, it meant to get lost."

"Oh, he's making it sound worse than it was," she said. "I got flustered. It was such a surprise. What I usually heard walking around New Haven or New York was, 'Hey, China doll,' or 'Hey, baby, I haven't seen anything like you since Nam.' "

"Guys say things like that?"

"Not anymore. Not when I'm with Robert."

"Anyway," Logan said, "we ended up negotiating. I'd teach her about China's past . . ."

"It's true," she interrupted, "he knows so much more than I do about my heritage."

". . . and she'd teach me the Chiuchow dialect."

Tom liked him. And especially her. "Your father did ask me, through the firm, to see how you were," he said. "I can certainly report that you're doing quite well. Of course, he'll soon be able to see for himself."

She turned, startled. "He's coming here?"

"You didn't know?"

"No. It's not important, though," she added hastily. "My father has his own way of doing things."

In the room where they ate, there was a photograph of a man with piercing eyes. "Is that your father?" Tom asked.

"Yes. And the other is of my mother. She died when I was born," she said. "I often think it was my fault. My father tells me not to be so silly."

"I'm also supposed to tell you," Tom said, "that I'm available for any professional advice and counsel you might need."

"I like you, Tom MacLean," she said. "I'll remember that."

Driving away, Tom saw Li-po and Logan still standing on the stoop in front of the house, holding hands. As he was about to turn onto the New England Thruway for the trip back to New York, he couldn't stop thinking about her. And her father, *his* client. There had been something other than surprise in her eyes when he told her Deng would be coming to the States shortly. It was, he decided, a flash of fear.

He suddenly braked at a pay phone and made a credit card call to his father, who lived on the eastern end of Long Island.

"Dad," he said. "I'm in Connecticut. New Haven. I know it's late, but if you don't have any plans, I'd like to take the ferry over from Bridgeport. Spend the night with you."

13

TOM MACLEAN DROVE east along the Montauk Highway on Long Island's south shore. Traffic dwindled, the roadside produce stands, to which summer vacationers flocked, were empty, potato and cornfields lay barren. In the last light, a wavering chevron of Canada geese crossed the leaden autumn sky.

He pondered how to raise the subject of Y. K. Deng. His father's former employment had always remained forbidden territory as a topic of discussion. It was as if he were a child in Hong Kong again.

Were the experiences of other CIA offspring the same? Or did their parents ignore the secrecy strictures? He laughed hollowly. Is there an advisory now for new recruits? "Warning: The Agency's Psychiatrist General has determined this can be dangerous to those whom you hold dear."

Darkness had fallen by the time Tom pulled up in front of his father's home in the old whaling port of Sag Harbor. The Federal-style clapboard house had been in his mother's family and her sole tangible inheritance. After John MacLean's retirement from the CIA, they had decided to reside there permanently. It appeared to be an idyllic arrangement, his mother in her rose garden, his father immersed in editorial and academic consulting. So deep was their attachment to one another, a secret world within a secret world, that at times Tom had felt himself an intruder. The separation had widened, both physically and psychologically, when he was left behind in the States to pursue first college and then law school while his father, following his Southeast Asia post, was assigned, under State Department cover, to Soviet bloc countries and, later, to Moscow itself.

Nine months ago, his mother had succumbed suddenly to an inoperable brain malignancy. After her death, Tom braced himself to cope with his father, envisioning a larger apartment in the city that the two of them would share. But John MacLean had never even raised that possibility. He would remain in Sag Harbor. It was evolving into a culturally active year-round community that included interesting writers and artists, and a vibrant regional theater, which flourished even in the dead of winter.

At the third rap of the brass knocker, John MacLean opened the door. Tom had not seen him for four months, not since late July when he had come out for a weekend. Then, as now, his father looked well, his body still fit, his face a bit more lined, the blond hair replaced by a shock of white. Tom had arrived for that earlier visit with the hope of redefining their relationship, but the frenetic social activity of summer in the Hamptons had dashed that possibility. Tom couldn't recall having more than ten quiet minutes with him. Perhaps it was his father's way of surviving the loss of a companion of close to forty years, a companion, moreover, who presumably was the only person in whom he could confide.

The moment his father opened the door, though, Tom sensed a change in him. John MacLean, in a cardigan sweater and corduroy trousers, embraced him with enthusiasm. "What a nice surprise," he exclaimed. "Come on in."

Maybe, Tom thought, the unexpectedness of his call had caught his father off guard. Didn't allow him enough time to don a behavioral mask. Usually, even when his mother was alive, their get-togethers were planned well in advance.

John MacLean led him into the study—paneled bookshelves, wide-planked oak floor, a hook rug, Windsor armchairs, pewter plates, a polished Early American tavern table, all in precise arrangement, as if to ward off life's disarray.

Fireplace logs crackled. A Beethoven piano sonata played on the stereo.

A photograph of his mother was in its usual place on one of the shelves. Then Tom saw that there was now another photograph alongside it, one of himself in an undergraduate cap and gown.

"God, I look so gawky," he said. "Where'd that come from?"

"Oh, I don't know. I was rummaging around a couple of months after your last visit and there it was. Had it framed to remind me of what a fine young man you've turned out to be. You've been on my mind a great deal recently, a regret really that I wasn't the kind of father to you that I should have been."

"Don't be ridiculous. I'm fine."

"I don't mean to suggest that you aren't. I think what I mean is that *I* was the one who missed out, sharing more in your growing up. My loss."

"Look, you had a wonderful relationship with Mom. I should be so lucky. And, after all, you were busy."

"Yes," his father sighed, "I was busy." Tom could almost feel the effort he was making to affect a cheerier tone. "Well, now, how's the new job suit you?"

"So far, so good."

"Excellent. You were in the government how long, eight years?"

"Just about."

"Time you left."

"That wasn't what you did."

"It was different for me. In my line of work, once you were in, you're pretty much in."

"Is that something you also regret?"

"When you've been around as long as I have, regrets aren't hard to find. Would I do it all over again? That's the question, I suppose. The world's very different now. Your mother and I used to talk about it quite a bit. Everything seemed so clear-cut at the time. The Cold War, the international Communist conspiracy."

John MacLean stared into the fire. "I grieve for your mother, for myself." Then, after a moment, he said, "Forgive the maudlin display. It's time for dinner. Your father is now an accomplished chef. My housekeeper, Mrs. Thomas, has left a delightful treat of bay scallops. All I have to do is sauté them in butter for a minute or so. She wanted to do the broccoli and have me heat it up in the microwave. But I said no, I wanted to show off for my son."

They ate in the big kitchen. "Now tell me more about this law firm you've joined."

"You might have heard of the senior partner, James Needham."

"Needham? The name strikes a bell. I don't know why."

"He was in the OSS. One of Wild Bill Donovan's boys, he tells me."

"Yes, that's it. Before my time. Strange, me saying something like that. I recall reading about him in one of the histories."

Well, the door's been opened, Tom thought. "Dad, what do you know about a Chinese? Name of Deng."

Tom saw the surprise register on his father's face. "Deng?"

"Yes, Deng. Y. K. Deng."

"Deng," John MacLean repeated with elaborate casualness. "Oh, you must mean Deng Yue-keung. That would be the right initials if he's anglicized his name. He wouldn't go any farther than that. Wouldn't take a Christian name, I expect. Very Chinese, very proud."

"Can you tell me anything more?"

"Mind explaining what this is all about?"

"From what I gather, he's one of the reasons Needham was so anxious to take me on. Apparently, Mr. Deng had some sort of a connection with you back when you were stationed in Hong Kong. And now he's about to establish himself in the U.S. Apparently, he's also quite well off—actually more than well off—and the firm went all-out to get him as a client, which it has. When I phoned you this afternoon, I'd just been with his daughter. She's a captivating girl, a student at Yale. You aren't aware of any of this?"

"*No!*"

Tom was taken aback at the sharpness in his father's voice. "Look, Dad, I know some things are out of bounds, but . . ."

Almost as if he hadn't heard him, as if he were musing out loud to himself, John MacLean said, "I knew Deng had remarried. I didn't know about the daughter. But by then I'd been reassigned and lost touch with him. I'm glad for him. I know he wanted children very much."

"What else can you say?"

"Deng was what we called an asset. He was, in fact, an invaluable asset before I met him, and presumably he continued to be one after I was gone. We worked together during the Vietnam War. Remember when I was away from Hong Kong so much? I was in Laos with him, and he was crucial in enlisting the indigenous hill tribesmen in our cause."

John MacLean finished the last of his scallops in silence. "There's one other thing. He saved my life."

"He did?"

"Yes. It was in Laos, near dusk. I wandered away from the camp. I can't think why. Maybe just to think. In any event, I was going along this mountain trail. The light was bad. I lost my footing and tumbled down a ravine. When I came to, it was pitch black. And, as it turned out, my ankle was broken. I tried to climb back up, but the incline was too steep. Conceivably, I could have made it through till morning, but spending a night in those circumstances in the Laotian jungle—a lot of slippery customers out there—isn't something you'd want to wish on your worst enemy. Suddenly, I saw some lanterns up where the trail was and I started yelling like crazy. It was Deng. He'd rounded up some tribesmen and was looking for me. Fortunately, he was successful."

"That's some story."

"And it's all you're going to hear. I've said far more than I should. Anyway, it doesn't involve you."

Of course it does, Tom thought. How could his father say that? He elected, though, not to press the issue.

"Coffee?"

"No, thanks. I've had a long day. I think I'll hit the sack after I help you clean up."

"I won't hear of it. There's hardly anything to do. I'm a practiced hand at putting things in the dishwasher. Off you go. You know where your room is. See you in the morning."

Asleep, under a down quilt, Tom was back in Hong Kong, in the forbidden tunnel with Freddie Carradine. All at once, Freddie wasn't there. Tom was lost. He heard a voice that said, "You're not supposed to be in here." He thought it was his father. But then he looked up and saw that it wasn't. The figure was blurry. He couldn't make out who it was. "Who are you?" Tom cried, and the figure said, "My name is Deng."

Tom jolted awake. Then he rolled over, thinking that all this CIA stuff was getting to him.

John MacLean did not go to bed. After he had tidied up, he returned to the study and helped himself to a glass of cognac. He added some logs to the dying fire and watched it leap up again. Sipping the cognac, he sat gazing into the fire, mesmerized by it. In the flames, an oil drum appeared, its water heating, raw opium and lime fertilizer being dumped in, steamy vapors rising. He heard Deng explaining this first step in the refinement process. Deng! In the study, he reached out for the cognac and refilled his glass. He couldn't keep his eyes away from the fire. The oil drum was still there.

He awoke much later, cramped, still in his chair. Except for a few glowing embers, the fire was out. He got up unsteadily and made his way to his bedroom. He stood there for a moment before he went to a blanket chest in the corner. He raised the top and removed a leather case and a cardboard tube. He snapped open the case and stared at the medallion with its red, white and blue ribbon nestled in fake velvet. In the center was a bald eagle, wings spread, claws gripping an olive branch and lightning bolts. On the eagle's breast were the radiating spokes of a compass covering all points of the globe. On the medallion's rim, it said "Central Intelligence Agency," and then "For Distinguished Service." He extracted the ersatz parchment paper from the tubing. It bore the CIA shield and said: "In Recognition of Outstanding Service of a Distinctly Exceptional Nature." There were no further details. John MacLean tossed them back into the chest. They had been hidden there because as long as he was alive, this, too, was a secret. As far as anyone was concerned, he'd been a Foreign Service troubleshooter.

He had never felt more weary, yet he could not sleep. Finally, at dawn's first light, he drifted off.

Next morning Tom noticed the puffiness under his father's eyes.

"I made a mistake," John MacLean said. "I treated myself to a brandy after you went upstairs. I should know better." He provided Tom with underwear and a cotton turtleneck. "We'll drive to the Candy Kitchen in Bridgehampton for breakfast. Get the Sunday papers."

Tom first phoned Shannon O'Shea. "I stayed with my father overnight here in Sag Harbor. I tried to reach you from New Haven, but you weren't home. And when I tried the office, they said you were on assignment."

"Yes, I got the message, but it was too late to call back. Still dealing with the White Eagle hit."

"Listen," Tom said. "I'll be leaving for the city in a while. You'll be home?"

"Yes. Can't wait."

The Candy Kitchen was a luncheonette on Bridgehampton's main street, in fact the only one. When they entered, his father waved to a group of elderly men gathered at the rear table. "That's the local power breakfast. We hash over all the world's problems, and then get down to really important topics, like the state of real estate out here."

After ordering eggs and country sausage, his father said, "I couldn't help overhearing you on the phone. You seeing someone special?"

"Yes. She's an FBI agent."

"Really?"

"And a former nun, to boot."

"Good lord. All this time, I thought I was the one with the exotic life."

Over a second cup of coffee, John MacLean said, "Do you have any Christmas plans? Why don't you come out here? Perhaps your friend would like to come, too."

"That'd be nice. I don't know about her. She's got family. But I'll ask."

Driving toward the city, Tom reflected on his client, Y. K. Deng. Actually, when you got right down to it, his father hadn't revealed all that much about him. Except that Deng apparently saved John MacLean's life in the jungles of Laos. The Chinese, it was said, fervently believe in relationships. But this one carried a burden that was spectacularly hard to beat. He couldn't help feeling the uneasy weight of it.

When Tom got to his apartment, there was a message from Shannon on his answering machine. She was at the Fifth Precinct in Chinatown. She left a number.

"Hey, what's up?" he said.

"I wanted to hear what Unicorn Frankie Chin had to say about his dead little brother when they brought him in for questioning. He's gone now. I know it's early, but I'm ravenous."

At six p.m., he met her in a small restaurant on Pell Street. On Sundays, filled with tourists, Chinatown looked like a theme park.

"I'll say this for Frankie," she said. "He puts up a good front. Wanted to cooperate any way he could. After all, as the *dai lo* of the White Eagles, he's lost big face. Supposed to take care of his people. I got the feeling he was enjoying every minute. That and a buck twenty-five gets me a ride on the subway. Could have been some rival gang, he said. He was going to get right on it. A homicide lieutenant even warned him not to take matters in his own hands."

"What about the other two you arrested in Flushing?"

"Nothing. Hadn't seen the victim—his name was Wu Lum, a/k/a Whiteface—for several days. The only possibility I can think of is that someone thought Whiteface was a bad security risk. I'll tell you, Tom, when the curtain goes down around here, it drops all the way."

After dinner, they walked north on Mulberry. In Little Italy, they stopped in a coffee bar and ordered cappuccino. "Cinnamon," Shannon said. "Lots of cinnamon."

Tom told her about his visit with Li-po, about how charming she was.

"You meet the boyfriend? I haven't had a chance to do a rundown on him yet."

"Yes, a very likable guy. The only odd thing was that she didn't know her father was coming here."

"He must have known you'd mention it."

"That's what I don't get."

"Maybe he's sending her a little shiver."

Then Tom told Shannon about the satisfying visit he'd had with his own father. "I can't tell you how good I feel about it. We weren't the closest family in the world, at least as far as I was concerned. It was like a lot of bad things were laid to rest. By the way, I told him about you."

"Nice things, I hope."

"Enough for him to ask me to ask you if you'd like to come for Christmas."

Her eyes suddenly sparkled. "He did?"

"I told him you probably had family obligations. But maybe we could work it out. The MacLeans usually celebrated on Christmas eve. Maybe you could manage a split shift."

Outside, on the sidewalk, she said, "You weren't kidding? He really did invite me?"

"Sure. Why would I make it up?"

"I don't know," she said, laughing. She took his hand, gripping it tightly. She didn't let go.

They walked through SoHo, crowded with uptowners downtown to visit the art galleries. Then they paused in Washington Square to watch the chess players, bundled against the chill, intent on the moves they were strategizing under streetlights.

His three-room apartment was on West Eleventh Street. Shannon was still holding his hand. She did not ask where they were going.

In the elevator, she smiled at him.

In the apartment, he took her in his arms and kissed her. He took off her coat and kissed her again. And again.

"I'll see you in bed," she whispered.

She came in from the bathroom wearing his terrycloth robe and let it fall to the floor. She had a slim body. Her breasts were small, but in perfect proportion to the rest of her.

"Hi," she said, slipping in next to him.

Tom felt her trembling. He stroked her hair and kept holding her. Gradually, the trembling subsided. He started to caress her. Her body tensed again, but this time it was from desire. She reached down and touched him.

He rose over Shannon and slowly entered her. She uttered a little gasp. There had been a moment when he thought she might be a virgin, but now he knew that this wasn't so. Inside her, he remained still for a time. Then he began to move and she responded.

He moved faster and she stayed with him. He tasted the perspiration on her upper lip. He could sense it building and then, all at once, he felt her spasms. "My God, oh, my God!" she cried. She clung to him as he let himself go.

He raised himself from her and cradled her head in the hollow of his shoulder. She drew a finger down his back. "Tom," she said. "My Tom."

The next afternoon, in her office, Shannon O'Shea phoned Tom. "I've been taking an unmerciful ribbing for the last two hours," she said. "There's a beautiful, single red rose on my desk in a thin crystal vase. Delivered anonymously. You wouldn't happen to know anything about this, would you?"

"Like it?"

"I love it!"

"See you tonight?"

"God willing. And, by the way, I ran a check on your Robert Logan," she said. "He's in the computer. But nothing remotely indicating he's bad news. Could provide little intelligence re current Beijing government. Spoke about discovery of fabulous cave drawings in the Chou period. FYI, that's circa nine hundred B.C. Last trip was different, though. Had gone concerning something about ancient skulls. Interviewing agent not clear what the significance is. Anyway, it was during the Tiananmen Square uprising, and one of his Chinese colleagues was imprisoned. Very disillusioning. Doesn't plan on returning unless things change."

"Much obliged."

"A rose will do it every time."

For the next hour or so, buoyed by thoughts of Tom, Shannon busied herself with paperwork. Then her phone rang. It was an agent named Kolinski in the Chicago field office.

"Tell me, Shannon," he said in his usual laconic manner. "What's black and blue and can be found floating in the Chicago river?"

"Somebody who tells Polish jokes?"

"Not bad. Try our prime-time CI re the White Eagles, Simon Hsu."

"You're joking."

"Sorry."

"When?"

"Coroner's best estimate was last night. They worked him over pretty good."

"Any leads?"

"*Nada.*"

The homicide was reported in the Chicago newspapers. Death was the result of garroting. There were unconfirmed rumors that the victim might have been a police informant. He also was said to have been an inveterate gambler. An unnamed local Chinatown source, identified only as a subscriber to Confucian wisdom, was quoted as saying, "One gambles to win, but one must pay one's debts if one loses."

Reading these stories brought a smile to the face of Unicorn Frankie Chin. He had them clipped and translated. He sent the originals and the translations via Federal Express to Stanley Chow in Hong Kong, adding a covering note in Chinese that said "From your dutiful nephew."

Then his thoughts turned to the *kwai lo* woman they called the Dragon Lady. In a futile attempt to save himself, Simon Hsu said she had been running the undercover operation that got Frankie into so much trouble.

14

IN SAG HARBOR, as soon as Tom left, John MacLean went to his Rolodex to find the unlisted home number in Vienna, Virginia, of Wayne Forrester, the current deputy director of CIA operations and former chief of the Far East Division.

"Wayne," he said. "John MacLean here. Sorry to intrude on a Sunday morning."

"No problem. Just settling in to watch the game on the tube."

"The game?"

"Yes, the Redskins. They're playing the Cowboys."

"Oh, right. I guess I'm out of the loop on pro football."

He heard Forrester chuckle. "John, you're never out of the loop when it counts."

Is that so? MacLean thought. "Wayne, something's come up that I have to see you about. I don't feel free to talk on the phone."

"When?"

"Tomorrow, if possible. I'll fly down."

"Hold on a minute." And then Forrester said, "I have a working lunch. Should be finished about two p.m. How's that sound?"

"Fine. I'll be there."

That afternoon, he drove to the cemetery. The gravestone read: "Gretchen Thyssen MacLean. 1929–1992."

"I wish you were here," he said. "What have I done?"

Overhead, swooping in from the bay, seagulls cawed.

At National Airport in Washington, John MacLean rented a car, then twenty minutes later, as directed, braked about fifty yards in front of the first security gate at CIA headquarters in Langley, Virginia. Over a speaker, he identified himself, recited his Social Security number and the purpose of his visit and was instructed to proceed. At the gate itself, after a guard inspected his driver's license bearing his photograph, he was provided with a preferred parking pass.

Obeying the twenty-mile speed limit, he drove about a quarter of a mile along a winding road past lunchtime joggers and turned left toward a massive, eight-story precast-concrete building. Still another guard, after he displayed his pass, waved him through.

No matter how many times he had been to Langley, John MacLean could not get over the change from the days of his own recruitment. Then, he had been processed in several ramshackle buildings on the Mall near the Lincoln Memorial that had been hastily constructed during World War II. And the old headquarters itself was scattered across Constitution Avenue in a cluster of yellow-brick structures once occupied by the Veterans Administration.

The original prospectus for the Langley site called for the atmosphere of a "college campus," a goal that had been monumentally missed. In addition to the great bunker-like concrete main edifice, there now stood behind it a second building, almost as big, with a four-story core and twin six-floor towers made of steel and green glass, lots of glass. When he first saw all the glass, he had quipped, "What about security" and whomever he had said this to earnestly replied, "Don't worry, John, it's state of the art. That glass is not only bulletproof, but impervious to any electronic listening devices beamed in its direction."

He walked by a bronze statue of the nation's first martyr spy, Nathan Hale, and up the steps leading to the main entrance with its flared canopy—pristine except for two sand-filled receptacles shaped like Grecian urns. A no-smoking edict had been adopted within headquarters and in each receptacle, left by employees seeking respite from world espionage action, were mounds of cigarette butts, at that moment being removed by a service attendant.

Inside the great central lobby, at yet another security checkpoint, he filled out additional forms, was given a visitor's badge and told to wait for his escort, a pleasant young man who said, "I'm honored to meet you, sir." They went down a hall featuring oil portraits of past CIA chiefs and into a private elevator requiring a key to operate. They rose to the top floor Holy of Holies, an imposing terraced complex containing the director's suite of offices and those of his deputies.

Wayne Forrester rose from his desk, flanked by the American and CIA flags. The windows offered a sweeping vista of the wooded northern Virginia landscape. The deputy director of operations, responsible for the CIA's global covert undertakings, was a fleshy-faced fellow whose round, rimless spectacles gave him an owlish look. He would have looked at home at a Rotary Club lunch. A Phi Beta Kappa key and chain were prominent on the vest of his three-piece suit.

"John!" he exclaimed with a broad smile. "How good to see you. How well you look." Then Forrester's visage turned somber. "That was terrible news about Gretchen. The directorate sent a wreath."

"I know. I hope I sent a thank-you note. Probably not. I wasn't really myself for a while."

"Not necessary. And quite understandable. My God! All our hearts went out to you." He guided MacLean to a chair. "Well, well, what brings this welcome surprise? You mentioned a matter of some urgency."

"Wayne, you must remember an important Chinese asset in Hong Kong, Deng Yue-keung—cryptonym DH/ROGUE. Is he still working for us?"

Forrester's face froze. "John, you know I can't answer that."

MacLean struggled to remain calm. "I've got to have some answers. My son, Tom, recently resigned as a federal prosecutor and joined the law firm of Needham & Lewis in New York. Deng's a client. From what I can gather, the fact that Tom's in the firm was a critical factor in Deng's decision to retain it. What the hell's going on?"

"John, it has nothing to do with you."

"Funny you should say that, Wayne. I found myself selling pretty much the same line to my son this weekend—that it didn't have anything to do with him. Well, it has plenty to do with *him* and *me*. You don't have to be clairvoyant to figure that out. Believe me, if I don't get some answers, I'm going to raise a real stink."

Forrester's eyes narrowed. Suddenly, he didn't look so owlish anymore. "That would be, ah, unfortunate. A clear criminal violation."

"I don't care. You know what Deng was doing in Laos at our behest. I was there and I saw it. And I know what happened. He isn't still in that stuff, is he?"

"Of course not. What do you think we are anyway, dope peddlers?"

"I think I'll pass on that one."

"Very amusing. I don't recall you being quite so witty in your active service days." Forrester peered at John MacLean for several seconds. "All right, for old time's sake, I can tell you this much. Deng's been extremely valuable. We hope to maintain our links to him. The problem is that because of the approaching changeover in Hong Kong, he wants to establish himself here, just to be on the safe side. He indicated a desire for some legal guidance in his business ventures, so we suggested Jim Needham, who's an old Company man, true blue. And without going into the details, we told Needham about your closeness to Deng. I mean, it's right in one of your evaluation reports, how Deng saved your life in the goddamn jungle. Deng still has an extensive network in China and we want him to know that we care about him. Continuity, relationships, connections are what it's all about with the Chinese, as you well know." Forrester drummed his fingers impatiently on his desk. "In a nutshell, that's it."

"So that's how Needham got onto my son?"

"Yes."

"Why wasn't I consulted?"

Forrester sighed audibly. "John, it wasn't anything personal," he said, as if addressing a child with a learning disability. "It's against the rules. As you yourself said, you're out of the loop. Remember, when you came in here a while ago, you didn't breeze through with your badge. You were processed like any visitor would be."

"That's all there is to this?"

"All there is. Look, I can understand your concern. It's the rules. Personally, I wish we could be more flexible. But we still live in dangerous times. The big beast may be gone, but there're hundreds of poisonous snakes out there, coiled and ready to strike."

"Very good, Wayne. That should be used in the next appropriations request."

Forrester looked pleased, even smug. "You think so? As a matter of fact, I included it in my draft contribution for the new director when he goes up to the Hill." He looked at his watch. "Well, nice seeing you, John. Really nice. I have to get to a briefing. Trust I've allayed your concern. There's nothing to worry about, believe me."

The same young man escorted MacLean back to the lobby. "Again, sir," he said, "it was an honor meeting you."

"Thank you. How long have you been here?"

The young man blushed. "I'm not permitted to say."

"*Right on!*" MacLean said. But the sarcastic edge to his voice went completely unnoticed. And why not? He might as well have been staring at himself forty years ago.

As he emerged outside, he noticed that the piles of cigarette butts in the twin receptacles were rapidly regaining their mountainous proportions.

Was Forrester to be believed? His explanation arguably made sense. John MacLean took a deep breath and slowly exhaled. He had never felt more angry, or impotent. The fact was he had no choice except to trust that Forrester was telling the truth. He could not stomach the prospect of saying to his son, "Listen, your client was a big heroin trafficker," and hear Tom say, "Really? And what were you doing all that time, Dad? Was that why Deng saved your ass in the jungle?"

15

IN NEW HAVEN, in bed, Li-po shivered in her flannel nightgown. She tried vainly to sleep, as she had every night since the visit of Tom MacLean three days before.

Not even Beverly Soo had been able to calm her. In her trepidation, Li-po felt herself careening helplessly away from everything she had learned from Beverly. There were, of course, other Chinese students on campus, but Beverly's saucy, insouciant manner instantly had drawn Li-po to her.

The first shock was that Beverly spoke not a word of Chinese. And then, even more astonishing, when Li-po asked her what branch of the Han race she was, she said, "I don't know." Her parents, Christian converts, had escaped to America in 1949 under the auspices of the Methodist church and settled in Los Angeles in an area where they were the only Chinese. "In my house, China was, like, forget it."

So for Li-po, she became both friend and mentor in this new land, truly American, yet sharing an inescapably visible, common heritage. "Are you two sisters?" people would ask.

And it was to Beverly that she confided her foreboding. "My father is coming," she said.

"So?"

"He will be very angry when he finds out about Robert."

"You mean you haven't told him?"

She remembered feeling herself blush furiously. "No."

"What did you tell him about staying here for the summer?"

"I said there were additional studies I wanted to undertake."

She didn't say that she thought surely her amah would have informed him and that his wrath would somehow provide her, the injured party,

with the spunk to stand her ground—the amah sleeping below, Auntie
Mei, who once told her not to swallow the seeds in oranges for an orange
tree would take root in her stomach and burst through her forehead, who
taught her how to conduct herself in public, never to gesticulate with her
hands, to lower her eyes demurely when men stared at her, to limit her
smile to a slight curve of her lips without ever exposing her teeth so as not
to appear forward. But not once in his weekly letters did her father mention Robert. As time went on, she felt increasingly trapped—and guilty.
Once she began a letter, "I have met the most wonderful man." But she
never mailed it.

How could she explain this to Beverly, whose parents had rejected all
things Chinese? Whose eyes twinkled merrily as she popped her bubble
gum, who said "Fuck off!" when some man whispered on the street, "Hey,
China doll."

Why couldn't she be like Beverly? She yearned for a mother to turn to.
"Tell me about my mother," she would say to Auntie Mei, who only made
Li-po feel more guilty by saying, "She was a woman of breeding, who
willingly sacrificed her life to give you to your father. In all things, you
must heed him in her memory." She must always follow the *ting hua,* Auntie Mei warned, the golden rule of obedience. "Your father expects great
things of you."

"What are you afraid of?" Beverly Soo said. "Did he beat you?"

Li-po was stunned. "Oh, no," she exclaimed. *He didn't have to.* She remembered how warily her classmates treated her at the parochial school
where she was sent to refine her English. Even the boys. *Especially the
boys!* How arrogant that made her feel. She must have been insufferable.
She now understood the fear he engendered in others.

It was Beverly to whom she went for advice after meeting Robert Logan. "Go for it, I hear he's a great guy," Beverly said.

Li-po recalled how correct her father had been to her in her adoles-
cence, careful always to hold her at arm's length to avoid any untoward in-
timacy, scrupulous about never entering her room without first knocking.
And she thought of nestling in bed with Robert Logan, thrilling to his gen-
tle touch. More waves of guilt washed over her. Of betraying her father.

Beverly, her almond-shaped eyes and oval face, her lustrous, waist-long,
raven-black hair, was almost a mirror image of herself, but all Li-po saw
now was the great cultural divide that actually separated them. Beverly
couldn't help her. She couldn't possibly comprehend.

But suddenly Beverly said, "Have you told Robert?"

"No," Li-po said, more miserable than ever. "I am ashamed to."

"Well, listen up, little sister. You love him, don't you?"

"With all my heart."

"Then do something about it! What is this, Romeo and Juliet time?"

16

IT HAD BEEN SIX MONTHS since Deng met secretly with General Li Wen-huen in Chiang Mai, Thailand's ancient northern capital, through which all the fruit of the Golden Triangle's poppy fields flowed south to Bangkok for overseas distribution.

Once, General Li commanded all the border crossings into Thailand. But supplied with an array of Soviet arms in the last years of the Cold War and a limitless supply of local tribal conscripts, the Burmese warlord, Shan Wa, had supplanted him.

"I am reduced to less than two thousand men at present, enough to defend my territory," General Li said, "but insufficient to pursue him to his lair across the Mekong River in Burma. The situation is worse than ever. The American drug agents pay the Thai Border Patrol to intercept the caravans and Shan Wa with his new wealth pays it to seize only my caravans. His arrogance knows no bounds. Just days ago, he captured one of my men and ordered his feet and hands chopped off and fed to a pack of dogs. My man observed himself being devoured while he was still alive. I ask you. Is that decent behavior?"

As good manners dictated, Deng indulged in a moment of silent commiseration, but it was precisely the general's plight, combined with the collapse of Shan Wa's Moscow benefactors, that had caused Deng to reach for control of the world's heroin supply.

He immediately saw the avarice in Li's eyes. "Fifty tons of opium? That presents no problem. The rains this spring have been bountiful. But even if the circumstances were different in Thailand, even if there was no Shan Wa, how can a shipment of that size be transported undetected?"

The moment had come. Deng savored it.

"First, it will all be refined in jungle laboratories. My brother, Ho Shu-shui, will supply the necessary equipment and chemists."

Then Deng quietly delivered his bombshell. "The shipment will not go through Thailand, my dear general. It will be taken north into our homeland itself, into Yunnan and then across the southern provinces to Canton."

Deng remembered how Li gasped, "You can't be serious. The southern provinces! Within the celestial moon, sixty-two drug dealers were executed in a public square in Guangxi before ten thousand witnesses."

"Yes, but that was because the *tai sei* was being sold locally. The contents of our shipment will not. I am informed that the regional commanders of the Red Army grow restless. They hear about the liberalization policies being preached in Beijing, of the immense profits being made in the new special economic zones, yet they receive no benefit." Deng grinned. "So it is natural that they would desire to create their own economic zones. They won't care if the product simply passes through. They particularly will not care if they receive payment for not caring. Indeed, they will applaud the prospect that it is destined for the veins and lungs of the barbarian *kwai lo*."

Now, the same week the Confederation agreed to back the shipment, Deng and Ho Shu-shui flew to Bangkok.

"I leave to see the general," Deng told Stanley Chow. "Do you wish to accompany me?"

"No, it's not necessary. You enjoy the relationship. Just keep me apprised."

Deng took a parting shot. "By the way, instruct your nephew in New York to halt all involvement in the white powder."

If Chow was surprised that Deng knew of his blood ties to Unicorn Frankie, he didn't show it. His face a mask, he replied, "It has been done."

From the moment Deng stepped from the plane, Bangkok's fetid heat washed over him like water, leaving him wringing wet, then chilled to his bones in the air-conditioned Mercedes. The twenty-mile trip on the traffic-choked highway from the airport took two hours.

In the city itself, the Mercedes lurched forward foot by foot in monumental gridlock that made Hong Kong's main thoroughfares look like racing circuits. Ahead, Deng saw an elephant, stalled as he was in the vehicular impasse, its tail switching impatiently.

Bangkok was a monument to improvisation. Gleaming glass office towers stood side by side with falling-down shanties along ancient canals choked with refuse. Stunning gold-gilded spires rose majestically above boxy prefabricated concrete housing, all built on reclaimed swampland. A blazing sun struggled to get through the polluted haze. Every corner cop, trying to maintain order, wore a surgical mask.

"Pungent, isn't it?" Ho observed as Deng first lowered and then quickly raised a window.

They passed by the pleasure palaces in the Patpong district. Even in broad daylight, it was neon-lit with signs that proclaimed "Pussy à Go-Go" and "Vagina Heaven." Another contribution of Western culture, Deng thought. The sex districts had begun to blossom during the Vietnam War when Bangkok became an R and R retreat for U.S. forces.

"It's said that more than a million tourists from the world over come each year just to sample the local delights," Ho observed. "Some in the brotherhood arrange profitable tours from as far away as Germany and Sweden. They also profit much," he added with a smile, "from ownership of health clinics that treat the venereal diseases."

When he and Ho had first journeyed to Thailand, Bangkok had seemed sublime. The sweltering heat, of course, had been present, but he had sensed a pleasant, languid feel to the city, a sweet softness. Well, things changed, Deng thought. *His* life was about to undergo momentous change.

The tree-shaded, peaceful gardens of the Oriental Hotel, the hint of a breeze coming off the Chao Phraya River, brought back memories of those days. In his suite, after bathing and dressing, he ordered a glass of freshly squeezed orange juice. Sipping it, Deng sat by the windows, observing the river activity. Where once the Chao Phraya had been a way to bypass the city's snarled streets, it was now almost as crowded with craft of every description. He watched a string of river barges head downstream, loaded with teak logs. It occurred to him that secreting the white powder in truckloads of teak crossing the southern Chinese provinces would be ideal for the shipment. Quite aside from the payoffs that would be required, they would attract little attention.

Promptly at four p.m., Ho rang him from the lobby.

General Li's Bangkok home was north of the Oriental near the original Chinatown. And in the quixotic nature of the city, he found himself entering a suddenly lush residential enclave with towering royal palm and leafy banana trees that swallowed up the chaotic din so pervasive elsewhere.

There was something new behind the old-fashioned grilled gates to Li's walled residence—a pair of heavy steel doors. At a signal from one of the two guards in front, in open shirts, slacks and sandals, AK-47s slung over their shoulders, the doors swung slowly open and Ho's chauffeur drove inside.

Rows of scarlet, white and yellow hibiscus lined the paths, along which more armed guards strolled. Orchids bloomed in profusion. Deng heard birds chirping.

As they approached the house with its imposing portico, General Li appeared to welcome them. He was wearing green silk pajamas and slippers. He had a black patch over his right eye.

After greeting him, Deng said, "I am pained by your ill fortune."

"The operation was yesterday. They say it went well. I return to the clinic tomorrow for further examination. They say it's a disease of the elderly. I don't feel so old. My third wife has just given me a newborn, a boy."

"The gods have truly blessed you," Deng said. "How many does that make?"

"Nine in all. My number-one son is now my adjutant." Li smiled broadly, displaying an expanse of yellowing teeth. "I must replenish my army with my own seed."

He led Deng and Ho into a sitting room. Tea was served. A box of cigars was brought in. "Cuban. I never smoke my own product," he said with another big grin. When Deng and Ho declined, Li bit off the end of a torpedo-shaped Montecristo and launched it expertly into a brass spittoon on the floor beside him.

"Ho has told me of the bombing assault by Shan Wa."

"The crater in front of the house was ten meters across and three meters deep. Luckily, I had departed an hour before. But the humiliation was great."

"Soon he will cease to concern you."

"That's what I don't understand. Your plan is brilliant. As you suggested, the generals in the southern provinces were most receptive. Fifty thousand dollars U.S. for each of them guarantees safe passage for the shipment. But Shan Wa will continue to operate as before."

"Trust me. You're aware of his transactions, are you not?"

"Of course. I still have many eyes and ears. Only the American drug agents remain ignorant."

"Perhaps, then, it's time they were enlightened," said Y. K. Deng with an enigmatic smile.

17

DENG HAD CONSIDERED the matter carefully. He would bring an entourage of eight with him to New York, an assistant dragon head who would act as liaison with Hong Kong, two accountants, the Chiuchow couple who for years had looked after his household wants and three *hung kwan,* red pole enforcers. Of these, only Deng's personal red pole, Chao Yu, was irreplaceable.

Forty years old, Chao possessed a body quite distinctive from most Chinese. He had a barrel chest, muscular shoulders and an unusually massive head resting on the thickest of necks. His thighs, bulging from tireless workouts, gave him the rolling gait of a sailor on the high seas. He was a ruthless, efficient killing machine.

He was also completely devoted to Deng. When Chao's father, a Swatow fisherman, died at sea, Deng spirited his mother out of China. Chao lived with her in Kowloon, eschewing marriage, contenting himself with call girls. Fortunately, the old woman had joined her ancestors two months ago, so there was no impediment to his leaving Hong Kong.

"I share the sorrow of your loss," Deng told Chao. "But I will have need of you in America. It will be good for you to get away. Your mother would approve."

"I will follow you anywhere, my *lung tao,*" Chao said. "But I must return for the Ching Ming." Ching Ming was the spring festival when graves were swept clean, inscriptions repainted and rice, wine and tea offered to the departed.

"Of course," Deng said drily. "I wouldn't have it any other way."

Although Chao alone in the group knew no English, it didn't matter. Armed with his fighting chain, three lengths of steel with steel-ring links, Chao spoke a universal language that was unmistakable.

At John F. Kennedy International Airport, Peter Pei anxiously watched the arrival screen, while the drivers of three limousines stood nearby. It had been a frenetic period for Pei, leasing a suitable residence for Deng that would have quarters for Chao—Deng had specified that—as well as the household staff, another apartment for the assistant dragon head, a third for the accountants to share and a place—Pei thought Chinatown would be best—for the two young enforcers.

Even more worrisome for Pei was the arrival of another mahjong delivery that had been sent before Ho Shu-shui received the fax requesting him to suspend future shipments.

What should he do? The decision had left him tossing restlessly at night for more than a week. Finally, he elected to proceed as before. He had received no instructions to the contrary. And it would be quite some time before Deng's master plan went into effect. Meanwhile, he could use the money. The losses he had incurred during recent excursions to the Atlantic City casinos were substantial.

He told Duncan Lau that it was time to return to the Jackson Heights apartment. He also told Duncan that this would be the last series of deposits. He expected Duncan to express dismay but, to his surprise, his nephew seemed quite relieved.

In the U.S. Customs office at JFK, a supervisor reminded agent Mike Larkin that a VIP party was aboard the United flight out of Hong Kong.

"Yeah, I see," Larkin said. "Deng, Y. K. Party of nine. Who's he?"

"Who knows? Who cares? It's straight from Washington. Why don't you check him out with the commissioner, you're so interested?"

"What's bugging you? Your wife find out about your girlfriend?"

"Keep it up, and you'll find your ass up on disciplinary charges, is what."

"OK, OK," Larkin said.

He got to the air bridge just as it was rolling out to meet the airliner. When the plane's door popped open, Larkin said to the senior flight attendant, "Hi, beautiful. Looking for a passenger. Deng, Y. K. First class, I bet."

As she led Larkin to Deng's seat, an announcement was made to the passengers preparing to disembark that there would be a brief delay.

"Mr. Deng?"

Deng nodded.

"Larkin, U.S. Customs. I'm here to assist you, sir. Is your party all here in first class?"

"No," Deng said, waving toward the rear of the plane. "Back there."

"Tell you what," Larkin said. "I'll wait for you inside the terminal. When everyone's together, we'll get you right through the formalities."

In the terminal, Larkin collected and counted the passports and declarations. "Let's see, you're nine in all. OK, follow me."

Larkin removed a chain barring entry to one of the Immigration stations and handed the passports to the man on duty. "Deng party," Larkin told him.

At baggage claim, he signaled a pair of porters with carts. "Take care of these people," he said.

As the baggage carousel began to move, Larkin found himself next to Chao Yu. "Ever been to the States before?" he asked.

Chao stared blankly at him.

One of Deng's accountants said, "He no speak English. No understand."

"Oh," Larkin said, taking another look at Chao. Jesus, he thought, this was a mean-looking fucker. Under normal circumstances, he would get a real Customs going over, the works.

Long lines had begun to form at the baggage inspection counters. Everything was being opened. Larkin felt compelled to explain. "It's like this with every flight from Hong Kong now. You know, because of all the dope."

"Yes," the accountant said. "It is very wise to be alert."

Out of the corner of his eye, Larkin spied a man approaching Deng. The man, dressed in a gray suit, had thinning blond hair and an ageless preppie face. Larkin watched the man shake Deng's hand, obviously introducing himself, and then whisper in his ear. Deng smiled. Larkin saw the man give Deng a card, shake his hand again and walk back to one of the side offices off the inspection area.

"Our luggage is all here," the accountant said.

Larkin escorted them down a wide center aisle, past the other travelers still inching forward and showed them through doors behind which relatives and friends impatiently congregated. He saw Peter Pei leap forward to embrace Deng.

"Glad to have met you, sir," Larkin said. "Have a nice day." But Deng, busy conversing with Pei, ignored him. Fucking Chinks, Larkin thought.

Back in the baggage claim area, he headed for his office. "Say," he said to another agent whose job it was to scrutinize suspicious passengers, "who was that guy?"

"Which guy?"

"The one in the gray suit. Looked like he talked with ice cream in his mouth. Who came up to that Chinaman I was shepherding."

"Oh, him. A spook, I heard."

"A spook?"

"Yeah. CIA, I think. Something like that."

Well, this at least solved the VIP mystery, Larkin thought. "Guess what?" he chuckled to his wife that night. "I saw a spy come in from the cold."

18

CHRISTMAS EVE DAY Tom MacLean picked up Shannon and they drove to Sag Harbor. She was wearing a string of pearls, a black turtleneck sweater and a gray flannel, pleated skirt.

"Don't ask," she said. "The pearls are fake. I know they're old-fashioned, but I like them anyway." She gave him a big hug. "I'm really looking forward to this." The plan was for her to stay overnight and then go to her parents in Queens on Christmas Day. "It's not worth fighting City Hall," she said. "There'll be my brother and his wife and their two kids, Mom and Pop, uncles, aunts, the whole nine yards. I'd never hear the end of it if I didn't show."

The expressway traffic was sparse. It was a Friday, and almost all the offices in the city had closed Thursday afternoon.

"So your man Deng is arriving when?" Shannon said.

"Sunday."

"You going to be at the airport?"

"Cut it out, Shannon. I'm his lawyer, not an indentured servant. I'm sure he can manage on his own."

"You're right. I'm sorry. Just being mean. I was wrong about him. He just seemed too good to be true. Maybe I should go back to the car-theft squad. Get my head straight. Banish paranoia. So, anyway, when will you meet him?"

"Needham only found out he was coming a couple of days ago. Maybe the middle of the week. Since it's the holidays, he was worried I might be taking off to the Caribbean or Colorado, like practically everyone else in the office."

As they passed through the Pine Barrens in eastern Long Island, there were patches of snow. "Oh, a white Christmas!" she exclaimed. "Well, semiwhite."

"It's left over from that big storm that moved up the coast last week. It doesn't last very long. The salt air does it in."

They drove by a pond. Tom remembered that when he had last visited his father, it was filled with wild ducks and geese. Now it had iced over and a bunch of kids were playing hockey on it.

"Maybe we could go skating sometime," she said. "You know how to skate?"

"Not very well. Do you?"

"No." She laughed. "Oh, Tom, I love you so much."

He braked abruptly, pulled off the road and put his arms around her and held her very tight. "Let's just head for the first motel," he said.

"Not on your life. That was only a test. And look," she said, pointing toward the pond. All the kids had stopped playing and were staring at them. "Let's get out of here before we're arrested on public morals charges."

In the village, they passed a group of carolers. The trees were ablaze with Christmas lights, as was the Douglas fir in a corner of John MacLean's sitting room.

"Delighted to meet you," he said to Shannon. "Come in, come in. Tom's told me so much about you."

"Uh, oh, I'm in trouble already."

"Not at all. From what I gather, he's a most lucky fellow."

"Stop, Dad. She's impossible as it is."

Upstairs, she told Tom, "He's nice. I can't believe he was so remote when you were growing up."

"I find it hard to believe myself. I'm just glad it turned out this way."

"And I can't get over this four-poster and the quilt," she said, bouncing on it. "I can't wait to snuggle in."

In the sitting room, John MacLean served mulled wine in glass cups.

"It's wonderful," Shannon said, "and it smells so good. What's in it?"

"Oh, cinnamon, orange rind, cloves, allspice, a little sugar. And, of course, the wine. Merlot. You live out here year round, you tend to learn such mysteries."

"That's my old man," Tom said. "Never misses a trick."

John MacLean gazed into his cup. He shook his head. As if he were addressing himself, he said ruefully, "I wish that was true."

There was an awkward pause.

Shannon said, "Tom told me you were in the Foreign Service in Hong Kong. Did you ever get to Taiwan?"

"On occasion."

"I was a missionary there."

"Yes, he told me. And that you speak several Chinese dialects. I envy you. I never got the chance to absorb much of the culture wherever I was. I was too busy advancing what was described as the best interests of America."

Dinner featured bluepoint oysters on the half shell followed by wild duck. "A neighbor of mine favored me with these mallards," John MacLean said. "Brought them down himself. Watch out for the bird shot. Another of life's lessons. There's always something to watch out for."

Afterward, over coffee and pecan pie in front of the fire, he said to Shannon, "Isn't being in narcotics enforcement dangerous?"

"It can be for the street agents. They're always on the line. You can never tell what might happen. But I'm in a supervisory role, so, really, it's not very hazardous."

"But can anyone stop the heroin traffic?" he continued. "Doesn't the problem lie elsewhere? I mean, don't people in the places where it's being used—in all the urban ghettos—turn to heroin because of the hopelessness in their lives, the grinding poverty they confront every day?" John Maclean groped for the words. "Isn't something like this simply inevitable?" he demanded, "no matter what?"

"Dad," Tom interjected. "You sound like you're arguing a case in court."

"He's got a point," Shannon said. "Mr. MacLean, I wish what you say wasn't so. But my job is to go after the ones who prey on the very people you're talking about. And the heroin traffickers are going all-out to expand the market. It isn't happening only in the ghettos. Let me tell you a story. The man was an ex-supermarket manager in a big mall up in Westchester County. Married, two kids. Vietnam vet, and a user. We caught him dealing to one of our undercover guys, and we flipped him. I sat in when they were questioning him. One of the agents said, 'How could somebody like you fall so low as to shove a needle in your arm?'

"He said, 'It didn't start out that way.' In Vietnam, he didn't use needles. The stuff was so pure and so available, he'd mix it with lemon juice and lace his cigarettes with it. Back in the States, after he got married and was a manager, he kept remembering those marvelous trips, how relaxed and fabulous he'd felt after those special cigarettes, and he was telling this to another vet, and the other vet said that the same pure China white was coming in now, and he put him in touch with a connection, and that's when he got hooked again. It was expensive, but, hey, he could afford it. Sometimes he'd smoke, other times snort.

"That's when he began crying. He got fired because suddenly they said his job performance was substandard. He couldn't afford the luxury of lacing cigarettes any longer, so he started skin popping to get the heroin in his bloodstream faster. He was still working at the mall as a salesman in a Kmart outlet. It was a real put-down, but he had no choice. Pretty soon, to save even more money, he was mainlining. By now, his wife and the kids, his house, were long gone. I remember how he looked at us and said, 'The worst part was I didn't care. All I cared about was my next fix.'

"Of course," Shannon said, "he lost the Kmart job, too, and began dealing himself to support his habit. We set up a stakeout for his connection, but the next delivery was never made. Obviously, word had gotten around. There are so many layers. The only way to have any real impact is to get the guys at the top." She shrugged. "Easier said than done."

"It's all from Southeast Asia?" John MacLean asked.

"The best grade of it is, like cigars from Cuba. You must have heard of China white when you were in Hong Kong. That's when the Golden Triangle started gearing up big-time."

"Yes, I suppose I did, but I had other things on my mind then." John MacLean fell silent. Then, all at once, he said, "I'm tired. If you'll excuse me, I'm off to bed."

"I hope it wasn't me," Shannon said to Tom. "I just got carried away. Not exactly ordinary Christmas Eve chitchat." She went over to him and held his hand. "I get this feeling something's troubling your father."

"If it is, it wasn't anything you said. After all, he brought the subject up. He's a little down probably because it's Christmas and he's thinking about my mother. He's gotten over it to some extent, but he never will completely. That's one of the reasons I was glad you came and why I'll stay out here until I hear from Needham."

In the morning, they exchanged presents. Tom had commissioned a silver charm bracelet. It had Blind Justice, a shamrock, a crucifix and the Chinese characters for "Dragon Lady."

"Oh, God," she said, giving him her gift, a pair of deerskin gloves with detachable cashmere linings, "I feel so uninspired."

"Hey, they're great," he said. "In a million years, I never would have gotten them for myself. That's what presents are all about."

After breakfast, he put her on the train for New York. In the afternoon, he jogged for miles along the deserted beach. The Atlantic surf pounded in. The sky was cloudless, the air delicious. He had never felt better.

On Wednesday, James Needham phoned him at his father's house and asked if he could come into the city for a Thursday meeting with Y. K. Deng.

It wasn't exactly phrased as a question.

Near Lexington, Kentucky, Li-po sat at a table laden with ham and smoked turkey, bowls of yams and corn pudding, her first American Christmas at the home of Robert's parents.

She had been nervous about how she would be received, but clearly, his mother and father, as well as two married brothers and a sister, were awed by him, the first in the family to go East to college on a scholarship and the first to travel anywhere abroad, much less to China. His mother had put her at ease at once when she showed Li-po to her room and said, "Now, honey, if there's the slightest little thing you might be needing, you just give a holler, hear."

Robert was born in the house, which had been in the Logan family for generations. The brick walls were six inches thick and he showed her some of the narrow openings for the flintlock rifles that were used to fight off Indians and the secret rooms where the children were hidden during raids. And she loved him all the more when he said, "It's a big macho part of our history, Daniel Boone and all that, but what we did to the Indians is unforgivable."

Robert's father, and his brothers who lived in their own homes on the property, grew Kentucky burley tobacco and he showed her the sheds where it was cured and she tried to imagine him working in them and in the fields as a boy. "Now I am the archaeologist, digging in *your* past," she said, giggling delightedly.

The surrounding countryside was filled with famous racing stables. They drove along miles of white fences, stopping now and then to watch the foals frolicking on spindly legs with their mares.

"Might we ride?" she asked.

"You know how?"

"Oh, yes. To ride was a required part of my education. My father is a member of the Jockey Club in Hong Kong."

So he arranged to use a neighbor's saddle horses and they rode for hours over the wintry fields. She had never felt so free. "This is wonderful," she exclaimed. "In Hong Kong, we were limited to a single bridle path."

Suddenly, one day, he said, "You hardly ever mention your father."

"He is a very private person. Sometimes I wonder if I really know him myself. He is not an easy man to talk to, but I think he cares very much for me. Once when I asked him if I were to blame for my mother's death, he became very angry."

Sensing the answer, he asked anyway. "Does he know we're seeing each other?"

She hoped her embarrassment didn't show. "No. But you heard the lawyer, Tom MacLean. He's coming here soon. I shall tell him then and present you." Then, remembering what Beverly Soo had told her, she clung to him and said, "It doesn't matter. I am my own woman." And in this setting, so removed from Hong Kong, even from Yale, her fears of Deng seemed to fade. Perhaps, she told herself, she had wildly exaggerated them.

And any lingering doubts she might have had about the man she had chosen disappeared the night they went into Lexington to see a movie. Two young men swaggered drunkenly past them. She heard one say, "You think their kids'll have slanty eyes?" while the other guffawed.

Instantly, she saw Robert turn back toward them and say in his soft-spoken way, "What was that you just said?"

"What's it to you?"

An instant later, the youth was sprawled out unconscious on the ground and the second one was backing away, hands up, yelling, "I didn't say nothin', mister."

In the car driving home, hunched over, she said finally, "Do you think about that, what he said?"

Robert drew her to him and said, "The only thing I think about is having children as beautiful as their mother."

19

PETER PEI HAD THE JITTERS as Deng inspected the apartment. He had spent days scouting the various possibilities. Of course, the apartment had to be suitably situated. But what about the furnishings? He knew he couldn't begin to duplicate the traditional Chinese furniture in Deng's house in Hong Kong. Finally he picked a location high above Central Park South whose interior decoration, all glass and black marble and leather, was reminiscent of the sleek interior of Deng's yacht, *Grass Sandal.* The rent—twenty thousand dollars a month—was not a concern.

Deng inspected all twelve rooms, including the quarters for the household staff and for Chao Yu. He even peeked into the refrigerator in the kitchen, which Pei had stocked with necessities to tide them over while they settled in.

At last, Deng, standing by the windows fronting on the park, expressed his approval.

Relieved, Pei said the *feng shui* master had informed him that there was no location in the city where he could enjoy better *ch'i,* the vital earth force that is the essence of life and fundamental to good *feng shui.*

"*You* consulted a *feng shui* master?"

"Yes," Pei replied proudly, gesturing at the park. "He said that the trees would tap positive energy and the placid water of the reservoir was most propitious."

Deng knew that Pei lived somewhere in Chinatown. He could just see in Pei's residence the *bat wa* mirrors—small, octagonal mirrors—strategically placed to deflect bad *feng shui,* turning it back to its source. All these years spent in America, Deng thought, and Pei had never truly left China. But did anyone?

"I compliment you on your foresight," he said with a straight face. "And now to business. I wish to dine tonight at my"—Deng corrected himself—"at *our* eating establishment. What's it called?"

"Inner Peace." Pei was pleased by Deng's courtesy, since the dragon head had put up ninety percent of the money to buy the building and construct the restaurant.

"I wish to be seen, and when I am seen with you, inquiries will be made and word will quickly reach the tong elders here. They know who I am, and yet they do not know. It will be good for them to dwell upon the significance of my arrival."

As Deng predicted, their presence in a Cadillac limousine slowly negotiating the narrow Chinatown streets attracted immediate attention, especially since they were not the usual *kwai lo* tourists the local residents were accustomed to seeing in such vehicles. In fact, because of the holiday season, there was scarcely a Caucasian face in sight.

By the time the Cadillac stopped in front of the Inner Peace, a large group of onlookers had gathered. As he was about to go in, Deng glanced up and smiled. He had been right about Pei. Above the entrance was a *bat wa* mirror aimed at a curio shop on the opposite street corner. Sharp angles were universally believed to project very bad *feng shui*.

At their table, besides Deng and Pei, were Chao Yu and the assistant dragon head, whose name was Ko Ping Lum. Ko's function was to stay in touch with the other three *fu lung tao* in Hong Kong overseeing the day-to-day affairs of the Righteous and Peaceful Society. Deng hadn't yet informed Ko of his grand scheme. Only Ho Shu-shui in Bangkok knew the details and Peter Pei, to a lesser extent. At this stage, even Stanley Chow's knowledge was limited to the fact that the shipment would cross southern China. Deng would need Chow's control of the dockworkers for what came next.

Halfway through the meal, Pei nudged Deng. "Word of your presence has indeed spread swiftly."

At the entrance, a bent old man gazed at them, his face webbed with wrinkles. Two younger men, barely out of their teens, were on each side of him, as if to catch him should he stumble.

"Who's he?"

"Paul Fu, the elder of the Fujian Merchants Association."

"Beckon him."

The old man shuffled forward, the other two moving in unison with him.

Rising, Pei said, "I wish to present Mr. Y. K. Deng."

"Ah, yes," Fu said with a gap-toothed grin, "his fame precedes him."

Deng, still seated, said, "Please join us for a moment if it does not interfere with your plans." He stared directly at Fu, making it clear that the invitation didn't include Fu's companions.

After a second's hesitation, Fu flicked a finger and the other two retreated to a nearby table.

"I am honored," Deng now said, having established his position.

"It is you who honor us. I congratulate you on your great success across the sea and on the recent victory of your racehorse."

"So you keep abreast of events in Hong Kong?"

"As they say, not to use one's eyes and ears desecrates a celestial blessing." Again, Fu grinned innocuously. "My Fujian clansman, Deacon Kau, advised me that you would be arriving and to extend you every welcome. Will you be staying long?"

"Permanently," Deng said. "I believe it is likely that Deacon Kau will join me."

He watched Fu's eyes widen as he digested this information. "That is most startling news. And," he quickly amended, "most pleasing."

"Many of us believe that the time has come to bring our resources here, all the more to enrich the growing Han community in America. We are troubled, however, by the activities of the youthful gangs who grow bolder each day, particularly in the traffic of the white powder."

"We?"

"The Confederation."

Fu's amiable mask vanished, unable to conceal his astonishment at Deng's bluntness. "You are of the Confederation?"

Deng smiled reassuringly. While Fu was aware of the Confederation's existence, the old man was certainly ignorant of its composition. "I am," he said, "but a humble emissary." Deng paused. "I am told there is a gang, the Gray Shadows, with ties to your association."

"That is true. We use them for necessary security in our businesses," Fu acknowledged. "As for the white powder, I cannot say."

"It would be well to offer them counsel on this subject. Your wisdom commands great respect," Deng said, pointedly adding, "or it should."

Fu decided not to challenge the gibe. "Yes, yes, as I think of it, you are quite correct. Perhaps that would be prudent, yes, speaking to them."

Deng abruptly dug into his food with his chopsticks, indicating that the conversation was over. He devoured a slice of chicken in a pepper and oyster sauce. "You must try this dish. I recommend it highly."

"Yes, yes," Fu repeated, getting up from his chair, shakier than ever. "I must rejoin my boys now. They're good boys, you know. I take them to dinner every Sunday night," he babbled on, as if words, any words, would hide the alarm binding his stomach. He turned to Peter Pei. "My compliments. An excellent establishment. A fortuitous encounter. Yes, by all means, I must try the chicken."

"Who are the other two with him," Deng inquired. "Gray Shadows?"

"Yes," Pei said.

"Remember their faces," Deng told Chao Yu.

On the way back to Central Park South, Pei said, "It's been many celestial years since anyone treated old Fu in that manner."

Deng waved a dismissive hand, as though it were of little concern to him. "Find this Frankie Chin," he said. "I wish to see him. Have him come to the apartment."

"Is that wise? Meeting him so directly?"

"I have no doubt that he already knows who I am and why I am here."

Deng pursed his lips. "Oh, yes. Have you made contact with the Italian, Frank Lucano?"

Pei squirmed in his seat. "I was waiting for your arrival. I have my method, but it is a delicate matter."

Deng grunted his displeasure. "It must be accomplished without delay. Lucano is vital to my plans."

Chao Yu held the car door open, swiveling his head up and down the street, as if hostile barbarian forces lurked in every dark doorway.

"One more thing," Deng whispered, pointing at Chao. "Arrange women for him. My faithful red pole grows tense without regular sexual exercise.

And lease one of these limousines with a driver of our race. Someone trustworthy who speaks Cantonese, but not Chiuchow."

Upstairs, in his bedroom, Deng examined the card that the man at the airport had given him. The man had said, "Allen Merser, CIA. If we can be of any assistance, call either of these numbers." There were two of them written on the card, one with a Manhattan area code, the other for northern Virginia. "As usual, ask for Mr. Sentry. We wish you a productive stay in the United States."

After he had undressed, bathed and donned silk pajamas, Deng strolled to the windows above Central Park and considered one problem he had yet to confront.

Li-po.

20

T HERE WERE MEETINGS.

Fretful elders of the four major tongs in New York, with chapters through-out the country, hastily convened at the national headquarters of the Greater Chinese Association. The five-story building was a Chinatown landmark with soaring tiled eaves painted green to signify harmony. A red and gold exterior proclaimed joy and heavenly glory. Cornices were festooned with carved lions, phoenixes and dragons.

In the conference room, joss sticks smoldered in urns. A portrait, said to be in the likeness of the Yellow Emperor, the father of the Han race, dominated one wall. He had a drooping mustache and a wispy chin beard, his clasped hands hidden in the sleeves of a white robe with a red sash. On the other walls were stilted photographs of deceased tong elders. Jas-mine-scented tea was served.

Tong meant a "hall" or "gathering place." Unlike the secret societies they sought to emulate, the tongs were not formed to drive barbarian in-vaders from the Central Country, but to offer a protective sense of com-munity to the first Chinese immigrants to the United States. And in that small community, they were all-powerful, dispensing justice to a people who would never dream of resorting to the *kwai lo* police or courts of law, exacting their own taxes and tribute and enforcing their codes of conduct. At first, they had been like snarling hyenas, fighting over the carcass of a small antelope. But gradually under the umbrella of the Greater Chinese Association led by Benny Wong, territorial areas of influence and control were delineated and observed. Criminality inevitably crept in—illegal gambling parlors, prostitution, extortion, opium dens—which was largely ignored outside the community. City officials, toting up dismal statistics of lawless behavior elsewhere, told themselves, "That's one thing you can say about Chinatown. There's no crime down there."

Everyone seated in the conference room knew the story. This closed society began to fall apart when the Chinese exclusion barriers were lowered. With the influx of immigrants came the youth gangs, first in San Francisco and then New York, and then in every city that had a Chinatown. While the tongs had patterned themselves after the secret societies and maintained links of a sort with them, they lacked the pervasive power of the *Hung* brotherhood, so they adapted, employing the gangs to protect their vested interests. The result was an uneasy truce, broken periodically by bloody shoot-outs. And not all the gangs had allied themselves with the tongs, most notably Unicorn Frankie Chin's White Eagles.

Now, suddenly, there was a new threat to established order, more ominous than anything that had preceded it.

Immediately following Paul Fu's encounter with Deng, calls were made to tong elders in San Francisco, Los Angeles and Chicago. Other calls were placed directly to Hong Kong. The sobering message, especially from Hong Kong, was always the same. Y. K. Deng was a man to be reckoned with, to be listened to. He did not walk alone.

"What orders did he give you?" Fu was asked.

"I tell you, he did not order anything. He just spoke in generalities. He spoke of his unhappiness with the activities of the youth gangs, which comes as no revelation to any of us. He did speak about trafficking in the white powder. I told him we, the elders, had nothing to do with that." Fu looked helplessly at them. "It was as if he hadn't heard me. He said that we should do something about it. He told me that if we didn't, they would."

"They?"

"The Confederation."

"He actually invoked the brotherhood?"

"Yes."

"But they remain so distant from us."

"He said he was going to reside here permanently. He suggested that others were soon coming as well."

"Ai!" one of the elders exclaimed, raising his hands in clenched supplication. "What is to be done?"

"We must accommodate ourselves," another said, "in order to retain what we have." They all knew what he referred to—the wealth they had accumulated in moneylending, Chinatown real estate, the illegal importation of slave labor in their textile sweatshops, the gambling dens, restaurants and other businesses under their control.

"What I do not comprehend," said a third, "is the concern about the white powder. It is well known that the brotherhood is immersed in it."

"We could report this to the police," someone said.

The suggestion was received in ghastly silence. To do that would mean abdicating all power, eliminating entirely the reason for their existence, an irretrievable loss of face.

Everybody looked at Benny Wong.

"You say he was with Peter Pei?" Wong said.

"Yes."

The memory of his lunch weeks ago with Pei raced through Wong's mind. Much of what Deng reportedly told Fu was similar to what Pei had said. At the time, Pei's words had stung him, but toward the end of the lunch, he sensed a nervousness in Pei caused by something he said. *What?* Ah, yes! It was after he had idly inquired about Pei's importation of the mahjong sets. Was it possible something was hidden in the tiles? But that didn't make sense in light of all the warnings about the youth gangs trading in the powder. Or did it? What did make sense was that Deng and Pei were Chiuchow and therefore not to be trusted. And what made the most sense, Wong grimly reflected, was that if Mr. Y. K. Deng from Hong Kong got his way, Benny Wong's status in the community was in imminent peril.

To the anxious men around him, he finally said, "It's the witless hare that is savaged. We must have patience. Watch what develops. In the meantime, it is wise to speak to the gangs. We are not without resources and they have grown too presumptuous."

Peter Pei, thirteen-year-old ship jumper to New York in 1934, American citizen no questions asked following U.S. Army service as an interpreter on the China-Burma front during World War II, founder of an export/import company financed by GI loans which brought renewed contacts with Chiuchow clansmen in Hong Kong and subsequent induction into the Righteous and Peaceful Society, used to transact business with Funzie Di-

Bello, then of the Green Berets, in a Saigon girlie bar.

Fidgeting, he waited for Funzie at a back table of the Ideal Restaurant in the old German neighborhood of Yorkville on Manhattan's upper East Side—far from Chinatown, far from Little Italy. They had been meeting here on the average of four times a year for nearly a quarter century, ever since Funzie got his honorable discharge and that same year became a made member of what was now the Lucano crime family in Cosa Nostra.

All this time, while various neighborhoods in the city underwent drastic change, and old landmarks fell, the Ideal, with its sawdust-covered floor, remained constant, serving ample portions of knockwurst and pig's knuckle and sauerkraut and boiled potatoes. Other than Pei and DiBello, certainly no Chinese and nobody remotely "Italian-looking" had ever been spied eating there.

Pei would leave a message at the home of DiBello's maiden aunt and DiBello would call back from a pay phone and Pei would say that he had a "piece," which was a unit of heroin number four, and DiBello would say, "OK," or, sometimes, "I could use two pieces, maybe."

The exchange always took place at the Ideal, around six p.m., before the dinner crowd came in. Pei's wholesale price over the years, of course, had risen. Still, at fifty thousand dollars per unit of unquestioned quality hidden in the mahjong tiles sent by Ho Shu-shui, it was far below what the current market brought in the mounting demand for China white. On the other hand, continuity counted for something and there was not a more risk-free heroin transaction in the entire city, much less the nation. And, best of all, it was cash income that Pei did not have to share with anyone.

The same waitress always presided over them, her once youthful figure turned formidable thanks to the Ideal's cuisine. They did not know her name or she theirs. She knew, however, where they preferred to sit and what they ate.

"A stein of lager, *ja?*" she said to Pei.

"Please."

"Your friend is coming?"

"Yes."

"So I make two places. I bring the sauerbraten and red cabbage and the wine for him when he is here."

Not even the dialogue with the waitress had changed. Pei sighed, wondering if this would be the last time he'd be sitting at this table. Now, with Y. K. Deng on the scene, everything was going to change. In Saigon, Deng had once told him, "You are our outpost in America. Some day we shall have further need of you."

DiBello hurried into the Ideal. "I just got your message. What's up?"

Pei passed him a package containing a unit of number four.

"Hey, I got no cash. Your message only said you wanted to see me."

"It is free."

"Free? What's that, free? Nothing's free. What's the hook?"

"In return, I would ask a small favor of you."

"Small, huh?"

"My, ah, how you say it? Yes, boss. My boss has arrived from the Far East. He wishes to meet with your boss, Mr. Lucano."

"You're kidding."

"No, I'm serious."

"Jeez, Peter, I can't swing that. I'm tight with Big Frank, but not that tight. I mean, how could I explain it?"

"I assure you, it will be very profitable for him. You would be in his gratitude."

Funzie looked at the package in his lap. He saw between ninety and a hundred thousand dollars net that he could expect within twenty-four hours from any one of the domestic heroin distributors he had quietly developed, unbeknownst to the rest of the family, especially unbeknownst to Big Frank Lucano. "Who is this guy, your boss?"

"He is a man of respect. Big respect."

"You know what you're saying? You catch my drift? What that means."

"Yes."

"OK, OK. So I'm not promising anything, but I'll give it a shot."

"Sauerbraten," said the waitress, suddenly hovering over them. "I bring you your sauerbraten. More beer? Another wine, *ja?*"

Pei and DiBello stared at one another.

"I'll get back to you," DiBello said.

Summoned to Deng's apartment, Unicorn Frankie Chin immediately realized he had made a tactical mistake. To exhibit a measure of defiance, he had come attired in his street uniform, a leather jacket decorated with metal studs, blue jeans and bikers' boots.

The magnificence of the living room with its sweeping park views wasn't what caused him to feel so ill at ease. It was Deng himself, seated by a window in his tailored suit, silk shirt and tie, jade cuff links inlaid with gold clearly visible, his mirthless eyes disdainfully surveying him up and down, *undressing him!*

And if that weren't enough, there was that man in a corner of the room to his right, also suited, *bulging* out of the suit, perched on the edge of a chair, leaning forward, like a pit bull poised to spring at him at the slightest provocation.

Frankie shuffled his feet.

Deng did not invite him to sit down.

Frankie cleared his throat. "Honorable sir," he began. Then his voice failed him. Suddenly, he did not know what to say.

Finally, Deng spoke, "Ah, the eight-million-dollar man," he sneered. "You have received a message from your uncle concerning me?"

"Yes."

"So I won't waste time going into that. You know what you are not to do?"

"Yes."

"Tell me, when did the youth gangs start selling the *tai sei* directly on the street?"

"About four years ago. Many blacks, the American blacks, came to us, as well as the others—they are black also, but different—called Dominicans. They were dealing South American cocaine, but now they also desired China white. 'Hey, man,'" Frankie mimicked, "'you got some of the good stuff? You got China white? We talkin' cash, man. Up front.' Sir, I assure you, it was very profitable."

"Then some of the buyers turned out to be undercover police."

"Yes, but it didn't seem to matter. So much was coming in."

"Except," Deng snapped, "it alerted the Drug Enforcement agents, the FBI, to the role of our people in this. I know how you were getting your product. What other methods are employed?"

"Members of the community will agree to receive packages in the mail for small sums that are big for them, half a year's pay. Couriers are used, mostly girls. Many are *kwai lo* girls who cannot live without the white powder. Others, of the Han, have fallen into gambling and are deeply in debt. I was thinking of employing a new courier, a *kwai lo* who wears the clothes of a Catholic priest. He will only accept merchandise delivered to Rome or Dublin. When he returns to New York in clerical dress, the Customs agents say, 'Oh, Father, did you see the pope? How was the weather in Ireland?' and he says, 'God be with you.' "

Even Deng couldn't suppress a smile. "Very clever," he said. "But very limited. So let us discuss the gangs. It will go hard on them if they don't change their ways. If they behave, they will be rewarded. If they don't, I am but the first of many to see that they do."

"I heard this afternoon that the tong elders already are telling the gangs to lay low. Only the Gray Shadows could be a problem. They're all ABCs. The brotherhood on the other side of the sea means little to them. They think it's all made up. They're employed by the Fujian Merchants Association, but they do as they please. Word will spread, however, that the White Eagles are no longer selling on the street, and they'll wonder about that. They'll wait to see what happens."

"This man you see here is Chao Yu," Deng said. "If he comes to you, he speaks for me."

"Yes, honorable sir."

Afterward, in the loft of the White Eagles on Division Street, Unicorn Frankie worked through the night with Fat Monster and Flying Pig on the package. He had planned it anyway, but there was another urgency now. He was sure it would regain him great face with Deng.

"I need Christmas wrapping paper," he said.

21

DENG WAS DUE at three p.m. When Tom strolled into Needham's paneled office, the grandfather clock in the corner indicated ten minutes to go. Behind Needham's desk, Wild Bill Donovan and William Casey stared down from the wall. Off to one side, a cream-colored settee and twin matching club chairs surrounded a mahogany butler's tray that served as a coffee table. A richly ornate Persian carpet covered the floor.

Needham bubbled with enthusiasm. The day before, the first monthly retainer check to be applied against billings had come in from Deng. "How do you like that?" Needham exclaimed. "Didn't even have to invoice him. Wonderful, doing business with a gentleman. Wish there were more like him!"

He drummed his fingers on the desktop. "Spent Christmas with your father, did you? Splendid. Old and young should join together at such a joyous time of the year. Too many of our partners head for the hills, forget their parents, family gatherings. I suppose skiing is acceptable. At least, there's snow. But sun and fun in the Caribbean? Remember once being talked into Christmas at Lyford Cay in Nassau, the Bahamas. Santa Claus arrived on water skis! Not my cup of tea, I can tell you." Suddenly Needham came upright in his highback chair. "*Tea!*" He pressed the intercom. "Ellen, don't forget to have the goddamn tea ready. You got the right kind, the kind the Chinese like? None of those tea bags, mind you. What's that? Jasmine, you say? Well, whatever. Just make sure it's right. And ready."

Needham turned back to Tom. "It's the little gestures that count." His eyes narrowed. "You convey my best wishes of the season to your father, even if I don't know him personally?"

"I did. He was very appreciative. He holds you in high esteem. He said you were a legend in his, uh, world."

Needham kept his gaze on Tom. "And our Mr. Deng? You mentioned him, I assume."

"I don't know if I did on this trip. But I have before. I guess I forgot to tell you. Yes, he remembers Deng quite well. They worked together on some sort of project when Dad was stationed in Hong Kong. Spent a good deal of time together during the Vietnam War."

"Good. Excellent. Relationships handed down from one generation to the next. Solid. The way it should be. Interesting how it all works out sometimes. Sow and you shall reap, eh?"

The chimes of the clock had barely ceased tolling the hour when Deng was announced and ushered in. Tom got an eerie impression of two different persons inside the same body. Deng's mouth was smiling broadly. His eyes weren't.

"Greetings, greetings," Needham said, coming to his feet. "Jim Needham. Welcome."

"Mr. Needham," Deng said. "A pleasure long looked forward to."

"This is my colleague, Tom MacLean."

"Ah, Mr. MacLean," Deng said, scrutinizing him.

Tom had the feeling of being a lab specimen under a microscope. This is not a guy to cross, he thought. Instantly, an image of Li-po sprang into his mind and of the tension that being Deng's daughter must entail.

"Over here," Needham said, waving toward the butler's tray arrangement. "More relaxed. Less formal, don't you think? Get to know one another."

He steered Deng to the settee. Then he and Tom sat in the club chairs. Needham tapped a silver cigarette case. "May I offer you one?"

"Thank you. I don't smoke."

"Nor me. Nor Tom. Used to. Like a chimney stack, three, four packs a day. No good for you, I say. Can't ignore all those warnings. Tea then. A spot of tea?"

"No, thank you."

Needham looked crestfallen.

Tom watched as Deng caught the expression on Needham's face and heard him say, "On reconsideration, yes. That's very kind of you. I didn't want to put you to any trouble."

"No trouble at all." Needham was on the intercom immediately. "Tea," he commanded.

Almost at once, Eldridge Jones appeared in a white jacket, bearing a tea service. Tom barely suppressed a smile. Eldridge must have been standing by right outside the door.

"Cream, sugar?" Needham asked.

"Thank you, no." Deng sniffed the aroma rising from his cup. "Ah, Chinese. Very thoughtful of you."

Needham beamed. "Well, now, when did you actually arrive?"

"Sunday. This is my first visit, so I seized the opportunity to examine your city. It is very vibrant. Filled with opportunity. Like Hong Kong."

"Get down to Chinatown, did you?"

"Not as yet," Deng said. "That would be, as you say, like carrying coals to Newcastle."

"I guess you have a point there," Needham chuckled. "But when you do go, I'd like to go with you. Never know what to order in those places. Uh, what I mean is I always depend upon expert counsel. What we intend to provide you here at Needham & Lewis."

Nice recovery, Tom thought, all things considered. Just when Needham seemed to be painting himself into a corner, he managed to turn it into something positive. Tom wondered if he didn't do it on purpose. It certainly got your attention.

"Precisely what I desire," Deng said.

"Well, then, can you give us an idea of your plans, where we can be of help?"

"Investments," Deng said, "particularly commercial properties. The commercial market in the United States has been in decline. It will come back. In Hong Kong, we have had similar ups and downs, but in the end it is always higher than the last high." Deng permitted himself a thin smile. "The secret for continued success is to maintain other, dependable sources of cash flow in times of distress."

This time, Tom thought, Deng's smile was as mirthless as his eyes.

"Couldn't have said it better myself," said Needham.

"As you know," Deng continued, "I have a casino, very profitable, in Macao. The great pleasure of my race is to gamble. I wish to make the proper contacts with the American gambling casinos, in Las Vegas, Atlantic City and so on. I want to incorporate a travel agency, specializing in charter flights from Asia, to bring to the United States myriads of these gamblers, many of whom are quite wealthy, but who would feel uncertain, unsure of themselves, if they came alone to a land whose customs are foreign to them. Additionally, I am confident that these casinos would pay a handsome fee for such a steady influx of players."

Deng took a perfunctory sip of tea. "My eventual goal, of course, would be to have my own casino. The Chinese population grows rapidly in this country. There are special games that would attract them—*sic bo* dice, *pai gow* poker, fan-tan—beside those that are normally offered."

Needham's bushy white eyebrows arched. "Could be problems there," he said. "The Mafia."

"Mafia?"

"Yes, the Italians. Organized crime. They run that sort of thing, I'm told. You hear about it all the time. All of a sudden, you get unwelcomed partners."

Tom interrupted. "Actually, there's been a change from the past. The Mafia, Cosa Nostra, whatever you want to call it, used to run the casinos. But the money required for these complexes, complete with huge hotels, got too big even for it, particularly when financing was lost from corrupt trade union pension funds. Still, these mobsters control many of the service aspects of a casino complex. So, to that extent at least, it's something you'd have to take into consideration."

"Thank you for your precious advice," Deng said.

"Not at all, not at all, what we're here for," Needham harrumphed. "I'll bow to Tom's expertise. He's fresh from the U.S. attorney's office, as you know."

"My chief interest, however, lies elsewhere," Deng went on. "In Hong Kong, and throughout Asia, I have noticed the proliferation of what you call fast-food establishments. I would reverse the process for America. A similar national chain in this country presenting Chinese food. Exotic, but familiar." He looked at Needham. "As you yourself said, in Chinatown you are always unsure what to order. On American highways, whether in California, Texas or New York, you would be comforted in the knowledge that you are getting exactly the same quantity and quality at the same price. I have a name. Definitely Chinese. But with an American connotation. It will be called Chow Chow. We will have regional distribution centers. Trucks bearing the Chow Chow logo, a golden pagoda, will be a familiar sight throughout your land."

"Chow Chow?" Needham repeated, rubbing his chin. "Yes! I get it. *Chow down!* Chow down at Chow Chow. Very good! Wish I'd thought of it myself. With the right marketing, it could be huge. Mr. Deng, you go ahead with this, you're looking at one of your first investors."

"Your response gratifies me," said Deng. He turned abruptly toward Tom. "Now, Mr. MacLean, I—"

"Please call me Tom."

"—yes, I, ah, Tom, what have you learned of this man who has been seeing my daughter?"

"I have to tell you that he appears to have a clean bill of health. Name's Robert Logan. No criminal record. Nothing subversive, which you indicated might be the case. Quite frankly, against my better judgment, I obtained an FBI rundown on him which didn't turn up anything at all derogatory."

"Against your better judgment?"

"Correct. As I told Mr. Needham, an inquiry like that coming directly from me could have caused him trouble. I managed to circumvent it. But barring an extraordinary situation, and without real grounds that something's there, I don't subscribe to this sort of thing."

"Isn't that for your client to decide?"

"Yes, after he gets his lawyer's input first."

"How is it, then, that Logan is allowed in remote areas of China where foreigners are normally forbidden?"

"I guess that's where the bones are buried. He's a respected archaeologist. And I must say I found your daughter's no fool, very intelligent, delightfully so, in fact."

"A young woman's head can be easily turned."

"Maybe so, but it seems to me that you're going to have to work this out with her yourself."

Glaring at Tom, Needham jumped in. "We'll keep an eye on this. I agree with you. Can't underestimate those Beijing fellows. Devious. Not unheard of to place someone like this Logan fellow in deep cover. Wouldn't put it past them for a minute."

Suddenly Deng threw up his hands, as if the matter was actually of no consequence. The tension evaporated. "You have been most helpful," he said.

Then, as Tom escorted him to the elevators, he introduced a new element into their relationship. "How is your father?"

"Fine, thank you. He told me he remembers you well. Why shouldn't he? He said you saved his life."

"It was nothing," Deng said. "He would have done the same for me, I am certain."

"Nevertheless, he, *I,* owe you."

"That comforts me greatly," Deng said. "I look forward to our next meeting."

When Tom returned to Needham's office, the managing partner was pacing back and forth. "Listen, son, you're not a prosecutor now. Be a little more politic, for Christ's sake. I'm talking about the daughter's boyfriend."

"Look, I'm not going to kid Deng or any other client I have. Otherwise, they're wasting their money and my time. Maybe you picked the wrong guy for this."

"No, you're not the wrong guy. I'm just trying to make you a *smarter* guy. Well, all right, except for that, it couldn't have gone better. Remember the way he thanked us for our advice? What did he say? Oh, yes. *Precious advice.* Couldn't have been more gracious, don't you think? Perhaps a little lesson there for you."

Five days later, chubby, apple-cheeked Miss Dotty Masterson, chief of the mail room, waddled into Shannon O'Shea's office bearing a Christmas-wrapped package.

Miss Dotty, as everyone called her, a recent celebrant of her thirty-fifth anniversary in the employ of the FBI, had hired on at age eighteen in the hope never realized of marrying the FBI agent of her dreams.

"Shannon dear, I brought this up myself because it got delivered so late. The post office is worse than ever these days," she clucked, "and I didn't want you waiting any longer. Besides, there's that new rule about personal mail and it could have stayed on the shelf downstairs another couple of days." As she departed, she said, "You got a fella? Don't make my mistake, holding out for Mr. Right. There isn't one, believe me. Just take the best you can."

"Well, Miss Dotty, it just might happen."

"Good."

At her desk, Shannon unwrapped the package. It was an attaché case. She tried to think. She needed a new one. Even complained to her secretary. Had Tom found out? The card must be inside.

She unlatched one of the clasps.

The phone rang.

One of the squad agents was on the line. A New York City cop had been picked up dealing heroin in his hometown in Suffolk County, out on Long Island. "And get this," the agent was saying. "He got the smack from a big dealer he was protecting uptown. Even was awarded a commendation in a shoot-out for knocking off another dealer who was trying to horn in."

Agitated, Shannon got up and stepped to the side of the desk, swinging the phone cord around with her. "God, what else?" she said, idly reaching over, unlatching the second clasp and raising the top of the attaché case.

The shot fired.

Screaming, she saw the hole in the wall behind her chair, chest high if she were still in it.

Other agents ran into her office. One of them gingerly raised the briefcase top again. There wasn't a gun. It was a sawed-off .22 caliber rifle barrel, nestled in Styrofoam and held in place with plastic twine. Behind it was a rattrap and a nail. They all could see how it worked. When the top was raised about four inches, the trap was sprung and drove the nail into the bullet with more than enough force to send it slamming through Shannon's body.

"Like the old zip guns," someone said.

"Lucky it wasn't a bomb," someone else said.

"Yes," Shannon said. "Lucky, lucky."

By now the assistant director for the New York office had arrived.

Shannon began laughing crazily.

"You all right?" he said. "Get her to a doctor."

"No, it's OK. I just remembered something. Over Christmas I was asked if this work was hazardous and I said being a supervisor wasn't hazardous at all."

22

HALFWAY AROUND THE WORLD, the next stage of Deng's plan began, a stage so secret that he had purposely kept it from the Confederation since many members of the brotherhood still depended on the poppy fields of the Burmese warlord, Shan Wa. Deng had confided only in his trusted lieutenant, Ho Shu-shui, and General Li.

Under the triple-canopied jungle just inside Burma, a khaki-clad scout from General Li's Third Chinese Irregular Forces watched one of Wa's mule caravans proceed slowly down a mountain trail on the opposite side of a gorge. The saddlebags of the mules were full. Uniformed soldiers guarded the caravan front and rear. It was headed toward the Thai border town of Mae Sai.

Early the next morning, in Thailand, the caravan halted at a remote cattle ranch. Three trucks were parked there, two of them already loaded with manure, fertilizer for the farms to the south. The contents of the saddlebags were removed, placed in heavy plastic bags and transferred to a third empty truck, which workers then covered with more manure. A contingent of the Thai Border Patrol stood nearby, passing the time of day with Shan Wa's guards.

The three trucks, throwing up plumes of dust, traveled down a dirt road and turned onto a two-lane paved highway for the six-hour trip to the city of Chiang Mai, where heroin traffickers could have a live cobra slit from head to tail right at their dinner table, its blood drained into wine glasses, which was said to be just the thing to bolster flagging libidos.

Chiang Mai has another feature—as exotic in its own way as the snake pits—the electronically secured, walled compound of the U.S. Drug Enforcement Administration. Complete with tennis courts, swimming pools, manicured lawns and houses, both ranch and duplex, with backyard barbeques, it was indistinguishable from any middle-class suburban development in America.

About an hour after the trucks had departed, the phone rang in the compound's command post. The agent who took the call listened for a moment and buzzed the DEA station chief, Terry McDonell. "Some guy," McDonell was told. "Sounds Chinese. Will only talk to you."

The voice on the phone said, "Three Toyota trucks coming south on highway ten-nineteen. Middle one has what you seek."

McDonell, deeply tanned, sporting Oakley wraparounds and a baseball cap that said L.A., summoned several agents.

"You think it's good info?" one of them asked.

"The guy didn't fuck around. No what's-in-it-for-me."

McDonell contacted the local police commandant. That was the best part for him. He had been in Chiang Mai for six months, totally dependent on tips, such as they were, from the Thai Border Patrol. Now the tables were being turned. Maybe.

The trucks were intercepted ten miles above Chiang Mai. A big air-conditioned tourist bus whizzed past. Along with dope, tourism was booming. A luxury hotel was even going up in the north, right at the edge of the Golden Triangle. A brochure promised adventure. See the poppy fields in all their natural beauty! McDonell had heard that the complex would include a casino. He had little doubt where the financing was coming from.

The Thai police lieutenant leading his detail wrinkled his nose in disgust. Although the humidity here in the uplands was nothing like Bangkok's, it was still plenty hot in the midday sun. The stench of the manure was overpowering. Flies swarmed in. A pair of Thai police reluctantly climbed each side of the truck and poked long poles into the manure. They looked back down at the lieutenant and shook their heads.

"Nothing," the lieutenant said.

"We have to empty it out," McDonell said.

The lieutenant's jaw set. Traffic on the road was backing up both ways. "We can't interrupt commerce like this," he said. "There will be many complaints. I have responsibilities."

McDonell saw a group of field-workers gawking at the scene. With his interpreter, he walked toward them, waving a fistful of bahts, the Thai currency. Delighted at the prospect of unexpected extra pay, they bent to the task. A third of the manure had been shoveled out before the first plastic bag was exposed. In all, there were four of them. Inside each were bricklike packages, also banded in plastic. McDonell slit one open, dug in a fingernail and tasted it. Heroin number four.

"Holy shit!" one of his agents exclaimed.

"I was hoping," McDonell said, smiling, "that I would be spared that."

The haul weighed in at four hundred units. Six hundred pounds. Close to three hundred kilos. The biggest seizure yet in the station's history. McDonell immediately cabled DEA headquarters in Arlington, Virginia.

Three days later, the same voice was on the line. This time, it was a ten-wheeler loaded with tons of bagged rice, headed out of Chiang Mai for Bangkok. Another Thai officer was on hand. When McDonell demanded that each bag be opened and resealed if it didn't contain heroin, the lieutenant protested, "But that will take the entire day."

The fifty-first bag held the units. So, conveniently, did the next two, a seizure even bigger than the first shipment. "Forget headquarters!" an agent yelled. "Call the *Guinness Book of Records.*"

The following week, it was eighty units in the trunk of a Honda sedan. *Only* eighty, McDonell thought. They were getting spoiled. He had said to the voice on the phone, "Who are you, friend?" and the voice replied, "Is what you say. A friend."

In his Burma retreat, Shan Wa raged, tossing down glass after glass of cognac. Word had been received from the heroin brokers in Thailand and Hong Kong that all advance payments were being halted. His instant thought was that General Li was somehow behind this. But he was told that nothing had been observed coming out of Laos destined for Chiang Mai. How would Li gain from this?

One of Wa's adjutants tried to inject a cheerier note. Not everything was being stopped. Some shipments were getting through.

Shan Wa sneered. Five units? Ten? He ordered the adjutant shot on the spot for insubordination. And before the assembled witnesses to the execution, he cried, "There is a betrayer among us. We will ferret him out and he will be fed to my dogs."

The tremors instantly reached the world markets. Like pork belly futures on the Chicago Commodities Exchange in anticipation of a corn belt drought, the wholesale price per unit of heroin number four began to creep up.

Besides McDonell in Chiang Mai, Y. K. Deng in New York was smiling.

23

F OR ONCE, BIG FRANK LUCANO forgot about the ever-present menace of the murderous Alphonse Carparti. In the office of his lawyer, Jack Koenigsberger, he could barely contain his fury.

"The way it sounds, Frank," Koenigsberger said, "the government's claiming extortion. You hear me? Monopoly price-fixing in garment center trucking."

"What monopoly? I got United Carriers, right? And that prick Carparti's got EEEZZZ Trucking, half of it, anyway, and he's pushing for more. Including my hide. Ain't that competition? All legal and aboveboard."

"Frank, the Feds set up a sting. They created a fake dress company. They called United and got a price. Then they called EEEZZZ Trucking, which said it didn't do pickups at that location and to call United. My sources tell me it's all on tape. They say United's offices were bugged for months. And they got witnesses."

"Who?" Lucano snapped, thinking of that loudmouth Goldie Goldstein of Hampton Fashions who tried to lead a manufacturers' boycott against United Carriers and who, thanks to Funzie DiBello, was recycled in the frame of a new-model car.

"*Frank,* come on," Koenigsberger cajoled.

"Well, Christ's sake, if it ain't one thing, it's another. I got them Chinks trying to undercut me, and now you're laying this on me."

Koenigsberger, biting down on an unlit cigar, said, "Chinks, what Chinks?"

"The Chinks that got them sweatshops around Chinatown. All of a sudden, they're bitching about our prices. They're starting to use their own vans. They got them crazy slant-eyed kids riding shotgun. I'm telling you, they're looking for trouble, they'll find it."

Jack Koenigsberger examined the mangled end of his cigar, threw it away and lit a new one. He puffed furiously for a moment. "Listen, Frank, that could be the solution."

"What?"

"The Chinks. Make a deal with them. Give them a piece of the action. Let them undercut you till this blows over. Create some competition."

"So who do I talk to?" Lucano said. "I don't know one Chinaman from the next." He glowered. "You should see what they're doing downtown, moving right into Mulberry Street. *Our* Mulberry Street."

"Frank, think about it. There has to be someone you can reach. Have I ever steered you wrong? Think about it."

"OK. I'll think, I'll think."

Funzie was waiting in the anteroom. They rode silently down in the elevator. One glance at Lucano informed Funzie that this was not the time for small talk. Finally, after Funzie checked the street, he ventured, "Boss, your face is kind of, like, all red. You OK? You want I should get you something?"

"Fucking A, I'm not all right," Lucano exploded. "You know what that fatassed Jewboy upstairs told me? I got to find some big boss in Chinatown, make a deal with him on the trucking contracts. How the fuck do I do that?"

Transfixed, Funzie hardly dared believe his ears. "Boss," he said, "I think maybe I could help you out on that."

In the car going to Deng's apartment, Big Frank Lucano said to Funzie, "How'd you meet this Chinaman again, what's his name?"

"Pei," DiBello said. "In Nam, boss. Around Saigon. He's good people. He's Chinese, but he's American. I mean, he's a citizen. And he's connected. The Chinese got a setup like ours over there in Hong Kong, organized and everything. Goes way back."

Lucano grunted. "So this other Chink, the guy we're seeing, he's a boss?"

"Hey, I don't know all the particulars. But Pei says he's a man of respect, like we say. Big-time. Pei don't make a move without him, I can tell you that. Like me with you."

Peter Pei greeted them at the door and once they were in the apartment, Funzie was relieved. He could see that Lucano was impressed that this was no fly-by-night guy. "Some view you got here," Lucano observed upon being introduced to Deng. "I got a pretty good one myself, you know, over in Staten Island. The city skyline. *And* the ocean."

"Funzie," Pei said, "I suggest we enjoy a walk and let these gentlemen discuss matters in private."

DiBello looked at Lucano. He nodded. Certainly, the hand of Alphonse Carparti was nowhere in evidence.

Pei had provided Deng with a supply of liquor. "Offer him this," he had advised, pointing to a bottle of Chianti Classico.

"Yeah, sure, *grazie,*" Lucano said, accepting a glass. Then, in a tone tinged with suspicion, "You ain't having any?"

"Ah, my liver unfortunately does not permit it."

"That's what my doctor says, that I got to watch it. Cut down. So I'll give it up for Lent."

"Lent?"

"Uh, that's a little complicated. It's sort of a religious thing. You don't know about it, it's hard to explain."

Deng poured himself some mineral water and raised his glass. "Welcome, Mr. Lucano."

"Hey, good health," Lucano said.

"Mr. Lucano, we share much in common."

"Yeah?"

"Yes. You, a Sicilian from Italy, and me, a Chiuchow from China, we have suffered ruthless foreign invaders who cruelly raped our land and tried to crush our people. I have read the history of what we both endured and how you, like us, formed a secret brotherhood to combat the savagery forced upon us, how we learned that so-called lawful authority was simply another instrument used to oppress us. How we banded together in blood oaths and with sealed lips, what you call *omerta,* to protect what was rightfully ours."

"Gee, the way you put it, that sounds right to me," Lucano said. "What's on your mind, you don't mind me asking."

"I propose that we join forces. This is a country that has been hostile to both our people. In the past, we have been treated like miserable dogs and there remains great prejudice against us."

Lucano's face darkened. "Let me tell you something. My old man, my father, he told me in his own words. He's sixteen, see, and he's working his way through high school, wants to make something of himself. Stays away from the tough guys, the Black Hand it was called in them days, and gets a job as a messenger for some fancy Wall Street firm. Works his fucking ass off. A couple of years later, he sees all these other kids with the right names sitting around doing nothing and getting promoted ahead of him. So he goes to the top guy and says, 'What's this?' and the guy says, 'Listen, you guinea bastard, you're lucky you got the job you got.' " Lucano gulped down his wine. "What's that mean? Join forces."

"My organization intends to settle here. We bring a valuable commodity. I offer you the opportunity to share in its profit."

"Commodity?"

"The white powder. Heroin."

"Uh, uh, no way," Lucano said. "Junk is out. Junk is what got the families in grief in the first place. I catch one of my guys dealing junk, he's whacked."

"Mr. Lucano. What you say is true, but it's too late now. Whether the families, as you call them, engage in heroin or not, everyone believes that they do. You therefore experience the pain without the benefit. I have the means to bring it here in bulk and to regulate the supply. It will be sold to your people at a favorable price and in each sale, because of your cooperation, you will receive a percentage as my partner without anyone knowing. Only I will know. I speak of vast profits, more, perhaps, than you have ever dreamed of. There is, for you, so little to lose and so much to gain."

Suddenly, as the content of what Deng was saying fully sank in, Lucano blurted, "Say, you checked this place out for bugs?"

"Bugs?"

"Yeah, *bugs*. You know, fucking hidden mikes. The fucking FBI has them everywhere."

"No, I don't believe I am of interest to the FBI. But your warning is well advised. I will take heed." Lucano's concern pleased Deng. If he was worried about these bugs, he had taken the bait.

Lucano shifted in his chair, frowning. "If this is so good, how come you're letting me in on it?"

"I will be honest, as I know you will be. While I have the commodity and the means of importation, you have what I lack. A distribution network, one already in place that can be enlarged as time goes on."

"Well, maybe so."

"Mr. Lucano, I am a serious man engaged in serious business. To demonstrate my good faith, I will render a service to you. I am told you have severe problems with another family boss, one Alphonse Carparti, who threatens the stability of your organization. Who threatens you personally. I will eliminate this Carparti on your behalf in a manner which will not involve you in any way."

"Who told you about Carparti?"

"My clansman, Pei."

"That fucking Funzie, he talks too much." Lucano's features turned sullen as he conjured up an image of Carparti, Carparti with his silk-suited strut, his lord-of-the-manor sneer. Finally, he said, "Well, yeah, it's true. I got to take him out, but I got to be careful. We can't afford no more all-out wars, that's what Carparti don't understand."

"As I say, I will do it for you."

"Hey, I appreciate the offer, but you ain't got no chance. Carparti's *pazzo,* you know, crazy, but crazy like a fox. He don't go nowhere, he ain't, like, with a little army. The guy on Channel Seven that does the weather, he says it's going to be sunny all day, not a cloud in the sky, Carparti makes sure to take his umbrella. The only place he goes regular is this restaurant on the East Side, way over, in the seventies, Villa Mia. One of his button men runs it, but Carparti's got a big piece, for sure. They say the button's a wonderful cook." Lucano looked morose. "Anyway, that's what I hear. I never ate there myself. But forget the Villa Mia. I mean, that's really asking for it."

"We Chiuchow have a saying," Deng said. "It is in his lair that the tiger sleeps."

"Yeah, well, believe me, this tiger Carparti sleeps with one eye open."

"If I perform this service, do we have, as you say, a deal?"

Lucano, tempted, hesitated. "I got to be honest, too. I got to talk to somebody about this first."

Deng nodded, as if acknowledging the sagacity of Lucano's caution. "I think we will go very well together. It is why I chose you. You will quickly inform me of your decision?"

"You got it," Lucano said. But first thing, he had to get to his brother, Father Paul, on this. Even though Paul had warned him to stay out of junk, this wasn't your ordinary everyday proposition. Paul would see all the pros and cons, get to the bottom line. Besides, he had to talk to Paul about the meeting with Jack Koenigsberger and the antitrust stuff. That was something Paul hadn't counted on. As he was about to leave, he realized he had forgotten about the trucking, and he turned to Deng. "Listen, there's something else maybe you could do."

"Yes?"

"Do you know any of these Chi"—Lucano stopped himself in the nick of time—"uh, Chinese guys that make dresses and so forth for the garment industry? I got to make a trucking deal with them. The government's giving me a hard time about, uh, unfair prices, you could say. I got to work out an arrangement, so it's like, there's competition, get the government off my back, and I don't know who the hell to talk to."

"Have your person provide the names to Pei and explain precisely what is required. I will take care of it."

Chink or no, Big Frank Lucano thought, this guy Deng was a man after his own heart, a man to be respected, a *pezzo grosso*.

In the morning, Lucano called the residence at the Church of the Holy Sepulcher and asked for Father Paul.

"Oh, you missed him," the old Irish biddy who worked the phone said. "He had a racquet ball date. Doctor Oliveri just picked him up."

That would be Tony Oliveri, the internist. They had all grown up together. "Where'd they go?" Lucano asked.

"Father Paul didn't say. He belongs to several clubs, you know, for golf, tennis, racquet ball."

Jesus! Lucano thought. The next thing she's going to reel off all his awards. He phoned again at two p.m., then three.

At four o'clock, he was about to try again. He was sitting in the kitchen of his mansion on Todt Hill, the highest point on Staten Island, playing gin rummy with Funzie. He preferred the kitchen. The rest of the house made him uncomfortable, filled with brocaded furnishings, gilt mirrors, romantic Sicilian scenes and copies of Roman statuary installed by some fancy decorator his wife, Louise, had found. He would like to get rid of the place, just as he would love dumping his son, Frank Jr., but it wasn't worth taking on Louise, who was now undoubtedly off on another shopping spree. Frank Jr., twenty-two, hadn't made it past the first semester of the local community college, so Big Frank set him up in a dress business and then had to find someone to actually run it. All the kid ever did was acquire new gold chains to dangle on his hairy chest, dance away the night at every club that opened up and fuck every model he could get his hands on.

Then the phone rang.

"Meestair Frank?" It was a woman's voice.

She sounded like she had a spic accent, Lucano thought. "Who's this?"

"Your brother, Father Paul!" she said. He could hear her breath coming in short, sharp takes.

"My brother Paul, what?"

"Please come quick. Is horrible."

"What's horrible?"

"You come. Please!"

"For Christ's sake, come where?"

She gave him an address, just off Fifth Avenue in Manhattan. "You press button PH. Is no name."

"Come on," Lucano said to Funzie DiBello. "Something's wrong with my brother."

Outside, Funzie's two young toughs leaped out of the Lincoln, one already holding the door open before Lucano was off the columned porch.

At his appearance, the two real Dobermans on the property pressed against their cage, hidden in the fifty thousand dollars' worth of rhododendron and blue spruce landscaping Louise had had planted.

"Boss, you want I should let the dogs out?"

"Forget it. We ain't got time. Give me a couple of Tums."

In the late afternoon traffic, the trip took nearly an hour. Lucano scanned the buttons in the foyer of the converted, six-story townhouse and found the one that said PH. It buzzed right back.

Lucano and DiBello got into the elevator. In a tight squeeze, it could have handled one more person. When they emerged, Big Frank pressed the bell.

He heard the same voice say, "Meestair Frank?"

"Yeah, open up."

The door opened partially. He saw big brown eyes peer warily out, dilated with fear. A premonition seized him. "You stay here," he instructed DiBello.

The door edged back farther and he stepped inside. Lucano gaped in astonishment when he got a complete look at her. The eyes were framed by a mass of dark brown curls, lipstick smeared, mascara a mess. Somehow, it only made her look sexier. She was about five feet four and barefoot. She was wearing a loosely bound robe. He could see her boobs. Like everything else about her, they were knockouts.

She clutched his arm and pulled him across the living room into another room. Then he saw Paul. He was naked, lying outstretched on the disheveled bed, face up. His eyes were open. And they weren't blinking.

Lucano could barely get the words out. "What the fuck happened?"

"He, I, we were . . ." She began sobbing. "He was on top of me and . . . and . . . he was suddenly no more. Like you see."

Lucano walked over to the body. Holy Christ! All the time Paul thought he was coming and all the time he was going.

He turned to the girl. "What's your name?"

"Maria. Maria Torrez."

"What's your racket?"

"I am . . . I was a dancer."

"Where you from?"

"Near San Juan. In Puerto Rico." She started crossing herself. "*Dios mio,*" she said. "Forgive me."

Big Frank reached into his pocket and extracted a wad of cash. He peeled off fifteen hundred-dollar bills and slapped them into her hand. "You listen to me good, Maria. You know who I am?"

"Yes, sair."

"Well, get dressed and pack up and hightail it right out to the airport back to San Juan. You ever show your fucking ass around here again, I catch you in any topless joint, whatever, your dancing days are over. Understand?"

When she was ready, Lucano told Funzie, "Take this cunt downstairs and put her in a cab. And stay down there till I buzz you. I got to think."

Lucano walked around the living room. There was a big TV screen in one corner. Next to it were stacks of porn films. The walls featured blowups of nudes, all with lusty figures. An end table had a sculpture on it, a man and a woman astride each other.

Big Frank shook his head. He had always wondered what Paul was spending his money on and now he knew. Anyway, he thought, you could say one thing about Paul. He wasn't diddling no little altar boys.

He found Paul's phone book.

The first call was to Monsignor McCarthy, the diocesan communications director.

"I'm sorry," he was told officiously, "but the monsignor is in a meeting. May I ask who's calling?"

"Father Paul Lucano," Big Frank said. "You tell the monsignor it's urgent, an emergency. I'll hold."

A minute later, McCarthy's nasal voice was on the line. Nasal and irritated. "This had better be good, Paul. I'm really tied up."

"This ain't Paul. It's Frank Lucano." He gave McCarthy the address. "You don't get right up here, the diocese, the cardinal, is in trouble like you've never seen."

The second call went to the office of Dr. Anthony Oliveri. An answering machine said, "The office is closed today. If it's an emergency, please . . ."

Lucano hung up. Luckily, Oliveri's home number in Pelham Manor was in the book. "Tony? Frank Lucano," he said.

"Frank! What a coincidence. I played racquet ball with Paul this very day. We had a swell workout."

"Yeah, well, Paul had another swell one this afternoon. Tony, here's where I'm at. You hop in your car now, no ifs, ands or buts. And Tony, you got one of them certificates you fill out for stiffs?"

"Yes, I think so. What's this all about?"

"Don't ask so many questions. Just bring the certificate."

The third call was to the Graziano Funeral Chapel on Mulberry Street. "Fredo," Lucano said after identifying himself, "I need you for a job in a couple of hours. A body pickup. But I don't want no hearse. You got a station wagon? Good. Don't move. I'll get back to you. And Fredo, I want you, just you, personal."

Alone in the room, Lucano stared at his dead brother, feeling rather pleased with himself. "Well, Paul," he said, "you can't say I ain't doing the right thing by you."

Monsignor Thomas McCarthy, slim, intense, with eyes that Savonarola would have envied, was the first on the scene.

"Welcome to Father Paul's little home away from home," Lucano said.

McCarthy immediately spotted the nudes on the wall and shuddered. Lucano took him to the bedroom. "You should've seen the broad. Don't worry, I sent her packing."

"You mean he died in . . . ah . . . ?"

Big Frank had to hand it to the monsignor, though. He went right to the side of the bed, knelt and proceeded to administer the last rites to his fellow priest.

"Mother of God, what'll we do?" McCarthy said after he finished. "This is disastrous. Think of the publicity."

"That's what I am thinking. Who's the top cop you know best?"

"Why the commissioner himself. He was just made a Knight of Malta. His eminence just had a private dinner in his honor."

"You get on the horn to the commissioner and tell him we don't want no police investigation on this, there's nothing to investigate."

"That's all? You're sure?"

"Yeah, I'll take care of the rest."

"Bless you," the monsignor said.

Doctor Oliveri arrived a half hour later.

"He was humping this broad," Big Frank said. "I guess a man his age shouldn't play racquet ball and fuck the same day. You shoulda seen her, though. Be tough on anybody's heart."

Oliveri looked as if he were falling apart. "Is that what it was, cardiac arrest?"

"How should I know? The broad said he was banging away and whamo! You got that paper?"

"That's what I'll put down." Oliveri started filling out the death certificate. "What was the time?"

"When'd you finish playing ball?"

"Around one. Afterward, we had lunch and I dropped him off. *Here.* Frank, I had no idea," he said.

"Who did, Christ's sake? Make it, let's see, about four. Yeah, four o'clock."

"God, Frank, I could lose my license."

Ignoring him, Lucano said, "Listen good, Tony. Take my word, nobody's going to stick their nose in this. But if you fuck up, you got a lot more to worry about than losing your fucking license. So beat it."

Then he dialed the Graziano Funeral Home. "Fredo, I'm ready for you. Funzie's downstairs waiting. Tell him I said to come up with you."

When the bell to the penthouse door rang and Lucano opened it, Funzie and Alfredo Graziano were standing outside.

"It's Paul, he's gone," Lucano said.

"Gee, boss," Funzie said.

"Frank, I express my profound sympathy," Graziano said. "As always, I stand ready to assist you in your hour of need."

The Graziano Funeral Home handled the obsequies of all the members of the Lucano family, both blood-related and occupational. Suddenly overcome by the emotion of the moment, tears coursed down Big Frank's cheeks as he embraced the two men. "I appreciate that, Fredo," he said. "I knew I could count on you."

In the bedroom, Graziano laid out the body bag he had brought with him. "Give him a hand, Funzie," Big Frank said.

"Right, boss. I done this plenty in Nam, let me tell you."

It was not an easy task. Rigor mortis had begun to set in. Once Paul was in the bag, Graziano glanced in dismay at the white-and-black-checked cashmere jacket and gray slacks folded over a chair and said, "Frank, are there any proper clothes?"

"Good thinking, Fredo," Lucano said, and in a closet he found a clerical suit and a pair of polished black shoes. A pleated silk black blouse and Roman collar were in a chest drawer. "Socks, where are the fucking socks?" he said.

"Don't worry," Graziano said, "I'll take care of that."

Holding Paul's body upright, Lucano and Graziano just managed to fit into the elevator. Funzie went down the stairs to prevent anyone in the building from using it. At the front entrance, he surveyed the street and announced, "All clear."

"Fredo, make him look good," Big Frank said, brushing away another tear. "It shouldn't be hard. He went happy."

The obituaries were uniformly laudatory. There were obligatory references, of course, to the fact that Father Paul was the brother of reputed mobster Frank (Big Frank) Lucano. But, it was pointed out, Father Paul had chosen another path in life. It was also noted that while Father Paul steadfastly denied the existence of the "so-called" Mafia, he had devoted himself to charitable works on behalf of the poor and the homeless, all those in society who had been disenfranchised.

The reported details of his death stated that Father Paul, to all intents in robust good health, spent his last day on earth with a childhood chum, the prominent physician Anthony Oliveri. The two had played racquet ball and then enjoyed lunch at a country club in Long Island. Upon driving the priest back to the city, the doctor had stopped by his office. And it was there, ironically, that Father Paul had suffered massive and terminal heart failure despite Oliveri's best efforts to revive him. A police department spokesman, questioned because of rumors of a vendetta between Father Paul's brother and another alleged crime boss, Alphonse Carparti, confirmed that there was nothing untoward in his demise.

Burial was in St. John's cemetery in Queens, a section of which contained the remains of legendary Cosa Nostra giants of yesteryear—among them, Lucky Luciano, Tommy Lucchese, Joe Profaci and Vito Genovese. Well, Lucano thought, now they would be comforted by a spiritual adviser who understood them quite well.

He sighed. He was on his own now. He turned to Funzie DiBello after the bronze coffin had been lowered into the ground and said, "Tell your Chink pal to tell his boss we got a deal."

24

On the phone, Deng listened to her say, "Hello."

He spoke in the Chiuchow dialect, "Daughter, it is your father."

"Father, where are you?"

"I am in New York."

"New York? But I didn't know. When did you arrive?"

He sensed her nervousness. "A short while ago."

"But why haven't you called me before?"

"I had business to attend to. Now much of it has been accomplished and I wish to see you."

"Of course, father. I will come straightaway."

"He's here, my father," she told Robert Logan. "I'm going to New York tomorrow to see him."

"Do you want me to go with you?"

"No!" she said, her voice shrill.

"Hey, come on, take it easy."

She took a deep breath. "I'm sorry. It's silly, isn't it. In America, you fall in love and you tell your parents and that's it. If they don't like it, too bad."

"This is America."

"I know. But China's in me, too. I can't escape it. Nobody can." She smiled. "Except, of course, Beverly Soo. And she's from nowhere. You of all people should know this. I have to do it my own way," she said. "I haven't seen him in a long time. It's best that I be alone with him first. After all, I owe him everything."

"Not the rest of your life."

"No, not that. I wish I could explain it better." She grew pensive. "I'll tell you a secret I haven't told anyone. Once in Hong Kong, he came to my school for some reason and I heard my classmates whisper that he was a dragon head."

"Li-po, you're kidding. A triad dragon head?"

"It was stupid. I didn't pay any attention to it. My father is a respected businessman. I'm only telling you because there's an aura about him that scares people. Me, too, a little."

She wore a navy blue silk cheongsam and a jade necklace he had given her on her eighteenth birthday. She felt funny about the cheongsam. She hadn't worn one once since she'd been on campus.

Deng greeted her with a chaste embrace. He stepped back and nodded approvingly. "You are as lovely as ever. My heart sings."

"Thank you, father. It's good to see you looking so well. I have missed you."

"I also. But that is now fortunately in the past."

"It is?"

"Yes, I intend to reside here more or less permanently. I have already begun preparations for investments in America. I cannot accept what will shortly occur in Hong Kong. My memories forbid it. Others may forget. I cannot."

She bowed her head in silence. She knew about his memories. She had been sixteen when she badgered him about the family history. What was his mother like, his father? All her friends had all kinds of stories about their grandparents. Why shouldn't she? So then he finally told her what had happened in Shanghai. "I do not wish to speak of this again," he had said. She remembered him saying, as she listened, horrified, "You do what you have to do to survive." And that was when, just because of the way he said it, she also remembered, she felt her first fear of him.

Deng stared at her. "I am most pleased with the progress of your studies. Very soon, you will be at my side."

She thought of Robert, who had awakened her sexuality. She felt his warmth and tenderness. How do you explain love? "Father," she said, her voice quavering, "there's someone important to me that I want you to meet."

"I have no interest in meeting him."

Him! So he does know. Of course, it was her amah. Her stomach turned over. Why hadn't she told him herself before! "Father, he is a wonderful man. I love him deeply."

"I have no time to discuss such infatuations. I have many plans for you. Why do you suppose so much effort has gone into your education?"

"Father, I appreciate everything you've—"

He cut her off. "Li-po, you are still a young woman unwise in the ways of the world. You are all that I have. One day you will come into great wealth. You must learn to manage all I have built. For my sake. For your sake and for the sake of the children you will bear. I value you as I would a son. In due course, you'll marry and it will be a correct marriage."

"I'm not your son!" she cried. "It's not fair."

"Fair? You dare speak to me, your father, of fairness?"

"Please understand," she begged him, "I must have my own life."

"You will come to your senses in due course."

"No, I have come to them now," she said and ran out of the apartment.

He made no effort to stop her. There would be a test of wills. He had handled it badly, but he had no doubt who would prevail in the end.

In the morning he called the number in Virginia he had been given at the airport. "I wish to speak to Mr. Sentry."

25

THE TWO ACCOUNTANTS Deng brought with him from Hong Kong listened attentively. Their names were Lee and Tam. "I assign you a mission of paramount importance," Deng told them.

They were to patronize an Italian restaurant, Villa Mia. He warned that there might be some hostility at their presence, but they must ignore any slights. At first, they were to arrive without reservations, as if they had wandered in on impulse. They should also arrive early in the evening, no later than six-thirty the first time, when there would be many empty tables. If asked, they were to say they were businessmen from Hong Kong, that they delighted in the Italian cuisine, that while there were Italian restaurants in Hong Kong, nothing certainly could compare with what was available in New York and that they desired to savor the best the city had to offer.

Deng instructed them to make it evident that their command of English was rudimentary, to be sure to order only the most expensive items on the menu and to leave a lavish tip. Finally, he provided them with a photograph of Alphonse Carparti that Pei had obtained from Funzie DiBello. They were to watch for this man.

The Villa Mia was on a residential stretch of York Avenue. A bar was on the right with two tables opposite it. The restaurant then expanded into a rectangular room with tables lining both sides. Round tables were in the center. In the far right corner was a larger round table, easily capable of seating eight or more people. There Alphonse Carparti held court, always with his back to the wall.

Rocco Rinaldi, a longtime button man for Carparti, happened to be in front checking the reservations list when Lee and Tam walked in. The Villa Mia had been his idea and he convinced Carparti to put up three-quarters of the financing. The truth was he loved cooking more than killing. And playing on Carparti's ambition to be a man-about-town, he had said, "Boss, you got to have a joint on the East Side."

It was an instant success. Anyone in the underworld who wished to curry Carparti's favor made sure to be in frequent attendance. And at cocktail parties up and down Park Avenue, people said, "*Well,* you'll never guess who I saw the other night. *Alphonse Carparti!* In the flesh. Yes, it's just opened, Villa Mia, practically around the corner, and very good. Nothing rough about it at all. Ties and jackets required."

For Rinaldi, the one drawback was when Caparti himself was present. That meant that the three tables in a semicircle directly in front of his table had to remain empty. Rinaldi hated the sight of those deserted tables and the thought of the money he was losing.

Chinks! Rinaldi thought. What the hell is this?

He approached Lee and Tam. "You in the right place?"

"Oh, velly, velly positive," Lee, slender and bespectacled, said, while the portly Tam bobbed his head enthusiastically. "Fliend say top establishment. Much good eat. We Hong Kong. On business, yes. Much delight of Italian food."

It was exactly six-thirty. Not another diner was present. He gave them the least desirable table he had, by the entrance at the end of the bar.

They ordered from every course on the menu, antipasto, pasta, fish, sliced prime steak with peppers and onions. They started off with a bottle of Recioto dei Capitelli that went for ninety dollars and then a Bricco dell Uccellone at one twenty-five.

That got Rinaldi's attention. He noticed that they weren't finishing every dish. Suddenly the anxious restaurateur, he said, "Something wrong? You don't like my kitchen?"

"Oh, yes," Lee exclaimed. "We sample. Is Chinese tradition."

This was a Tuesday night. According to Lucano, Carparti regularly came in on Tuesday and again on Friday, which was traditionally boys' night out for mafiosi and their girlfriends. Lee and Tam had just ordered cannoli for dessert when there was a stir in the now-crowded Villa Mia.

Carparti, right on schedule, accompanied by a half-dozen men, strode past them and headed for his table, pausing en route to oblige two autograph requests.

Shortly thereafter, Lee asked for the bill.

Rinaldi whistled softly when it was added up. Five hundred and twenty dollars. Best of all, it was paid in cash. Plus a one-fifty-buck tip, he noticed.

"Hey, come again," he said.

Nodding and smiling, they said they would.

They returned on Thursday at approximately the same hour. Rinaldi moved them into the main part of the restaurant.

On Friday night, they were again given preferred seating. As predicted, when Carparti arrived, he was with two other men and three women. The women, Lee and Tam reported to Deng, were young and had large, exposed bosoms. Unlike the previous time, there was much laughter and carrying-on at his table. Carparti appeared to drink a considerable amount of wine.

The following Tuesday night, Deng told them not to go to the Villa Mia until nine-thirty. Carparti was already there and every table was taken, except the three immediately around him.

Rinaldi groaned. "Why didn't you call?" he said.

"Velly solly," Lee replied. "Work late." Lee looked properly dejected. "We must go?"

"No, wait, hang on a minute," Rinaldi said. He went to Carparti, bent down and whispered in his ear. "Boss, you see them two Chinks standing over there? Been coming in a lot. From Hong Kong. Real big spenders. You mind I put them by you?" he said, pointing at the middle one of the three empty tables. "Believe me, they don't know from nothing. Can't hardly speak no English."

Carparti smiled his famous smile, the one that caused *GQ* magazine to dub him the Dandy Don. "Hey, why not?" he said. "We're in business, right? And that fucking Lucano tries anything funny, hey, they're in the way."

Rinaldi froze. "Boss! Don't even say it as a joke."

"Love you, Rocco, baby. You're my man."

Lee and Tam, avoiding any eye contact with Carparti's table, gabbed away with one another in Chiuchow. Once more, their bill was enormous and paid in cash.

On Friday evening, when Lee and Tam again arrived at nine-thirty, they were promptly led to the same table in front of Carparti. He was seated with the two men and three women who had been with him the week before.

Lee said to Rinaldi, "Expecting two fliends. Is permitted? Just in from Hong Kong."

"No problem," Rinaldi said. "Hey, the more the merrier."

Right after ten o'clock, the two red poles that Chao Yu had chosen to bring to New York entered the restaurant. Lee rose and waved to them. One, trailing behind the other, was carrying an attaché case. As they reached the table, Tam also stood to greet them.

The first red pole pulled a nine-millimeter semiautomatic from his shoulder holster and shot Lee in the face. Then he shot Tam.

At that instant, the second red pole, having snapped open the attaché case, yanked out a Cobray M-11 semiautomatic machine pistol, altered for automatic fire capable of delivering nearly a thousand rounds per minute, and began to spray Carparti's table, aiming initially at Carparti himself. A forkful of linguine dribbling from his mouth, Carparti pitched forward. Blood spurted in a jagged line above the breasts of the woman who had been nuzzling him.

The red pole with the Cobray continued to fire with professional coolness, feet braced, moving the barrel slightly left and right. The two men with Carparti toppled off their chairs. The other two women slumped on the table.

The sound of the shooting was deafening. For a moment, there was silence. Then the first screams could be heard. Almost everyone dining in the room had dived to the floor. A few customers at the tables along both walls were hunched down, hands shielding their faces.

At the bar, a stunned Rinaldi reached beneath the cash register and came up with a revolver. Nobody had noticed Chao Yu at the door, a Cobray at his side. One burst cut down Rinaldi.

The first red pole observed that Tam was still alive and put another bullet into him. As the two red poles backed away, some heads peeked over the tabletops. A gun was seen in a hand belonging to one of the heads. Chao Yu stepped into the room and raked it, aiming at the ceiling. Every head disappeared. So did the hand holding the gun.

Chao Yu let loose a final volley and then he and the red poles exited, dropping their weapons by the bar.

Except for traffic in and out of the Villa Mia, this block of York Avenue at this hour was usually deserted. Chao Yu and the two red poles calmly crossed the sidewalk to the car double-parked, engine running. The Cantonese driver, whom Pei had hired for Deng, had no idea of what had happened.

"We go," Chao told him.

An hour later, in his kitchen on Todt Hill, Big Frank Lucano first heard the news from a reporter calling to ask for his reaction. "I don't know nothing," he shouted. "I been home all night."

At that point, all the reporter could tell Lucano was that Carparti had been whacked. Lucano immediately phoned Funzie DiBello and told him to get over to his place with plenty of men. Then he checked the alarm system and made certain that the Dobermans were on the prowl. He next phoned his key capos and told them to prepare for trouble.

By morning, though, scanning the headlines, he knew that there was no cause for alarm. Carparti's death was on the front page of every paper. The headline in the *Daily News* summed it up:

MOB BOSS SLAIN IN
CHINESE SHOOT-OUT

The thrust of all the stories was identical. The alleged top boss of organized crime had been dining in an East Side restaurant in which he was said to have had a secret interest. At approximately ten-thirty p.m., three gunmen, apparently Chinese, entered the premises and shot to death two other Chinese, whose papers indicated that they were Hong Kong citizens.

Caught in the hail of bullets, Alphonse Carparti, who was portrayed as having a notoriety unrivaled in gangland circles since the imprisonment of John Gotti, became a hapless victim. In sidebar features, much was made of the strange quirk of fate that had Carparti, himself a man of violence, sitting in the wrong place at the wrong time.

Police theorized that one Rocco Rinaldi, reputedly a close associate of

Carparti's and the ostensible owner of the restaurant, was slain while trying to thwart the assassins.

Other than stating that the gunmen appeared to be Chinese, shaken witnesses had little of substance to offer. The chief of detectives was quoted as saying, "Asian crime is on the rise. So far it's been confined to Chinatown. This doesn't bode well for the future." He added that the weapons left at the scene were being checked for fingerprints, although he had little hope that this would amount to anything, especially if, as he phrased it, "the perpetrators didn't come from here."

Reading these stories over and over again, Lucano shuddered. Who were the Chinks Deng set up? It had to be a setup. Whatever else they were, he reasoned, not even Chinks were crazy enough to get themselves knocked off willingly. For sure, that fucking Deng was nobody to fuck around with.

26

TOM HAD BEEN TRAVELING with Deng when Shannon O'Shea received her Christmas package. In a bistro near his apartment, he said, "Why didn't you call me? My secretary knew where I was."

"What was I supposed to say? Guess what? I'm alive."

"Thank God, it wasn't a bomb."

"Yes, that seems to be the conventional wisdom."

He ignored the sarcasm. "Anything new on it?"

"What's new is we now have a security screening system. All incoming mail is X-rayed."

"I can't believe it wasn't being done before."

She shrugged. "Nobody ever tried to whack an FBI agent in his or, in my case, *her* office. Live and learn, as they say. The first thing the assistant director did was circulate a memo warning everybody to keep mum about it. Rather embarrassing, you know."

"So what do you think?"

"Oriental cunning. What else? Even if X rays were in place, it probably would have gotten through. Remember, it wasn't a gun, at least the kind you'd be looking for. Who and why is the question."

A waiter came for their drink order. "I don't think a beer will do it for me tonight," she said. "Bourbon on the rocks, please. Make it a double." She downed almost half of it in one swallow.

Tom had never seen her so on edge. "Maybe you ought to take a little time off," he said.

"Don't worry. It's not the damn package. You should have been at the meeting I was at this afternoon. Headquarter's all worked up about big heroin seizures the DEA's suddenly making in Thailand. Headquarters wants to know when we're going to stop twiddling our thumbs up here."

The old story, he thought, the ugly little secret of law enforcement. The main battle, as always, was for turf and credit. He was glad he was out of it.

"If that wasn't bad enough, DEA had a press conference touting its triumphs. Even managed to ridicule a two-kilo grab my undercover guys made a couple of days ago. The sellers were three Gray Shadows, one of the gangs we've been targeting. So, naturally, with all the heat, my boss, that pompous clown Wakefield—I think you met him the night of the raid in Flushing—was all over me with wonderful lines like 'Let's get with it, shall we?' I suggested to him that maybe we weren't making bigger seizures because the stuff wasn't coming in the way it's been. And that's the truth. There's a real shortage. Right now, on the street, a unit is going for over a hundred thousand wholesale."

She drained her glass and motioned to the waiter.

"Make it a single this time," Tom said.

"I was about to switch to beer. I don't need any lectures." Then she abruptly told the waiter, "On second thought, give me another. Another *double*."

She glowered at Tom, as if challenging him to say something. When he didn't, she ranted on about Wakefield, "So he said, 'Oh, is that what you want me to put in my report? Because of the excellent work of the DEA, the FBI finds itself irrelevant as regards trafficking in heroin.' I tell you, I wanted to spit in his eye. Anyway, that's that. How was the trip with the fabulous Mr. Deng? You don't look all that happy yourself."

"Oh, it went fine. In D.C., we met both New York senators. Deng told them about his plans for a fast-food chain. He also talked about other investments, real estate and so forth. Wanted to do everything he could to help revitalize the economy. Create jobs. They asked about Asian street crime and he said that many youths had lost touch with their ancient heritage of courtesy, respect and honest labor that marks the Chinese culture. He hoped to be a role model that would redirect them into productive, law-abiding paths, adding a most positive mix, as he put it, to the great ethnic melting pot of America."

"Very uplifting," Shannon said. "I'll bet there wasn't a dry eye in the house."

"Then we hit the road to scout franchise locations. Amazing. No matter where we went—Atlanta, Dallas, L.A., San Francisco, of course, and Chicago, there were Chiuchow. Clansmen, he called them. Tomorrow we're closing on a midtown tower he wants. And I've got to start on the tax implications of incorporating all his Hong Kong holdings here."

"So why the furrowed brow? You should be laughing all the way to the bank."

"It's boring. I miss the action in court."

"Isn't that what your job is? To keep clients out of court?"

"Yeah, but Deng makes it too easy. Maybe after I've gotten him settled in, I'll get some big cases. Show everybody I trained downtown they still have a lot to learn when they go up against me."

They both ordered steak, rare, and *pommes frites*. "Now I'll have the beer," she said.

"Glad I'm so persuasive."

"Oh, come off it."

On the way back to his apartment, she asked, "Speaking of clients, what's the latest with Deng's daughter?"

"He hasn't mentioned her again. I guess no news is good news. Anyhow, it's not my problem."

In retrospect, he should have known better. All the ominous signs of tension and frustration were there.

They made love. But it was different. More out of pure physical desire. No words of endearment. With an undercurrent of anger. As if it were a contest in which, when it was over, Tom felt he had performed exceedingly well, sensing her absolute dependence on him to bring her to orgasm. And it was this hubris that caused him to say afterward, as she lay limp beside him, "Why'd you become a nun?"

She stiffened at once. "*Please,* for God's sake."

"Come on, there's got to be a reason. And spare me that community service stuff."

"Look, I don't want to talk about it, OK?"

But he didn't let it go. "What's the big deal?" he persisted.

"Tom, just lay off, will you?"

"Why won't you tell me? I want to know. What's to hide? There's nothing to be ashamed of, is there, being God's handmaiden?"

Suddenly, she sat upright and turned on the bed lamp, facing him. That should have been warning enough. She was usually quite shy about exposing her body.

"So you have to know, huh? All right," she cried, "do you know what it's like to have a mother and a father who go to Mass every day? Do you know what it's like to have your father tell you to stop seeing that boy—David was his name—because he's Jewish and you're sixteen years old and you think you love him more than life itself? Do you know what it's like to find out one day that inside your belly, there's a baby, David's baby?"

She was beginning to sob now and he tried to stop her. "Look, forget it. I'm sorry." But it was too late.

"Oh, no! You wanted to know and now you're going to know. Can you imagine what it's like for a good little Catholic girl to think about telling that to her father on the way to Mass? So, of course, you don't. You can't. So what do you do? You sneak off to some sleaze doctor David's found because you're sure not going to some clinic where your father or your mother, who's a nurse, could find out, and you have yourself an abortion. You murder that baby inside of you that you've never seen, never will see!"

Her entire body was shaking. She covered her face with her hands. It was as if she weren't even talking to him anymore.

"You have committed the most mortal of sins and you're going to suffer the fires of Hell for all eternity. You pray for guidance. How can you redeem yourself? So you offer yourself to God in the hope that somehow He in His infinite mercy will forgive you. You enter a convent. And it takes years to discover that your motivation is wrong, that being driven endlessly by guilt isn't exactly the healthiest thing for God or for you, and that you have to get on with your life on your own terms."

Tears continued to stream down her face. She dropped her hands to her sides and stared at him.

"Come on," he said. "Aren't you being a little overdramatic? Not then. I mean now. Lots of women have abortions."

"You are truly some piece of work. I was stupid enough to want to have a baby with you and I'm scared to death I can't ever have another baby, period."

"Look, what I meant—"

She cut him off. Standing by the bed, naked, her face hardened. "You satisfied with your cross-examination, Mr. Prince of Darkness? Got everything you wanted? Well, fuck off. I'm out of here."

She began to dress.

He started to get off the bed.

"Don't move," she said. "Don't get near me. Don't even think about it."

Tom watched her storm out of the bedroom. He heard her footsteps in the hall and then the front door open. He braced himself for it to slam shut behind her. But it didn't. He heard her retracing her steps. She's coming back, he thought.

When she marched into the room, however, not even looking at him, she went straight to her SIG-Sauer lying on the dresser.

"Sorry," she snapped. "I forgot my gun."

The two-kilo seizure by Shannon's undercover agents and the arrest of three Gray Shadows had not escaped Deng's notice. That same night, after returning to the city with Tom, Deng dined in solitude in his apartment.

Completing his meal, he called for his faithful red pole, Chao Yu, to join him in a cup of Chiuchow tea.

Near midnight, Chao pushed aside the two newest recruits in the Gray Shadows standing guard at the gang's storefront club on East Broadway.

About a dozen members were inside. Some were sitting around a table playing thirteen-card poker. Others were watching a porn movie on a video recorder. Startled, they all looked at Chao.

He spotted the two who had been with Paul Fu at the Inner Peace restaurant. Both were at the card table. Chao jerked one of them out of his chair and hurled him against a wall. He drew his fighting chain from his hip pocket and whipped it across the boy's face. Blood poured from his smashed nose as he slid to the floor. Chao expertly brought the chain down on the boy's right leg just below the knee. There was an audible crack as the tibia parted.

The other Gray Shadow flung himself at Chao, trying to wrest away the chain. Chao threw him aside as if he were a minor nuisance and immediately delivered a vicious, roundhouse kick called a *liau ing tui* to his groin. As the boy doubled up helplessly, Chao proceeded to break both his arms with the chain.

Everyone else, paralyzed by fear and shock, froze in place. Chao gazed at each of them, one by one. He folded the lengths of steel that made up the chain and returned it to his pocket. The moans of his two victims mingled with the moans of fake ecstasy from a girl in the video.

"No more white powder," he said and walked out of the storefront.

The last thought anyone present had was to seek hospital assistance. That would bring the police. And, they were certain, a return visit from this monster who had suddenly appeared in their midst.

Finally, one of the gang, after taking a nervous gulp of cognac, peered outside to make sure Chao was gone and then ran to the home of Paul Fu and routed the elder of the Fujian Merchants Association out of bed. Fu listened to what had occurred and phoned a doctor who was a tong member.

When the doctor arrived at the scene, he injected morphine into the two boys to kill the pain. He dressed the lacerations on the face of the first one and set their broken limbs as best he could with temporary splints. They would have to get through the night, he said, and come to his office in the morning for further ministration.

Fu, of course, remained at home. Over the phone, the doctor reported the extent of the injuries he had treated. The tibia fracture was compound, he said. Jagged edges of bone had pierced the skin. The doctor doubted that the boy would ever be able to walk normally again.

"Ai!" Fu exclaimed. The next day, he sought out Benny Wong and recited the events of the previous night. "You must do something," he yelled at Wong.

27

AT HER PRIORITY SERVICE TELLER'S WINDOW in Citibank's Fifty-sixth Street and Broadway branch, Pam Erikson from Cleveland, Ohio, floated in euphoria.

It was her twentieth birthday. That morning Duncan Lau had given her a pair of gold earrings with little sapphires. In the evening he was taking her to a Broadway musical, the first she had ever seen. Afterward, they would have dinner at a famous restaurant, the 21 Club. If they could only see her in Cleveland now!

During her lunch break, she rushed off to Bergdorf Goodman and made the most extravagant purchases in her life, a blue satin dress that perfectly showed off the swell of her bosom. She also bought blue satin pumps to go with it. She laughed giddily as she surveyed herself, gaily swirling in front of a dressing-room mirror.

For the past month, Duncan had been totally occupied with his take-out restaurant and messenger service, and Pam had assumed responsibility for the cash deposits and wire transfers to Hong Kong. That morning he had also given her five envelopes, the amounts marked on them adding up to forty-four thousand dollars. There would be no more, Duncan told her. Competition had become so severe in the pirated video business, he said, that the people who employed him had decided to turn to other enterprises.

"Well, sweetheart, if they ever need you for anything else," she replied, "I'll handle it. It's no trouble."

She completed three deposits in the morning before buying the dress and shoes and then did the other two that afternoon. Since it was her birthday, Pam was allowed to leave early when the branch closed its doors at three p.m.

The plan was for her to meet Duncan at the theater. She went to a beauty salon to have her hair and nails done. Then she got on the subway to return to the Gramercy Park apartment to put on her new outfit.

On the subway, she daydreamed about the evening ahead. Determined to provide Duncan with the best sex he had ever had, she had purchased and carefully studied an illustrated book titled *A Hundred and One New Ways to Please a Man.*

Suddenly, she clapped a hand to her mouth. It dawned on her that she had just made a terrible mistake. In her haste to get out of the bank, she had made the final two deposits in the same account number, the one thing Duncan had always warned her about. It was too late to rectify the error. Should she tell him? *No!* She wasn't going to allow anything to spoil the night. Besides, she consoled herself, there must have been thousands of similar transactions, tens of thousands probably, throughout the bank's branches during the day.

Who would notice? she thought.

Pam's slips were reconciled, as were those of the other tellers. They were brought by messenger to Citibank's Manhattan operations center, where clerks separated and sorted them, along with all the slips from every other branch in the borough. The information was fed into computers designed to detect anomalies, including cash deposits of ten thousand dollars or more that had the same account number no matter how many branches were involved. It was an oversight a lot of people made trying to beat the system. Burt Richards, an assistant manager at the center, laughed about it all the time.

Around six p.m., Richards heard a bell ring. He walked over to a printer and watched it spew out Pam Erikson's last two cash deposits, amounting to seventeen thousand nine hundred dollars. Small potatoes, he thought. Maybe the CTR hadn't been properly executed. A CTR was a Currency Transaction Report that went to the IRS. Still, he dutifully transmitted the information to Citibank's internal security office across the East River in Long Island City.

In the morning, the first thing a security officer named Bob Cusack did was to check for the CTR. When he found there wasn't one, he requested copies of the actual deposit slips from the operations center to make sure there hadn't been a human error in the data that went into the computers. Then he punched up the account number and saw that, in the past month, there were three other deposits from the same branch, each under ten thousand dollars, amounting to twenty-seven thousand four hundred dollars. Sure he had something now, he continued to search back, looking for other activity in the account during the past year. He found thirteen more deposits, one at Broadway and Fifty-sixth Street, the rest at other branches.

Punching up additional information, Cusack not only saw the deposits, but the wire transfers to somewhere else in the worldwide Citibank network. To learn exactly where, he called the wire room.

"Hong Kong," he was told.

"Everything?"

"Yeah."

On Thursday morning, the day after Pam's birthday, Cusack labeled her deposit slips "suspicious transactions" and reported his findings to the chief of internal security, an ex-FBI supervisor named John Twomey. Going by the book, Twomey told Cusack to contact IRS. Then, out of his old loyalty to the FBI, he put in a call to Shannon O'Shea. "I don't know," he said, "but there might be something here for you."

Friday morning Shannon and Tony LaPerla from the IRS criminal division met with Twomey and Cusack. Shannon was glad to see that LaPerla was the IRS man on the job. They had worked together before and, like her, Tony was not into law-enforcement turf disputes. Getting the bad guys was the important thing.

"Do we know who any of the tellers are?" Shannon asked. "Could be they'll remember something."

"Yes," Cusack said. "And it's *a* teller, not tellers."

Every cash deposit slip was stamped with a teller identification number and Cusack had noticed right off that the two slips initially in question had the same ID stamp.

"Who is he?" LaPerla asked.

"It's a she," Cusack said. He had already obtained Pam's personnel file. "Erikson, Pamela. Born February twenty-eight, nineteen seventy-three. Cleveland, Ohio. Father a bus driver. Mother, a homemaker. High school graduate. One year in the billing department of the local Sears in Cleveland. Been here at Citibank almost three years. Recent address change, care of Duncan Lau, Nineteen East Nineteenth Street, Manhattan."

"Sounds Chinese," LaPerla said.

"That's what got me real interested," Cusack said. "When I pulled all her work for the month, guess what? Not only a total of five deposits in this account, but twenty-six more in other accounts. Same MO."

"What about Hong Kong?"

"The account that started the bells ringing," Twomey said, "is corporate. Opened up over there with a twenty-five-hundred-dollar deposit. The corporation, it seems, is fictitious. We're working on the other accounts, some are corporate, some personal. It'll take a while."

"What about Pam Erikson's own account?" LaPerla asked.

"Her current weekly take-home is three twenty-seven, fifty-one cents. Goes into her account automatically. No other deposits showing. Biggest expenditure for the past year was last Wednesday. Two purchases on her Citibank Visa at Bergdorf Goodman for seven hundred forty-nine and change. Fifty dollars a week in savings, like clockwork." Cusack smirked. "I guess Duncan's taking pretty good care of her."

"I think it's time for a little chat with her," Shannon said. "Any objections, fellows?"

"That's what we're here for," Twomey said. "To help."

Pam was in a funk.

Her birthday had been wonderful. But then, this very Friday morning, just like that, Duncan announced he would be away for the weekend. He was going to Atlantic City with his uncle, he said, without identifying who his uncle was. You really couldn't trust men, she thought—in Cleveland or New York. It sounded to her like this uncle was made up.

"Why can't I go, too?" she asked.

"It's a family affair," he said.

Family? she thought. So she wasn't family! Is that what Duncan was saying?

"He's Chinese," Duncan said, as if that explained everything.

"Go to hell, then!" she yelled, storming out of the apartment.

And now, at lunchtime on Friday, as Pam left the Citibank branch,

O'Shea and LaPerla stepped alongside her and identified themselves.

Oh, my God, she thought, feeling her stomach turn over. The FBI! The IRS! She knew it had to be about the deposits. How had they found out so soon? "What do you want?" she asked.

"We'd like to talk to you," Shannon said.

"But I have to be back at work in half an hour."

"Don't worry about it," LaPerla said. "It's been taken care of."

Taken care of, she thought. What did that mean? Had she lost her job? "Where are you taking me?" she asked, her voice quavering.

O'Shea and LaPerla had already decided that he would play the hard guy. So Shannon said, "How about your apartment, downtown?"

The suggestion comforted Pam. At least they weren't taking her to jail, or to some other terrible place. But she said, "It's really not my apartment."

"You live there, don't you?" LaPerla retorted.

"Yes."

"Then it's your apartment, too."

Yes, it is, she thought, thinking of all the things she had done to fix it up. In the car, Shannon asked, "Do you get back to Cleveland much?"

So they know that! she thought. What else do they know?

In the apartment, LaPerla said, "Where's your boyfriend?"

They know everything, she told herself. "He's in Atlantic City," she said. "For the weekend, he said."

Shannon said, "We'd like to talk about those two cash deposits to the same account you signed off on Wednesday."

On the way down to the apartment, in the car, Pam had already rehearsed her answer. "What deposits?" she said. "I can't remember all the deposits that people make everyday."

LaPerla, straddling a chair, leaned over the back of it toward Pam. "The same account for three other cash deposits last month with your teller's stamp on them. And twenty-six others you processed in other accounts." Locking eyes with her, he said, "When did you start dealing heroin?"

Pam felt her world start to crumble. "Heroin!" she cried. "I don't know anything about heroin. He said it was pirated video tapes."

"*He?*" Shannon said. "Who's he?"

"My boyfriend, Duncan Lau." She told them how she first met Duncan at the Madison Avenue bank branch and then later at Broadway and Fifty-sixth and had asked him what these cash deposits were all about, and how he had explained about the video tapes being pirated so that poor, hard-working Chinese could afford some entertainment.

"You telling us you bought that line?" LaPerla demanded.

"Yes," she said, sobbing now. "Why shouldn't I? I love him."

Shannon nodded at Tony and they went into the kitchen alcove. "I think she's telling the truth," Shannon said.

"I agree."

Returning, Shannon said, "Pam, do you do drugs?"

Pam Erikson, still sobbing, shook her head violently.

LaPerla searched the studio apartment, the bathroom, closets, the kitchen cupboards, her purse. He looked at Shannon. Nothing.

"You're in trouble, Pam," Shannon said. "Big trouble. You could go to prison for a long time. Even if you weren't involved in heroin, you've broken serious laws. But I think you've been used. Look, maybe your boyfriend was used, too. But you have to make a choice. You have the right to call a lawyer. I can't make any promises, but if you cooperate, Tony here and I will do our best for you. I must warn you, however, that you may even have to testify in court. Are you willing to do that?"

Through her tears, scared out of her wits, Pam mumbled, "Yes." In her whole life, she had never expected that anything like this would happen.

LaPerla went back into the kitchen. Shannon joined him. "We've got to find out where this goes," she said. She phoned Twomey. "John, we're with the girl. Looks like she's a pawn. We're going to hold her as a material witness and we have to ice her for a while. Got any ideas?"

Twomey instantly knew what Shannon was driving at. She wanted Citibank to pick up the tab to avoid screams from the bean counters at either the FBI or IRS. The unsaid quid pro quo was that Citibank would not suffer any unfavorable publicity. "They're installing a new computer system for Citibank Visa headquarters in Sioux Falls, South Dakota," Twomey said. "We're sending trainees there. How much ice do you have in mind?"

"A couple of weeks, minimum."

"You've got it."

Shannon gave Twomey the address and apartment number. "John," she said, "I know it's late in the day, but could you get a letter right over instructing her to leave immediately?"

When the letter arrived, Shannon had Pam tape it to the bathroom mirror along with a note that said "I wanted to call you, but I didn't know how to reach you."

"It's time to pack a bag," Shannon said.

"Take something real warm," LaPerla said. "It's a little chilly where you're going."

He flipped a coin. "Heads or tails?" Shannon lost, so an FBI agent drove Pam Erikson to the airport for a Northwest flight via Minneapolis. At the changeover in Minneapolis, another agent was on hand to ensure that she boarded a plane for Sioux Falls.

In New York, LaPerla said to O'Shea, "We lucked out with the girl. But what do we really have?"

"I'm not sure yet. But you can bet the farm it isn't pirated video tapes."

Shannon placed a surveillance on Duncan Lau when he returned from Atlantic City, his head still swimming with the grandeur of the experience. He and Uncle Pei had stayed at the Taj Mahal hotel and casino. "It is a reward for your most excellent work in completing the deposits," Uncle Pei said.

Their suite was magnificent, with separate rooms and baths that had huge sunken tubs and gold-plated fixtures. Duncan was amazed at the respect they received at the Taj Mahal. "It is because I am known as a high roller," his uncle explained.

On Saturday night, they enjoyed a sumptuous meal and then a floor show filled with gorgeous women, the sequins on their scanty costumes glittering in a sea of colored, shifting spotlights. After they retired for the evening, there was a knock on the door. Duncan opened it and found two beautiful young women standing outside, one blond, the other a brunette. Uncle Pei seemed amused at his evident astonishment. "The dark-haired one is for you," he said.

As Duncan unlocked the door to his apartment, he wondered if Pam was still in a snit. Well, he would make it up to her. She had to realize, though, that he had become a man of affairs. Then he saw the Citibank letter and her note. Why couldn't she have waited until he got back? he wondered. Then he decided it was her way of getting back at him. She would get over it.

Early Monday morning, he boarded a No. 7 subway for Queens. Uncle Pei had one more chore for him. He was to clean out the Jackson Heights apartment.

An agent observed him going into it. Duncan took down all the charts he had on the wall, cross-indexed for account numbers and bank branches, and stuffed them into a canvas bag, one that had held the last batch of cash. He dumped the bag in a sidewalk trash can and reboarded a train for Manhattan.

The bag with the charts was retrieved by a member of the surveillance team. Duncan was followed as he checked his various messenger-service clients. Late in the day, he took the subway to Chinatown and entered Uncle Pei's liquor store. He had neglected to give his uncle copies of the final round of deposit slips.

Uncle Pei scowled when he saw him and immediately led him into the back room, where he slapped Duncan across the face. "You fool," he shouted. "I instructed you never to come here."

The following day, after receiving the surveillance reports, Shannon O'Shea searched the computer files in vain for anything on a Peter Pei.

Near noon, she took the short walk over to the Fifth Precinct station house on Elizabeth Street, which covered Chinatown and what was left of Little Italy. On the way, she passed Pei's liquor store near the corner of Mott and Pell. She hadn't noticed it before. As a matter of fact, she hadn't noticed any retail liquor stores in Chinatown. And then she did remember there was another one on the Bowery.

The station house, built in 1880, was one of the oldest in the city. It was on a block lined with tenements of the same vintage. Shannon spoke to a beefy desk sergeant named Dowd, who looked as battered as his surroundings.

Dowd couldn't hide his surprise when she showed him her shield.

"They take all kinds these days, don't they?" she gibed.

"You said it, not me," Dowd huffed, face reddening.

"Ever run across a Chinese named Peter Pei? Has a liquor store down on Mott."

"Yeah, why?"

"It's nothing, really. His name came up in an investigation we're doing that maybe he could help on. I just wanted to check out his reliability."

"Listen, if everybody in Chinatown was like him, we wouldn't have no trouble, believe me."

"Is that so?"

"In the big war, he even volunteered. You go into his store, there's his honorable discharge, framed and everything. Not like them other new Chinks rolling in, you never know what they're thinking."

"How long have you known him?"

"Ever since I been here."

"How long's that?"

"Better than eleven years now."

"That's pretty long to be in one precinct."

"Yeah, well, you know, I started out as a beat cop and I picked up some speakee Chinee. So they kept me here. I got some good lines into the community. I need to know something about something, I drop in on Peter Pei, for sure."

I'll bet, especially around Christmas time, Shannon thought. "Well, thanks a lot, sergeant," she said, "you've been very helpful."

"Say, you mind telling me," Dowd said, "how did you end up in the FBI?"

"It's a long story," Shannon said.

Her problem was whom to continue surveilling, Duncan Lau or Pei? There was nothing definite enough to justify an additional manpower request. Not a speck of heroin so far. No deal in the offing.

And then her problem was resolved.

The phone call came that afternoon.

"Missy Dragon Lady?" a voice said in English.

"Yes."

The voice switched to Cantonese. It had an urgent tone. "I must see you. Important information."

"Who is this?"

"You will learn."

"When?"

"I meet you today. Four o'clock Staten Island ferry. You come alone."

Not bad, Shannon thought. Good public place for a private meeting.

Plenty of time to see who else might be skulking around.

At a quarter to four, she stood to one side as the first wave of homeward-bound commuters gathered at the ferry slip gates, headed for the city's outer borough.

Then she saw him, the only Chinese face in sight. Mr. Chinatown himself, Benny Wong. There was no mistake. He was looking directly at her from his vantage point on the far side of the crowd.

When she boarded the ferry, she stayed back on the glass-enclosed deck while most the passengers moved forward. March winds whipped up whitecaps in New York's Upper Bay.

Five minutes elapsed before Wong sidled alongside her.

He had thought long and hard about calling this FBI woman and even more about what to say to her. But after Paul Tu had come to him about the havoc Deng's man had wrought on the Gray Shadows, the delicate balance of power that had prevailed for so long in Chinatown was clearly being undermined.

But he dared not utter Deng's name. The mere thought of that, and the retribution it could bring, had driven him instantly to two steaming cups of ginseng tonic to quell the uproar in his stomach. Nor could he say anything that would cause him to be a witness, or that could be traced back to him. No, he would simply be a tipster, as the *kwai lo* called it. He would show the way and then remove himself from the picture.

As the ferry passed the Statue of Liberty, Wong said, "How inspiring! A cry of succor to the downtrodden of the world."

"Yes," said Shannon, gazing out the window.

"A light that offers refuge to my people as well, although there was a time when this was not so."

"Yes," Shannon repeated.

Silence ensued. Then Wong sighed. "There is much unrest in Chinatown," he said.

She nodded gravely, twice, as if recognizing the profundity of his words.

"I think it is because of the white powder."

Now we're getting somewhere, Shannon thought.

"There are whispers about a man in Chinatown who is said to engage in it."

"A man?"

"Yes. His name is Peter Pei. I know nothing personally," Wong hastily added. "I have only heard it. I have heard he imports white powder in sets of mahjong. He has a business called Swatow Trading."

Trying to encourage him to reveal more, she said, "We also have heard of him. What else can you tell me?"

Wong was elated. So they knew about Pei! He could honestly say he had nothing to do with this. Thank the celestial gods that he had come forward, however. This Dragon Lady had seen him with Pei at the Inner Peace establishment. Had she been trying to trick him? *Ai!* You had to be so careful. "No," he told Shannon. "I have said everything I have heard."

He moved quickly away to the opposite side of the ferry. They remained apart for the return trip and she watched him scurry off ahead of her.

At eight o'clock the next night, Peter Pei walked up Mott to Canal Street, turned west and waited at the northeast corner of Lafayette.

A Lincoln Town Car pulled up to the curb and Pei got in. "Good evening, Mr. Lucano," he said, and then, glancing around, asked, "Where is Mr. Funzie?"

"He's got the flu, or something." Big Frank shifted in his seat. "I could get up there on my own, you know. You don't have to hold my hand."

"It's Mr. Deng's desire, sir, that I escort you. To show proper respect."

At the apartment building on Central Park South, Lucano and Pei got out. About twenty minutes later, Pei exited the building alone and hailed a cab.

The two FBI agents in the surveillance car didn't quite know what to do. But their orders were to trail Pei, so they followed the cab back to his residence in Chinatown on Bayard Street.

About then, Shannon O'Shea returned to her own apartment. Leaning against her door was a big bouquet of long-stemmed red roses. There was a note from the super. "I signed for these," it said. Shannon reminded herself to tip him.

Inside the bouquet was another note. From Tom. It simply said, "Please!"

Her heart melted. She was about to phone him when her beeper went off. When she called back, one of the surveillance agents, Don Flagg, was on the line.

"We just signed off on Pei," he said. "But that's not why I'm calling. About eight p.m., he got picked up by car downtown and got out on Central Park South. Guess who got out with him? Frank Lucano. *The* Frank Lucano. Big Frank himself."

"You're kidding."

"I'm not. They went into an apartment house. Billy Holzman talked to the guy at the desk. He said they went up to the apartment of another Chinaman, a Y. K. Deng."

"*Who?*"

"Deng, D-e-n-g. Like I said, initials Y. K."

Shannon felt a rush of adrenaline. "Then what?"

"Then Pei came out. By himself. So we tailed him. That's the drill, isn't it? He went home. You want us to go back up and see what's with Lucano?"

"No, that's it. Go home yourselves. Great work."

She had to think. There was no way she could call Tom now. Suddenly, they were on opposite sides of a big fence.

In bed, she tossed restlessly, trying to grasp a thought that eluded her. In the morning, over coffee, it came to her.

In the office, she pulled the clips on the Villa Mia shooting and read how the death of Alphonse Carparti left Big Frank Lucano as Cosa Nostra's reputed number one in the city. Then she found the names of the two Chinese residents of Hong Kong who were the ostensible targets of the attack. Lee Hei and Tam Tso-lin.

She tried regional Customs at the World Trade Center first and held for a computer check.

"Yeah, we have them coming in December twenty-six. JFK. United from Hong Kong."

"Anything more?"

"That'll take time. I have to check the paperwork downstairs in the archives."

That afternoon she was told that both Lee and Tam were "red pens" marked "IA." The red ink signaled VIP. "IA." meant immediate attention.

Shannon drove out to JFK. In Customs, she asked, "Anyone around who was on duty the day after Christmas?"

"Mike Larkin, over there."

Sure, Larkin said, he remembered them. Party of nine.

"How come you remember them so well?"

"The question is how could I forget."

Then he told Shannon how the top guy in the group, a guy named Deng, had been met at baggage claims by a CIA spook. He had even mentioned it to his wife that night, Larkin said.

Deng and Lucano! *And the CIA.* Then she remembered the notation she had received from the Hong Kong police that Deng had been seen in the company of a man believed to be the new local station chief.

Oh, boy, Tom, Shannon thought.

28

W HEN PEI WAS SPOTTED with Lucano, it had been Big Frank's third visit to Deng's apartment.

After their initial wariness, the two men had become quite fond of one another. And despite the apparent gulf between them in custom and language and culture, they had discovered that they shared much in common.

They had even laughed about it once. Deng said it first. After all, he had observed, it was an Italian, Marco Polo, who first opened China to the West.

"Yeah," Lucano replied. "I guess he saw something nobody else did."

Big Frank never inquired into the details of the Carparti hit. He was still shaken, though, about what he knew had to have happened. All he said was, "You took care of that fuck pretty good," and Deng said only, "You do what you have to do."

But he had thanked Deng directly for setting up and controlling an artificial competitiveness in garment center trucking. He could still see the prosecutor's red face when his lawyer, Koenigsberger, pointed out that Chinese manufacturers were starting to use truckers of their own, who charged less.

"And you're telling me you're letting them get away with it?"

"Hey, it's free enterprise, right?" Lucano had said. "My people are union. So I got to find a way to meet the price, is all. Offer better quality service, like AT&T."

And he owed Deng something else. Although it was too personal a subject to bring up, with Carparti out of the way, he could at last return safely to the pleasurable company of his manicurist mistress, Miriam Feinstein.

This Deng, Lucano thought, reminded him of what he had heard about the founder of Cosa Nostra in America, the Sicilian Salvatore Maranzano, a student of Julius Caesar, who had negotiated a truce between Sicilians, Neapolitans and Calabrians and unified them, structuring them into an underworld army that for decades had controlled organized crime. Of course, Maranzano, as smart as he was, was too rigid, had wanted to retain too much power, wouldn't adapt to new times, and in the end got knocked off by Charlie Lucky Luciano, Vito Genovese and the others.

"From what Funzie tells me," Lucano said, "your outfit goes way back."

"Yes, many centuries," Deng said, and he told Lucano some of the history of the *Hung* brotherhood, and how it was formed to fight the Manchu invaders and then the Communists. But how it learned that it had to protect its own interests as well.

"Hey, that's the way it was with us in the old country," Lucano said. His father had told him. Wave after wave of cruel invaders. His father told him how the Mafia sprang up to defend the people. Mafia meant place of refuge, his father said.

"So Cosa Nostra is what?"

"It's, like, Americanized. *Our Thing.* It's the same old story. We got to look out for ourselves."

But what, Deng wanted to know, had caused Cosa Nostra's recent decline?

"Greed," Lucano said. "They forgot the old ways. Like that cocksucker Carparti, strutting around like some fucking peacock, not leaving well enough alone, not staying in the shadows." Lucano's features darkened. "And also them ratfink canaries. For fifty, whatever, years, it was: 'Is there or ain't there a Mafia?' Even the FBI said there wasn't no Mafia here. Well, they was right. It was Cosa Nostra. But that rat Joe Valachi took care of that, giving out the right name, spilling his guts about the initiation and everything. It was like that English guy that broke the four-minute mile. For a hundred years, they're trying to break the four-minute mile and then this Limey comes along and done it and before you know it, everybody else is doing it. They turned so many rats after Joe Valachi, they had to invent the Witness Protection Program, which like my brother Father Paul, God rest his soul, said was really a big literary agency. As soon as some two-bit button man ratted, he got an agent and the next thing you know he was out peddling his story and the public was lapping it up. And that got the Feds going and they passed all them new racketeering laws and that's where we are today."

Recapitulating this depressing turn of events, Lucano had begun pacing in tight little circles. "How come you people don't have them headaches?" he asked.

"The *Hung* brotherhood is not a secret, you see, yet it is," Deng said. "Our people know it is there and yet they do not know. That is our strength."

"And you don't have no wars, like, between families?"

"No, we divide our interests equitably."

"Maybe we should have took a leaf out of your book," Big Frank said. "Of course," he added defensively, "you're talking about how it is over there. Over here, it could be different."

And now, that night, after Peter Pei departed and was followed home by Shannon's surveillance team, Deng said to Lucano, "You appear disgruntled, my friend. Is something troubling you?"

"Ah, it ain't nothing. It's my kid, the boy, if you want to know. He's worse than useless. Spoiled rotten by his mother. Throws his weight around, only it's my weight he's throwing. I set him up in business and I got to bring in people to run it for him. Dances and screws around all night and sleeps all day. I'd toss him out in a second, if it wasn't for my old lady. You got kids?"

"I have a daughter, yes."

"These kids, they give you a heartache. They don't know what you go through to give them a life. I suppose you guys don't have to worry about that."

Deng felt the anger course through him at the thought of Li-po. So he was not alone. But he simply observed, "Children can be troublesome." It was important to maintain the superior position that he had achieved with Lucano.

"So what do you do about it?" Lucano pressed him.

"You must be stern. You must maintain your position. We have a saying. A father must protect his assets."

"Yeah, you're right. I think I'll lay down the law with the kid. Teach him what's what."

The two crime chieftains brooded silently about the burdens of parenthood. Finally, Lucano said, "When's the junk coming in?"

"Soon. Very soon. Everything is in preparation."

"I let the word go out already. On junk, everybody's on their own. The death penalty for dealing is off. It didn't work, anyway, is why. But personally, I'm against it, I'm saying."

Big Frank was not the only one with questions about the details of the shooting at the Villa Mia restaurant.

In Hong Kong, Stanley Chow read the local press accounts. Their focus was not on the demise of Alphonse Carparti, but on the violent fate of Lee and Tam.

Both were identified as employees of a reputable Kowloon accounting firm. A spokesman for the firm was quoted as saying that the two men were in New York to help with real estate investments for a client whose identity, as with all the firm's clients, was confidential. He was at a loss to explain what happened to them. He declared, however, that New York was widely known as a most dangerous place for visitors and further questioned whether the gunmen were, in fact, Chinese as the police insisted. The American police, he said, overwhelmed with street crime, constantly tried to cover up their inability to cope with it by blaming such unfortunate incidents on foreigners. In this regard, the bias against Asians and so-called Asian crime was especially blatant.

Chow knew that the firm was secretly owned by Deng and that the two accountants were most certainly members of the Righteous and Peaceful Society. What madness was Deng up to in New York? he wondered. But to inquire directly would entail too great a loss of face.

Just keep me apprised, he had said. Perhaps he should have kept closer watch on Deng. So far, all he knew was that the laboratories in Laos were in full production and that Deng had arranged safe passage for the shipment across the mainland's southern provinces. He knew, too, what his dockworkers were to do once it reached Hong Kong. The scheme, Chow had to admit, was brilliant. What rankled was that as a result, Deng would enjoy even greater prestige among the dragon heads.

Chow sent a message by courier to Unicorn Frankie Chin to gather every particle of information, every rumor, concerning Deng's activities. And to be prepared to come to Hong Kong.

29

L<small>I-PO HAD SPENT</small> most of the gray March day in the library.

In the afternoon, as she was about to turn into her block, she heard Beverly Soo shouting, "Stop, wait!" And then Beverly, breathless, was saying, "Don't go home. They're there, looking for you."

"*Who?* What are you talking about?"

"The Immigration men."

"The *what?*"

"I was in the administration building when they were asking where you lived. They said your papers weren't in order. I didn't get all of it. One of them started looking kind of funny at *me,* so I didn't hang around. But it's, like, you're here illegally. Or something."

"That's ridiculous."

"I know it is. I'm only telling you what I heard."

She and Beverly peeked around the corner.

Two cars were double-parked in front of her house. Two men were standing on the sidewalk. And then two other men came out of the house with Auntie Mei between them. She was carrying a suitcase. Li-po watched them put her in one of the cars and drive away.

The other two men remained stationed outside her house, blowing on their hands and stamping their feet.

Suddenly, Li-po began shivering.

"We better get over to Robert's," Beverly said. "He'll know what to do."

"Suppose they're there, too?"

"I'll go first and make sure the coast is clear."

Li-po felt helpless, cowering behind a tree while Beverly went up to

Robert's off-campus garden apartment. At least here there were no dou-ble-parked cars or strange men in sight.

A minute later, she saw Robert with Beverly beckoning her. She threw herself in his arms. Inside, sobbing inconsolably, she cried, "It's my father. I know it. He's having me deported."

"Li-po," Robert said, "this isn't China. There must be some mistake. We'll get it straightened out."

"No, you still don't understand how powerful my father is. He gets his way no matter what. I have displeased him and he is punishing me." Her tears came again. "I didn't mean to bring you such trouble."

The doorbell rang.

Beverly peered out the window. "It's the same men who were at Li-po's house."

"Get in the bedroom," Logan said. "The two of you."

When he opened the door, one of the men said, "Professor Logan?"

"What can I do for you?"

"Harry Johnson. Immigration and Naturalization. We understand that you have, uh, a close relationship with a student, a Li-po Deng."

"What's that supposed to mean?"

"Look, *Professor,* I'm not here to debate the finer points. We are look-ing for Li-po Deng and we have reason to believe you may know where she is. Like maybe she's here. Is she? If we have to, we can get a warrant."

"No, she isn't and, no, you can't come in. I'm in the middle of a re-search project and I've got papers all over the place that I don't want dis-turbed. What the hell's this about, anyway?"

"Li-po Deng's student visa's been revoked. Moral turpitude." Johnson grinned, a man-to-man leer. "You wouldn't know about that, now would you?"

"No, actually I wouldn't."

"You know," said Johnson, still leering, "I read a lot these days about how horny professors are seducing young female college students. I can see another story now on the front page of the *Times.* Just what Yale needs."

"Nice meeting you. Go get your warrant," Robert Logan said, slam-ming the door.

Beverly scurried to the window again. "They're standing on the side-walk, talking. Oh, they're getting in the car. And driving off, I think. I can't see that far down the block."

"Forgive me, Robert, I'm so sorry," Li-po whispered.

"For what?"

Her face ashen, she started to sway. He caught her and helped her to a sofa. He told Beverly, "There's a bottle of bourbon in the kitchen cupboard to the left of the sink. Bring it and a glass."

He made Li-po take a sip. And another. She started to cough. Some color returned to her face. "Ugh!" she said.

"Kentucky medicine," he said. "Cures all."

Beverly had a glass in her hand. "Give me the bottle," she said. "I think I could use a little medicine myself. God, what'll we do? They're sure to be back."

"Maybe we could call that lawyer, Tom MacLean," Li-po said. "I liked him. He said that if I ever needed anything I should contact him."

"No way," Logan said. "Remember. He's your father's lawyer."

Li-po buried her face in her hands. She started shaking again.

Logan was holding her, stroking her hair. "Listen to me. What we're going to do is get out of here fast." He removed her hands from her face and looked into her eyes. "And then we're going to get married. Let's see what Immigration does with that. And your wonderful father. Christ almighty! Moral turpitude. Can you believe it?"

"Robert, I can't ask you to do something like that, not this way."

"You're not asking. *I am!* Will you? Will you marry me?"

She managed a smile through her tears. She clung to him. "I love you," she said. She said it over and over.

They left by the back door, through the garden and along an alley to the next street. They waited outside Beverly's dorm while she went in to pack some things for Li-po and herself. And they drove with Beverly to La Guardia Airport, where Logan phoned his parents that they were coming to Kentucky.

Two days later, they were married in the Presbyterian church where Robert had been christened. The same minister officiated. Beverly was Li-po's maid of honor. Both of Robert Logan's brothers wanted to be best man, and both were.

At the wedding lunch in the Logan home, Robert's father, champagne glass in hand, rose to give a toast. "I'm not real good at words," he said. "I'd just like to say how pleased we all are to welcome Li-po into our family."

She burst into tears.

The old man appeared taken aback.

"Forgive me," Li-po said softly. "I am so happy. For we who are Chinese, nothing is more important than family."

30

In New York, Shannon O'Shea was on the phone again to Washington, speaking with FBI liaison to the CIA.

"What do you mean, they don't have anything on Deng?"

"I didn't say that. I said they said their initial file search didn't show anything. They'll keep looking. They've got a lot of different files for security."

"That's baloney."

"What do you suggest? A search and seizure at Langley? This happens all the time over there. They're not exactly our pals."

She hung up. Another blind alley.

Continued surveillance of Peter Pei had proved fruitless. He had been seen twice in Deng's company for dinner at the Inner Peace restaurant, but there had been no Lucano in attendance. And no Duncan Lau.

Shannon arranged a monitored phone call to Duncan from Pam Erikson in Sioux Falls. It ended up in a lovers' quarrel. "Why didn't you let me know you were going away?" Lau demanded and Pam said, "I would have, if I knew how to reach you and *your uncle*."

"When are you coming back?"

"When they let me."

Shannon could, of course, bring in Lau, but to do so ran the risk of tipping off Pei, and she wasn't prepared to take that step yet. She considered bugging Deng, but it would require a court order, which was getting tougher and tougher to get authorized, and the plain fact was that she still did not have sufficient justification. And even if she managed to obtain a court order, there would be a translation problem. The probability was high that the key conversations would be in Chinese. Cantonese or Mandarin presented no difficulty. But Chiuchow? She couldn't think of a single translator currently available to the FBI fluent in the dialect.

Finally, she called Tom.

"Listen," he said, "I can't tell you how bad I feel about what I—"

She cut him off. "It's OK. Let's put it behind us. You were out of line and I went overboard. We're both to blame, so let's promise ourselves not to let something like that ever happen again."

"I miss you," he said.

She hesitated, trying to find the right words. "Tom, something's come up that I have to see you about."

"What?"

"I'd rather talk about it in person."

"Great. I've got Knicks tickets tonight."

"That's not quite the setting I had in mind."

"This must be serious."

"It is."

"Don't tell me you're seeing someone else."

"Oh, God, no, Tom. It's nothing like that."

They met at a restaurant downtown, west of Soho, called Allison's on Dominick Street. It was Tom's choice. The food was superb and it had a wonderfully romantic aura, a rendezvous for lovers.

Shannon looked as adorable as ever, but when Tom hugged her, he could feel her tenseness. And then he saw the bluish smudges of stress under her eyes. Had she been as tormented by their separation as he? Well, he thought, they were together again. That was what counted.

"New York water," she said when the waiter came for their drink order.

"What's that, a new brand?"

"No," she said, smiling faintly, "it's what comes right out of the tap and doesn't leave a hangover."

"I'll have the same," he said.

Still smiling, she clinked glasses with him, and then he saw her frown and her jaw set.

"Tom," she said, "like the song goes, we got trouble, right here in River City."

"We?"

She began with Pam Erikson's two telltale deposit slips. And explained how Duncan Lau led them to the Jackson Heights apartment with the charts showing all the cross-indexed accounts and bank branches. "It's obviously a heroin money-laundering scheme," she said. She told him how Lau next led them to Pei. And how Pei was then seen with the boss of the Lucano crime family. "Guess who they were visiting?" She paused for dramatic effect. "Your client. Mr. Y. K. Deng."

"So."

"What do you mean, *so?*"

"Just that. How do you know heroin's involved?"

"I have a CI that says Pei's been smuggling heroin into the country in mahjong sets."

"Why not arrest Pei?"

"I don't want to blow this investigation. I think we've located the tip of an awesome iceberg here. I can smell it. I mean, how does a supposedly reputable Hong Kong tycoon suddenly get cozy with someone like Big Frank Lucano?"

"I don't know. There could be all sorts of reasons."

"Come off it! Stop being a defense attorney."

"What do you want me to do? Advise my client that the FBI's informed me he's been seen with an alleged Chinese drug dealer and a Cosa Nostra godfather?"

"You wouldn't dare!"

"Wouldn't I? You want me to recite the Canons of Ethics? A lawyer's duty is to counsel and assist a client in protecting and furthering his interests. Do I have to remind you that my last case as a prosecutor was putting away a lawyer who did just the opposite?"

"Look," Shannon said, irritated, "we're talking heroin here, not bilking some insurance company. We are talking about hundreds of thousands of ruined lives, maybe millions before it's over. Kids, husbands, mothers. What about a lawyer's responsibility to them?"

"Give me a break. Short of aiding and abetting his client in the commission of a crime, a lawyer's client comes first."

"Maybe you're aiding and abetting him without knowing it. Tom, you want to know what I want? I want to know what he's doing. What he's got you working on. Maybe somewhere in it is the answer. What he's up to."

"Shannon, there's a classic case they teach in law school involving a leasing company. It was called OPM. Which actually stood for 'Other People's Money.' And that's exactly what the company was using in a massive fraud to get big bank loans with phony leasing contracts as collateral.

Its law firm got suspicious. The question was whether suspicions were enough for the firm to inform a third party like, say, the Securities and Exchange Commission. Or did it have to know for certain that its client was breaking the law?"

"And?"

"The firm brought in a distinguished law professor as outside counsel who advised that the most the firm could do was to withdraw its representation, period."

"That's protecting the public? No wonder lawyers are so beloved."

"Look, Shannon, whether you like it or not, we're a nation of laws and we have to abide by the rules. If I had a client who told me he'd just sunk an ax in somebody's head, there's nothing I could do. I'm bound by client/lawyer confidentiality. Like a priest in a confessional. I can only act if I know ahead of time for sure that my client's intending to commit a crime that could cause imminent death or substantial bodily harm and that I can prevent it."

They glared at each other, their dinner untouched on the plates between them.

"If you were still a prosecutor, you wouldn't be saying this."

"Yeah, well, I'm not. I love you, but you're a cop. What you're asking me to do is professionally and morally wrong. You want me to give up everything I believe in. It strikes right at the heart of our legal system, which may not be perfect, but it's all we have. And since you brought it up, if I were still a prosecutor, I wouldn't even go to a judge for a wiretap because he'd turn me down flat. All you've got is a bunch of hypotheticals you're trying to fit into some preconceived theory you've worked out. You keep talking about heroin. Where is it? From day one, you've been on me about Deng. But suppose I decided you were right. All I could do is tell Deng I can't represent him anymore. I'd also owe him an explanation."

"I know I'm right," Shannon said. "And I'm going to keep on this. I have to."

"There's nothing I can do about that."

"Under the circumstances, then maybe we better not see each other until it's resolved. I mean," she said acidly, "I wouldn't want to overhear anything you might say in your sleep."

Tom remembered thinking earlier that, after this evening, everything would be right between them. "It's your call," he said.

"There's one other interesting item about your client," she said. "When I sent you those clips on him, I didn't include a Hong Kong police intelligence report that he'd been seen with the CIA's local station chief. And when he arrived at JFK, guess who was on hand to meet him? Someone from Langley. I did a little research. Do you know one of the things the CIA was doing during the war in Vietnam? Keeping the hill tribes on our side by helping to market their big cash crop, heroin number four. In Laos. Be funny if Deng was in Laos, too, wouldn't it?"

"Did you check with the CIA?"

"Of course. Stop the presses! They claim there's nothing there." She stood up. "Well, maybe when all this is over, we can see each other again. Like I told you once," she said, "it's tough being female and an FBI agent." Then she walked out.

Tom sat aghast. He might as well have been kicked in the stomach with the news Shannon had unwittingly imparted. My God, he thought, was it possible? Deng. Heroin. The CIA. Laos. *My father?* No! It couldn't be.

The waiter came over. "Will that be all?"

"Give me a Macallan's on the rocks," he said. "Make it a double."

In the morning, at Needham & Lewis, Tom tried to focus on the legal paperwork for Deng.

There was the mortgage for the Manhattan tower Deng wanted to buy. There were also the tax implications of transferring Deng's properties in Hong Kong to a U.S. holding company. It was the same for his shipping interests, five medium-size freighters owned outright and five more under long-term lease. Find the most advantageous foreign flag for them to sail under, Deng had said. And there were also the preliminary steps that had to be taken for an eventual private placement of a minority interest in the Chow Chow restaurant chain to American investors.

At least, Tom had closed on the one acquisition Deng has been hounding him about—a warehouse north of the city in the Rockland County town of Suffern. It was needed, Deng said, to store all the special kitchen equipment that had to be imported and, later, for use as a regional service center. When Tom argued that the purchase might be premature, Deng retorted that the price would never be better. In the boom of the 1980s, the area had been overbuilt and was now in a severely depressed state that wasn't going to last forever. Besides, said Deng, the location was ideal, right by a web of interstate highways.

Around four p.m., Tom couldn't stand it any longer. And it was not the paperwork. Suppose Shannon was right in what she said about Deng?

Twenty minutes later, he confronted Deng in his apartment. "We have a problem. As you know, I was a government prosecutor before joining Needham & Lewis."

"Of course," Deng replied. "That is why I was so pleased to have someone like you to counsel me on the correctness of my endeavors."

"Sir, a federal agent informs me that you've been seen meeting recently with a notorious Mafia boss named Frank Lucano."

To Tom's astonishment, Deng didn't blink an eye. "That is so," he said. "Have I broken some law?"

"No. But it's raised a lot of eyebrows. Which was why I was told about it. What's going on?"

"Thank you for your concern. But you will recall that when I first met with you and Mr. Needham, I expressed an interest in casino gambling and Mr. Needham advised that I would encounter much trouble with this Mafia. We Chinese believe in *guangxi,* what you call connections, and so I thought it prudent to speak directly with Mr. Frank Lucano to ascertain what these troubles might be and to determine how they might be avoided."

Pretty good, Tom thought. And it could be true. "Mr. Deng, that's not the point," he said. "During that first meeting we had, you'll also recall that I made it clear that, to do my job, I had to be consulted about any business decisions you were contemplating. Apparently, that's not your style. So I suggest that it might be better all around if you retain another attorney to represent you."

Tom was barely back in his office when Needham stormed in. For once, the managing partner got right to it. "Have you gone bonkers? I just got a call from Deng. Very upset. He says you think he's in bed with the Mafia, for God's sake! He explained what it was all about and, for my money, he made perfectly good sense. He's used to doing things his way. Appreciates your concern. Values you. Says it won't happen again. What more do you want? I expect you to finish up what you've been doing for him. You're so big on legal ethics, so honor your commitments. To him. And to the firm."

Tom looked hard at Needham. "If he steps off the reservation one more time . . ."

"Don't worry," Needham broke in. "Son, take it from me. From now on, he won't be doing anything on his own. Thanks to you, he's learned his lesson."

31

In Bangkok, following instructions from Deng to check on the refinement process, Ho Shu-shui boarded a plane for the hour-long flight to Chiang Mai. And in a car driven by an adjutant of General Li's, he continued north, passing an endless expanse of rice paddies. At a village on the Laotian border, they were ferried across the Mekong River by shallow-draft boat into Laos. Ho climbed into a waiting Toyota land cruiser and was driven along a dirt road through jungle vegetation so dense that the sky was only occasionally glimpsed. Gradually, the road began to wind upward. Saw-toothed ridges and deep, narrow valleys appeared through openings in the branches and vines that slapped at the land cruiser. Three times they were halted at outposts manned by General Li's troops. The air became distinctly crisper and cooler. Ho saw the first slashed hillsides, indicating an elevation of at least three thousand feet, where the poppy that produced China white—it was called the Yunnan poppy—flourished.

General Li's headquarters was located in a high valley traversed by a clear mountain stream. Ho entered through a massive teak archway with a carved sunburst painted white, the standard of Chiang Kai-shek's old China. The sturdy wood houses topped with tin roofs in which the general's troops and their families lived had an air of permanence. They were laid out in a grid pattern, all quite immaculate compared to the scruffy Thai towns that Ho had traveled through the day before. There was a reflecting pool with lily pads, a field for games and military drills, even a children's playground complete with swings. Generators supplied power for running water and electricity.

The general's personal quarters, shaded by giant banyan and teak trees, sat on the slope of a hill. While it had none of the opulence of his Bangkok residence, it was quite comfortable, resembling the hunting or fishing lodge of a wealthy sportsman. Li's eyes actually twinkled when he greeted Ho. Production quotas were being met, almost two hundred units daily, which pleased the general as much as the successful interdiction of Shan Wa's heroin pipeline. "He doesn't know yet," Li observed, "but he's already being eaten alive by my dogs." After dinner, he showed Ho to a guest house, where a young woman soon appeared.

In the morning, Ho toured the laboratories in an adjacent valley. Each of them, four in all, was about a hundred feet long and thirty wide, divided into two sections, the first to convert the opium into morphine base and the second to refine the base into heroin number four. The laboratories were enclosed by fences of bamboo slats lashed together. They were roofless to allow the noxious fumes to escape. It never ceased to amaze Ho how the seemingly primitive, jerry-built tangle of tubing, of suction pumps, flasks, stainless steel drums, reflux condensers, funnels, filters and charcoal-fed fires could produce such miraculous results.

After the conversion of the opium to morphine base, it was combined with an equal amount of acetic anhydride. The mix was then heated at exactly one hundred and eighty-five degrees Fahrenheit, which was the stage that caused the foulest odors, usually lasting some six hours. This produced heroin in an impure form. Next, other substances were added, including sodium carbonate and chloroform. The final stage, the introduction of highly volatile ether, presented the most danger. A single windblown spark from one of the charcoal fires could set off the ether, destroying the laboratory and killing everyone in it. "We have been most fortunate," General Li said. "The order will be complete before week's end. The trucks carrying the teak logs beneath which it will be hidden are already here."

Gratified by what he had witnessed, Ho gave Li the code word to be used at a Bangkok finance shop, one of the outlets of the Chiuchow underground banking system, where a first payment of two million American dollars in either gold or currency awaited his pleasure.

After returning to Bangkok, Ho faxed Deng in New York, "Our forecasts are being met. The time draws near."

Then Ho flew to Hong Kong to brief Stanley Chow personally in his Kowloon office overlooking the container port.

"Wonderful," said Chow.

Within an hour after Ho's departure, Chow had another, entirely unexpected visitor. He was a Hakka clansman and deputy minister in Red China's Ministry of Public Security, which included the secret police.

"My minister conveys warm greetings," he said in the Hakka dialect, attempting to quickly establish a special bond.

"Really?" Chow replied, barely able to conceal his amazement. "I am honored. What prompts such a gracious sentiment?"

"First, naturally, is the recognition of your exalted status in the Glorious Together Association."

Ah, Chow thought, as he suspected, Beijing, or at least the Ministry of Public Security, knew precisely who the dragon heads were.

"Second, many changes will be occurring in Hong Kong. The minister envisions much of mutual interest—and benefit."

"Please continue. As is often said of me, I'm all ears."

"There are already many changes in the Central Country. While the Soviet Union lies in ruins, we have embarked on our own road. The Ministry of Public Security now owns and operates the most modern Western-style hotel in Shanghai. It has an employment service to provide personnel for barbarian corporations wishing to do business in the Central Country. In Shenzhen, it has recently formed its own export/import company. We call it 'Socialism with Chinese characteristics.' We are the way to the future."

No, thought Chow, you are mistaken. It is the way of the past, the ancient passion of the Han race to make money.

The deputy minister pressed his fingertips lightly together. "In the coming absorption of Hong Kong, my minister anticipates many additional areas of profit from an association with a man of your experience. As the minister has wisely said, 'The best way to prevent our socialism from becoming capitalism is precisely to import capitalistic expertise.' "

Chow said, "I thought Beijing regarded our societies as criminal."

"My minister says not all societies. Unlike your colleague Deng Yuekeung, you are not only at heart patriotic, but pragmatic. Deng is a zealot. We have evidence that he has for many years been a lackey of the American spy service. You have never done that."

Stanley Chow was impressed. So they seemed to know all about Deng as well. "Yes, that's true. I've always said fuck the Americans. But what does your minister want of me?"

"He would like a meeting."

"Where?"

"If he came to Hong Kong, it would attract undue attention. He suggests a private place in Shenzhen."

Chow considered the proposal. The Shenzhen special economic zone was in Guangdong Province across the border, beyond Hong Kong's New Territories, the last piece of China that Britain annexed in 1898. Access was now relatively free. Still, Chow had to be cautious. For all the deputy minister's assurances, he had been an enemy of the state since his escape after Mao achieved power. Finally, he said, "Yes, perhaps. I would require, however, a direct signal from your minister."

After the deputy left, Chow reflected that interesting possibilities had surfaced, although to what end, he wasn't sure. Brotherhood or not, he decided to keep them to himself, to privately observe further developments.

He did not have to wait long.

An interview with Red China's minister of public security appeared two days later in the Chinese-language newspaper *Ming Pao*. While acknowledging an upsurge in domestic crime, the minister insisted that the police could easily control the problem. Asked about the triads, he stated that there was little evidence of their rebirth on the mainland.

And what about Hong Kong?

That, he said, was another matter. Many triads there were engaged in nefarious criminal activity, which would be of great concern when Beijing took over the English colony.

He added, however, that certain of the secret societies were quite patriotic in nature. "As for them," he declared, "as long as they remain concerned with Hong Kong's prosperity and stability, we should unite with them. I believe the more people with whom we unite the better."

Chow had received his invitation to the dance.

He took an express train alone for Guangzhou, as Beijing now called Canton. Less than an hour and a half later, he crossed into Shenzhen. When he had last seen it, it was an alluvial plain, part of the rich Pearl River delta, filled with rice paddies, fields of sweet potatoes, sugar cane and jute, fish-rearing ponds and hog farms. Now everywhere he looked, there were newly built factories and office buildings, some fifty stories high.

He was met by the Hakka deputy minister of public security in a Mercedes-Benz sedan driven by a uniformed policeman. He saw a huge banner that proclaimed "Unity, Progress, Friendship." Another exhorted "Time Is Money."

The minister himself, Zhu Jintao, received Chow in a large modern villa. Zhu was wearing a suit and tie. He had a jovial manner, more in keeping with an energetic business executive than a man who ran a police establishment that had jurisdiction over all China. Chow judged him to be in his late forties, exceptionally young for his position, a mere child who had been barely past infancy when Chow had departed the Central Country.

Zhu got briskly to the point, not even bothering to inquire whether Chow had enjoyed a pleasant journey. Speaking Mandarin, he said that he trusted this would be the first of many face-to-face encounters. What he was looking forward to, he told Chow, were "joint business ventures," in which Chow's advice and participation would be invaluable. What organization, after all, better knew the intricacies of Hong Kong than the Confederation? Zhu smiled expansively. He had carefully studied the five dragon heads and concluded that Chow was the one among them who had the flexibility and independence of spirit necessary for the foundation of a fruitful relationship.

"Joint ventures?"

"Yes. As a matter of fact, I have one immediately in mind. A shipment of, ah, teak, yes, *teak,* that is soon to cross the southern provinces."

It took every ounce of willpower Chow possessed to maintain his composure. He felt a muscle twitching in his jaw. He hoped that it wasn't noticeable.

Zhu was still talking. "A shipment, I believe, that is under the protection of three separate regional commanding generals."

"Your knowledge," Chow finally managed, "is extensive."

Zhu shrugged. "That's my job. To know things. But I'm curious. Did you expect the protection to continue down the Pearl River to the sea?"

"That was the expectation, yes."

"You may require additional help."

So this, finally, was what it was all about. The minister of public security not only knew about the shipment but wanted to deal himself in. Sensing now a kindred spirit, Chow said, "Not surprisingly, that very thought has just occurred to me."

"It would be a great police undertaking to make sure that not one bit of the shipment remains within our borders. That, of course, would be most unacceptable. What happens to it afterward, in the *kwai lo* world, is no concern of mine."

"We think as one."

The minister pursed his lips. "There is a problem, however. Under no circumstances can Deng be part of this. He is a sworn enemy of the state. He is not to be trusted."

"I will see what I can do."

"I'm sure you will," Zhu said. "You really have no choice. What would Deng have received?"

"One hundred twenty-five million U.S."

"That sum is acceptable to me for now. There is much teak yet to be harvested. I will leave that for a future discussion."

Four days later, in Kowloon, Unicorn Frankie Chin stood at attention before his uncle.

"What was behind the shooting in New York?" Chow asked.

"No one knows. But I am sure Deng was involved. The description of one of the gunmen—big shoulders, a massive head—convinces me it was his red pole, Chao Yu."

"Ah, Chao. A strange man. Not to be trifled with. Never married. Devoted to his mother, they say."

"His mere presence in Chinatown terrifies everybody," Unicorn Frankie said. "He arrives there at least twice a week, striding down the street as if no one else is present. You must leap out of his path. He goes to a *chiu ka* run by a Madame Chang, but the young girls there fear him greatly. He is dissatisfied and has asked me if I know any women for him. Real women, strong ones, he said."

Suddenly emboldened, Frankie added, "Uncle, it is crazy to limit ourselves to importation of the white powder and let the Italians have all the distribution. We should do it also and triple our profit. The youth gangs grow restless. My idea is to band the gangs together as one, remove them from the influence of the tongs. So what if there are arrests. There will be so much powder that it won't matter. And there are many other activities we can engage in. We are well situated throughout the United States. It's time to strike. The day of the Italians is finished."

Chow pondered the prospect. There was merit in what his nephew said. Deng, naturally, would never countenance it. But things had changed dramatically. Chow now had a new partner, Zhu Jintao. The public security minister was not bluffing when he said Deng had to be out of the picture. *And without Zhu, there would be no shipment.*

Still, what to do about Deng? Never, in the history of the brotherhood, had a *lung tao* been removed by others than those within his own society. It would destroy the fabric of the Confederation. Chow's fellow dragon heads would not accept it, no matter what the reason.

He had told them nothing about his visit to Zhu. The dragon heads picked him to be their representative. And he knew they would be delighted not only with the profits filling their vaults as the powder spread across America but overjoyed that they could remain in Hong Kong as long as they desired because he, Stanley Chow, now had *guangxi,* big connections, in Beijing. He would be recognized as the first among equals, displacing the pretentious Deng and his condescending ways.

"You say the gangs are restless?" he asked.

"Yes. Soon, they'll even stop listening to me."

Chow brooded. Perhaps that was the solution. If certain incidents occurred in New York, how could he be blamed? Wasn't he here in Hong Kong all the time?

"Listen carefully," he said. "You are on the verge of a great leap forward. You must not touch the person of Deng. But he has a vulnerability, a daughter, Li-po, a student at Yale University."

"I know where it is, Uncle. What should I do?"

Chow felt his temple throbbing. Even now, he couldn't bring himself to say it plainly. "Ah, I will leave that to you. But the message you convey through her to Deng must be one he cannot mistake. And one more thing," he said, "rid us of the red pole, Chao."

32

UNDER GENERAL LI'S WATCHFUL EYE, the refined heroin was pressed into bricks, wrapped in plastic sealed with white tape, then encased in more plastic. Divided into loads of a ton each, it was placed under protective housing on the beds of big diesel-engine trucks, then covered with teak logs.

Belching oily exhaust fumes, the trucks moved out of Laos, escorted by two Red Army scout cars. A third scout car was positioned a quarter of a mile ahead, clearing the narrow two-lane road of other trucks, ox-drawn carts and windowless buses crammed with passengers and piled high with luggage that threatened to overturn them at every curve. The road rose from the jungle toward Yunnan's central plateau, winding around steep hills called the Home of the Clouds, their nearly vertical slopes etched with hundreds of contoured rice terraces.

Below Kunming, the convoy turned southeast, passing an expanse of fantastically shaped limestone pillars, sculpted over the aeons by the wind and rain into what appeared from a distance to be an eerie, treeless forest.

For a time, the road paralleled the narrow-gauge railway built by the French at the turn of the century linking Kunming with Hanoi in Vietnam. Then heading due east, the convoy picked up a new escort as it entered the subtropical agricultural basin of Guangxi. Near the city of Wuzhou, it went past China's largest snake warehouse, where thousands of cobras, vipers, tree snakes and water snakes were housed in wire cages awaiting live transport to Canton and Hong Kong, where they would be served up to tickle the palates of gourmets. In Guangdong, with still another escort team, the convoy reached the lush Pearl River delta, crossing countless tributary streams and running alongside barge-filled canals.

At nightfall on the sixth day of the journey, the shipment reached Canton's port of Whampoa, where it was met and guarded by a special detachment of the *Gonganju,* the public security police.

In a last-minute deal, Chow had agreed to turn over the teak to Zhu Jintao. It would be fashioned by local woodworkers into furniture and other household objects, and also into carved animal figures and Buddhas for export at high prices. In practicing the new socialism with Chinese characteristics, Chow reflected, Minister Zhu was not missing a bet.

There was only one mishap. A policeman was caught trying to filch a unit as the shipment was being loaded on barges for the trip down the Pearl River to Kowloon's container port. He was summarily executed.

Even Stanley Chow had to admire Deng's ingenuity in conceiving the next step in the plan. In Kowloon, under the care of trusted dockworkers of the Glorious Together Association, three hundred units of the heroin bricks were hidden, as directed, on a New York-bound container ship, *Sea Dragon.*

The remaining units, now not quite five tons, were packed into an ocean-going container and hoisted aboard a sister ship, *Sea Horse,* which would also sail for New York. Both ships were owned by Deng's Hong Kong/Kowloon Shipping, Ltd.

Chow couldn't resist the temptation to stroll through the arc-lit glow to the pier where the ships were docked, gazing up at their rusted hulls, smiling at what they held. Yes, he decided. Why not? He would go this night to the fan-tan tables in Macao and help himself to a little more of Deng's money.

In New York, upon confirmation from Ho Shu-shui that the ships had departed, Deng dined with Chao and Peter Pei at the Inner Peace. "Inform Lucano's man that the shipment is en route," he told Pei. After his encounter with Tom MacLean, Deng had no intention of meeting with the Italian again, at least for a while. Lucano must be under constant surveillance and he castigated himself for not foreseeing that possibility. It was annoying to have made such an obvious mistake. But he was comforted by Needham's assurance that young MacLean would continue to represent his interests. Deng was quite aware of the privileged status of lawyer/client relations under American law.

Chao excused himself from the table.

"Let him have his enjoyment," Deng said.

Pei essayed a small joke. "Not the Gray Shadows again?"

Deng didn't laugh.

To have any chance at all, Unicorn Frankie knew he would have to take Chao by surprise.

She was Chinatown's most famous whore, Eurasian, her mother Hakka and her father, it was rumored, a Spanish sailor, which accounted for her ripe, sensual beauty. She lived on Division Street and he had seen many chauffeured limousines parked in front of her building. It was said that she could fulfill the needs of any man, no matter what they were, and that her price was as much as a thousand dollars a visit. In Chinatown, she was called *Tu Mu,* the Earth Mother. Her uptown *kwai lo* clientele knew her as Mistress Saturnia.

When the White Eagles robbed a jewelry store, Frankie would always offer her the first selection. It had to be the best. The second time he showed her what he had for sale, she humbled him, sweeping the gold rings and chains off the table, forcing him to go down on his hands and knees to recover them. "Don't waste my time," she sneered.

Yes, he thought, she would be strong enough to handle Chao. Frankie made an appointment for him that evening and gave her a thousand dollars. "Be careful. This man could be rough," he said.

The next day he asked her how it had gone.

"Handcuffs," she said.

"Handcuffs," he said, wincing, thinking that she would demand additional money, "he made you put on handcuffs?"

"No," she said. "The handcuffs were for him."

"For him?"

"Yes. I handcuffed him to the posts at the head of the bed and bound his feet with silken cords to the posts at the bottom. Then he wanted me to pee on him. He kept crying out, 'Mother! Mother!' "

"Then what?"

"Then I sat on him and he came."

"Ai, unbelievable!" Unicorn Frankie exclaimed.

She laughed. "It wasn't so unusual. Why do you think I have handcuffs and masks and whips?"

"When is his next visit?"

She consulted her appointment book. The following Tuesday, she said. Seven p.m.

"I will pay you ten thousand dollars if you will hide me here before he arrives."

She laughed again. "I do charge for watching. That reminds me. You haven't brought me any jewelry recently."

In New Haven, on the Yale campus, a little brother of the White Eagles was directed to the administration building. His face had a freshly scrubbed look, his hair was neatly combed. He wore a white buttoned-down shirt, a blue and red striped tie, a blue blazer, khaki trousers and polished penny loafers.

"I am from Hong Kong," he told a woman at the desk, blushing slightly, as if in awe of his surroundings. "I am looking for my cousin, Deng Li-po. Stupidly, I have lost her address, and I want to surprise her. She doesn't know I'm in the States."

The woman studied the blushing young man. He was so polite and attractive. "You say you're her cousin?"

"Yes, my mother was her mother's younger sister."

"Well, your cousin isn't Deng anymore. She's Mrs. Robert Logan. Professor Logan's wife."

The young man seemed genuinely confused, blushing even more furiously. "Oh, I didn't know."

"It happened rather suddenly." She flipped through a card file and gave him Logan's address. "I really shouldn't be doing this, but I don't want to ruin your surprise."

"I'm so happy you told me my cousin is married. Because now I will buy her a wedding present and she will be doubly surprised."

After he left, the woman turned to another woman at the desk behind her and said, "Aren't those Chinese kids something else, real nice and respectful. They're not like a lot of spoiled brats around here."

33

T HE *SEA HORSE*, with nearly five tons of heroin number four on board, and the second container ship, *Sea Dragon,* carrying four hundred and fifty pounds, plowed eastward across the Pacific, maintaining the same speed, fifty miles apart.

On schedule, both ships entered the locks of the Panama Canal, one after the other, and then turned north through the Caribbean, steaming up the U.S. coast toward Port Newark, part of the marine complex of the Port Authority of New York and New Jersey.

Near Suffern, New York, immediately north of the New Jersey line, work proceeded on the renovation of a warehouse that would serve as a regional center for the projected Chow Chow chain of Chinese fast-food restaurants. It was an area dotted with warehouse facilities because of its proximity to the New York State Thruway heading north and west and the New Jersey Turnpike running south. The Rockland County *Journal-News* had featured a story on Deng's acquisition of the warehouse, pointing to it as another sign of revitalization following the recession. Deng himself was quoted as saying, "I have come to this country because of my faith in its future."

Deng's shipping agent informed him that the two ships were off the Virginia Capes. And now the last, crucial element in his plan was put into motion. He faxed Ho Shu-shui in Bangkok, "All is ready. Proceed."

Within the hour, in Chiang Mai's DEA compound, Terry McDonell received a telephone call. Because of his still-unknown informant, more than a ton of Shan Wa's heroin, two thousand nine hundred pounds, had been intercepted in nineteen separate seizures. In Arlington, Virginia, DEA headquarters was ecstatic, especially because the FBI was lobbying to take over all narcotics operations. This would show everyone in law enforcement who was doing what.

McDonell, however, hadn't heard the familiar, anonymous voice for almost a month.

"What do you have for me?" he asked.

The voice said, "I regret an unfortunate oversight. Three hundred units passed through Chiang Mai without our knowledge. They reached Bangkok and went by trawler to Hong Kong, where they were placed aboard a ship. Her name is *Sea Dragon*. I am unable to say where the units are hidden. My information is that *Sea Dragon* will soon dock in New York. Again, I regret this short notice. Be well."

"Hello, hello?" McDonell shouted. But the line was dead.

He immediately dispatched an urgent, coded cable to Arlington.

34

CROUCHED IN A CLOSET, the sweat coursing down him, Unicorn Frankie Chin kept his eye glued to the inch-wide crack in the door as a naked Chao Yu lay spread-eagled on the bed. He watched the Earth Mother attach the handcuffs to Chao's wrists and then to the wooden bedposts. She was wearing black stiletto heels and gloves. She had on black stockings and a garter belt. She wore a black mask over her eyes.

Chao began to whimper. "Mother, please don't hurt me."

"Quiet!" she commanded, leaning over him, her breasts brushing his face. "You've been a naughty boy." She slapped him and moved out of Frankie's view.

"Please don't tie my ankles too tight," he heard Chao plead. How could this be, he thought, coming from a man who so terrorized other men?

"Quiet, I say!"

Frankie closed his eyes, praying for courage. The moment had come. He leaped out of the closet, a meat cleaver raised high in his hand, its edge honed razor sharp. He aimed for Chao's neck, intending to sever it. At the last second, Chao saw him and lurched his head violently away, so that the cleaver came down on the left side of his neck just above the collar bone. Dark blood shot up in spurts from the carotid artery that went directly from his heart to his brain.

Chao howled.

The cleaver slipped from Frankie's grasp. He shrank against the wall. Blood continued to pump from Chao's neck, like a miniature geyser. But to his horror, Frankie saw Chao suddenly arch upward. Incredibly, he jerked his handcuffed right hand forward and snapped off the bedpost. One of Chao's bound feet came free. He saw Chao grip the post and start to swing it toward him.

"No!" he cried. Then, all at once, he saw Chao fall back on the bed, his face contorted, mouth wide open, wordless, trying to gulp in air that never came.

Unicorn Frankie slumped to the floor.

He saw the Earth Mother standing in the far corner of the room. She removed her mask and studied him impassively. "This is going to cost you more than ten thousand dollars," she said.

He nodded dumbly. He rose clumsily to his feet and approached her. He took a ball of tissue paper out of his pocket, unfolded it and presented her with a large cut emerald. She held it up in the light, appraising it, and smiled approvingly.

Then she said, "Who's going to clean up this mess?"

Finally recovering his voice, he said, "Don't worry about it." He went to the phone. About ten minutes later, three White Eagles arrived. Chao's body was lugged to a bathtub and dismembered with the cleaver and a saw.

His remains were placed in three trash bags.

Later that night, the bags were swallowed by a New York City sanitation truck.

In New Haven, the next afternoon, Robert Logan never had a chance to defend himself.

When the bell rang, he looked through the small front-door window and saw a young Chinese in a blue blazer and blue and red striped tie. Thinking him a student he hadn't seen before, he opened the door.

"Professor Logan?"

"Yes, come in."

The boy stepped forward, arm extended as if to shake Logan's hand. Then, abruptly, he lowered his head and charged, butting his head against Logan's chest. Five more White Eagles rushed in behind him. Then came Unicorn Frankie Chin.

Logan was bigger than any of them and in excellent physical condition. But as he toppled backward, attempting to regain his balance, his head slammed against the edge of the doorjamb at the end of the hallway. Stunned, he started sliding down. They swarmed all over him. Hands gripped his arms, other hands grabbed his legs, pulling them out from under him, pinioning him to the floor. He tried thrashing one way and another, but their combined weight on him was too much.

Unicorn Frankie leaned over and ripped Logan's shirt sleeve from his left arm. Frankie wrapped a length of rubber tubing around it, just above the bicep. And then, when the vein was prominently visible, he stuck in the syringe. It was a "hot shot," ninety percent pure heroin. Even for a longtime user, fifty milligrams would have been a lethal dose. Frankie injected Robert Logan with one hundred and fifty milligrams. In about three minutes, Logan stopped struggling. His eyes were closed. Frankie lifted a lid. The pupil was rapidly contracting.

They dragged Logan into the bedroom. Frankie saw the lump and a small cut on the back of his head, so they placed him partially off the bed, to make it appear as if he had fallen during his deadly stupor. Frankie told a White Eagle to stuff the torn shirt in his jacket.

Li-po arrived half an hour afterward. She called out, "Robert, I'm home." They were her last words. She weighed barely a hundred pounds and was helpless before them. She managed to bite the hand that was clapped over her mouth and tried to scream, but a fist hit her, cutting her lip.

They held her, standing up, as Unicorn Frankie injected her also with a lethal dose of heroin. She began to sag. They carried her to the bed and stretched her out. She had a trace of a smile. Right then, as Li-po lay dying, she had never felt better.

Within her body, the heroin onslaught was in full fury. As with Robert, the moment it was in her bloodstream, enzymes from her liver started breaking it back down to morphine. It sped into her limbic system, the brain's nerve groupings that trigger pleasure. There was a marvelous, reassuring drowsiness from the medulla at the base of her brain which controlled breathing and the beat of her heart. Less than five minutes had elapsed.

Gradually, Li-po's breathing slowed, from perhaps thirteen or fourteen breaths a minute to three or four. Carbon dioxide built up relentlessly. From the massive dosage Unicorn Frankie administered, her brain began to slip into irreversible coma. The air sacs in her lungs filled with fluid. She was also drowning. As Frankie watched, a whitish froth oozed from her mouth and nose. It looked like shaving cream. It turned pinkish. Frankie heard a gurgling sound. And then a faint snoring that came now not more than once a minute.

Then it ceased. Lacking oxygen, Li-po was brain-dead. But her heart continued to beat, feebly. Her pupils were mere pinpoints. Frankie sent the other White Eagles away. He stayed. He had to be sure. He remembered his present to the Dragon Lady. He still didn't know what went wrong.

At last there was no breathing, no pulse. He started to leave the room, then froze in sudden horror. He had heard the gurgling again, her body's final reflexive spasm of protest. He whirled, half expecting to find Li-po rising from the dead, pointing at him, demanding vengeance. But she remained inert, lips slightly parted.

"Sweet dreams, lovers," Frankie said.

The bodies were discovered at noon the following day by Logan's cleaning lady.

In New York, Tom MacLean was having a sandwich at his desk when his secretary said, "There's a Beverly Soo on the line. She says she was a friend of Li-po Deng. She sounds hysterical."

Was? Tom thought. He reached for the phone.

35

T OM WENT to the New Haven morgue with Beverly Soo. They were joined there by a homicide detective named Angelo Bertoni and the assistant medical examiner, a Dr. Milton Fleischman.

When Tom viewed Li-po, she looked so vulnerable and innocent. That was the crazy part. No sign of torment, pain. No hint of an agonizing death.

"It was real pure, as close to a hundred percent as you can get, is why," Bertoni said. "We already tested the residue in one of the bags. No bad stuff."

Tom couldn't stop staring at her waxen face.

I like you, Tom MacLean.

He remembered how her laugh made him want to laugh, too. And then the fleeting fear in her eyes at his mention of her father.

He's coming here?

"What are you putting this down as?" he asked Bertoni.

The detective appeared surprised. "What else? ODs. Both of them."

"She, *they,* weren't dopers," Beverly whispered. "I knew them. I was with them all the time."

"I could retire, I get a buck for every doper around here who isn't a doper," Bertoni said.

Tom pulled back the sheet and pointed to Li-po's arm. "Except for that one mark, where are the tracks if they were such big users?"

"Hey, maybe they were smoking and snorting and it wasn't doing as much for them anymore. So they go for the needle for a bigger kick and overdid it. Forgot what a wallop this smack had. Happens all the time. The street purity level has really jumped. So have ODs."

"What about that bruise on the corner of her mouth?"

"Look, counselor, I don't have all the answers. But it didn't kill her, for sure. Maybe the good professor slapped her around a little. How the hell should I know what they did in their bedroom. He's got a lump and a cut on the back of his head. Must've happened when he flopped off the bed. Unless you got a theory that they had a big fight first and she popped him with something, object unknown."

"I can't bear to listen to this," Beverly said. "They adored each other."

"Do we know how much heroin was involved?" Tom asked.

"No," Fleischman interrupted. "That's always the problem. Unless you get the body right away, it breaks down so fast that you can't really tell how much was injected. You can't say with any degree of certainty if it's an accidental OD or a suicide. So the MO is you classify it as drug abuse or undetermined death."

"Or," Tom said, "a homicide?"

"That's right," Bertoni said. "Not a bad way to whack somebody, I grant you. Except you have to have a suspect. About a year ago we had a real good case against a dealer. The chief witness was his girlfriend. And the day before trial, she was laid out right here, like this one. That wasn't too hard to figure out. You got any perps in mind, Mr. MacLean?"

It was inconceivable that Deng could have had his own daughter murdered. "No," Tom had to admit.

"There wasn't any sign of a forced entry into the apartment. The front door was locked when the cleaning lady who found the bodies came the next day. So was the rear door to the garden. Nothing else was disturbed. She had a pretty expensive collection of jewelry, including a real fancy jade necklace," Bertoni said. "None of which is missing, according to Miss Soo. But all the paraphernalia was there for some partying. Bags, needle, mixing spoon, the works. Absent any suspects, I guess that's it. You say her father is her only relative. How do I reach him?"

"I'll take care of it," Tom said.

"Sorry about your friend," Bertoni told Beverly. "Better take good care of yourself."

Afterward, Beverly Soo said, "Can you imagine the nerve of that detective? He practically said I was into heroin."

"He meant well," Tom said. "He just has difficulty expressing himself."

"Like the way he trashed Li-po and Robert? Look, last night we were supposed to meet for a recital to hear a young Chinese pianist. Li-po was raving about him all week. I wondered where they were. I phoned, but there was no answer." Tears streamed down her face. "If I had only gone over there. Mr. MacLean, I can't tell you what a standup girl Li-po was. She did everything she could to placate her father. It tore her apart, trying to be the dutiful Chinese daughter. But she was deliriously happy with Robert."

When she composed herself, he said, "You say they got married about three weeks ago?"

"Yes. It was so romantic. *And* scary, what with the Immigration people her father sent."

"They arrived out of the blue?"

"Yes. Like I told you, if I hadn't overheard what I did, who knows where she'd be."

"How do you know her father was behind that?"

"I don't. But Li-po was sure, and that's good enough for me. She'd gone to New York to see him. She told him about Robert. He hit the ceiling. Practically disowned her on the spot."

"Why didn't she call me?"

"She did suggest it to Robert. But he said what could you do? You were *his* lawyer. The only reason I called you was because she said how much she liked you. I wasn't about to call *him*."

"You don't think for a second he had anything to do with this?"

"Look, Mr. MacLean, I don't know what to think. I only know Li-po and Robert didn't do it to themselves, no matter what the police say. Somebody else did it. They were murdered. It's that simple. And somehow, her father has to be mixed up in it. How else could it have happened? I mean, wasn't everything fine for Li-po until he showed up?"

Beverly had a key to the apartment.

When they went in, Tom surveyed the bedroom. There were photographs on the dresser in silver frames.

"Those three were taken at the wedding," she said. "And that's Robert's family. The other one of Li-Po and Robert on horseback was at Christmas." Beverly started to cry again.

"Who's that?" Tom asked, pointing to the portrait of a Chinese woman.

"Her mother."

Looking at the photographs, he realized that the one of Deng that he had seen the first, and only, time he had met Li-po, was nowhere in sight.

Driving back to New York, he felt his rage building.

Around six p.m. that evening on Central Park South, Deng was advised that the two ships would arrive in the morning. The decoy ship, *Sea Dragon,* would come in first, followed by the *Sea Horse.*

He relayed the news to Peter Pei in Chinatown. "Tell the boy, Chin, to be prepared." Then he said, "What have you learned of Chao Yu? He's been missing for two nights."

"I have searched throughout the community. Madame Chang tells me he has not visited her establishment. She asks herself where he is. Should I make inquiries with the police? I have my contacts."

"Under no circumstances. He has undoubtedly found other pleasures. New York has gone to his head. I'll deal with him myself."

Still, a vague uneasiness seized Deng. Chao had never disappeared like this.

But then he comforted himself with the thought that his grand design, so dazzling in its concept, so many months in execution, would soon be a reality. This first shipment was only the beginning. After the United States would come Western Europe, within which goods could now move freely across national borders. *And* Eastern Europe with its chaotic new freedom. Even in the former Soviet Union itself with its rampaging crime syndicates.

Deng's household staff was asleep. He answered the building's intercom himself. A Mr. Thomas MacLean was in the lobby. Insisted on seeing him.

He felt a flicker of annoyance at this interruption of his reverie, this late-night intrusion.

He felt still more annoyance as Tom pushed rudely past him into the apartment. "I don't think you'll want any of your neighbors to overhear what I'm saying," Tom said. "I'm here about your daughter."

"I no longer have a daughter," Deng replied coldly. After a second's hesitation, he amended this. "At least for the time being."

"No, you were right the first time. You don't have one. She's dead."

"*What?*" Deng appeared to shrink in front of Tom. He tottered back, reaching for a chair. He sat down. "Dead? What are you talking about, MacLean? Where is she? I must go to her."

"It's a little late. She's in a morgue in New Haven, Connecticut. I've just come from there. The police say it was caused by an overdose of heroin."

"Heroin?" Deng's anthracite eyes bore into Tom. "Are you mad? My daughter doesn't take heroin."

"For once, I agree with you. I'm sure she was murdered. But in any case, it was heroin. You know about heroin pretty good, don't you, *Mister* Deng? You go back a long way with it, like, maybe, in Laos during the Vietnam War. With my father."

"Your father told you this?" Deng asked, hands fiercely clenched, knuckles white.

"No, he didn't. He didn't have to. I've gotten enough information to figure that out for myself. And I've got a few other tidbits I haven't told you. Besides knowing you met with Big Frank Lucano, the FBI knows that he was brought to you by your friend downtown, Peter Pei. And they know Pei's been smuggling heroin into the States. I don't know what you're mixed up in, but as your lawyer, about to be ex-lawyer, I'm telling you that you won't be reaping any of the benefits. You're finished. They are hot on your trail. Try leaving the country and see how far you get."

"Are you suggesting I had my own daughter killed?"

"No, I don't think you ordered it. But she was killed because of you. As far as I'm concerned, you're as much her murderer as whoever did it."

Tom drew a deep breath. They stared at one another, like two exhausted fighters in a ring. At last, wearily, Deng said, "Li-po. I must make arrangements."

"Don't worry, it's the least I can do for her. Call me tomorrow. But obviously, I can't represent you any longer." Tom turned toward the door. And turned back. "You son of bitch! All Li-po ever wanted was her own life."

Deng sat there, immobile.

He gazed out the window. The dark expanse of the park stretched below, bathed in the surreal glow of a full moon. The buildings surrounding the park were outlined in its light.

But Deng saw none of this. He sat in his own darkness.

What he saw were the hacked, disemboweled bodies of his mother and father and sister.

He saw himself lighting the joss sticks in memory of An-shui. *Brother, my wife, your sister, is no more.*

He heard himself saying to the doctor of his second wife, "I want the child." And he saw Li-po's face, wide-eyed, floating in front of him.

He remained motionless. For the first time in his life, tears rolled down Deng's face. A pent-up, racking sob escaped him.

Dawn spread across the park. Had he dozed off? He couldn't be certain. He shaded his eyes. Hundreds of windows blindingly reflected the sunrise.

In the light of day, his grief was replaced by fury. Who could have done this? Who would have dared? His mind darted over the possibilities. Shan Wa in his Burma retreat? That made no sense. How could he know of Li-po? *Who* knew about her?

Stanley Chow? Absurd. Chow would not throw away millions of dollars, nor would anyone in the Confederation.

A terrible thought insinuated itself. *Had* Li-po indulged in the white powder? He dismissed it. He was grasping wildly at straws. MacLean was right. Whatever it was, it involved him.

At eight a.m., the phone rang. He seized it, thinking the answer was at hand. But it was the shipping agent calling. The two vessels had left the Ambrose Lightship, where the world's shipping lanes converged on Lower New York Bay. Harbor pilots were on board.

"Yes, thank you for your precious advice."

Deng slammed down on the phone. *Where was Chao Yu?* Why wasn't he here?

His cook brought him breakfast. He had her take it back.

He heard the doorbell ring. The cook timidly reappeared with a package. He ripped it open. And then he did have the answer. Inside was a severed finger with a gold ring. He recognized the ring at once. Engraved on it was the character for "Tsoi," the surname of one of the Five First Ancestors of the brotherhood. He had presented it to Chao upon his elevation to a red pole.

A note was also enclosed. It said, "Remove yourself while you are able."

Only one person could be behind its challenging, mocking tone. It had to be Chow! What was going on? Slumping in his chair, he remembered Lucano's words. *And you don't have no wars, like, between families?*

He considered his options for vengeance, for that was all he thought of now. Slowly, the plan evolved to destroy all who sought to destroy him, and in a manner that no one could anticipate.

He would become the Ice Man again.

The threat that he couldn't get out of the country posed no concern. If he had to, he would find a way. But to what end? To go where? And for what? And why? He no longer had family. He was, finally, alone.

First, he sent a fax containing explicit instructions to Ho Shu-shui.

Then he wrote a letter addressed to Thomas MacLean, Esq. It took him nearly an hour. He gave the envelope to his houseman to be delivered late the same afternoon. After that, he retired to his bedroom, leaving instructions that he was not to be disturbed. No exceptions.

In the bedroom, he dialed the law offices of Needham & Lewis. "I wish to speak to Mr. MacLean," he said.

Stanley Chow had finally miscounted the buttons under the fan-tan bowl.

36

THE *SEA DRAGON* moved that Friday morning through the Narrows, between Staten Island and Brooklyn, beneath the Verrazano Bridge and entered the Upper Bay. Ahead lay the Statue of Liberty. She turned left into the Kill van Kull passage that separated Staten Island from New Jersey. Once past the Bayonne Bridge linking the two, she was met by tugs that guided her up Newark Bay and brought her into the Port Newark berthing channel.

She was one of approximately fifty thousand merchant ships that would dock during the year, ninety percent of their cargo packed in steel containers, more than a million and a half containers in all. In the War on Drugs, almost every intercept was based on informant reports. As for the rest of this vast incoming cargo, about one percent was subject to random inspection. And only one percent of this one percent was thoroughly examined, containers opened, as well as the crates inside. To do otherwise, considering the manpower available to the U.S. Customs Service, would tie up the port facilities in economically unacceptable gridlock.

The Port Newark channel ran east to west. It had thirty-four berths. Shortly after eleven a.m., tugs edged the *Sea Dragon* alongside Berth One, the farthest in on the channel's north side.

As a result of Terry McDonell's urgent cable from Chiang Mai, ten DEA agents and twenty-two Customs inspectors waited on the quay, along with four Labrador retrievers, trained to sniff out caches of narcotics. Two Boston whalers belonging to Customs cruised back and forth in the channel close by the ship.

Since McDonell's mysterious informant had not specified the whereabouts of the suspected heroin, the search would be massive. First, the crewmen were mustered in the crew's lounge so their quarters could be ransacked. Then the five-hundred-foot-long *Sea Dragon* was divided into sections with teams of inspectors and agents assigned to each. There were literally scores of hiding places above and below deck. While the three hundred units alleged to be on board would take up considerable room, they might have been broken down into smaller parts. Topside, there were scores of inviting cavities in the deck knuckles for the container cranes, in the forepeak boatswain's storage areas, in the mast housing. Below, it was even worse, false floor plates in oil, bilge, water and ballast tanks, false walls in the sides of the hull itself, in the empty space between the ship's double bottom.

About an hour later, her sister ship, the *Sea Horse,* nosed in and tied up at Berth Two, on the south side of the channel, directly opposite the *Sea Dragon.*

As the containers from the *Sea Horse* were being unloaded, it took a while for a commercial shipping agent to locate Charlie Gaffney, the Customs inspector on duty for Berth Two. Gaffney was intent on the proceedings aboard the *Sea Dragon,* across the channel, three hundred yards distant.

"What's all the commotion?" the agent asked.

"They say it's a big load of smack," Gaffney said. "They've been all over her ever since she came in. Real good overtime for the boys."

"Sorry to be late on this," the agent said, brandishing paperwork. "But I got it late myself."

"What's that?"

"A container of kitchen equipment. On *Sea Horse.* This is her, isn't it?"

"Yeah. Same as the one they're searching. Kitchen equipment, huh?"

"They're going to franchise a chain of fast-food restaurants, like, you know, McDonald's. Only Chinese."

"They got to bring kitchen equipment in from over there?"

"It's all specialized stuff. Look at the invoice. Wok tables. Bean sprout machines. Roast pork ovens. Rice cookers. What have you. The pickup's for this afternoon. They want to get this stuff fast."

"OK," Gaffney said. "Come on in the office. I'll stamp the bill of lading for you and you're all done."

"Jeez, if somebody wanted to sneak a little something else in," the agent laughed, "this'd be the day to do it. Looks like nobody around here is thinking about anything except what's on that other ship."

At Berth Two, giant forklifts trundled containers from the *Sea Horse* to a staging area or placed them on tractor-drawn, sixteen-wheel flatbed trailers that were lined up.

The driver of a leased rig gave Gaffney a duplicate set of papers for a container carrying kitchen equipment. In the tractor cab with the driver were Unicorn Frankie Chin and his chief lieutenant in the White Eagles, Fat Monster.

In Tom MacLean's office, his secretary buzzed him. "It's Mr. Deng."

Well, Tom thought, he would get this over with in a hurry. Then he heard Deng say, "What the FBI is looking for is on one of my ships, *Sea Horse*. She has arrived today."

"I'm sorry. Would you repeat that?"

But Deng had hung up.

He tried calling him back. There was no answer.

Moments later, he was dialing Shannon.

"Miracle of miracles," she said. "A voice from the past."

"Listen, Shannon," he said, "I don't have time to go into it, but a lot's happened. The thing is I just got a call from Deng. You were right. He's up to his eyeballs in heroin. He told me there's a big shipment on one of his boats. In port somewhere, *now*. Name's *Sea Horse*."

"You speaking as his attorney, Tom?"

"That's another long story. But what's that got to do with anything?"

"Because he's still throwing you curve balls, is what. You should see the gloom and doom around here. The DEA knows about the shipment. They're scrambling all over the ship. And her name, for your information, isn't *Sea Horse*. It's *Sea Dragon*."

"Are you sure? I'm positive he said *Sea Horse*."

"Tom, when are you going to come to your senses?"

He tried phoning Deng again. Still no answer.

37

A<small>FTER AN INDECISIVE MOMENT</small>, Tom had his secretary look up the Port Authority number and dialed it himself. An automatic voice came on, reciting his various options if he was using a Touch-Tone phone. At last he was informed of a button number that sounded as if it might provide ocean shipping news. Another robotic voice said, "Please hold, all our lines are busy." Then the line he was on went dead. He tried the general number again and this time pressed the button for operator assistance. After perhaps twenty rings, he finally heard a human voice, "Can I help you?" He told the operator what he wanted and she said, "I'll connect you." More interminable rings until a man responded, "Port Newark/Port Elizabeth Marine Terminal."

"I'm trying to find out if a ship docked today. Her name is *Sea Horse.*"

"Hold on," the man said. Then he said, "Yeah, she's here. Berth Two. Port Newark channel."

Tom started to ask for directions. But the line went dead once more.

He asked his secretary to call the car service the firm used. "Make sure the driver knows how to get to the Port Newark marine terminal in Jersey."

It took over an hour to get through the Lincoln Tunnel and more time for the driver to find the right gate.

The vastness of the scene around Tom was staggering. Endless rows of containers, *miles* of them. Row upon row of of flatbeds as far as he could see. Tractor trailers roared behind him on the New Jersey Turnpike. A

long freight train filled with containers rumbled along the adjacent Con-
rail tracks. On the other side of the turnpike and tracks, jets screamed out
of Newark International Airport. In the distant haze, he could make out
the Lower Manhattan skyline.

A security guard was holding up his hand. "You have a pass?"

Tom got out of the car and showed him his business card. "I want to
get to Berth Two. There's a ship there, the *Sea Horse*. I'm the attorney for
her owner."

"No pass, no go."

"Look, all I want to do is see the Customs guy. You can come with me."

"I can't leave my post."

As Tom started to argue, he heard a car horn honk. He looked behind
him. It was Shannon in the Ford sedan the FBI had assigned her.

"Hey, surprise, surprise," he said. "I can't believe it."

"I checked shipping arrivals after you called," she said. "I owe you one.
Saw that there really was one called *Sea Horse* in today. Maybe something
fishy's going on, after all. I tried to call you back, but your secretary said
you'd already left for Port Newark."

She showed the guard her shield.

"Oh, FBI? OK," he said, glowering at Tom.

He signed a receipt for his driver. As he followed Shannon to her car,
he said, "How come you're wearing a skirt on the job? New fashion
trend?"

She snorted, "No. I had a court appearance this morning. Some of the
judges are a little touchy about proper decorum."

In the car, wending their way to Berth Two through acres of containers
stacked three high, he said, "Deng's daughter is dead."

"*What!*"

"Heroin OD. Also her husband, Logan. Apparently, they got married
about three weeks ago."

"Don't tell me. Users?"

"I'm sure not. It has to be murder. But I don't know why. When I confronted Deng last night, he was genuinely shocked. Anyway, I told him to
get another lawyer."

"So how come he called you today about the *Sea Horse?*"

"I don't know that, either. He hung up on me right afterward."

"I put out a stop on him in case he tries to skip the country. If he does,
I don't know what I'll do. You're my only source. If he gets a new lawyer,
they'll say whatever he told you was privileged and can't be used in court."

They found Gaffney still observing the search on the other side of the channel.

Shannon flashed her shield again. "That's the *Sea Dragon* over there?"

"Yep."

"Found anything?"

"Not yet. And they've been at it all day. See those launches? They brought in scuba divers a while ago to do the outside. Wait a minute! Look at that. See that one in the water? He's signaling thumbs up."

Tom saw the figures on the deck across the way rushing to the rail, looking down at the diver. He heard cheers. Later, it would turn out, the three hundred units were sealed in torpedo-shaped plastic blisters welded to the hull.

"Well, I guess that's it," Tom said. "You're right. Deng was pulling a fast one."

Shannon put up a cautionary hand. Pointing at the *Sea Horse* looming over them, she said to Gaffney, "Everything unloaded?"

"Yep."

"Anything unusual come off her?"

"What do you mean?"

"Like, what was she carrying?"

"Textiles. Mostly cotton goods. Damn near two hundred containers. And shoes."

Shannon and Tom started to walk away.

"There was one thing different," Gaffney called after them. "A container full of kitchen equipment."

"Kitchen equipment?" Shannon said.

"Right. I was talking about it with one of the shipping agents. For some new Chinese restaurant chain."

Tom grabbed Shannon's arm. "I know where the container is." Then he told her about the warehouse in Rockland County.

Shannon went back to her car, opened the trunk and took out a bag. "Is there a ladies' room?" she asked Gaffney.

"Over there, in the office."

She reappeared in a few minutes. "OK, I'm ready."

"Where to?" Tom said.

"The warehouse."

"You don't think we need backup?"

"Let's be sure, first. Find out what's what. So far, the DEA's come up big. I don't want a lot of potential egg on my face."

They drove north on I-95, the New Jersey Turnpike, a full moon again rising in the twilight sky.

Tom said, "There's something I want to tell you. I dug pretty hard into your past, when I had no right to."

"*Please.* I told you. It's over. Forget it."

"Well, I want to even things up. I've got a buried secret, too. My dad wasn't in the State Department. He was CIA. And he was in Laos, a long time ago, during the Vietnam War. With Deng. What I didn't have an inkling of was that heroin might be involved back then. Not until the night you brought it up. I damn near keeled over at the table."

He looked at her. She was staring straight ahead, both hands gripping the wheel.

"Have you spoken to your father?" she finally asked.

"About this? What would I say? What would *he* say? That the world was different? And, of course, I guess it was. He's more than hinted that he has many regrets. And then I thought about your situation with your father and how you've never said anything to him. So I thought, What's the point? Mistakes were made and they can't be fixed. I'm just glad I have a good relationship with him now. I don't know. What do you think?"

She reached over and squeezed his hand. "I think you've done the right thing," she said.

38

SHANNON CONTINUED north on the turnpike until the George Washington Bridge and then along the Palisades Parkway up the west side of the Hudson River. It was night by now. Tom glimpsed the shimmering expanse of water below.

"Did your father ever say exactly what Deng was doing in Laos?" she asked.

"Only that he was helping us in the war. And that once, in the jungle, he saved Dad's life."

"That certainly gave Deng a hook into you."

"I guess. But whatever was going on before, I can't believe that Dad knew he was still trafficking. I mean, he was so out of touch, he didn't even know Deng had a daughter. He seemed really startled when Deng popped up again through me. And when you get down to it, it's hard to believe the CIA knew about it, either."

"Maybe Langley had another agenda," Shannon said. "It's clear the CIA and Deng are tight. When I first saw that Hong Kong police report, I thought Deng might be just putting on a show. Get it on record what a swell friend of ours he was, in case somebody like me decided to take a look at him. But it's got to be more than that. The CIA fellow meeting him at JFK is all you need to know. And there's something else. Deng came in with an entourage, including those two Chinese accountants who were shot with Carparti. I tried to trace when and how their visas were obtained. Ran into a stone wall. That smells CIA all over. It's not the first time it's happened. Those covert guys think they have all the answers. What they have is world-class myopia. So maybe it was Deng who controlled the agenda from the beginning."

They crossed the New York State line, exited the parkway and drove west through the Ramapo Valley. "You say the warehouse is in Suffern?"

"Near there," Tom said. "I think it's technically in the village of Sloatsburg, a mile or so away. I don't know where precisely, but Deng's purchase got major local coverage. Stop in Suffern and we'll ask directions. Somebody's sure to know about it."

Close by, Tom could see the dark, jagged Ramapo Mountains looming over them. Incongruous in this rural setting were dozens of warehouses, big, medium and small, many of them with halogen light towers, announcing the presence of stored automobile parts, computers, books, clothes, brand-name household appliances. Some had for sale or lease signs. Occasionally, one had a big sticker plastered on it that proclaimed "Sold!"

"Deng couldn't have picked a better neighborhood for his distribution center," Shannon said. "Just another warehouse. Sometimes, Colombian coke rings outsmart themselves. Last year one of them bought a farm in upstate New York and turned it into a crack factory. Stuck out like a sore thumb in the middle of all the cornfields and cows."

Tom fell silent. Then he said, "I can't help thinking. Isn't this a case of the chickens coming home to roost! The West forced opium on China and now we're getting it back in spades. How's that for poetic justice?"

"Darling Tom," Shannon said. "Are you saying two wrongs make a right? There's no big deal here. All it ever was, was about money. Then. And now."

"I keep forgetting my true love's a cop."

Lafayette Avenue, Suffern's main street, appeared to have remained essentially unchanged through much of the century. It was lined by one- and two-story brick and wood structures with insurance and legal offices and small retail shops that were closed for the night. They passed a movie theater with an old-fashioned marquee and winking lightbulbs.

The avenue dead-ended at a railroad station. Shannon turned right on a street paralleling the tracks. On the next corner, there was a tavern featuring two neon shamrocks in the window.

"My people," Shannon said. "I'll ask there. The Irish make it their business to know everybody's business. A lot of recent arrivals have settled around here. Half of them are probably illegals and would be diving out the windows if they knew who my employer is. You want to talk about justice, try what the Brits are doing in Northern Ireland."

"I think I'll skip that one," Tom said.

When Shannon returned, she said, "OK, we're almost there. But it's a little complicated, because of that," she added, pointing to a giant overpass on the other side of the tracks. "That's the New York State Thruway and a major interchange is being constructed to connect it with all the regional highways, so everything's screwed up with detours. Anyway, the warehouse is on Route Seventeen just past Sloatsburg, which they say you could miss if you blink at the wrong moment. The locals are quite put out because the warehouse is being renovated and apparently only Chinese are being used to do the work."

"Listen," Tom said. "Don't you think it's really time to call in some support?"

"I want to take a look first. Make sure. They said the warehouse is set back from the road. If we miss it, there'll be a rinky-dink motel for truckers on the left and on the right the entrance to a hilltop Japanese steak house."

"You're kidding. Up here in the middle of this?"

"Yes, and an inn to go with it."

Shannon veered left and then right along the railroad tracks, past a huge pet-food warehouse and under the Thruway overpass. The car climbed a steep, winding incline. Shannon went left, right and left again until she announced, "What do you know. Route Seventeen. Should be about a quarter of a mile north. On the right."

Then, a minute later, Tom said, "There it is."

Shannon kept going until they got to a road leading to the Japanese steak house. She made a U-turn, drove back toward the warehouse and pulled off the highway about fifty yards past its gated entrance.

They hustled across the highway and made their way through the trees and bushes to a razor-wire-topped chain-link fence at least twelve feet high that enclosed the warehouse and its grounds. Hundreds of feet above them, off to their left, they could see the glowing lanterns of the restaurant.

Through the fence, the warehouse was clearly visible. It nestled in a hollow, perpendicular to the highway. The near end had eight windows on the ground floor. There was another row of them on the second level. The ground-floor windows were lighted. Like most of the warehouses in the area, the exterior was corrugated steel. It had a flat roof. They heard the faint sound of music. Along the right side of the warehouse were six bays. A container on its flatbed was backed into one of them.

"OK," Tom said, "let's go. We know the container's here."

"Yes, but we still don't know what was in it. I can see the headlines. And my bosses' faces. FBI Raid Nets Ten Wok Tables."

They crept along the fence until they reached the gate. It was padlocked with a heavy chain.

"Now you're going to tell me you can pick the lock," Tom said.

"No," she said. "We have specialists for that. Wait here. I'll be right back."

When she returned, she handed him bolt cutters.

"Where'd you get them?"

"In the trunk of my car. Remind me someday to show you what else every agent is required to carry."

Grunting, Tom severed the chain and gingerly pushed open the gate. "Do you think there's a security system?"

"I didn't see any cameras," Shannon said. "If they're renovating, even if there is one, it's probably not activated. We would have heard something by now."

Crouching, they moved toward the lighted, ground-floor windows. The music got louder. Heavy metal. They peered in. There were perhaps a dozen young Chinese. Two of them were dancing to the music. The rest, partying, were swigging bottles of beer and cognac.

"OK, that's it," Shannon whispered. "See that guy sitting at the head of the table with the big mole between his eyes? That's Unicorn Frankie Chin. Now we can call in the troops. He's not here to assemble wok tables."

Tom started to back away. And stopped dead in his tracks. The cold metal of a gun was pressing against the nape of his neck. A voice said, "Freeze."

Out of the corner of his eye, Tom saw that Shannon was also being held at gunpoint.

Tom felt the pressure on his neck ease. The voice said, "Both of you, stand up and turn around. Slowly."

Two Chinese had automatics trained on them. They were wearing sneakers. That and the sound of the music had covered their approach.

Tom and Shannon were marched into the warehouse office. Instantly, someone cut off the music. Unicorn Frankie rose, a little unsteadily, shaking his head in disbelief. Tom saw the trepidation in his eyes.

"Who else is out there?" he yelled at the two gang members who had caught them, and who still had their guns on them.

"No one. We looked. We saw only their car. It's parked across the highway."

"Who's got the keys?" Frankie demanded, hand out.

"I do," Shannon said and gave them to him.

"Bring the car in the lot," Frankie ordered one of the White Eagles.

Pacing back and forth, Unicorn Frankie began to gather himself. Still, Tom could sense his lingering uncertainty. The last thing he had expected was the appearance of an FBI agent.

It was one of his lieutenants, Flying Pig, who bucked him up. Waving a beer bottle drunkenly, he sauntered up to Shannon and bowed theatrically, "You, Missy Dragon Lady. You going to arrest us?"

With that, Frankie's confidence seemed restored. "Search them," he ordered. One of the White Eagles jerked open Shannon's jacket and found the nine-millimeter at her waist. Then he patted her down, spending too much time on her breasts for Tom's liking. He started toward the White Eagle, a fist clenched.

"Cool it," Shannon said. "You can't take them all on."

Then Tom was searched.

"Who you?" Frankie said.

"My name is MacLean. I am the attorney for Mr. Y. K. Deng. He sent me to check on his shipment. How do you think I know about this warehouse?"

"He sent you with *her?*" Unicorn Frankie said, smirking now.

"Listen, Frankie," Shannon said. "Use your head. It's finished. If my office doesn't hear from me in an hour, FBI agents are going to be swarming all over the place. Is that how you want to end your days?"

"Hey, Missy Dragon Lady, you what I want," Frankie's other lieutenant, Fat Monster, interrupted, unzipping his fly. "Find out if you got real fire in your cunt."

As Tom lunged toward him, he felt the side of his skull explode.

As he regained consciousness, the pain came in pulsing waves. Tom, bound hand and foot, was facedown on the concrete warehouse floor. He groaned.

"You all right?" he heard Shannon say.

"I think so." He twisted his head sideways and saw her about six feet away. She was in a chair, tied to an I-beam.

"No more dumb Galahad plays," she said. "You could have been blown away right then and there."

"How long have I been out?"

"About half an hour."

"Where are we?"

"In the main part of the warehouse. Take a look to your left. See what's involved here. But do it slowly. There's a White Eagle guarding us. And he's got heavy artillery. A MAC-ten submachine gun with an extra clip."

Tom saw the wooden crates, piled at least eight feet high. Three of them had been pried open, revealing plastic-wrapped bricks of heroin. "Christ," he said. "How much is there?"

"I'd say enough to keep the United States of America nodding off for the rest of the year. No wonder there's been such a dearth of product on the street. Pretty diabolical. First they cut off the supply. Then they sacrifice a few hundred pounds, so they can bring tons more. No worries about Customs intercepts. Complete control. And I'll bet whacking Carparti has something to do with this."

Tom groaned again. "What's that funny smell?"

"They haven't finished painting the inside."

"So what do we do now?"

"Obviously, they can't let us go," Shannon said, her voice low. "After you were clocked, and while they were bringing us in here, Frankie was already on the phone. And obviously not to Deng. My guess is he called somebody else who's involved in the shipment, probably at the Hong Kong end. Frankie's still shaken. Wants advice about what to do with us, or to get the go-ahead to do it on his own."

In his frustration, Tom attempted to turn over, squirming, trying to break out of his bonds. He felt a sharp jab from the MAC-10 in his back.

"Listen up," Shannon said. "My hunch is this guy doesn't speak English. Frankie gave him his instructions in Hakka. I'm going to give it a shot."

Tom heard her say to the White Eagle, "Fuck your mother."

There was no response.

"OK," she said to Tom. "I've got a backup gun inside my thigh. Remember when I went to the ladies' room in Port Newark? I strapped it on there. Just don't move."

She switched to Hakka. "I have to go to the bathroom. I have to pee."

The White Eagle giggled. "Pee where you are."

"Is that how your mother raised you?" Shannon said. "Is that how she taught you to behave?"

Silence. Then Tom heard the White Eagle mumble something. He shuffled into Tom's view. He looked to be perhaps eighteen years old. Tom saw him untie Shannon. That was all he saw.

Shannon walked to the lavatory, the White Eagle behind her, his MAC-10 prodding her in the spine. She opened the lavatory door and went in. There was a toilet and wash basin. When she tried to close the door, the White Eagle said, "No."

"You mean you're going to stand there and watch me pee?"

The White Eagle nodded eagerly, giggling again.

Shannon shrugged, sat on the toilet, hiking up her skirt, pretending to lower her panty hose. The hidden gun was a five-shot Smith & Wesson Chief's Special. Made of light alloy, it weighed slightly more than two pounds. The thigh holster was like a garter belt. It had a neoprene waist and thigh band with an adjustable, connecting strap that held the holster. On the firing range, she could score a bull's-eye with it at thirty feet. But the circumstances now weren't quite the same. She saw the White Eagle leering at her, perhaps twelve feet away. He was holding the MAC-10 a little more loosely, craning to get a better look at her. She tried to relax. As she brought up the Chief's Special, he stepped back, open-mouthed.

"Drop your gun," she commanded in Hakka.

Instead, he swung the MAC-10 at her.

She fired.

Sheer luck, she thought. He fell without uttering a sound, a bullet hole between his eyes. She jumped forward, searching his pockets. She knew almost every gang member carried a knife. She found it, picked up the MAC-10 and ran toward Tom.

She had just released him when the ground-floor office door opened and a White Eagle surveyed the storage area. When he spotted them, he immediately disappeared. Shannon could hear his cries of alarm.

She helped Tom get to his feet. He staggered, flopping like a rag doll, his leg muscles cramping. She took him by the arm and pulled him toward stairs that led to a mesh-steel catwalk circling the warehouse. They scrambled up it. When they got to the catwalk, they hurried around it to the side opposite the stairs.

From there, in the fluorescent lights hanging from the ceiling, he could see that the warehouse space was about two hundred by eighty feet. At the end where they had been taken captive, there was a laminated wood partition that enclosed the offices. The second story had windows overlooking the storage area. The ground floor only had the door.

Suddenly, the office door was flung open and a half-dozen White Eagles poured out. Shannon let off a burst from the MAC-10 and they scattered. A fusillade of bullets whined off the catwalk under their feet.

Shannon gave Tom her Chief's Special. "You know how to shoot?"

"Sure, I used to practice up at the firing range with some of the agents." He didn't mention how poorly he scored.

"Don't use it unless you're up close. And remember, you've only got four rounds."

Below, a quartet of White Eagles raced toward the catwalk stairs. Shannon sprayed the bottom of the stairs with the MAC-10. One of the White Eagles went down. The others retreated behind I-beam ceiling supports.

We're trapped, Tom thought. There was no way out. It would be simply a matter of time.

"Oh, boy," Shannon said, pointing to buckets of paint and brushes in jars on the catwalk. "Paint thinner. Just what the doctor ordered. Good as gasoline." She emptied two of the jars and filled them with the thinner. She stuffed rags into the tops of the jars. "You have a light?" she said.

"You know I don't smoke," Tom said.

She stood up, frantically patting her jacket pockets. And smiled. "Thank God, I collect matchbooks—to remember those big moments in my life." She held up one that said Allison's on Dominick Street.

She handed the MAC-10 to Tom. "Cover me." She lit the rag in one of the jars and ran toward the wooden office partition. She hurled the jar through a window. There was an instant explosion. Flames began to leap up.

She ran back along the catwalk and retrieved the MAC-10 from Tom. "There's a fire door at the other end," she said. "Open it, so we get a draft going."

Bent low, he made it to the door. As he got there, the fluorescent lights were switched off. It was the best thing that could have happened to him. Yanking the door open, he came face to face with Fat Monster. Tom shot him twice at point-blank range. He toppled backward down the outside stairs, slamming into two other surprised White Eagles who were following him. Tom crouched outside on the landing. He had only two rounds left. But the two gang members had vanished.

Shannon lit the second Molotov cocktail. She tossed it on the crates of heroin below her. It also exploded. The tinder-dry crates caught fire at once. And then the plastic.

In the darkness, a pair of White Eagles had managed to get up the stairs to the catwalk. Tom and Shannon lay flat as gunfire raked them from across the storage area.

Then the fluorescent lights went on again. Peering over the edge of the catwalk, Shannon saw Unicorn Frankie Chin darting toward the burning crates. He had a fire extinguisher. Despite the bullets flying over her and Tom, she sighted the MAC-10 and let loose with another burst. She heard him scream as he crumpled to the floor.

The office end of the warehouse, fanned by the draft Tom had created, had become a wall of flames. More flames danced up from the crates. Thick, acrid smoke billowed as the heroin also began to burn slowly.

"We've got to make a move," Shannon said.

She and Tom groped their way to the open fire door. Tom looked out. In the moonlight, he could see the two White Eagles who had been with Fat Monster. They were standing at the bottom of the stairs. Tom fired his last two rounds at them and they scurried around the corner of the warehouse.

"I'm out of ammunition," Shannon said.

"So am I."

John and Harriet Abernathy, residents of Suffern, had just finished a dinner of sushi, assorted tempura and rolled beef with scallions at the hilltop Japanese restaurant. "What a wonderful meal," Harriet was saying as John started down the winding drive to Route 17. And then she said, "My God, look! That whole place is burning up."

Tom and Shannon heard the wail of fire trucks. And then the engines of cars in the parking lot starting up as the remaining White Eagles, their leader dead, fled in panic.

They stayed at the scene for several hours as local police, state police and FBI agents began converging on the burned-out warehouse. After the last glowing embers were extinguished, about a third of the heroin in the crates had congealed into a black, tarlike substance. The bodies of Unicorn Frankie, Fat Monster, Flying Pig and a fourth White Eagle were found and removed.

Shannon said to one of the agents, "The guy we want is named Y. K. Deng. He lives in Manhattan on Central Park South. Tom, what's the address?"

Then she said, "I've got to get some sleep. I'll file a full report in the morning."

"You want somebody to drive you and Mr. MacLean home?"

"No, it's OK. I've got my car. I'm up to that. At this hour, what's it take? Thirty minutes."

Exhausted, Tom and Shannon stayed silent on the trip into Manhattan. Then, crossing the George Washington Bridge, he said, "You were fantastic. I should have listened to you about Deng."

"You were, too," Shannon said. "And I'm the one who should have listened to you about backup."

He reached over and stroked her hair. "I'm never going out again without you. Look, don't drive me all the way downtown. I'll grab a cab."

She found a parking spot near her building. He kissed her good night, holding her very tight. "I love you," he said. In the taxi going down Second Avenue, he saw the late Friday night crowd leaving the various bars. Some Friday night, he thought.

In Hong Kong, Ho Shu-shui had received the instructions contained in Deng's fax sent the day before. He acted on them at once.

And at that same hour, local time, as Stanley Chow turned the key of his Lamborghini, both he and it promptly blew up. The police announced that the cause of the explosion was a sophisticated bomb planted by persons unknown. But many in the colony's Chinese population preferred to think differently. Stanley, they said, had tempted fate far too long with the four sevens on his license plate.

39

Shortly after nine o'clock in the morning, Tom's phone rang. It was Shannon. "They found Deng," she said. "In his apartment. Dead. Hanged himself in his bathroom."

"Was there a note?"

"Nothing."

"Where are you?"

"At the office. I'll be here all day."

He couldn't go back to sleep. He checked his answering machine. There was a call, late yesterday afternoon, from his secretary. She said, "An envelope arrived by messenger from Mr. Deng. I didn't know how to reach you, so I left it on your desk."

He showered and went to Needham & Lewis. When he opened the envelope, he first found a covering letter.

"My dear MacLean," it began. "I bid you good-bye. The time has come for me to embark on a journey.

"I have always believed in controlling my own destiny, but I realize now that, from the very beginning, I allowed it to control me.

"Life has dealt me harsh blows and in an attempt to overcome them, I lost myself. That is to say, I lost my humanity.

"I deceived you and I regret it. Upon reflection, I should have heeded you regarding my beloved Li-po. It was my final chance to set matters right and I failed. Hubris is a terrible thing.

"I cannot rectify what has happened. But you can help me, as no one else can, to make some effort to right an unrightable wrong. I trust that you will, for I have no one else to turn to.

"You were correct in your judgment about my actions toward my daughter, in fact, if not in every particular. It is because of me that she is no longer on earth.

"As I write this, I am alone. There is nothing left for me here. So I gladly go to rejoin my family. To rejoin Li-po and to ask her forgiveness."

The second letter was in the form of a will.

It appointed Tom the executor of Deng's estate. A foundation was to be created for the advancement of Chinese studies in Li-po's name and for major archaeological explorations in China. It was to be funded with interest derived from capital investments selected by Tom as the foundation's sole trustee.

Both letters were signed by Deng in English and in Mandarin.

That Saturday afternoon, the CIA's Wayne Forrester summoned Allen Merser, Deng's last Mr. Sentry, to an emergency session in his Langley office.

"What went wrong with the business of Deng's daughter?" Forrester demanded.

"What went wrong was she ran off and married that professor. Made it a bit difficult to demonstrate moral turpitude."

"Are we in the clear?"

"Three cutouts were used to get to Immigration, all verbal. Anyhow, the girl's dead."

"Deng?"

"I don't know. The New Haven police are carrying it as a heroin OD."

"All right," Forrester said. "Let's wipe the slate clean. See that all files concerning DH/ROGUE are expunged. That means all computer records and any paper that might still be around. That understood?"

"Yes, sir."

In the evening, Tom and Shannon met at Allison's on Dominick Street. It was her choice. "I know this was where we had the fight," she said. "On the other hand, if I hadn't picked up that book of matches, we wouldn't be around."

Tom told her about Deng's letter to him and the will.

"Are you going to do it?"

"Of course. If nothing else, I owe it to Li-po. But I'm going to make one change. The foundation will also bear Robert Logan's name. I know she'd want that." Then he said, "Your bosses must be happy."

"Believe it," she said. "Yesterday, they were walking around with hangdog looks, like the world had come to an end. Today, even though it was Saturday, they were all in the office. The word is, Who needs DEA? The biggest seizure in history. Tomorrow, they're bringing in TV crews to film the heroin. The director's flying up himself to pose with it. I hear the White House is getting in the act. They'll say they've cut off the dragon's head. There'll be a cautionary note. But it'll be in the fine print. It's revolting."

Tom resigned from Needham & Lewis. Deng's estate was valued in the tens of millions of dollars. Tom's statutory fee entitled him to two percent of all moneys received or paid out. He reduced this to a half percent instead, which was more than sufficient to launch his own legal practice, specializing in advising securities and corporate clients on appropriate legal and moral behavior.

He kept urging Shannon to quit the FBI. "Come on," he said. "It's time for you and me."

"I can't. I have a lot of loose ends to tie up. For instance, they've decided to grant immunity to Duncan Lau to nail Pei and that's my case."

A week later, however, she walked into Tom's office and said, "I'm still staying on to wrap up Pei, but I've decided to make a career change, after all."

"You're kidding. How come?"

"I'm thinking of getting married. Turns out something else happened when I was chasing Deng and it's impossible to be an agent *and* a mother, at least for me. I just found out."

He started to laugh. "Who's the lucky father?"

Shannon sat in his lap. "Oh, Tom, funny, funny," she said.

EPILOGUE

As the early morning mist began to dissipate in the Laotian uplands, a venerable tribesman crouched under a towering teak tree and gazed with satisfaction at the clearing that sloped away below him.

The clearing measured three hectares, about seven and a half acres. During the dry season, the tribesman's sons had hacked and slashed at the forest growth to create it. Once the felled trees and brush had dried out, they raced through the area with torches. Instantly, there was an awesome explosion of fire. Flames shot hundreds of feet in the air, soon followed by a mile-high plume of smoke that drifted over the landscape. All through the Golden Triangle, similar plumes could be seen.

When the flames died, the rich wood ash was worked into the soil, fertilizing it and creating a fire-hardened surface to seal in the moisture. Then the women in the tribesman's family sowed the poppy seeds just before the first seasonal rains came.

And now, in the autumn, the petals, mostly scarlet, some purplish-red, a few of them brilliant orange or creamy white, had begun to fall from the poppy plants, leaving green, egg-shaped pods on top of the four-foot-high stems.

Each evening for the past week, the women, and the more responsible grandsons and granddaughters, using small, sharp hooked knives, had cut vertical incisions in the pods, from which oozed the milky white sap of raw opium. Overnight, it congealed, turned brownish-black and in the morning was removed with a flat flexible blade much like a painter's scraper.

On this fourth and final morning of the harvest, the aged tribesman watched as the turbaned women, in their red, embroidered yarn jackets and black trousers, lifted off the last of the pea-sized particles of opium, placing them first in cupped poppy petals and then transferring them to teak boxes that hung from their necks.

At midday, when all the opium had been collected in one central box, the tribesman carted it with him along a path to his village a short distance away, past his own raised, bamboo, thatched-roofed house. Around it, chickens ran free. A sow nursed a half-dozen piglets.

Ahead of him, he saw other villagers gathering around a young officer, clad in the khaki cap and quilted jacket of General Li's Third Chinese Irregular Forces. The tribesman had heard that General Li was in a continuing battle with another renegade warlord general in Burma named Shan Wa for control of the opium trade in the Golden Triangle, but this mattered little to him. Right then, all he cared about was receiving enough money to replace his thatched roof with tin and to purchase household necessities—pots, pans, tools, matches, salt, cloth, batteries for his transistor radio.

The young officer had two soldiers with him who weighed the raw opium before it was placed in the saddlebags of waiting mules. For the tribesman's opium, the officer paid him two thousand two hundred and fifty dollars in Thai bahts, the preferred currency, since the goods he intended to buy would be smuggled into Laos from Thailand. In cities across the United States, this particular batch, once refined, would fetch a price of eight hundred thousand dollars at the wholesale level. And in the retail market, on the street, in wretched slum hallways and roach-infested rooms, in sleek suburban malls and elegantly appointed executive suites, repackaged in small glassine bags, its total value soared into millions of dollars.

As he waited in line, the tribesman noticed that the officer spoke the local dialect. And made bold by the knowledge that he would be able to afford the luxury of a new tin roof, he said, "Sir, by chance, can you tell me what happened to Mr. Deng?"

"Never heard of him. I don't know who you're talking about."

"Yes, I've asked before. It's been many, many years since he was here, but I remember Mr. Deng was such a nice man, young like you." The tribesman started to turn away, then hesitated, as if additional clues might be helpful. "He would often come with a blond-haired foreigner, an American."

"Old man," the young officer snapped, "stop wasting my time."

Author's Note

While this book is a work of fiction, it is by no means based on fantasy.

Over the past decade, heroin trafficking into the U.S. by the Chinese triads, after first rising gradually like the early stages of a flood, now suddenly threatens to become a tidal wave. The signs are everywhere. In 1993, the number of people seeking hospital emergency-room help because of heroin addiction reached an all-time high. More than half a ton of heroin in a single shipment was seized in 1992 in a random search by U.S. Customs inspectors in Oakland, a record that is certain to be broken. Because of the new purity available—eliminating the need for injection—heroin's popularity is soaring on college campuses. Mainland China has now become a major export route for the product of the Golden Triangle's poppy fields. In 1994, a new high-level post was created in the Department of Justice to cope expressly with the sinister rise of Asian organized crime and the influx of China white.

For the reader interested in learning more about how and why this has happened, I suggest:

The Underground Empire by James Mills (Doubleday).

Warlords of Crime by Gerald L. Posner (McGraw-Hill).

The Politics of Heroin by Alfred W. McCoy (Lawrence Hill Books).

Chinatown by Gwen Kinkead (HarperCollins).

Dead on Delivery by Robert M. Stutman and Richard Esposito (Warner Books).

Chinese Subculture and Criminality by Ko-Lin Chin (Greenwood).

Triad Societies in Hong Kong by W. P. Morgan (Government Press/Hong Kong).

And for a detailed study of the Chinese diaspora, the greatest overseas migration in history:

Sons of the Yellow Emperor by Lynn Pan (Little, Brown).